"What are ye doing in my bed, Ian MacDonald?"

Sìleas lit the candle and turned furious eyes on him.

"It's *my* bed, too," he said.

"How dare ye come in here when I'm fast asleep and think ye can have your way with me."

"You're my wife," Ian said. "That means I can have my way with ye."

"So I'm your wife now, am I? Ye didn't think so before."

"I'm ready to take ye for my wife now," he said, giving her a slow look up and down. "Quite ready."

"Are ye now? And what has made ye come to this decision after all this time?"

"I know ye heard me say some unfortunate words about ye before I left. But I find ye appealing now. Verra appealing."

"What you're saying is that ye want to take me to bed."

He stood and pulled her against him.

"We are going to bed, eventually, Sìl," he said against her ear. "Don't make me wait."

Praise for the novels of
Margaret Mallory

KNIGHT OF PASSION

"Top Pick! As in the previous book in her All the King's Men series, Mallory brings history to life, creating dramatic and gut-wrenching stories. Her characters are incredibly alive and readers will feel and believe their sensual and passionate adventures. Mallory raises the genre to new levels."

—RT Book Reviews

"A story full of revenge, love, hope, and pain...Beautifully written. Mallory is extremely talented...[She] has obviously done a great deal of research for this trilogy— it certainly paid off! And if you're addicted to historical romance, you're going to want to get your hands on this book."

—RexRobotReviews.com

"Another hit for this wonderful series!"
—TheMysticCastle.com

"I really enjoyed this story...Very intense...Fans of medieval historicals will especially love this one."
—CoffeeTimeRomance.com

"Intriguing and enjoyable...truly a great romance that you won't be able to put down!"
—RomanceJunkiesReviews.com

"An amazing story...a series that readers won't want to miss...Filled with hot romance as well as adventure with a fascinating historical background."

—RomRevToday.com

KNIGHT OF PLEASURE

"4 Stars! A riveting story...Such depth and sensuality are a rare treat."

—RT Book Reviews

"Fascinating...An excellent historical romance. Ms. Mallory gives us amazingly vivid details of the characters, romance, and intrigue of England. You're not just reading a novel, you are stepping into the story and feeling all the emotions of each character...*Knight of Pleasure* is amazing and I highly recommend it."

—TheRomanceReadersConnection.com

"An absolute delight...captivating...Combining a luscious romantic story with a fascinating look at an intriguing time in history, Mallory captures her readers' attention."

—FreshFiction.com

"If you like heated romance sprinkled liberally with royal politics, you can't miss this book."

—RomanceJunkiesReviews.com

"Thrilling, romantic, and just plain good reading...an enjoyable, historically accurate, and very well written novel."

—RomRevToday.com

The
GUARDIAN

MARGARET
MALLORY

FOREVER

NEW YORK   BOSTON

This book is a work of fiction. Names, characters, places, and incidents are the product of the author's imagination or are used fictitiously. Any resemblance to actual events, locales, or persons, living or dead, is coincidental.

Book design by Giorgetta Bell McRee

Forever
Hachette Book Group
237 Park Avenue
New York, NY 10017
Visit our website at www.HachetteBookGroup.com

Forever is an imprint of Grand Central Publishing.
The Forever name and logo is a trademark of Hachette Book Group, Inc.

The publisher is not responsible for websites (or their content) that are not owned by the publisher.

Printed in the United States of America

First Printing: May 2011

10 9 8 7 6 5 4 3 2 1

ATTENTION CORPORATIONS AND ORGANIZATIONS:
Most HACHETTE BOOK GROUP books are available at quantity discounts with bulk purchase for educational, business, or sales promotional use. For information, please call or write:

Special Markets Department, Hachette Book Group
237 Park Avenue, New York, NY 10017
Telephone: 1-800-222-6747 Fax: 1-800-477-5925

This book is dedicated to the red-haired women in my family—my sister, daughter, and three nieces—who were clamoring for a red-haired heroine. Sìleas (SHEE-las) is for you.

ACKNOWLEDGMENTS

My biggest thanks goes to my long-suffering husband, who—among other trials—gracefully puts up with jokes about where I get the inspiration for my love scenes.

I am grateful to my editor, Alex Logan, and the rest of the crew at Grand Central Publishing for all they do for me. This time, I owe a special thanks to Amy Pierpont and Alex for suggesting I try my hand at writing Scottish historicals. If I'd known how much fun I'd have with my Highlanders, I would have done this sooner. I'm giving a wild cheer for Diane Luger and the art department for the gorgeous cover with a hero who looks exactly as I wrote him.

Many thanks to my agent, Kevan Lyon, for her enthusiastic support and wise counsel. Warm thanks also goes to Anthea, Wanda, and Ginny for their helpful comments on the draft—and for reviewing it in an unreasonably short time. I am grateful to my RWA chapter-mates and the many romance authors who continue to help me along the way.

D. J. Macleod, Honorary Librarian for the Gaelic Society of Inverness, was very kind to send me a copy of the Society's invaluable but out-of-print article, *Marriage, Divorce and Concubinage in Gaelic Scotland*, by David Sellar. Finally, thanks to Sharron Gunn, who helped me with Gaelic and other things Scottish.

Is minic a rinne bromach gioblach capall cumasach.
Many a ragged colt becomes a noble horse.

The GUARDIAN

PROLOGUE

ISLE OF SKYE
Scotland
1500

Teàrlag MacDonald, the oldest living member of her clan and a seer of some repute, let her good eye travel slowly from boy to boy. Visitors to her tiny cottage at the edge of the sea were rare.

"What brings ye lads to come see me on this blustery night?"

"We want to know our future, Teàrlag," young Connor said. "Can ye tell us what ye see for us?"

The boy who spoke was the chieftain's second son, a strapping lad of twelve with the pitch-black hair of his mother's side.

"Are ye sure ye want to hear?" she asked. "Most often I foretell death, did ye not know?"

The four lads exchanged glances, but none took a step toward the door. They were braver than most. Still, she wondered what led them to be crowding her cottage and dripping rain on her floor this particular night.

"Ye feared I might die before I foretold somethin' about ye, is that it?"

She fixed her good eye on the youngest, a lad of ten with black hair like his cousin Connor's and eyes as blue as the summer sky. The lad blushed, confirming her suspicion.

"Well, I don't expect to die as soon as ye think, Ian MacDonald."

Ian raised his eyebrows. "So ye know me, Teàrlag?"

"'Course I know ye. The three of ye," she said, pointing her finger at Ian and his cousins Alex and Connor, "are my blood relations."

Learning they were related to a woman with one eye and a hunched back did not appear to please them. She chuckled to herself as she turned to toss a handful of herbs on the fire. As it crackled and spit, she leaned forward to breathe in the tangy fumes. She could not call upon the sight at will, but sometimes the herbs made the vision clearer.

As soon as the boys entered her cottage, smelling of dogs, damp wool, and the sea, she had seen the orangey glow about them that signaled a vision was coming. It was unusual for her to see the glow around more than one person at a time. She suspected it was because the lads were close as thieves, but it was not for her to question her gift.

"Ye first," she said, curling her finger at Ian.

The lad's eyes grew big, but when one of the other boys gave him a shove, he came around the table to stand beside her.

Quick as a wink, she slipped a small, smooth stone into his gaping mouth. The stone did not help her see, but it added to the mystery and would keep him quiet.

"Don't swallow the stone, laddie," she said, "or it'll kill ye."

Ian turned wide eyes on his cousin Connor, who gave

him a reassuring nod. She rested her hand on Ian's head and closed her eyes. The vision, already forming from the moment he passed through her door, came quickly.

"Ye shall wed twice," she said. "Once in anger and once in love."

"Two wives!" Alex, the one with the fair hair of his Viking ancestors, hooted with laughter. "That will keep ye busy."

Ian spit out the stone into his hand. "I didn't want to know that, Teàrlag. Can ye not tell me something interesting...like how many battles I'll fight in...or if I'll die at sea?"

"I can't command the sight, lad. If it chooses to speak of love and women, then so be it." She looked to the others. "What of the rest of ye?"

The other three made faces as if she had given them one of her bitter-tasting remedies.

She cackled and slapped the table. "No so brave now, are ye, lads?"

"It is no fair for ye to hear about my two wives," Ian said to the others, "unless I hear about yours."

Alex gave the other two lads a lopsided grin and exchanged places with Ian.

"I don't need the sight to know ye were born to give trouble to the lasses." She shook her head. The boys would all be handsome men, but this one had the devil in his eye. "Shame, but there is nothin' to be done about it."

Alex grinned. "Sounds verra good to me."

"Ach." She popped a second stone from the dish on the table into Alex's mouth and put her hand on his head. 'Twas good luck she had gathered pretty stones from the shore that morning.

"Tsk, tsk, this is no good at all. One day, ye'll come across a woman so beautiful as to hurt your eyes, sittin' on a rock in the sea." She opened her eyes and thumped Alex on the chest. "Watch out for her, for she might be a selkie taking on her human form to lure ye to your death."

"I'd rather have a selkie than two wives," Ian grumbled from across the table.

For a MacDonald of Sleat to put away one wife to take another was common as grass. It seemed the way of it for them to break the hearts of the women who loved them.

Teàrlag closed her eyes again—and laughed so hard it made her cough. Ach, this was a surprise, for certain.

"Alex, I see ye courtin' an ugly, pockmarked lass," she said, wiping her eyes on her shawl. "I fear she is quite stout as well. And I don't mean pleasing plump, mind ye."

The other boys doubled over laughing until they were red-faced.

"I think ye are having fun with me," Alex said, looking sideways at her. "Since I've no intention of marrying, I am sure that if I do, the lass would have to be verra, verra pretty."

"I see what I see." She gave Alex a push and motioned to Duncan. He was a big, red-haired lad whose mother had served as Connor's nursemaid.

"This one has the blood of both the MacKinnon Sea Witch and the Celtic warrior queen, Scáthach, so mind ye keep him on your side," she said, wagging her finger at the other three. To Duncan, she said, "That's where ye get your fierceness—and your temper."

Duncan stood still, his expression serious, as she put a stone in his mouth and rested her hand on his head.

Almost at once, a powerful feeling of loss and longing

stole over her and weighed down her spirit. She lifted her hand, being too old to bear it for long.

"Are ye sure ye want to hear, laddie?" she asked softly.

Duncan gave her a level look and nodded.

"I fear you've sad days before ye," she said, squeezing his shoulder. "But I will tell ye this. Sometimes, a man can change his future."

Duncan spit out the stone and gave her a polite "Thank ye."

The chieftain's son was last.

"What I want to know is the future of our clan," Connor said around the stone in his mouth. "Will we be safe and prosper in the years to come?"

His father had come to ask her the same question not long ago. All she had been able to tell him was that one day he would have to send this son away to keep him safe.

When she put her hand on Connor's head, she heard the moans of the dying and saw men of her clan lying in a field soaked in Scottish blood. Then she saw the four lads as strong, young men, on a ship, crossing the sea. She grew weary as the visions continued, one after the other.

"Teàrlag, are ye well?" Connor asked.

When she opened her eyes, Alex handed her a cup of her own whiskey, saying, "A wee nip will do ye good."

She narrowed her good eye at him as she drained the cup, wondering how he'd found it.

"I see many perils ahead for all of ye," she said. "Ye must keep each other close, if ye are to have any hope of survivin'."

The lads appeared unimpressed. As Highlanders, they knew without foretelling that their future held danger. And as lads, they found the notion more exciting than worrisome.

They were young, and a wise woman did not tell all she knew. After considering what might be of use for them to know, she said to Connor, "Ye want to know what ye must do to help the clan?"

"Aye, Teàrlag, I do."

"Then I will tell ye," she said, "the clan's future will rest on ye choosin' the right wife."

"Me? But it's my brother who will be chieftain."

She shrugged. He would learn soon enough of the sorrows to come.

"Can ye tell me what woman I must choose, then?" Connor asked, worry furrowing his brow.

"Ach, the lass will choose ye," she said, and pinched his cheek. "Ye just must be wise enough to know it."

She looked to the cottage door just before the sound of the knock. Alex, who was closest, opened it and laughed when he saw the little girl with wild, unkempt red hair standing there.

"'Tis only Ian's wee friend Sìleas," he said, as he pulled her inside and shut the door against the cold.

The girl's large green eyes took in the room, then settled on Ian.

"What are ye doing wandering alone outside in the dark?" Ian asked her.

"I came to find ye, Ian," the girl said.

"How many times must I tell ye to be careful?" Ian tightened his mantle and turned to the others. "I'd best take her back to her da."

The old woman thought the lass's da should be skinned alive for letting the wee bairn wander about as he did. But he was not the sort of man who had much use for a daughter.

"Were ye no afraid the faeries would snatch ye?" she asked.

Sìleas shook her head. Ach, the poor child knew that the faeries steal only the children who are most precious to their parents.

"Come on, then," Ian said, taking the wee girl's hand. "I'll tell ye a story about a selkie as we walk."

Sìleas looked up at the lad, and her eyes shone as if God himself had sent the strongest and bravest warrior in all the Highlands to be her protector.

CHAPTER 1

ISLE OF SKYE
Scotland
1508

Sìleas's outstretched hands bumped and scraped against the rough earthen walls, touch replacing sight, as she raced through the blackness. Small creatures skittered before her, running in fear as she did.

But there was no echo of footsteps behind her. Yet.

A circle of gray light appeared ahead, signaling the end of the tunnel. When she reached it, Sìleas dropped to her hands and knees and crawled through the narrow opening, mud dragging at her skirts.

Brambles scratched her face and hands as she scrambled out the other side. A burst of clean sea air surrounded her, blowing away the dank, new-grave smell of the tunnel. Sìleas sucked in great lungfuls of it, but she had no time to stop.

Startled sheep stared or trotted out of her way as Sìleas clambered up the hill. She prayed that she had not already missed him. When she finally reached the path, she flattened herself behind a boulder to wait. Before she could catch her breath, she heard hoofbeats.

She had to be certain it was Ian. With her heart thudding in her ears, she peeked around the boulder.

As soon as the rider rounded the bend, she shouted his name and jumped out onto the path.

"That was dangerous, Sìl," Ian said, after pulling his horse up hard. "I nearly rode over ye."

Ian looked so handsome on his fine horse, with his dark hair flying and the glow of sunset shining all about him, that for a long moment Sìleas forgot the urgency of her trouble.

"What are ye doing out here?" Ian asked. "And how did ye get so filthy?"

"I'm escaping my step-da," Sìleas said, coming back to herself. "I came out the secret tunnel when I saw them turn ye away at the front gate."

"I was going to stay the night on my way home," he said, "but they told me half the castle was ill with some pestilence and sent me away."

"They lied to ye," she said, reaching her hand up to him. "We must hurry before they notice I'm gone."

Ian hoisted her up in front of him. Though her back stung like the devil, she leaned against him and sighed. She was safe.

She'd missed Ian these last months when he was off at the Scottish court and fighting on the border. This felt like old times, when she was a wee girl and Ian was always helping her out of one scrape or another.

But she was in trouble as never before. If she'd had a doubt about how dire her situation was, seeing the Green Lady hover over her bed weeping was a clear warning.

When Ian turned the horse back in the direction of the castle, she jerked upright and spun around to face him. "What are ye doing?"

"I'm taking ye back," Ian said. "I'm no going to be accused of kidnapping."

"But ye must get me away! The bastard intends to marry me to the worst of the MacKinnons."

"Mind your tongue," Ian said. "Ye shouldn't call your step-da a bastard."

"You're no listening to me. The man is going to make me wed *Angus MacKinnon*."

Ian stopped his horse. "Ye must be mistaken. Even your bastard of a step-da wouldn't do that. All the same, I promise I'll tell my da and uncle what ye said."

"I'll tell them myself when ye take me to them."

Ian shook his head. "I'm no starting a clan war by stealing ye away. Even if what ye say is true, there will be no wedding soon. You're a child yet."

"I'm no child," Sìleas said, folding her arms. "I'm thirteen."

"Well, you've got no breasts," Ian said, "and no man is going to want to marry ye until ye do—*Oof!* No need to jab me with that pointy elbow of yours just for speaking the truth."

Sìleas fought against the sting in her eyes. After all that had happened to her today, this was hard to bear— especially coming from the man she planned to marry.

"If ye won't help me, Ian MacDonald, I'll walk."

When she tried to slide down off the horse, Ian caught and held her. He took her face in his hand and rubbed his thumb lightly across her cheek—which made it devilishly difficult not to cry.

"I don't mean to hurt your feelings, little one," he said. "Ye can't go off on your own. It's a long way to the next house, and it's near dark."

"I'm no going back to the castle," she said.

"I suppose if I take ye back, you'll just sneak out the secret passageway again?"

"I will," she said.

Ian sighed and turned his horse. "Then we'd best move fast. But if I'm hung for kidnapping, it'll be on your head."

Ian stopped to make camp when it grew too dark to see. If he didn't have Sìleas with him, he'd be tempted to continue. But his family's home was a fair distance yet, and it was risky to ride in the black of night.

He handed Sìleas half of his oatcakes and cheese, and they ate in silence. There would be hell to pay for this, all because she let that imagination of hers run wild again.

He glanced sideways at her. Poor Sìl. Her beautiful name, pronounced with a soft "Shh," like a whisper in the ear, mocked her. She was a pathetic, scrawny thing with teeth too big for her and unruly red hair so bright it hurt the eyes. Even once she had breasts, no man was going to wed her for her looks.

At least she'd washed the mud off her face.

Ian rolled out his blanket and gave her a warning look. "Lie down and don't say a word."

"'Tis no my fault—"

"It is," he said, "though ye know verra well no one is going to blame you."

Sìleas scrunched herself into a ball on one side of the blanket and tucked her feet under her cloak.

Ian lay down with his back to her and wrapped his plaid around himself. It had been a long day of travel, and he was tired.

Just as he was drifting off to sleep, Sìleas shook his shoulder. "I hear something."

Ian grabbed his claymore and sat up to listen.

"I think it's a wild boar," she whispered. "Or a verra large bear."

Ian flopped back down with a groan. "'Tis only the wind blowing the trees. Have ye not tortured me enough for one day?"

He couldn't go back to sleep with the wee lass shivering beside him. She had no meat on her bones to keep her warm.

"Sìl, are ye cold?" he asked.

"I am near death with it," she said in a weak, mournful voice.

With a sigh, he rolled onto his back and spread his plaid over both of them.

Now he was wide awake. After staring at the tree branches whipping in the wind above him for a long while, he whispered, "Sìl, are ye awake?"

"Aye."

"I'm going to be married soon," he said, and couldn't help grinning to himself. "I met her at court in Stirling. I've come home to tell my parents."

He felt Sìleas stiffen beside him.

"I'm as surprised as you," he said. "I didn't plan to wed for a few years yet, but when a man meets the right woman...Ah, Sìl, she is everything I want."

Sìleas was quiet for a long time, then she asked in that funny, hoarse voice of hers, "What makes ye know she is right for ye?"

"Philippa is a rare beauty, I tell ye. She's got sparkling eyes and silky, fair hair—and curves to make a man forget to breathe."

"Hmmph. Is there nothing but her looks ye can say about this Philippa?"

"She's as graceful as a faerie queen," he said. "And she has a lovely, tinkling laugh."

"And that is why ye want to marry her?"

Ian chuckled at Sìleas's skeptical tone. "I shouldn't tell ye this, little one. But there are women a man can have without marriage, and women he cannot. This one is of the second kind, and I want her verra, verra badly."

He dropped an arm across Sìleas's shoulder and drifted toward sleep with a smile on his face.

He must have slept like the dead, for he remembered nothing until he awoke to the sound of horses. In an instant, he threw off his plaid and stood with his claymore in his hands as three horsemen rode into their camp and began circling them. Though Ian recognized them as his clansmen, he did not lower his sword.

He glanced over his shoulder at Sìleas to be sure she was all right. She was sitting up with his plaid pulled over her head and was peering out at them from a peephole she had made in it.

"Could this be our own young Ian, back from fighting on the border?" one of the horsemen said.

"Why, so it is! We hear you had great success fighting the English," another said, as the three continued circling. "It must be that the English sleep verra late."

"I hear they wait politely for ye to choose the time and place to fight," said the third. "For how else could a man sleep so soundly he doesn't hear horses before they ride through his camp?"

Ian gritted his teeth as the men continued enjoying themselves at his expense.

"The English fight like women, so what can ye expect?" the first one said, as three more riders crowded into their camp.

"Speaking of women, who is the brave wench who is no afraid to share a bed with our fierce warrior?" another man called out.

"Your mother will murder ye for bringing a whore home," another said, causing a round of laughter.

"I want to be there when she finds out," the first one said. "Come, Ian, let us have a look at her."

"I've no woman with me," Ian said, flipping back the plaid to reveal the girl. "It is only Sìleas."

Sìleas yanked the plaid back over herself and glared at all of them.

The horsemen went quiet. Following their gazes, Ian looked over his shoulder. His father and his uncle, who was the chieftain of their clan, had drawn their horses up at the edge of the camp.

There was no sound now, except for the horses' snorting, as his father's eyes moved from Ian to Sìleas, then back to Ian with a grim fury.

"Return home now, lads," his uncle ordered the others. "We'll follow shortly."

His father dismounted but waited to speak until the other men were out of earshot.

"Explain yourself, Ian MacDonald," his father said in a tone that used to signal that Ian was in for a rare beating.

"I don't know how I could sleep through the approach of your horses, da. I—"

"Don't play the fool with me," his father shouted. "Ye know verra well I'm asking why ye are traveling alone with Sìleas—and why we find ye sharing a bed with her."

"But I am not, da. Well, I suppose I am traveling with her, though I didn't intend to," Ian fumbled. "But we are no sharing a bed!"

His father's face went from red to purple. "Don't tell me I'm no seeing what's plain as day before my eyes. There can be but one explanation for this. You'd best tell me the two of ye have run off and married in secret."

"Of course we've not married."

All the way home, Ian had imagined how his father's eyes would fill with pride when he heard of Ian's exploits fighting the English on the border. Instead, his father was speaking to him as if he were a lad guilty of a dangerous prank.

"We were no sharing a bed in the sense ye are suggesting, da," Ian said, trying and failing to stay calm. "That would be disgusting. How could ye think it?"

"So why is the lass here with ye?" his father asked.

"Sìleas got it into her head that her step-da intends to wed her to one of the MacKinnons. I swear, she was going to run off alone if I didn't bring her with me."

His father squatted down next to Sìleas. "Are ye all right, lass?"

"I am, thank ye." She looked pathetic, her skin pale against her tousled red hair and huddling like a small bird under his plaid.

His father gently took her hand between his huge ones. "Can you tell me what happened, lass?"

This was too much. His father was speaking to Sìleas as if she were the innocent in all of this.

"'Tis true that Ian didn't want to help me. But I forced his hand because my step-da means to wed me to his son so they can claim Knock Castle." She dropped her eyes and said in a shaky voice, "And it wasn't just that, but I don't wish to speak of the rest."

Sìleas was always one to exaggerate. If she didn't have Ian's father in her hands before, she surely did now.

"'Tis a lucky chance the lass learned of their plan and got away," Ian's uncle said. "We can't let the MacKinnons steal Knock Castle out from under us."

His father stood and rested his hand on Ian's shoulder. "I know ye didn't intend to, but you've compromised Sìleas's virtue."

Ian's stomach sank to his feet as he felt disaster coming. "But, da, that can't be true. I've known Sìleas all her life. And she is so young, no one will think anything of my spending the night in the woods with her."

"The men who found ye already believe the worst," his father said. "'Tis bound to become known to others."

"But nothing happened," Ian insisted. "I never even thought of it!"

"That doesn't matter," his father said.

"This isn't about Sìleas's virtue, is it?" Ian said, leaning toward his father with his fists clenched. "It's about keeping her lands from the MacKinnons."

"There is that as well," his father owned. "But ye have ruined Sìleas's reputation, and there is only one way to set that aright. The two of you will be wed as soon as we get to the house."

Ian was aghast. "No. I will not do it."

"What ye will not do is shame your mother and me," his father said, his eyes as hard as steel. "I expect honorable behavior from my sons, even when it is hard. Especially when it is hard."

"But I—"

"Ye have a duty here, to the lass and to your clan," his father said. "You're a MacDonald, and ye will do what is required."

"I'll gather the men," his uncle said. "I don't expect the MacKinnons will be pleased when they hear the news."

Sìleas was crying soundlessly, holding Ian's plaid to her face and rocking back and forth.

"Pack up your things, lass," his father said, giving her an awkward pat. "Ye must be wed before the MacKinnons come looking for ye."

CHAPTER 2

THE DUNGEON IN DUART CASTLE
Isle of Mull
OCTOBER 1513

"**D**amnable vermin! The straw is alive with the wee critters." Ian got to his feet and scratched his arms. "I hate to say it, but the Maclean hospitality is sadly lacking."

"'Tis the Maclean vermin on two legs that concern me," Duncan said. "Ye know they are upstairs debating what to do with us—and I've no faith they'll chose mercy."

Connor rubbed his temples. "After five years of fighting in France, to be taken by the Macleans the day we set foot in Scotland…"

Ian felt the humiliation as keenly as his cousin. And they were needed at home. They had left France as soon as the news reached them of the disastrous loss to the English at Flodden.

"'Tis time we made our escape," Ian told the others. "I expect even the Macleans will show us the courtesy of feeding us dinner before they kill us. We must take our chance then."

"Aye." Connor came to stand beside him and peered

through the iron grate into the darkness beyond. "As soon as the guard opens this door, we'll—"

"Ach, there's no need for violence, cousin," Alex said, speaking for the first time. He lay with his long legs stretched out on the filthy straw, untroubled by what crawled there.

"And why is that?" Ian asked, giving Alex a kick with his boot.

"I'm no saying it is a bad plan," Alex said, "just that we won't be needing it."

Ian crossed his arms, amused in spite of himself. "Will ye be calling on the faeries to open the door for us?"

Alex was a master storyteller and let the silence grow to be sure he had their full attention before he spoke. "When they took me up for my turn at being questioned, they got a bit rough. The chieftain's wife happened to come in, and she insisted on seeing to my wounds."

Connor groaned. "Alex, tell me ye didn't..."

"Well, she stripped me bare and applied a sweet-smelling salve to every scratch from head to toe. The lady was impressed with my battle scars—and ye know how I like that in a woman," Alex said, lifting one hand, palm up. "It was all rather excitin' for both of us. To make a long story short—"

"Ye fooked the wife of the man who's holding us? What is wrong with ye?" Duncan shouted. "We'd best be ready, lads, for I expect the debate on whether to kill us will be a short one."

"Now there is gratitude, after I sacrificed my virtue to set ye free," Alex said. "The lady's no going to tell her husband what we done, and she swore she could get us out."

"So when's she going to do it?" Ian didn't question

whether the lady would come; women were always doing unlikely things for Alex.

"Tonight," Alex said. "And it wasn't just my pretty face, lads, that persuaded her to help us. The lady is a Campbell. Shaggy Maclean wed her to make peace between their two clans. She hates him, of course, and does her best to thwart him at every turn."

"Ha!" Ian said, pointing his finger at Connor. "Let that be a lesson to ye, when you go choosing a wife among our enemies."

Connor rubbed his forehead. As their chieftain's son, he would be expected to make a marriage alliance with one of the other clans. With so many men dead after Flodden, a number of clans would be looking to negotiate such a match.

"Interesting that ye should be giving advice on wives," Alex said, raising his eyebrows at Ian. "When it doesn't appear ye know what to do with yours."

"I have no wife," Ian said with a deliberate warning in his voice. "So long as it hasn't been consummated, it's no a marriage."

While in France, Ian had done his best to forget his marriage vows. But now that he was returning home to Skye, he would put an end to his false marriage.

Alex sat up. "Anyone willing to make a wager on it? My money says our lad will no escape this marriage."

Duncan grabbed Ian before he could beat the smile off Alex's face.

"That's enough, Alex," Connor said.

"Ye are a sorry lot," Alex said, getting to his feet and stretching. "Ian, married but doesn't believe it. Duncan, who refused to wed his true love."

Ah, poor Duncan. Ian glared at Alex—the tale was too sad for jesting.

"And then there's Connor," Alex continued in his heedless way, "who must try to guess which of a dozen chieftains with unwed daughters would be the most dangerous to offend."

"Ach, my da's brothers will likely kill me first and save me the trouble of choosing," Connor said.

"Not with us watching your back," Duncan said.

Connor's half-uncles would be pleased to have one less obstacle between them and leadership of the clan. Connor's grandfather, the first chieftain of the MacDonalds of Sleat, had six sons by six different women. The sons had all hated each other from birth, and the ones still alive were always at each other's throats.

"I hope when my brother is chieftain he'll save the clan trouble by keeping to one woman," Connor said, shaking his head.

Alex snorted. "Ragnall?"

That was a false hope if there ever was one, though Ian wouldn't say it. Connor's older brother was no different from his father and grandfather when it came to women.

"So who will you wed, Alex?" Duncan asked. "What Highland lass will put up with your philandering without sticking a dirk in your back?"

"None," Alex said, the humor thin in his voice. "I've told ye. I'll never marry."

Alex's parents had been feuding for as long as Ian could remember. Even in the Highlands, where emotions tended to run high, the violence of their animosity was renowned. Of the three sisters who were Ian's, Alex's, and Connor's mothers, only Ian's had found happiness in marriage.

At the sound of footsteps, Ian and the others reached for their belts where their dirks should have been.

"Time to leave this hellhole, lads," Ian said in a low voice. He flattened himself against the wall by the door and nodded to the others. Plan or no, they would take the guards.

"Alexander!" A woman's voice came out of the darkness from the other side of the iron bars, followed by the jangle of keys.

Ian drew in a deep breath of the salty air. It felt good to be sailing again. They had stolen Shaggy's favorite galley, which went a long way toward restoring their pride. It was sleek and fast, and they were making good time in the brisk October wind. The jug of whiskey they passed kept Ian warm enough. He grew up sailing these waters. Every rock and current was as familiar to him as the mountain peaks in the distance.

Ian fixed his gaze on the darkening outline of the Isle of Skye. Despite all the trouble that awaited him there, the sight of home stirred a deep longing inside him.

And trouble there would be aplenty. They had spoken little during the long hours on the water since the Campbell woman had given them the terrible news that both their chieftain and Connor's brother Ragnall had been killed at Flodden. It was a staggering loss to the clan.

Duncan was playing sweet, mournful tunes on the small whistle he always carried, his music reflecting both their sadness and yearning. He tucked the whistle away inside his plaid and said to Connor, "Your father was a great chieftain."

Their chieftain had not been loved, but he was respected

as a strong leader and ferocious warrior, which counted for more in the Highlands. Ian found it hard to imagine him dead.

He took a long pull from the jug. "I can't believe we lost them both," he said, clasping Connor's shoulder as he passed him the whiskey. "To tell ye the truth, I didn't think there was a man alive who could take your brother Ragnall."

Ian knew that the loss of his brother was the harder blow for Connor. Ragnall had been fierce, hotheaded, and accepted as the successor to the chieftainship. He had also been devoted to his younger brother.

"I suspected something," Duncan said, "for if either of them was alive Shaggy wouldn't have risked a clan war by taking us."

"Even with our chieftain fallen, Shaggy should expect a reprisal from our clan," Ian said after taking another drink. "So I'm wondering why he didn't."

"Ian's right," Alex said, nodding at him. "When Shaggy said he was going to drop our lifeless bodies into the sea, he didn't look like a worried man to me."

"He had no extra guard posted outside the castle," Ian said. "Something's no right there."

"What are ye suggesting?" Connor said.

"Ye know damn well what they're suggesting. One of your da's brothers is behind this," Duncan said. "They knew we'd return as soon as news of Flodden reached us, so one of them asked Shaggy to keep an eye out for us."

"They're all wily, mean bastards," Alex said. "But which of them would ye say wants the chieftainship most?"

"Hugh Dubh," Connor said, using Hugh's nickname, "Black Hugh," given to him for his black heart. "Hugh never thought he got his rightful share when my grand-father died, and he's been burning with resentment ever since. The others have made homes for themselves on the nearby islands, but not Hugh."

"What I want to know," Ian said, "is what Hugh prom-ised Shaggy to make sure ye never showed your face on Skye again."

"You're jumping to conclusions, all of ye," Connor said. "There's no affection between my uncle and me, but I won't believe he would have me murdered."

"Hmmph," Alex snorted. "I wouldn't trust Hugh fur-ther than old Teàrlag could toss him."

"I didn't say I trusted him," Connor said. "I wouldn't trust any of my da's brothers."

"I'll wager Hugh has already set himself up as chief-tain and is living in Dunscaith Castle," Duncan said.

Ian suspected Duncan was right. By tradition, the clan chose their leader from among the men with chieftain's blood. With Connor's father and brother both dead and Connor in France, that left only Connor's uncles. If half the stories told about them were true, they were a pack of murderers, rapists, and thieves. How a man as honor-able as Connor could share blood with them was a mys-tery. Some would say the faeries had done their mischief switching babies.

They were nearing the shore. Without needing to exchange a word, he and Duncan lowered the sail, then took up the oars with the others. They pulled together in a steady rhythm that came as naturally to Ian as breathing.

"I know you're no ready to discuss it, Connor," Ian said between pulls. "But sooner or later you'll have to fight Hugh for the chieftainship."

"You're right," Connor said. "I'm no ready to discuss it."

"Ach!" Alex said. "Ye can't mean to let that horse's arse be our chieftain."

"What I don't mean to do is to cause strife within the clan," Connor said. "After our losses at Flodden, a fight for the chieftainship would weaken us further and make us vulnerable to our enemies."

"I agree ye need to lay low at first," Ian said. After an absence of five years, Connor couldn't simply walk into Dunscaith Castle and claim the chieftainship—especially if Hugh already had control of the castle. "Let the men know you're home and see they have an alternative to Hugh. Then, when Hugh shows he puts his own interests above the clan's—as he surely will—we'll put ye forward as the better man to lead."

Alex turned to Duncan, who was on the oar opposite his. "You and I are like innocent babes next to my conniving cousins."

"All great chieftains are conniving," Ian said with a grin. "'Tis a required trait."

"Connor will need to be conniving just to stay alive," Duncan said without a trace of humor. "Hugh has been pirating in the Western Isles for years without being caught. That means he's clever and ruthless—and lucky as well."

They were quiet again for a time. Connor may not be ready to admit it aloud yet, but Ian agreed with Duncan—Connor's life was in danger on Skye.

"If you're going to the castle, I'm going with ye," Ian said. "Ye don't know what awaits ye there."

"Ye don't know what awaits you either," Connor said. "Ye must go home and see how your family fares."

Ian sent up a prayer that his own father had survived the battle. He regretted that their parting had been angry—and regretted still more that he had ignored his father's letters ordering him home. He should have fought alongside his father and clansman at Flodden. He would carry the guilt of not being there to his grave.

"And ye need to settle matters with the lass," Connor added. "Five years is long enough to keep her waiting."

Ian had managed to forget about the problem of Sìleas while they talked of Connor and the chieftainship—and he didn't want to think about it now. He took another swig from the whiskey jug at his feet while they rested their oars and glided to shore. As soon as the boat scraped bottom, he and the others dropped over the side into the icy water and hauled the boat up onto the shore of Skye.

After five years gone, he was home.

"I'll wait to go to Dunscaith Castle until I know which way the wind blows," Connor said, as they dragged the boat above the tide line. "Duncan and I will take Shaggy's boat to the other side of Sleat and find out the sentiment there."

"I still think I should go with ye," Ian said.

Connor shook his head. "We'll send word or come find ye in two or three days. In the meantime, talk to your father. He'll know what the men are thinking on this part of the island."

"I know ye can't mean to leave your best fighting man out of this," Alex said. "Should I come with ye or go north to hear what the folks there are saying?"

"Stay with Ian," Connor said, the white of his teeth bright in the growing darkness. "He faces the greatest danger."

"Verra funny." At the thought of Sìleas, he took another

swig from the jug—and choked when Alex elbowed him hard in the ribs.

"You'd best give Ian a full week," Alex said. "Ye don't want him leaving his poor wife wanting after such a long wait."

The others laughed for the first time since they had heard the news about Connor's father.

Ian, however, was not amused.

"I have no wife," he repeated.

"Sìleas's lands are important to the clan, especially Knock Castle," Connor said, draping an arm across Ian's shoulders. "It protects our lands on the eastern shore. We can't have it falling into the hands of the MacKinnons."

"What are ye saying?" Ian asked between clenched teeth.

"Ye know verra well my father did not force ye to wed Sìleas out of concern for the girl's virtue. He wanted Knock Castle in the hands of his nephew."

"Ye can't be trying to tell me to accept Sìleas as my wife."

Connor squeezed Ian's shoulder. "All I'm asking is that you consider the needs of the clan."

Ian shrugged Connor's hand off him. "I'm telling ye now, I'll no keep this marriage."

"Well, if ye don't," Connor said, "then ye must find a man we can trust to take your place."

"Perhaps ye should wait until you're chieftain before ye start giving orders," Ian snapped.

CHAPTER 3

ON THE SLEAT PENINSULA
OF THE ISLE OF SKYE

The wind whipped at Sìleas's cloak as she stood with their nearest neighbor, Gòrdan Graumach MacDonald, on a rocky outcrop overlooking the sea. The mountains of the mainland were black against the darkening sky. Despite the damp cold that penetrated her bones and the need to get home to help with supper, something held her.

"How much longer will ye give Ian?" Gòrdan asked.

Sìleas watched a boat crossing the strait, its outline barely visible in the fading light, as she considered his question.

When she didn't answer, Gòrdan said, "'Tis past time you gave up on him."

Give up on Ian? Could she do that? It was the question she asked herself every day now.

She had loved Ian for as long as she could remember. Almost from the time she could walk, she had planned to marry him. She smiled to herself, remembering how kind he had been to her, despite the teasing he got from the men and other lads for letting a wee lass half his size follow him like a lost puppy.

"Five years he's kept ye waiting," Gòrdan pressed. "That's more time than any man deserves."

"That's true enough." Sìleas brushed back the hair whipping across her face.

Her wedding was the worst memory of her life—and she was a woman with plenty of bad memories to choose from. There had been no time for the usual traditions that made a wedding a celebration and brought luck to a new marriage. No gifts and well-wishes from the neighbors. No washing of the bride's feet. No ring. No carrying the bride over the threshold.

And certainly no sprinkling of the bed with holy water—not with Ian threatening to toss the priest down the stairs when he attempted to go with them up to the bedchamber.

None of the traditions for luck were kept, save for the one. Ian's mother insisted Sìleas wear a new gown, though Sìleas didn't see how a bit more bad luck on top of what she already had could make a difference. Regardless, Ian's mother wouldn't hear of her wearing the filthy gown she had arrived in. Unfortunately, the only new gown to be had upon an hour's notice was one Ian's mother had made for herself.

Sìleas rushed through her bath, barely washing, so she would be out and dressed before Ian's mother returned to help her. Quickly, she dabbed at the long gashes across her back so she would leave no telltale blood on the borrowed gown.

When she slipped the gown over her head, it floated about her like a sack. She looked down at where the bodice sagged, exaggerating her lack. If that were not bad enough, she wanted to weep at the color. Such a violent shade of red would look lovely on Ian's dark-haired mother, but it made Sìleas's hair look orange and her skin blotchy.

When Ian's mother burst in the room, her startled expression before she smoothed it confirmed Sìleas's worst fears.

"'Tis a shame we can't alter it," his mother said, clucking her tongue. "But ye know that brings a bride bad luck."

Sìleas was sure the gown's color canceled out any good luck its unaltered state was likely to bring her. A bride was supposed to wear blue.

Then came the worst part of all. As she descended the stairs, with his mother's hand at her back pushing her forward, she heard Ian shouting at his father. His words were the last blow that nearly felled her.

Have ye taken a good look at her, da? I tell ye, I will not have her. I'll no say my vows.

But with his father, his chieftain, and a dozen armed clansman surrounding him, Ian did say them.

Sìleas blinked when Gòrdan stepped in front of her and took hold of her shoulders, bringing her sharply back to the present.

"Don't try to kiss me again," she said, turning her head. "Ye know it's not right."

"What I know is that ye deserve a husband who will love and honor ye," Gòrdan said. "I want to be that man."

"You're a good man, and I like ye." Gòrdan was fine looking as well, with rich brown hair and warm hazel eyes. "But I keep thinking that once Ian returns, he'll..."

He'll what? Fall on his knees and beg my forgiveness? Tell me he regretted every single day he was away?

Truth be told, she wasn't ready to be married when they wed. She had needed another year or two before becoming a true wife. But five years! Each day Ian didn't return deepened the wound. By now, she should have a babe in her arms and another grabbing at their skirts, like most women her age. She wanted children. And a husband.

Sìleas drew in a deep breath of the sharp, salty air. It was one humiliation after another. Ian could pretend they were not wed, because he was living among a thousand French folk who did not know it. But she lived with his family on this island in the midst of their clan.

Where every last person knows Ian has left me here waiting.

"If you cannot ask for an annulment..." Gòrdan let the question hang unfinished.

Though she could ask for an annulment, she could not tell even Gòrdan that—at least, not yet. She had been lectured on that point quite severely by both Ian's father and the chieftain. If her MacKinnon relatives heard that her marriage was never consummated, they would attempt to steal her away, declare the marriage invalid, and force her to wed one of their own.

Yet her marriage to Ian was not a trial marriage, as most were. Through some miracle, the chieftain had found a priest. The chieftain had wanted them bound—and her castle firmly in the hands of the MacDonalds of Sleat.

For the same reason, it would have been useless to ask her chieftain to support a petition to annul her marriage. A bishop wouldn't send a petition to Rome on her request alone. Consequently, she had written a letter to King James seeking his help. For six months, the letter lay hidden away in her chest, awaiting her decision to send it.

But now, both King James and her chieftain were dead.

"If you can't ask for an annulment," Gòrdan said, "then simply divorce Ian and marry me."

"Your mother would no be pleased with that," she said with a dry laugh. "I don't know if she would faint dead away or take a dirk to ye."

Although it was common in the Highlands to wed and divorce without the church's blessing, Gòrdan's mother had notions about the sort of woman her precious only son should wed. A "used" woman was unlikely to satisfy her.

"'Tis no my mother's decision," Gòrdan said. "I love ye, Sìleas, and I'm set on having ye for my wife."

Sìleas sighed. It was a precious gift to have a good man tell her he loved her, even if he was the wrong man. "Ye know I can't think of leaving Ian's family now."

"Then promise ye will give me an answer as soon as ye are able," Gòrdan said. "There are many men who would want ye, but I'll be good to ye. I'm a steadfast man. I'd never leave ye as Ian did."

Though he meant to reassure her, his words pierced her heart.

"'Tis time we returned to the house." She turned and started toward the path. "I've been gone too long."

"Ach, no one will begrudge ye a wee time away after you've been working so hard," Gòrdan said, taking her arm. "And if ye marry me, they'll have to learn to do without ye."

As they walked up the path, Sìleas looked over her shoulder at the dark water. *Where was Ian now?* Even after all this time, she missed the boy who had been her friend and protector. But she didn't think she still wanted the angry young man who had left her—even if he deigned to return to claim her after all this time.

Five years she had waited for Ian. It was long enough. Tomorrow, she would rewrite her letter and send it to the dead king's widow.

. . .

"Perhaps ye should ease up on the whiskey," Alex said.

"Ye can't expect me to face this sober," Ian said.

Ian tipped the jug back one more time to be sure it was empty then tossed it aside. When they rounded the next bend, he saw the smoke from the chimneys of his family home curling against the darkened sky and felt a piercing longing for his family. It would be good to be home... if not for having to face the problem of Sìleas.

"Most women don't appreciate a man who is slobbering drunk, cousin," Alex said. "I hope ye haven't had so much you'll have trouble doing your husbandly duty."

"Will ye no leave it alone?"

"Ach," Alex said, rubbing his arm where Ian had punched him, "I only meant to cheer ye up with a wee bit a teasing."

"'Tis good you're coming home with me," Ian said. "Since Sìleas will be needing another husband in the clan, it may as well be you."

"And I thought ye were fond of the lass," Alex said.

In truth, Ian was fond of Sìleas. He wanted a good husband for her.

He just didn't want it to be him.

For five years, he had this false marriage hanging over him. Not that he'd let it constrain him, but it was always there in the back of his mind like a sore that wouldn't heal. Now that he had come home to Skye, it was time to take his place in his clan. He supposed he would have to take a wife—which meant he had to deal with the problem of Sìleas first. He still got angry every time he thought of how he'd been forced to wed her. And whether she'd done it on purpose or not, it was her fault.

Once he was out from under the marriage, he could forgive her.

A dog barked somewhere in the darkness to herald his homecoming. The smell of cows and horses filled his nose as they passed between the familiar black shapes of the byre and the old cottage where his parents had first lived. Just ahead, lamplight filtered through the shutters of the two-story house his father had built before Ian was born.

Swaying just a wee bit, Ian found the latch and lifted it. The earthy smell of the peat fire enveloped him as he eased inside the door.

Ignoring Alex's nudge from behind, he paused in the dark foyer to survey the people gathered around the hearth. His mother sat on the far side. Her face was still beautiful, but she was too thin, and her thick, black braid had streaks of white.

Across from her, a couple sat on a bench with their backs to the door. Neighbors, most likely. Between them and his mother, a young man with his brother's chestnut hair was sprawled on the floor, as if he lived here. Could this long-limbed fellow, talking in a deep voice, be his "little" brother Niall?

There was no sign of his father or Sìleas, so he would have the easy greetings first.

"Hello Mam!" he called, as he stepped into the hall.

His mother shrieked his name and ran across the room to leap into his arms. He twirled her around before setting her back down.

"Mam, mam, don't weep." Her bones felt sharp under his hands as he patted her back to soothe her. "Ye can see I am well."

"Ye are a wretched son to stay away so long." She

slapped his arm, but she was smiling at him through her tears.

"Auntie Beitris, I know ye missed me, too," Alex said, as he held his arms out to Ian's mother.

"And who is this braw man?" Ian said, turning to his brother.

Their mother had lost three babes, all of them girls, before Niall was born, so there was a nine-year gap between Ian and his brother. When Ian left for France, his brother had barely reached his shoulder. Now, at fifteen, Niall stood eye to eye with him.

"Surely, this cannot be my baby brother." Ian locked his arm around Niall's neck and rubbed his head with his knuckles, then passed him to Alex, who did the same.

"Look at ye," Alex said. "I'd wager all the lasses on the island have been after ye, since I wasn't here to divert them."

Niall and Alex exchanged a couple of good-natured punches, then Niall caught Ian's eye and cocked his head. Ian had forgotten all about the couple on the bench, but at his brother's signal, he turned around to greet them.

The room fell away as Ian stared at the young woman who now stood in the glow of the firelight with her eyes fixed on the floor and her hands clenched before her. Her hair was the most beautiful shade of red he had ever seen. It fell in gleaming waves over her shoulders and breasts and framed a face so lovely it squeezed his heart to look at her.

When she lifted her gaze and met his, the air went out of him. Her eyes were a bright emerald, and they seemed to be asking a question as if her very life depended upon it.

Whatever this lass's question was, his answer was aye.

CHAPTER 4

There was something very familiar about this lovely, green-eyed lass, but Ian could not place her.

"Ian." Alex jabbed him in the ribs.

Ian knew he should stop staring at her, but he couldn't help himself. And why should he, when the lass was staring right back at him? He wondered vaguely if the man at her side was her husband—and hoped he wasn't.

"Hmmph," Alex grunted, as he pushed past Ian. He strode across the room and greeted the young woman with a kiss on her cheek, as if he knew her well.

"Ach, you are a sight to behold," Alex said, standing back and holding her hands. "If I were your husband, Sìleas, ye can be sure I wouldn't have kept ye waiting a single day."

Sìleas? Ian shook his head. Nay, this could not be...

The young woman was nothing like the scrawny thirteen-year-old he remembered. Instead of gawky limbs and pointed elbows, she had graceful lines and rounded curves that made his throat go dry.

And yet...that was Sìleas's upturned nose. And he

supposed that glorious mass of curling red hair could be hers, if it were brushed and combed—a state he'd never seen it in before.

"Welcome home," the young woman said to Alex in the kind of throaty voice a man wanted to hear in the dark.

Sìleas never had one of those high-pitched little girl voices... but this beauty could not truly be her.

"Ye two must be hungry after your travels. Come, Sìleas, let us get these men fed," his mother said, taking the lass by the arm. His mother gave him a wide-eyed look over her shoulder, the kind she used to give him when he was a lad and had committed some grievous error in front of company.

When he started to follow the two women to the table, Alex hauled him back. "Are ye an idiot?" Alex hissed in his face. "Ye didn't even greet Sìleas. What's the matter with ye?"

"Are ye sure that's Sìleas?" Ian said, leaning to the side so he could see past Alex to the red-haired lass.

"Of course it is, ye fool," Alex said. "Did ye no hear your mam just say her name?"

Ian had to tear his gaze away from her when Niall and the other man joined them. Now that he took a good look at the man, he saw it was their neighbor, Gòrdan Graumach MacDonald.

"Ian, Alex," Gòrdan said, giving them each a curt nod.

Ian met the man's stubborn hazel eyes. "Gòrdan."

"You've been gone a long time," Gòrdan said, sounding as though Ian could not be gone long enough to make him happy. "A good deal has changed here in your absence."

"Has it now?" Ian said, knowing a challenge when

he heard one. "Well, ye can expect it all to change again, now that I'm back."

Gòrdan scowled at him before turning on his heel to join the women, who were busy setting food on the table on the other side of the room.

"Thank ye kindly for supper," Gòrdan said to them.

"Ye are always welcome to join us. 'Tis small thanks for all you've done for us," his mother said, beaming at Gòrdan. "'Twas kind of ye to take Sìleas out for a stroll today."

What in the name of all the saints was his mother doing, thanking that conniving Gòrdan?

"If ye need me for . . . for anything at all," Gòrdan said to Sìleas in a low voice, "ye know where to find me." Gòrdan touched her arm as he spoke to her, and an unaccountable surge of anger rose in Ian's chest, choking him.

If Sìleas answered, Ian didn't hear it over the blood pounding in his ears. Just what was going on between Sìleas and Gòrdan Graumach MacDonald? He was about to help Gòrdan out the door, when the man showed the good sense to leave.

"Ye won't have far to look to find a man to replace ye," Alex said in Ian's ear. "That is what ye wanted, no?"

"That doesn't mean I'll let Gòrdan make a cuckold of me," Ian ground out through his teeth.

Ian didn't know whether to regret drinking so much whiskey—or to wish he had drunk a good deal more. After traveling half the world, he felt disoriented in his own home. Everyone had changed—his brother, his mother. And most of all, Sìleas. He still could not quite believe it was her.

"Where's da?" he asked his mother.

"Come have some supper," his mother said, and disappeared into the kitchen. She returned a moment later with a steaming bowl. "I've got your favorite fish stew."

Ian's stomach rumbled as the savory smell reached him. He was near starved.

"Where's da?" he asked again, as he sat down at the table.

From the corner of his eye, he saw the back of Sìleas's skirt disappearing up the stairs.

He stopped with his spoon halfway to his mouth as it occurred to him he had the right to follow her up and take her to bed. Tonight. Right now. Before supper, if he wanted. And again, after. The part of him between his legs was giving him an emphatic *Aye!*

His reaction startled him. For five long years, he had planned to end the marriage as soon as he returned. He'd harbored not a single doubt. The only question had been how to do it with the least embarrassment to Sìleas—and the least difficulty for him.

But he made that plan before she turned into this enchanting lass with a voice that was like velvet sliding over his skin—and curves that would have him dreaming of her naked as soon as he closed his eyes.

Aye, he most definitely wanted to take Sìleas to bed. Any man would. The question, however, was whether he wanted her to be the last woman he ever took to his bed. He wasn't prepared to decide that tonight. Hell, he didn't even know Sìleas anymore. Was the woman anything like the wild-haired bairn who used to follow him about and always need rescuing?

Ian knew he should say something to her. But what? He couldn't tell her he was ready to be her husband and bind his life to hers forever. Though he had no idea what he would say, he got up from his chair, stomach rumbling, to follow her upstairs.

Before he had taken two steps, he was stopped by a loud crash in the next room. He turned in time to catch his mother and brother exchanging glances.

At the sound of a second crash, Niall jumped to his feet. "I'll get him."

Sìleas ignored the crash of pottery and the bellowing that followed as she ran up the stairs. This once, they would have to manage without her. She slammed the bedchamber door, leaned against it, and gulped in deep breaths. Damn him! She had wept for Ian MacDonald too many times over the last five years, and she was not going to do it again.

Her head pounded, her chest hurt, and she could not get enough air.

The foolish plans she'd held on to since she was a wee girl were shattering like the crockery Ian's father was hurling against the wall downstairs. She had lied to herself. Lied, when she told herself she had put her childish dreams away. Lied, when she said she'd ceased expecting Ian to want to share a life with her when he finally returned.

If she had given up her dreams, her heart would not be breaking from the loss of them now.

When Ian embraced his mother first, she understood. That was only right. And she hardly resented it at all when he greeted Niall next, for Niall had missed Ian almost as much as she had. But then, it was her turn. She fixed her gaze on the floor and held her breath, waiting. He was the one who left; he should come to her. In any case, her feet would not move.

Then the room went silent, and she felt his gaze on her. Slowly, she lifted her head and looked into the bluest eyes in the Highlands. Her fingers were ice, her palms sweaty, and her bodice felt too tight. For five years, she had waited for this moment.

She had imagined it a thousand times. Ian would give her a wide smile that warmed his eyes and pull her into his arms. He would tell her how much he missed her and how glad he was to be home. Then, in front of God and his family, he would call her wife and give her a kiss—her first real kiss.

In her more realistic moments, she thought it might be awkward between them at first, but that Ian would attempt to make it right and seek her forgiveness. Never did she imagine he would not speak to her.

Not a single word.

With her heart in her throat, she implored him with her eyes to do as he ought. Instead, he stared at her as if she had grown a tail and fins. If he didn't want to claim her, he could have had the courtesy to greet her as the old friend she was, then told her in private he did not wish to be her husband. His public dismissal was both insulting and heartless.

Sìleas paced up and down her bedchamber, clenching her hands until her nails pierced the skin. The boy she had known would never have been so unkind. The angry young man who had called her repulsive, however, was capable of such cruelty. All this time, she had made excuses for him. Even now, she was tempted—but failing to acknowledge her in some small way was simply unforgiveable.

Ian's words from their wedding day rang in her ears. *Have ye taken a good look at her, da?* Ach! She gave the door a good kick—they wouldn't hear it below over the yelling.

She tilted her head back. "Dear God, did ye have to make him more handsome than ever? Was that truly necessary?"

Ian had been a lovely boy, with kind, sky-blue eyes framed by thick, dark lashes—the sort all the mothers cooed over. But there was nothing left of the sweet lad in the man who strode into the house tonight. True enough, his eyes were as blue as ever and his hair the same shiny black of a selkie. But the man had a rough, dangerous air about him.

It was possible he'd been like this when he returned from fighting on the borders, and she had been too young to recognize it. But the moment he burst into the room tonight, she felt it, recognized it, knew it for the danger it was. And instead of making her wary, a ripple of excitement shivered through her, right down to the tips of her toes. She wanted to be next to him, to feel the power of his presence, to touch the vibrating energy that coursed through him.

She felt it, wanted it...and Ian ignored her.

She needed to be gone from this house. Nay, she would not be married to a man who did not want her. She jerked the cloth sack off the hook on the back of her door, threw it on the bed, and started tossing things into it.

Not all men found her disgusting. She knew several clansmen who would be pleased to have her for a wife—and *not* just for her lands.

As she looked around the room, deciding what to take

with her, her gaze lingered on the quilt his mother had made her...the colored stones Niall had collected with her...the wooden box Ian's father had carved for her.

She'd lived here for five years, but she'd been wrong to think of this as her home. No matter how much she loved Ian's family, they were *his* blood, *his* family. Not hers.

Sìleas looked down at the gown in her hand and remembered how she and Ian's mother had talked by the fire as they worked on it together. All her life, she had longed for a family, for a home where people laughed at the table and cared for each other. She had been happy here, despite the waiting.

Ian's family had welcomed her from the start, and eventually accepted and loved her. His father had taken the longest to win over—but she had. Losing the family she had come to think of as her own would be hard. Very hard, indeed. But she was here as Ian's wife. If she wasn't that, she could not stay.

But where could she go?

Sìleas sank to the floor and leaned her head against the side of the bed. She had no family to take her in, no home to go to. Although she was heir to Knock Castle, her step-da, Murdoc MacKinnon, had it now. After he took it, she feared he would come for her too.

She could go to Gòrdan, of course, but she wasn't ready to make that decision.

Despair weighed down on her as she looked at the moonless black sky outside her window. Traveling in the dark would be foolish—and she had no place to go. Besides, she couldn't just abandon the family after all they had done for her. There were things she must see to before she could leave.

She was so tired she felt light-headed. The last weeks had been difficult—and tonight, worse. In the morning, she would make a plan for her future.

She pulled the half-filled bag off the bed and let it drop to the floor with a thump. As she crawled into bed, Sìleas tried to forget that this was meant to be her marriage bed.

Ian's stomach tightened. "Mam, what is it? Has something happened to da?"

"Your father was wounded at Flodden." His mother gave him a thin, tense smile. "But he's much better now."

She flinched at the sound of another crash and broken crockery falling to the floor. This time, it was followed by his father's voice, bellowing, "Leave me be, damn ye!"

Ian sprinted through the doorway to the small room that used to serve as a servant's bedchamber. He stopped in his tracks when he saw the man on the bed.

His father lay under a quilt, looking thinner than seemed possible. A bandage covered the top of his head and one eye. Below the bandage, a red gash ran down the side of his face to below his jaw. The part of his face that wasn't covered by bandages was parchment white, rather than its usual ruddy color.

In all his memories, his father was a tall, powerfully built warrior who could swing a claymore with enough force to cut an enemy in half. He was a man who spent his time outdoors, in the mountains or on the sea. Finding him a bed-ridden invalid shook Ian to his foundations.

"Hello, da," he said, forcing his voice to be steady.

"It took ye a damned long time to come home." His father's voice sounded raspy, as if he had to fight to draw breath to speak. His father's gaze went past him to Alex, who had come in on his heels. "The same goes for you, Alex Bàn MacDonald. Have Duncan and Connor returned as well?"

"Aye," Alex said. "They've gone to the west to have a look about."

Ian's mouth went dry. The quilt covering his father lay flat on the bed where his father's left leg should have been.

Ian tore his gaze from the missing leg, guilt weighing on his chest like a stone. "You're right, da. I should have come home sooner. I should have been here to fight with ye at Flodden."

"Ye think ye could have saved my leg, is that it?" his father said, his face flushing with anger. Then, in a quieter voice, he said, "No, son, I would not have wished ye there. Ye would have been lost like the others, and the family needs ye now that I'm useless."

Regardless of the outcome, Ian should have fought at his father's side. His father's words did not absolve him. Redemption was something a man had to earn.

"But if ye had been at the battle, I know ye would have let me die like a man," his father said with a vicious look at Niall.

Ian glanced at Niall, realizing for the first time that his young brother must have fought at Flodden. A strong fifteen-year-old who was trained to fight would not be left home with the women and children.

The muscles in Niall's jaw clenched, before he said, "Come, da, let me help ye sit up."

When Niall tried to take his arm, his father shook him off. "I said, let me be!"

Something more than losing a leg had changed in his father. Payton MacDonald had been a warrior who sent terror into the hearts of his enemies, but he had also been a man who showed warmth and kindness to his family.

"Give Ian the chair and go," his father barked without looking at Niall. "Alex, get out of the doorway and come in. I must tell the two of ye of our clan's misfortunes, for the future of the MacDonalds of Sleat rests with ye."

CHAPTER 5

"Do ye think we should be leaving so soon?" Alex asked, as they crossed the yard to the byre. "We only just arrived."

"We need to find Connor and Duncan and make our plan," Ian said.

His father's grim news had kept Ian and Alex up talking far into the night. As they had feared, Hugh Dubh and his rough, clanless men had taken control of Dunscaith, the chieftain's castle, as soon as the men returned from Flodden bearing the body of their dead chieftain. Hugh had proclaimed himself the new chieftain. And then, the new "chieftain" had stood by and done nothing while the MacKinnons attacked Knock Castle.

Ach, it made Ian blind with fury.

"Connor said he'd come for us when he wants us," Alex said.

"I can't sit here on my arse doing nothing with so much at stake," Ian said.

Besides, he needed to escape, if only for a day or two.

Nothing at home was as he expected. Finding his father crippled had shaken him badly. And seeing Sìleas had confused him.

"So what are ye going to do about Sìleas?" Alex asked.

"I don't know."

"Ye think being away from her will help ye decide?" Alex asked. "Ye must know that's utter foolishness, cousin."

Foolish or no, that was what Ian was doing. Because he was forced to say vows when he'd committed no offense, he'd never considered keeping them. But if he took Sìleas as his true wife now, that would be an entirely different matter. It would be his decision, and he would feel honor-bound to keep his vows. *'Til death.*

"I need time to decide," Ian said.

"So ye think it's your choice, do ye?" Alex said. "Are ye so sure Sìleas wants ye?"

Ian turned to look at Alex to see if he was serious. "She's been living with my family all this time, waiting for me." With a grin, he added, "The whole clan knows the lass has adored me since she was a child."

"Ach, but she's not an ignorant child now," Alex said over his shoulder as he pulled open the door to the byre.

Alex stopped so abruptly that Ian ran into him. When Ian pushed past him, he saw what—or rather, who—had caught Alex by surprise.

Sìleas was dressed in a man's shirt and old boots, and she was mucking out a stall with a pitchfork. With streaks of dirt on her face and bits of straw tangled in her hair, she looked more like the Sìleas that Ian remembered.

Her pitchfork was half-raised when she saw them. Her eyes widened, and then, very slowly, she rested the wooden end of the pitchfork on the dirt floor.

"Do not tell me ye have it in your head to leave," she said, looking at Ian.

"Just for a few days," Ian said, feeling unaccountably guilty. He had every reason to go.

"Ye cannot mean it," she said, her voice rising. "You've seen how it is here. You've seen what's happened to your da."

"Sìl, a man must do what he must," Ian said. "The future of the clan is at stake."

"Hugh Dubh has been sitting in the chieftain's castle for weeks," she said, planting one hand on her hip. "I believe we can survive another day or two with him in it."

"Delay will only make things worse," Ian said.

"Ye cannot spare your mother more than an evening after the poor woman didn't lay eyes on ye for five years?" Sìleas said.

Ian felt a twinge of guilt about that, but he had to go. To divert her—and because he was curious—he asked, "What are ye doing dressed like that and mucking out the stalls?"

"Someone has to," Sìleas said, her eyes sparking green fire. "Your da can't do it. And your brother can't do everything himself, try as he might."

"There are other men who can do this," Ian said.

"Do ye see any men here to help?" she said, sweeping one arm out to the side. Her other hand gripped the pitchfork so tightly her knuckles were white. "We lost some men in the battle, and Hugh Dubh has forbidden the rest from working our lands."

Ian's father had not told him of this insult.

"Give me that, Sìl," Alex said, using the voice he used to gentle horses. "I understand why you want to use it on him, but Ian won't be good to anyone if you stick that pitchfork into his heart."

When she glared at Alex and banged the end of the pitchfork against the ground, Alex lifted his hands palms out and stepped back.

"I can see," he said in a low voice to Ian, "the lass adores ye still."

Ian decided to try his luck. When he started toward her, Sìleas braced the pitchfork in front of her.

"Don't ye try to tell me what a man must do," she said, so angry that tears filled her eyes, "because the truth is ye are just playing at being a man."

She was straining his patience now. How dare she mock him? "Protecting the clan is not playing."

"A true man doesn't desert his family when they need him," she said. "And protecting the clan starts with your family."

This time, the truth of her words burned through him.

"I'll stay until we hear from Connor," Ian said, and reached out for the pitchfork. "Go inside, Sìleas. I'll do this."

She hurled the pitchfork against the wall with a loud clatter that set the horses snorting, and stormed past him.

At the door, Sìleas spun around to fling one last remark at him. "It's time ye grew up, Ian MacDonald, because your family needs ye."

Ian and Alex went to the creek to clean up, rather than dirty his mother's kitchen washing in the tub there.

"Mucking out the byre was not how I thought we'd be serving the clan," Alex said, sounding amused.

"It is a waste of our talents. We're warriors!" Ian said, Alex's good humor annoying him further. "We should be using our claymores, fighting our way into the castle, and tossing Hugh over the wall for the fish to eat."

"While Sìleas mucks out the stalls for ye?" Alex said, raising an eyebrow and grinning. "Hugh Dubh has as much right to seek the chieftainship as Connor. We can't just toss him in the sea, as satisfying as that would be."

"But he's claiming it without being chosen, and he's no right to do that," Ian said. "He made a mistake by not calling a gathering and forcing the selection before Connor returned."

"I expect Hugh was waiting until he could share the sad news of Connor's demise," Alex said.

"It won't be easy to convince the men to go against Hugh while he holds Dunscaith Castle," Ian said. "We must find a way to show them that Connor is the better man."

"I'm starving," Alex said, tossing his dirty towel at Ian. "It must be time to eat, aye?"

"Something da said about what happened at the battle troubles me," Ian said, as they headed toward the house.

"What's that?" Alex asked.

"He said the English surprised him, striking from behind," Ian said. "You've fought with my father—the man fights like he's got eyes in the back of his head. How did the English get past him without him knowing it?"

Alex squeezed Ian's shoulder. "In his prime, your father was a great warrior—but he's grown old."

"Aye, he has," Ian said, his spirits sinking as he recalled his father's sallow cheeks and graying hair. "I should have been there to protect his back."

"How are ye feeling today, Payton?" Sìleas asked, as she set the tray on the small table next to the bed.

"I'm missing a leg, so how do ye think I am?" he said.

She stopped herself from helping him sit up, knowing it would annoy him. Though she had a hundred things to do, Sìleas took the chair beside him and forced her hands to be still.

"What are ye all upset about?" Payton asked, slanting his eyes at her as he lifted an oatcake to his mouth.

Sìleas pressed her lips together.

"Come, Sìleas, you're so furious it's making your hair curl."

"Your son is an idiot," she blurted out—and regretted it as soon as the words were out of her mouth.

"Which of my idiot sons are ye referring to?" Payton asked.

"I'll not hear ye say another word against Niall, and ye know it," she said. "It's time ye stopped blaming him for doing what he had to do."

"So it's Ian, is it?" Payton said.

"I fail to see why this is the first thing to amuse ye in weeks," she snapped. Despite her annoyance, Sìleas was pleased to see a glimmer of his old self.

"What's Ian done to get on your wrong side so soon?"

She couldn't tell him that Ian had not seen fit to acknowledge her or their marriage—she had her pride— so she shared Ian's latest offense.

"He's no notion of what must be done with the crops and livestock," she said, folding her arms. It was Ian's responsibility now, and he would just have to learn.

"I raised Ian to be a warrior, not a farmer, lass. He has more important things to attend to," Payton said, his expression turning stern. "I told him how that devil took Knock Castle."

Sìleas said nothing, knowing that the loss of her castle was a festering wound to Payton's pride—and to the whole clan. Her step-da had bided his time for five years, then struck in the wake of Flodden when the MacDonalds were weak.

Payton set his plate on the tray and sank back on the pillows, looking pale.

"If it's any comfort to ye, I expect the Knock Castle ghost is haunting my step-da," she said, giving him a wink. "I doubt the Green Lady has let Murdoc have a single good night's sleep."

"'Tis a shame your ghost doesn't carry a dirk," Payton said in a tired voice.

"Shall I tell ye how she warned me to leave that day?" she asked.

"Aye, lass." Payton closed his eyes as she began and was asleep before she was halfway through the old story. It hurt her to see the great man so weakened.

The hands resting on the bedcovers were marked by battle scars that told a tale of their own. Yet she remembered how gently those big hands had encompassed hers the morning Payton had found her and Ian sleeping in the wood. Without waking him, Sìleas lifted the hand closest to her and held it.

Payton was getting stronger every day. She could leave soon. With Ian here, he would do just fine without her. They all would.

But she feared that when she left she would be like Payton, always missing a part of her that was gone.

CHAPTER 6

Ian stood in the doorway watching Sìleas. This was the new Sìleas again, all clean and combed in a moss-green gown—and so lovely he had to remind himself to breathe. She must have bathed in the tub in the kitchen, for her cheeks were pink and a damp curl was stuck to the side of her face.

He was surprised his father would let her hold his hand as if he were a child, until he realized his da was asleep. Though he was careful not to make a sound, she sensed his presence and turned. Today her eyes were the same dark mossy green as her gown, but touched with dew from tears that welled in her eyes.

"My mother said to tell ye dinner is ready," he said in a hushed voice. "Are ye all right?"

Sìleas nodded and picked up the tray as she got up. When Ian stepped aside to let her pass, she said, "He's not a well man. Ye shouldn't have kept him up so late."

Apparently, Sìleas had kindness in her heart for every member of his family but him.

"My father wanted to talk," Ian said, "and I think it did him good."

"I suppose you're right," she said with a sigh. "But have a care with him."

Ian followed the provocative sway of her hips until she disappeared into the kitchen.

He continued watching her as they ate their midday meal. With that full bottom lip, her mouth was made for kissing. Every time she puckered and blew on her stew, his heart did an odd little leap in his chest. And his heart was not the only part of him affected. His cock was standing to attention, stiff as an English soldier.

Likely, Sìleas was foul-tempered toward him for not making his intentions clear. He had trouble recalling his reasons for waiting as he watched her take a spoonful into her mouth, smile with pleasure at the taste, and run her pink tongue across her top lip.

Perhaps he should just take her to bed now and have done with it. If the price of following his desire was gaining a wife, well, it was time he had one anyway.

Alex, the devil, was sitting next to Sìleas and plying her with his legendary charm. She threw her head back laughing at something he said. It was a lovely laugh— full-throated and sensual.

"I don't believe a word you're saying, Alex Bàn Mac-Donald!" Sìleas pressed her hand to her bosom as if she couldn't get her breath. "Five men, ye say? How did ye ever escape?"

"Ye mean, how did *they* get away?" Alex asked. " 'Twas nothing, really. I told them they could run, or they could die."

It irked Ian the way Sìleas leaned forward with her

eyes fixed on Alex, as if she were swallowing Alex's tale whole.

"There were only three of them, not five," Ian corrected, his words sounding peevish to his own ears.

Sìleas turned to face him, her smile fading. Lord, but she had pretty eyes, even when they were dead serious, as they were now. The scent of summer heather tickled his nose. Did she use dried heather in her bath water? Ah, that meant every inch of her skin would have that lovely smell.

"Now that we've mucked out the byre," Ian said, "Alex and I are going to go speak to some of the men on this side of the island."

"And why do ye need to do that?" Sìleas asked.

Ian raised his eyebrows. "Not that ye need to know, mind ye, but we intend to find out how the men feel about the prospect of having Hugh as their chieftain."

"I can tell ye the sentiment toward Hugh, as can Niall," Sìleas said, slicing her meat with enough vigor to cut through the table. "But if ye must ask the men yourself, they'll all be at the church tomorrow."

"A priest is visiting the island," his mother explained. "Father Brian will be baptizing all the children born since he was here a year ago."

There was always a shortage of priests in the Highlands. Unlike in France, the church here was poor. Though Highland chieftains might allow God the use of their lands for churches and monasteries, they did not give their lands away. Because the church could provide little to support them, few men joined the priesthood, and a priest who married was not turned out. As with divorce and marriage, the rules of the church were not strictly followed in the Highlands.

"Waiting to see the men at the church seems a good plan," Alex said, giving Sìleas a bright smile. "Wouldn't ye agree, Ian?"

Ian nodded, though he would rather go now, if only to feel he was doing something.

"And don't ignore the womenfolk," his mother put in. "*Ná bac éinne ná bíonn buíochas na mban air.*" Pay no heed to anyone that the womenfolk do not respect.

"Sìleas," Alex said, "what do ye say to you and me going out in the boat this afternoon?"

Alex was trying to taunt him; Ian glared at him to let him know he did not find it amusing.

"That sounds lovely," Sìleas said with a soft smile for Alex. "But after I clean up the kitchen, I must have a word with Ian here."

She said his name like she might say *pig shite*.

Then she turned to level a hard look at him. "When ye have finished your meal, can ye spare a wee bit of time to speak with me?"

Sìleas might not look the same, but she was as direct as when she was a lass running wild. Clearly, she wanted to know where she stood with him. Her sharp words reminded him that he would be wise to give himself time before deciding his fate.

"Do ye have no woman to help in the kitchen?" Ian asked, only partly because he wanted to divert her. They had always had one clanswoman or another who needed a home, living with them and helping his mother.

"Some of the men came to ask your da's advice regarding the selection of a new chieftain," his mother said. "He urged them to wait for Connor's return—and Hugh Dubh has been punishing us ever since."

"When Hugh threatened everyone who worked here," Sìleas said, "we told them to leave."

"Go along now and talk with Ian," his mother said, taking the bowls from Sìleas. "I'll clean up."

As Ian got to his feet, Niall came in through the door. Instead of giving him the sharp edge of her tongue for missing dinner, Sìleas's expression softened when she saw him.

"Niall, can ye join Ian and me?"

Now, why would she be asking Niall to join them?

"Whatever ye need, I'm there," Niall said, smiling at her as he hung his cap by the door.

"I appreciate it." Sìleas's voice wavered a bit, as if Niall had done something special that touched her—when all she showed Ian was irritation.

As he followed Sìleas up the stairs, the smell of heather filled his nose. He couldn't help taking in her slim ankles and the sway of her skirts as she climbed the steep steps. Lifting his gaze, he imagined her smooth, rounded bottom beneath the skirts.

She led them into the room that had been his bedchamber growing up. It looked different now, with pretty stones lining the windowsill and dried flowers in a jug on the table. His stomach tightened with the memory of the last time he was in this room—their "wedding" night, when he had spent a long, restless night on the hard floor.

He glanced at his old bed—the bed she slept in now. If he chose, he could sleep here with her every night. He was hard just thinking about it. If he stayed with her, he would build a new bed for them suitable for Knock Castle, with posts and heavy curtains like he had seen in France.

After taking a chair at the table, she gestured for him

and Niall to do the same. Niall sat opposite her, as if by habit, leaving Ian to pull up a stool between them, facing the wall.

"I don't know if ye realize how verra badly injured your da was when we first got him back." Sìleas spoke in a soft voice and fixed her gaze on the table.

"Da didn't wake for a fortnight," Niall put in. "'Twas a miracle he lived."

His father wished to God he hadn't, crippled as he was. In his place, Ian would feel the same.

"Since ye were not here, Niall and I have been making the decisions that needed to be made these last few weeks," Sìleas said, her tone becoming clipped again. "I hope you'll be satisfied with what we've done."

"What sort of decisions?" Ian asked.

Sìleas stood to take down a sheaf of papers from the shelf above the table. "How many cattle to slaughter for the winter, which sheep to sell or trade, that sort of thing."

What could be more tedious?

Sìleas sat down and pushed the stack of papers across the table to him. "Now that you are here, these are your decisions to make." She paused, then added, "At least until your da is well."

Ian glanced down. There were figures all down the first page. "What do ye expect me to do with these?"

"Sìleas will have to explain it to ye," Niall said, grinning at her. "She's been helping da manage our lands and tenants for years. Ye should hear him, always bragging about how clever she is."

His father? Letting a lass help him and boasting about it? Ian didn't want to accuse his brother of lying, but, truly, this was hard to fathom.

Ian watched Sìleas as she spoke about cattle and crops, listening more to the sound of her voice than her words. He did notice how she repeatedly brought Niall into her recitation. What impressed him as much as her enthusiasm for the tedious details was how she recognized his brother's need to be relied upon as a man.

His father certainly showed no concern for Niall's pride. Remembering his father's harshness toward Niall, Ian felt a rush of warmth toward Sìleas for her kindness to his brother. He would have to ask her why his da was so angry with Niall.

With his mind on Niall and his father, he didn't realize she was finished going over the accounts until she was on her feet.

"I must go now," she said, smoothing her skirts, "or the clothes will never be washed and you'll have no supper."

Without thinking, Ian said, "Isn't running the household my mother's responsibility?" This brought a second question to mind that had been nagging him. Gesturing to the sheaf of papers before him, he said, "Why was she not the one to make these decisions in da's place?"

"Do ye think I took it from her?" Sìleas asked, her voice barely above a whisper. "Is that what ye think?"

The hurt in Sìleas's eyes cut him to the quick.

"I did not mean—," he started to say, but she cut him off.

"It doesn't matter," she said, though clearly it did. "You'll be taking over the task now, so I'll leave ye to it."

"Wait," Ian said, catching her arm. "You've done a fine job with it, and I'd be happy to have ye continue."

"'Tis no my place to do it now," she said in a tight voice.

Ach, he felt lower than dirt. But before he could get out

a word of apology, she was out the door. No sooner was she gone, than his brother slammed his fist on the table.

"Ye have no notion what it's been like here, while you've been off having your adventures," Niall said.

Ian met his brother's angry gaze. "Then you'll have to tell me."

"Da was barely alive when I got him home." Niall worked his jaw as he leaned forward and stared at his hands. "I don't know what we would have done without Sìleas. She was the one who washed his wounds every day and put on the salve she got from Teàrlag."

Grief and guilt curled together in Ian's gut. He would never know if he could have saved his father from injury had he been at his side in the battle. But he was as good as any man with a sword, so he might have made a difference.

"During the time da did not waken," Niall said, "Sìleas spent hours at his bedside, talking and reading to him as if he could hear every word."

It struck Ian as odd that Niall spoke only of Sìleas taking care of their father. "What about mam?"

"Mam stopped speaking when she thought da was dying. She was like the walking dead herself." Niall kept his eyes fixed on his hands and spoke in a low, rough voice. "Sìl and I did our best to make her eat, but she grew so weak we feared we would lose her, too."

Guilt was bitter in Ian's throat. Niall was far too young for the burden he'd been carrying—and it was Ian's burden.

"Mam's been much better since da woke up a couple of weeks ago. But da..." Niall turned to gaze out the small window. "Well, it's been almost worse since he awoke and found his leg was gone."

Ian leaned across the table and squeezed his brother's

shoulder. "I'm sorry I wasn't here. We came as soon as we heard the news of the battle."

"Ye should have been here long before then," Niall said, his voice hard. "For Sìleas, ye should have been here. You've shamed her by leaving her for so long."

Ian had never considered that his absence might shame her. Until he returned, he had thought of her as an awkward girl not ready for marriage.

"One way or another, I will make it right," Ian said. "I am grateful to ye for taking care of the family in my absence."

"It's Sìleas ye should be thanking, not me." His brother stood abruptly, jostling the table. He was shaking with anger. "Sìleas has worked herself to the bone, keeping the family going these last weeks. Did ye not see the circles under her eyes? I do my best to help her, but it's no enough."

"I'll see to things now," Ian said, keeping his voice quiet.

"Then you'd best convince her to stay," Niall said, "for we cannot do without her."

"Sìleas is not going anywhere soon." At least not until he made up his mind.

"'Tis a wonder she hasn't left ye yet," Niall said, his eyes burning into Ian. "If ye don't know it, there is a line of men just waiting for her to lose patience with ye."

CHAPTER 7

Ian listened to Alex's snoring in the next bed and watched the sky grow light through the crack in the shutters of the old cottage as he thought about the day ahead. It was an important day, for him and for the clan. After weighing the advantages and disadvantages over the two days since his return, he had decided to accept Sìleas as his true wife. He would tell her today, after the gathering at the church.

In the end, it was an easy choice. Sìleas had become the peg that held his family together. After not being here when they needed him, he would not take her away from them now. They were all very fond of her. In fact, he was a trifle concerned Niall's feelings toward her were not entirely brotherly, but the lad was young and would get over it soon enough.

For his mother, Sìleas filled the hole in her heart left by the baby daughters she had lost. What surprised him was the closeness between Sìleas and his father. Busy as Sìleas was, Ian found her at his father's bedside several times a day. Her presence seemed to soothe him.

Although his father had never openly mourned the loss of their daughters as his mother had, perhaps he, too, had carried a wound that Sìleas healed.

If for no other reason, Ian would have kept Sìleas for the sake of his family. Added to that, she was heir to Knock Castle, a good manager, and she made his blood run hot. What more could a man ask for?

Now that he'd come home to take his place in the clan, he needed a wife. There was no good reason to upset the basket when he already had one that suited. The only objection he could claim was that he hadn't chosen Sìleas in the first place. It would be just pigheaded to let that stop him when everything else weighed in favor of the marriage.

Now that he'd made up his mind, it was only a matter of getting Sìleas alone so he could tell her. Saving the clan from Hugh Dubh came first, of course. He would speak to her after the business at the church today.

Then he could join Sìleas in the bed upstairs.

He smiled to himself. That particular advantage had weighed heavily in favor of keeping the marriage. No more sleeping in the old cottage with Alex. And once he told Sìleas of his decision, she would stop giving him the sharp edge of her tongue.

He could think of other uses for that tongue...

"Are ye going to lie abed all morning?" Alex said, and Ian turned to find his cousin dressed and strapping on his claymore.

Ian grinned at him, feeling better than he had since returning home. He could hardly wait to see Sìl's face when he told her. He remembered how she used to look up to him, with that glow in her eyes, as if he was the strongest and bravest person she could ever hope to meet.

When he told her, she would look at him that way
again—but with a woman's eyes. And a woman's desire.
Then he'd pull her into his arms and kiss her as he'd been
wanting to. Ah, it had been years since he'd given a lass
her first kiss.

And then there would be all the other firsts...

God's blood, he'd never bedded a virgin before. He had
done his best to avoid innocents up until now. It surprised
him that he found the prospect of bedding a virgin...
exciting. At least, this particular virgin. Sìleas would be
his alone, now and forever.

"Ian," Alex said, jarring him back to the present.

As he got out of bed, Ian grabbed his plaid to cover his
throbbing erection. God's beard, he was in pain. Tonight.
Tonight, he would get to take Sìleas to bed.

But first, there was the gathering. Work before pleasure.

"I see you're going to church prepared," Ian said to
Alex, as he strapped on his own claymore.

"I don't wish to count on Hugh respecting the house of
God without encouragement."

Word of Ian and Alex's arrival would have reached
Hugh's ears, and their presence was bound to make Hugh
nervous. Hugh was no one's fool. He'd know that if they
were here, Connor and Duncan could not be far behind.

"How many blades are ye taking?" Ian asked, as he
slipped a dirk into the side of his boot.

"I only have two dirks," Alex said, pulling a face.

"Here," Ian said, tossing him another. "I got extra from
the house last night."

"You're a good man," Alex said, catching it.

Sìleas wasn't downstairs when they had their breakfast, but she was waiting at the gate with Ian's mother when

Ian, Alex, and Niall brought the horses to the front of the house.

"You're sure you'll be fine without me?" Sìleas asked his mother.

"Ye worry too much," his mother said, patting her hand. "I'm feeling my old self again. Payton and I will manage just fine."

Sìleas kissed his mother on the cheek and turned to where the three of them were waiting on their horses. "It's such a fine day," she said. "We could walk."

"We're riding," Ian said.

It was true that the rain was no more than a light mist, which made it a fine day for mid-October in the Highlands. But he wanted the horses in case they needed to make a quick departure.

When Sìleas started toward Niall's horse, Ian nudged his forward to block her way. He held out his hand. "Ride with me."

For a moment, she looked as if she would refuse, which annoyed him. He reminded himself that she didn't know yet of his decision. When she finally gave him her hand, he swung her up in front of him. He pulled her tight against him as he kicked his horse into a trot. When he turned to wave good-bye to his mother, she gave him an approving nod.

He'd make two women happy by his decision to make a true marriage with Sìleas.

It was hard to think with the smell of her hair in his nose and her bottom snug between his thighs. But the ride was short, so he forced his thoughts to what he would say to the men when they got there.

As they neared the church, they had to pass Dunscaith Castle, the seat of their clan chieftain. The castle was

made famous by two women, both of whom—if Teàrlag
was to be believed—were Duncan's ancestors. According
to the old stories, Dunscaith was built in a single night by
a sea witch. It was here, too, that the great Celtic warrior
queen, Scáthach, ran her legendary School for Heroes.

Ian had seen Dunscaith a thousand times before, but
today he looked at it for the first time as an attacker. The
castle stood on a rock island just offshore, with a gap of
twenty feet between it and the main island. If the sheer
rock was not enough to deter an attack by sea, the five-
foot-thick curtain wall on top of it surely would.

To get into the castle, an attacker either had to come in
by the sea gate on the far side, which was easily blocked,
or cross the walled bridge that spanned the gap. If you
made it across the bridge, the castle's defenders could
raise the drawbridge at their end of it to stop you. And if
you made it past the drawbridge, you still had to fight your
way up a walled flight of stairs that was too narrow for
two men to go abreast swinging their swords.

"An easy castle to defend and a hard one to take," Alex
said, echoing Ian's thoughts.

"Aye." As they rode past, Ian narrowed his eyes at the
castle's tower. Was Hugh there now, watching them from
his perch?

It was hard to bear that a greedy, honorless man held
the castle where Scáthach had trained her celebrated warriors of old.

Ian could see that there was already a large gathering
of people outside the church, which was no more than a
stone's throw past the bridge to the castle. The church was
a humble, whitewashed building, a poor relation to the
cathedrals he had seen in France.

With his thoughts on Hugh and the tasks ahead, Ian realized that he hadn't spoken a word to Sìleas—but he didn't have time now.

"Watch after her," Ian said to his brother, as he helped her dismount. "I need to talk to the men."

As planned, he and Alex moved separately through the gathered men to discover what they thought of Hugh proclaiming himself chieftain. After welcoming him home, a few spoke quietly to Ian about Hugh's mistreatment of them or their family. One who was not so quiet was Tait MacDonald, a wiry man of thirty.

"Hugh violated my sister and left her carrying a babe," Tait said, his eyes burning with hate.

"I suspect ye don't wish to wait for Judgment Day to see him punished," Ian said. "I know I wouldn't."

"Hugh had best watch his back." Tait sidled closer and added, "A lot of men would support ye if ye put yourself forward for the chieftainship."

"I am not of the chieftain's blood." Ian was as skilled a warrior as any, and he could lead men in battle. But the best of chieftains needed to be patient schemers as well, and patience was one trait he did not share with his cousin.

"No, it has to be Connor," he told Tait. "He's back, and he'll be a great chieftain, even better than his father."

"Tell Connor I'm with him," Tait said.

Ian looked the man over and surmised that Tait's quickness would more than make up for his short stature in a fight. "He'll be glad to have ye on his side."

It was a start, and others would follow. As the saying went, one cow breaks the fence, and a dozen leap it.

"The problem is that Connor is still a lad in the men's memory," Tait said. "He's been gone a long time."

Tait was right. The men needed to see Connor to judge his mettle as a man. Showing himself openly too soon, however, could get him killed.

"On the other hand," Tait said, "the men are outraged that after calling himself chieftain, Hugh sat by while the MacKinnons attacked Knock Castle. And they don't understand why he hasn't tried to take it back."

The loss of Knock Castle was one more weight in the chain of guilt around Ian's neck. Even though he hadn't wanted it, holding Knock Castle had been his duty.

The morning after his "wedding," Ian and his chieftain surprised Sìleas's stepfather with the news of the marriage—and an overwhelming force. As soon as the MacKinnons surrendered the castle, Ian sailed for France, not caring who his chieftain chose to hold the castle in his name. But fury, tinged with shame, burned in his belly now. The clansman who stood in his place as defender of the castle had been killed in the MacKinnon attack.

As Ian moved through the crowd, he heard again and again the complaint about the loss of Knock Castle.

"What are ye going to do about your wife's castle?" more than one man asked him. "We're ready to fight for it, but we need a chieftain to lead us."

Speak of the devil.

When the men around Ian shifted their gazes and stepped back, he turned to see Hugh Dubh emerge from the castle's bridge followed by a score of men. Ian exchanged a glance with Alex over the heads of the other men to be sure Alex had seen Hugh. Alex nodded and headed his way.

Ian caught the priest by the arm. "Father, get the women and children inside the church."

The priest turned and saw Hugh and his men. "I'll get

them inside, but I'm warning ye, I'll have no violence here in the churchyard."

"That's up to Hugh," Ian said. "All I can promise is that I won't be starting it."

Ian found Sìleas and Niall next. "Go inside now," he said, putting his hand to the curve of her back to push her along.

Sìleas glared at the approaching men over her shoulder. "I'm not afraid of Hugh."

"Ye should be," Ian said, gripping her arm hard so she would know he meant it. "Niall, see that she gets inside, then help the priest with the others."

Niall and Sìleas both scowled at him, but he didn't have time to argue.

"Go now, both of ye."

He moved to stand next to Alex just as Hugh and his men entered the churchyard. Hugh's gaze was fixed on him, which was fine with Ian.

I am ready to cut your ballocks off, Hugh Dubh.

Hugh halted a yard in front of him and stood with his legs apart in a wide stance. For a long moment, they took each other's measure. Hugh was a big, square-faced man who bore a strong resemblance to Connor's father and Ragnall. As the youngest of his father's six sons, he couldn't be much over thirty, though his years at sea made him look older.

When Connor's father was made chieftain, Hugh took up pirating. Judging from the colorful stories told about him, Hugh was successful at his trade. Some believed he could call up a sea mist at will, because of the way his boats disappeared after an attack. Others said Hugh had a large stash of gold hidden on the Isle of Uist—and that he fed captured children to the sea dragon that guarded it.

"I heard the two of ye were back," Hugh said, resting his hand on the hilt of the long dirk in his belt. "Ye should have come to the castle to pay your respects."

"If the men who used to work our land still did," Ian said, "perhaps I could have spared the time for a wee visit."

"The rest of ye stand back," Hugh said, and lifted his hand. "I need a private word with the prodigal sons here."

He waited to speak until the others backed away a few paces.

"I was merely encouraging your da to pledge his loyalty," Hugh said, his eyes glinting with amusement. "But now that you're here, I'll accept your pledge in his place."

Anger pulsed through Ian; his hand itched to reach for the claymore strapped to his back. One good swing and he could rid the clan of this vermin.

Ian made no effort to keep his voice down. "While my father lives, I'll no be making decisions for him." *Ye slimy bastard.*

"I hear he's lost his mind, as well as his leg," Hugh said. "It's your duty to step up and take his place as head of your family."

"As all the men here know," Ian said in a loud voice, as he swept his arm out to encompass the men gathered around them in the churchyard, "my father fought in many battles with the Lord of the Isles to protect our clan. He merits the respect of his son and his clan."

The men responded with nods and grunts of approval.

"I will not take my father's place nor give his pledge," Ian said, glaring at Hugh.

"And where does your father stand, Alexander Bàn MacDonald?" Hugh asked.

"If ye have to ask, my guess is he hasn't given ye his

support," Alex said with a smile that suggested he knew very well his father wouldn't favor Hugh. "Ye don't suppose he has reservations about your ability to lead, do ye?"

The vein in Hugh's neck pulsed as he flicked his gaze between Alex and Ian.

"In the end, he'll bend his knee with all the rest of ye," Hugh snapped. "Ye can tell Connor the same when ye see him."

Ian turned to speak to the men behind him, leaving Alex to cover his back.

"As the son of Payton, a nephew to our dead chieftain, and a man of this clan," Ian shouted, "I call for a gathering of the clan to choose our next chieftain, as is our custom."

When Ian turned back, Hugh looked as if he would have liked to plant his claymore in his chest, but another round of approving grunts had him thinking better of it.

"That's a fine idea," Hugh said through his teeth. "We can all go into the hall of the castle and do it right now."

Hugh's men, a rough lot from his pirating days, raised their fists and shouted their agreement. For a moment, Ian feared he had lost control of the crowd, but it was soon evident from the silence of the other men that they did not agree with Hugh's suggestion.

"Every man is entitled to a voice in the selection of our chieftain," Tait called out. "Word must be sent to every member of the clan, with a date certain."

There was a loud murmur of agreement.

Hugh could read the crowd as well as Ian. "We'll confirm my place as chieftain at the Samhain gathering," he said. "I'll send word out that I expect every man to come to the castle and make his pledge."

Alex raised an eyebrow at Ian. At least they wouldn't

have to fight their way into Dunscaith, since Hugh had agreed to a formal gathering to select a chieftain.

"Now, let's see those babes christened." Hugh signaled to his men, and the crowd parted for them as they headed for the church door.

"You've got ballocks," Ian said to Alex, as they waited for the other men to go inside the church. "Do ye suppose my father has reservations about your ability to lead?"

"Me? I was just trying to make Hugh's eyes bulge as much as you did."

They shared a dry laugh, then started for the church.

"Samhain is less than three weeks away," Alex said, worry tugging at his voice.

"It might be easier to take the castle by force," Ian said, "than to persuade so many hard-headed MacDonalds of anything in so short a time."

"Pity Hugh's mother didn't drown him at birth," Alex said.

"Aye, 'tis a damn shame."

The priest, who had a warrior's build to go with his manner, stood at the doorway, making every man leave his weapons outside. "Now lads, ye can put your claymores in this pile and your dirks in that one. They'll be no weapons in my church."

"Did ye make Hugh Dubh and his men leave theirs?" Ian asked when it was his turn.

"I did," the priest said. "And ye will leave yours as well."

"You're a brave man," Ian said in a low voice. "If you're a good one, too, then ye know that Hugh is the devil's tool."

The priest's dark eyes flashed, and he gave Ian a slight nod.

"Ye can be sure that Hugh and his men kept a few

dirks hidden from ye," Ian said. "I mean no disrespect, but that means my cousin and I must keep ours as well."

"Keep them well hidden," the priest said in a low voice.

Ian leaned close to speak in the priest's ear. "When the time comes, we'll need every good man, including you, Father."

"God will reward the righteous," the priest said. "Now ye are holding up God's work, so get inside."

One look from Ian, and the boys who were sitting in the back pew got up to find other seats. He and Alex needed to sit closest to the door—and the piles of weapons outside. After they sat down, Ian searched the crowded church for Sìleas. It didn't take long to find her near the front. Hair as bright as hers stood out, even among this many redheads.

"Who is that beside her?" he hissed at Alex.

"Beside who?"

"Ach, ye know damned well I meant Sìleas."

Alex didn't try to hide his smile. "I believe that's your neighbor, Gòrdan." After a pause, he added, "Gòrdan is a fine man. I'd wager the lasses find him handsome as well."

Ian stewed as a dozen squalling babes were sprinkled and prayed over.

"By the saints, how many babes were born this year?" he complained.

"I'd say the men had a verra good winter," Alex said.

Ian and Alex were the first ones out the door after the last babe was baptized. The drops of holy water didn't have time to dry on the babe's wee head before they had their weapons in their hands.

" 'Tis good to have her again," Alex said, kissing the blade of his claymore.

He and Alex stood side by side with their blades

unsheathed as Hugh and his entourage filed out of the church.

Hugh stopped in front of them. "Mark my words, unless you're dead by Samhain," he hissed in a low voice, "you'll be on your knees before me at the gathering."

"One of us will be dead before that happens," Ian said.

Ian met the gaze of each man as they came out of the church and passed him. He recognized most of them. Every man understood that the return of the Highlanders from France had shifted the balance of power here on Skye. Each man would have to choose sides.

When the last of Hugh's men was on the bridge to the castle, Ian caught sight of Ilysa, Duncan's sister. She was such a slight thing, it was hard to believe she and Duncan came from the same mother. In a shapeless gown and with her hair covered in a drab kerchief like a grandmother, Ilysa blended in with the married women. He only noticed her when she looked up and gave him a razor-sharp glance. Then she tilted her head, signaling she wanted to talk with him.

When he approached the group of women, they crowded around him asking about his travels. It took him some time to ease Ilysa away.

"I am sorry to hear you lost your husband at Flodden," he said once they were out of the hearing of the others.

An emotion he couldn't read crossed Ilysa's face before she dropped her gaze and nodded to acknowledge his condolence.

"Where are ye living?" he asked.

"I'm back at the castle."

Ian stared at her. "That can't be safe. Hugh and his men are a rough lot."

Ilysa and Duncan had grown up in the castle, but Ian had assumed she was living with her husband's family.

"Ach, no one notices me," Ilysa said with a small smile. "And just to be sure they keep their distance, I let it be known that I'm learning magic from Teàrlag."

"I can't believe Duncan is letting ye stay there," Ian said.

"As if I'd let Duncan tell me what to do," she said, rolling her eyes. "I managed without his instruction while the four of ye were gone. He did try, but I'm twice as stubborn as he is."

That was saying something.

"But why stay at the castle?" Ian said. "If ye don't want to go to your husband's family, you're welcome to stay at our house."

"Connor needs eyes and ears in the castle, and none of ye can do that for him," she said. "Hugh thinks so little of women, he has no notion I'm spying on him."

If Duncan hadn't been able to convince her, Ian wouldn't be able to. "Ye be careful now. Don't take any chances."

"I have a message from Connor and Duncan," Ilysa said in a low voice. "Ye are to meet them in the cave below Teàrlag's cottage day after tomorrow."

Alex came up behind them and put his arm around Ilysa's narrow shoulders. "So how is Duncan's baby sister?"

"I am just fine, and ye can take your hands off me, Alexander Bàn," Ilysa said good-naturedly as she pushed Alex's arm off. "What trouble are ye up to?"

"Trouble, me? No, I've been doing a good deed," Alex said, with a devilish grin. Turning to Ian, he said, "I found a woman to help your mother and Sìleas in the kitchen."

"Did ye now?" Ian scratched his neck. "Let me guess. Does the woman ye found happen to be an attractive lass with loose morals?"

"Here I am, trying to help out a poor kinswoman whose been thrown out by her husband," Alex said, shaking his head, "and all ye want to do is criticize."

"Ye don't mean Dina, do ye?" Ilysa asked.

Dina? Ian had a vague memory of a dark-eyed, curvy lass who was a couple of years older than he was. He'd been between her thighs once or twice when he was barely old enough to know what to do.

"Good luck with that," Ilysa said. "I must get back now. I've got Hugh believing no one else can make sure there's plenty of food and ale on the table."

When she had gone, Ian said, "Perhaps ye should have asked me before inviting someone to live in my house."

"I didn't see you finding anyone to help your poor mother and wife." Alex shrugged. "But if ye don't care that they are working their fingers to the bone, well . . ."

At the mention of Sìleas, Ian swept his gaze over the few women still in the churchyard.

"Have ye seen Sìleas?" he asked, thinking she must have gone back into the church.

"She left with Gòrdan"—Alex cleared his throat—"for their *usual* Sunday stroll."

"Their what?"

"Don't fret—she said they'll meet us at the house," Alex said. "Ye see, Gòrdan's joining the family for Sunday dinner. As usual."

"What does Sìleas think she's doing?" Ian felt as if his head was exploding.

"Strolling, I suppose," Alex said.

Ian wanted to smash his fist into the middle of Alex's grinning face.

That sneaking Gòrdan. Ian found his brother by their horses and grabbed him by the arm. "Tell me what's been going on with Sìleas and Gòrdan."

Niall jerked his arm away. "Gòrdan's been protecting her, just as we all have, *in your absence*."

With that, Niall swung up onto his horse, slapped the reins, and galloped off. Ian blew out his breath and wondered what had happened to the young lad who used to look up to him. He would have to have a talk with his brother. But first, he would deal with Sìleas.

On the ride back to the house, he ignored Alex's attempts at conversation. He was in no mood for it. He kept his eyes out for Gòrdan and Sìleas, but he did not catch a glimpse of the wandering pair all the way back.

If they were not on the path, where in the hell were they?

CHAPTER 8

When they reached the house, Alex went to the byre, saying he preferred the beasts' company to Ian's. Niall must have taken himself off somewhere as well, for there was no sign of him. Ian found his mother alone, stitching by the fire.

"How's da?" he asked.

"Sleeping."

Ian sat with his arms folded, waiting for Sìleas and Gòrdan.

His mother looked up from her sewing. "What's troubling ye, son?"

"I am trying to understand why my family appears to have encouraged Sìleas to go off alone with Gòrdan every chance she gets," he said, grinding out the words. "Ye know how that looks, mam. Sìl didn't have a mother who taught her that sort of behavior could earn her a reputation, but ye know better. Why did ye not tell her?"

His mother arched her eyebrows. "If ye were concerned about your wife's behavior, perhaps ye should have come home sooner."

"I didn't know she was traipsing all over the Isle of Skye with Gòrdan Graumach MacDonald." And traipsing had damned well better be all she was doing with Gòrdan.

"Ach, men," his mother murmured and went back to her stitching. "What ye should be doing is thanking Gòrdan for looking after her."

"I should be thanking him?" Ian said, working hard not to shout at his mother.

"Ye can't expect her to stay cooped up in the house all the time," his mother said. "Your da never let her go out alone for fear her MacKinnon relations would try to snatch her. Since he was injured and the other men quit working our lands, Gòrdan has been kind enough to accompany Sìleas when your brother can't."

"Hmmph," Ian snorted. "Gòrdan has something in mind other than protecting her."

"Gòrdan is an honorable man," his mother said. "If ye don't want Sìleas for a wife, I'd be glad for her to have Gòrdan as her husband."

Ian sat up straight. "As her husband, ye say?"

"Keep your voice down. You'll wake your da."

Before Ian came home, his plan had been to see Sìleas settled with a good man. But Gòrdan? He would never do for her.

"It would be a good match for our Sìleas—except for Gòrdan's mother, of course." She clucked her tongue. "That woman will be a trial to any daughter-in-law."

"It would be a good match—*except for his mother*?" Ian bit out. He couldn't believe he was hearing this.

"Aye, it would," his mother, breaking the thread with her teeth. "Losing Sìleas would be like losing my baby daughters all over again. If she isn't going to remain part of our family, then it would please me to have her close by."

"What makes ye think I'll let Gòrdan have her?"

His mother set her sewing aside and gave him a soft smile. "If ye want Sìleas as your wife, don't ye think it's time ye told her?"

At the sound of the door opening, Ian jumped to his feet. Sìleas came in, looking over her shoulder and laughing. She was a vision, with her cheeks rosy from the cold and loose tendrils of hair curling about her face.

Her laughter died when she turned and saw him.

"Where have ye been?" Ian stood in front of her waiting for an explanation.

"With Gòrdan," she said, as she slipped off her cloak and handed it to Gòrdan to hang by the door.

"I did not see ye on the path," Ian said.

"We weren't on the path," she said, then turned to speak to his mother. "Such a lovely afternoon for this time of year. No, don't get up, Beitris. I'll see to supper."

She brushed past Ian and headed for the kitchen without so much as a glance at him. He was about to follow her when Alex stuck his head through the front door.

"Niall and I could use your help with one of the horses," Alex called, then shut the door again.

Ian stormed outside and found Alex waiting for him by the byre. "What do ye need me for? You're the best man with horses."

"I didn't call ye out for help with the damned horses," Alex said in a low voice. "Your brother is in the byre, and he's in such a fury he's like to put the cows off their milk."

"I don't have time now," Ian said, clenching his fists. "I need to talk with Sìleas."

"Just now, I think ye need to speak with your brother more. I've tried telling Niall that ye are not the horse's ass ye seem to be, but I fear I wasn't too convincing." Alex slapped Ian on the back. "Go talk to the lad."

"Ach!" Ian banged into the byre and found Niall brushing his horse down.

When Niall looked up and saw him, he threw the brush against the wall.

Ian grabbed Niall as he stormed past him. "Niall, what is—"

"Go back to France!" Niall shouted in his face.

Ian blocked Niall's arm when he tried to drive his fist into Ian's face. Before Niall could punch him with his other hand, Ian spun him around and held him by the neck. His own temper was flaming now.

"You're a long way from taking your big brother, so I suggest ye not try that again," Ian hissed in Naill's ear.

There was no point in talking when they were both so angry, so he let his brother go.

Ian watched Niall's stiff back as he stalked out of the byre with his fists clenched. So much for following Alex's advice. Ian finished brushing the horse to calm himself before going back to the house.

By the time he got to the table, his brother and Gòrdan were sitting on either side of Sìleas, and Alex had taken the seat across from her. He sat down and glared at Alex as he started shoveling his food down.

His mother was speaking to him, but Ian couldn't follow what she was saying when it was plain as day that Gòrdan was set on stealing Sìleas away—right under his own roof. God's bones, the man's gaze never left her face.

And what was Alex up to? He was putting on a full

show of his dazzling charm. And from the way Sìl laughed at Alex's foolish remarks, his charm was working.

Ian could hardly choke down his food.

Sìleas was determined to be cheerful. Damn Ian Mac-Donald anyway. First, he demands she ride with him, leading her to believe he was going to play the part of her husband before half the clan at the church. Then, as soon as they arrive, he sends her off as if she were still a child.

She threw her head back and laughed at Alex's joke, though she had missed the first half of it entirely.

Was it too much to ask Ian to sit beside her? For five years, she'd had to listen to the women's remarks about her missing husband. If one more matron had given her a look of sympathy today, she would have screamed right there in the church. And then the women would have even more to talk about.

She should be used to the humiliation by now. But it had been harder than she expected to watch mother after mother bring her babe forward to be baptized, while her own arms were empty.

Ian wasn't even waiting for her at the church door. Fortunately, Gòrdan had been kind enough to take her home as soon as the ordeal was over. Of course, that meant she had to suffer Gòrdan's pleading looks, but at least he had the good sense not to press her today.

"We need to tell them about the men we saw," Gòrdan said in a low voice while the others were talking.

"No," she mouthed.

Gòrdan didn't look happy about it, but he'd do as she asked. She didn't want to worry Beitris and Payton over nothing, just when they were both getting so much better. When she and Gòrdan saw the three strangers coming toward them on the path, she panicked, thinking they could be MacKinnons coming after her.

It was foolish. Why would they come for her after all this time? All the same, she and Gòrdan slipped off the path. They took the shortcut to his house, where he gave her a nip of whiskey while his mother scowled at her.

"What's that you're saying?" Ian asked, glaring at Gòrdan from the far end of the table.

She kicked Gòrdan to remind him of his promise to say nothing.

"That I'd best be getting home," Gòrdan said and stood up. "My mother will be waiting."

She tilted her head back and gave Gòrdan a grateful smile for not telling. "Thanks for seeing me home safe."

No sooner had Gòrdan gone than there was a knocking at the door.

"I'll get it," Alex said.

When he opened the door, in came Dina, a woman men followed around as if she had some dark secret to share with them. Sìleas heard at the church today that Dina's husband caught her in their bed with another man—which was no surprise to anyone but him—and tossed her out.

Unease settled in Sìleas's stomach when Dina dropped a heavy cloth bag inside the door.

"Thank ye for taking me in," Dina said, dipping her head to Ian's mother. "I'm a good cook, and I'll do my best to lend a hand wherever ye need it."

From the startled look on Beitris's face, the invitation to join their household had not come from her.

"Ian and I told Dina ye would be happy for her help," Alex said.

Sìleas shot a look at Ian, who was glaring at Alex, as if he was not pleased with Alex for mentioning his role in this. How could Ian do this to her, on top of everything else? It was one humiliation too many.

The awful memory flooded her vision. She must have been nine years old. Ian had told her—repeatedly—that he was "a man now" and couldn't have her following him everywhere anymore. Of course, she had paid no heed.

Until the day she came upon him behind a shepherd's hut with Dina's legs wrapped around his waist.

Ach, he'd forgotten all about Dina. He should have warned his mother. Why did Alex have to go and invite her? Wasn't there enough trouble in the house?

"I'll take Payton's supper to him," Sìleas said, getting up without so much as a glance Ian's way. "Ye must be hungry, Dina. Take my seat."

Ian noticed Sìleas had not touched her own supper.

After they finished their meal, he and Alex went in to talk with Payton. When Ian attempted to catch Sìleas's eye, she abruptly left the room, leaving a cold frost in her wake.

Ian wanted to go after her, but his father was waiting to hear what happened at the church. He showed some of his old spirit as they discussed what needed to be done next. Since his father had taken a long nap, he didn't tire for a good long while.

By the time Ian and Alex returned to the hall, it was empty.

"Damn it," Ian said. "I wanted to talk to Sìleas tonight."

"Talk?" Alex said, elbowing him. "I thought your plan was to take that lass to bed and make a proper wife of her today."

"She doesn't make it easy," Ian said, taking down the jug of whiskey and two cups from the shelf. "The looks she gives me could fry eggs."

"Ach, Sìleas is just upset because you've kept her waiting." Alex patted his chest. "Ye can be sure I wouldn't have."

"Oh, aye, for certain ye would be ready to jump into marriage," Ian said, then tossed back his first drink.

"Not me, but we both know ye are the sort to marry." Alex drank his own cup down and signaled for more. "Ye will do no better than Sìleas. That lass has fire in her."

Before drinking down their second round, they clinked their cups together and chanted, "It's no health if the glass is not emptied."

"What can I do?" Ian said, wiping his mouth. "She acts as if she hates me. And she's always running off with that Gòrdan Graumach."

"Ye can't let Gòrdan have her—he's too dull for a lass with her spark." Alex waggled his eyebrows. "I'd know what to do with that spark."

"This is no time for your joking," Ian said, his irritation rising. "And I'm more than a wee bit tired of hearing what ye would do in my place."

"Who says I'm joking?" Alex lifted one shoulder. "Wouldn't ye rather see her with me than with Gòrdan? Ach, she'd be wasted on a man with so little imagination."

"I don't appreciate ye speaking about my wife that way," Ian said, clenching his fists.

"If ye are so foolish as to let Sìleas go without fighting for her, ye don't deserve her." Alex leaned forward, his expression serious. "And if ye don't make her your true wife soon, ye are going to lose her."

"She is my wife," Ian said through his teeth. "And I intend to keep her."

"Then you'd best do something about it," Alex said. "I grew up with a bitter woman, so I can tell ye—a woman will only forgive so much before she comes to hate ye."

That was a depressing thought; they both took another drink.

"Speaking of your folks," Ian said, "when are ye going to go see them?"

"No matter which I see first, I'll never hear the end of it from the other." Alex blew out a long breath. "I'll wait until the Samhain gathering, so I can see them both at once."

"How many times has your mother tried to poison your da?" Ian asked, without expecting an answer. "Doesn't it strike ye as odd that neither of them married again?"

"Praise God they haven't undertaken to torture anyone else. The only thing the two of them can agree upon is that I should make the same mistake. They want me to marry and produce an heir." Alex shook his head. "Perhaps I should rescue Sìleas from Gòrdan. It would be no hardship to set to work on getting an heir with her."

Ian reached across the table and grabbed Alex by the front of his shirt. "I warned ye not to speak of her that way."

He was stopped from punching his cousin in the face by a light laugh behind him. He turned to see Dina saunter in from the kitchen.

"Fighting over me already, are ye?" she said.

"Don't hurry to the cottage," Alex said to Ian before he pushed himself up from the table. He put his arm around Dina's shoulders and walked with her toward the door.

Ian tipped more whiskey into his cup and swirled the golden liquid. He'd take good Scottish whiskey over French wine any day. He felt the pleasant burn as it slid down his throat. Hell, he'd take bad Scottish whiskey over the best French wine.

What was he doing sleeping in a cold bed every night— next to Alex, for God's sake. Sìleas was his wife, wasn't she? She was sleeping in his room—in his bed, no less.

They'd said vows before a priest. Surely that meant something? True, he'd been ready to give Sìleas up, but that was before he'd returned to find her all grown up.

Lord help him, Sìleas had grown up fine.

He thought of her full breasts, the mesmerizing swish of her skirts as she climbed the stairs, the sparkle in her green eyes, the creamy skin that showed at her throat above her gown.

His cup was empty, so he took a long pull straight from the jug.

He wanted to see more of that creamy skin. To smell it. To run his tongue over every inch of it. And there was no reason he shouldn't. Sìleas belonged to him. The church had joined them.

Damn it, he shouldn't have hesitated. That was where the problem lay. All he needed to do now was show her he wanted to be a husband to her.

But was he ready to give up other women? Was he ready to say she would be the last woman he bedded? He thought about it for a moment.

Hell, yes.

He would show her just how much he wanted her. Sìl was a fiery thing, always was. She'd be everything he wanted in bed, he knew it without a doubt. And he'd be everything she wanted. She damned well wouldn't look twice at that Gòrdan Graumach again.

He slammed his cup down on the table. It was time. His decision was made. By God, he was ready to commit himself.

It was going to be a night to remember.

CHAPTER 9

Ian took off his boots and stepped quietly up the stairs. No need to let the entire household know his intentions. He lifted the latch to Sìleas's bedchamber door—*their* bedchamber door—and slipped inside. Blackness enveloped him as he eased the door shut behind him.

He felt for the bar and slid it across. He wanted no early-morning interruptions. Someone else would have to do the morning chores; he intended to keep Sìleas in bed late. Perhaps they wouldn't get up at all tomorrow.

He stood near the door, every muscle taunt with anticipation, and waited for his eyes to adjust. His cock was painfully hard already. In the stillness, he heard her breathing, soft as sighs.

Gradually, he could make out her form on the bed. She lay on her back, with one arm flung up, framing her head on the pillow. He swallowed. He would carry this image of her from their first night together with him for the rest of his life. A wave of tenderness swelled in his chest. This woman was his to protect. His wife.

He was ready for the responsibility.

His throbbing cock reminded him he was more than ready for the pleasure. His breathing came in short, shallow breaths as he stepped to the edge of the bed.

Lying with her would not be like lying with other women. This was his wife. This was Sìleas.

The muscles of his stomach were tight, and his throat dry. He couldn't wait to touch her. To remove her nightshift and run his hands over that creamy white skin for the first time. To sink his fingers into her mass of red hair as he kissed and caressed her.

They would be naked. Aye, definitely naked. Skin to skin, with the smell of heather in his nose.

He unwound his plaid and pulled his shirt over his head, letting them both drop to the floor at his feet. She gave a sigh as he lifted the covers and slipped beneath the blankets. With his heart thundering in his ears, he reached for her.

He caught the edge of her nightshift, the cloth stiff beneath his fingertips, as she rolled away from him with another sigh. He moved closer and rested his hand on the curve of her waist.

Lust roared through him like a wild beast. For God's sake, she was a virgin. He told himself he must go slowly, but it was not going to be easy.

He pulled her against him and bit his lip against the surge of desire that swamped his senses and tested his will. He made himself take in slow, deep breaths. He meant to savor every part of this first time: holding his wife in bed, the smell of her hair in his face, the warmth of her body next to his.

He pushed her heavy hair to the side and kissed her neck.

"Mmmmm." The sound came from deep in her throat.

He smiled against her skin as he breathed her in. He thought he might have to persuade her, but she had been waiting for him to come to her.

"Sìl," he whispered in her ear, "I'm going to take your nightshift off now."

When he nuzzled her neck, she made that low "Mmmmm" sound again, which set a fire deep in his belly. Then the breath went out of him in a rush as she pressed against him, making his cock throb against the crevice between her buttocks.

He worked her nightshift up, anticipating the feel of bare skin. Slowly, he eased it over her hip—*ahhhh*. Her skin was even softer than he imagined. One more tug on the shift and his shaft rested against her bare buttocks.

"Ye can't know how good that feels," he said in a choked whisper. So good, he nearly bit her shoulder. But this was going better than he expected, and he didn't want to frighten her. So he kissed her shoulder softly, instead, and forced himself not to move against her. She drew in a deep breath that sounded so contented he wondered if he was worrying too much.

He wished he had lit a candle. He wanted to see her, but nothing could get him out of this bed now. It was pleasurable torture to run his hand slowly up and down the curve of her hip. Of its own volition, his hand moved to cup her breast.

Oh Jesu! The heavy softness of her full breast felt glorious in his hand. The nipple hardened and pressed against his palm—and he was a lost man. Blood pounded in his ears. His hunger was urgent, demanding. Now. He needed her under him now.

His resolution to go slow was a lost ship in the raging storm of his lust. All he wanted in this world was to be buried inside her. In an instant, he had her on her back. His hands were on her breasts under her nightgown, and his cock pressed against the inside of her thigh while he kissed her throat.

"Ian! What are ye doing?"

Ach, what was he doing? He dragged himself back from the edge. *A virgin. She's a virgin.*

A virgin shouldn't feel this good beneath him. He took her face in his hands and lowered his mouth to hers. Her kiss was so innocent, it shook him.

"Aw, Sìl, ye are a wonder to me," he said.

He ran his tongue across her bottom lip and heard her draw in her breath. At first she seemed to resist his kisses, but gradually she softened. When he urged her mouth open, she jerked back, startled, but in another moment she softened for him again. When her tongue moved against his he saw a glimpse of the heaven to come. Soon he was drowning in her kisses.

It was all perfect. She was perfect.

He clutched his hands in her hair.

"Don't be afraid. I'll be careful. It won't hurt much," he whispered in her ear as he inched forward. He gasped when the head of his cock found its goal and touched her sweet center.

"Get off me!" Sìleas shouted, and started pounding her fists against his shoulders and chest.

"What? What's wrong?" She didn't answer, but she was clawing at him and squirming like a fish, so he rolled off her. "Sìl, what did I do?"

She threw off the covers and leaped out of the bed. He

caught a glimpse of long legs in the moonlight from the window before she jerked her shift down.

She lit the candle and turned furious eyes on him. "What are ye doing in my bed, Ian MacDonald?"

"It's my bed, too," he said, trying to get his brain to work. His cock was so hard it hurt him. He had been so close...

"How dare ye come in here when I'm fast asleep and think ye can have your way with me."

"You're my wife," Ian said. "That means I can have my way with ye."

"So I'm your wife now, am I? Ye didn't think so before." She folded her arms beneath her breasts, and his throat went dry.

"I...I've decided to accept the situation," he said, his eyes and thoughts on her breasts. The skin of his palms tingled with the memory of the feel of them in his hands. "I'm ready to take ye for my wife now. Quite ready."

"Are ye now? And what has made ye come to this decision after all this time?"

She was tapping her foot, not a good sign. Ach, Sìl even had pretty ankles...

"Ian!" she said to get his attention. "I asked what made ye decide ye wanted to be married to me. I thought I 'disgusted' ye."

He swung his legs over the side of the bed and gave her a slow look up and down.

"Ye don't disgust me now," he said, his voice thick. "And I don't disgust you either, judging from the way ye were kissing me." He couldn't help grinning when he said it, which was probably a mistake.

"I was asleep!" She had her hands on her hips now, and her foot was tapping furiously.

"Maybe ye were at first," he said, finding he was enjoying teasing her, "but I don't believe ye were sleeping when ye kissed me back."

"I thought I was dreaming," she snapped. "I didn't know what I was doing."

"For not knowing, ye were doing fine," he said, grinning at her. "Verra fine indeed."

Her cheeks flushed, and she looked prettier still. He grabbed a handful of her voluminous nightshift and pulled her closer.

"I know ye heard me say some unfortunate words about ye before I left, and I'm sorry I hurt your feelings. But I find ye appealing now." He dropped his gaze to the lovely, rounded breasts just inches from his face. "Verra appealing."

When he looked up, her eyes were boring holes into him. He couldn't think for the life of him what he was saying wrong now. What woman didn't like to hear a compliment?

"What you're saying is that ye want to take me to bed," she said.

"Absolutely," he said.

"And that's the reason ye want to be my husband."

"It's one of the reasons," he said, speaking carefully now. "I've also seen all you've done for my family, and how attached they are to ye. My mother is very fond of ye."

"So ye want to keep me because your mother is fond of me," she said. "That would be a rare comfort to any woman."

The conversation had somehow gone awry. The problem was that there was too much conversation altogether. If he could just get her into bed again, he could make her forget whatever nonsense she was fussing about.

He stood up and pulled her against him.

"I am sorry if I can't find the right words, but ye feel so good," he murmured against her hair, "and ye smell so good, I cannot think."

She gasped when he cupped her breast. Finally, she seemed at a loss for words.

"We are going to bed eventually, Sìl," he said against her ear. "Don't make me wait. I want ye badly."

She shoved him away. "There's nothing special about wanting to take me to bed, Ian MacDonald." Flinging her arm to the side, she said, "Half the men in the clan could say that. At least, I don't think many would refuse if I made the offer."

Blood pounded in his ears. "If ye offered? If ye offered!"

"Ye wanting me in bed is not a good enough reason for me." She stomped across the room. At the door, she turned and shouted over her shoulder, "You're not good enough for me."

She slammed the door so hard her pretty rocks on the windowsill bounced.

He was more than a wee bit annoyed himself. *If she offered.* How could she say such a thing?

He grabbed his shirt from the floor, pulled it over his head as he crossed the room in three long strides, and took off after her down the stairs. "You are the one who wanted to be married to me in the first place. Ye can't deny it."

"Just stay away from me," she shouted back. "Or I swear, I'll stick a dirk in ye."

"You planned the whole thing because ye wanted to be away from your step-da," he bellowed, as he followed her through the hall and into the kitchen. "And I wasn't supposed to have any say over it, was I? Everyone would get what they wanted—but me."

They were in the kitchen now, with the worktable between them. When he reached around the side to get a hold of her nightshift, she grabbed a skillet from the table and swung it at his head.

"Now that I want ye to be a true wife, ye change your mind," he shouted. "Just what did ye think you were getting into? Did ye no expect a husband to want ye in his bed?"

"Perhaps I did expect it—a year ago. Or a month ago," she shouted back. "Or a few days ago, when ye finally decided to bless us with your presence."

"I am prepared to be your husband now," Ian said, gritting his teeth.

"Oh, thank ye." She rolled her eyes and patted her chest. "My heart is all aflutter over it."

"You picked me, and like it or no, I am your husband," he said. "And I don't want to ever again hear my wife talking about other men and what they'd do *if ye offered*."

That was when she caught him on the side of the head with the skillet.

"Jesus, Mary, and Joseph, ye hit me!" He doubled over holding his head. It hurt like hell.

Sìleas looked as shocked by what she'd done as he was. He decided that if she were in a forgiving mood, so was he.

"Come, lass, this is no way to start our married life."

"No, it isn't," she said in a shaky voice.

He noticed that she had a kitchen knife in her other hand now and reached for it. "Put the blade down, Sìl, and come to bed."

That was when she hit him the second time.

He woke up on the floor with Sìleas standing over him,

the kitchen blade still in her hand. Judging from the fire in her eyes, she was debating just where to stick it into him.

"I think you're safe from the beast without having to use my best kitchen knife on him."

At the sound of his mother's voice, Ian risked taking his eyes off Sìleas long enough to see his mother standing in the doorway in her nightshift and cap. Her long, black and gray braid hung over her shoulder, and her hands were planted on her hips.

Ian rolled out of the way as the knife fell from Sìleas's hand, and it clattered to the floor where he had been lying. Sìleas opened her mouth as if she were trying to form a reply to his mother, then she clamped her hand over her mouth and ran from the room.

"Thanks, mam," Ian said as he got to his feet. He shook his head, trying to get his bearings and make sense of what just happened. One minute, he was kissing Sìleas in bed, and the next she was trying to kill him.

"And just what did ye think ye were doing?" his mother asked.

"Me?" he asked, thumping his chest. "Sìleas was the one attempting to murder me in your kitchen."

"Ach, even half drunk as ye are, I expect ye could get away from a wee lass like Sìleas." His mother waved a dismissive hand. "Now, are ye going to tell me how it is that sweet lass was chasing ye around the kitchen with a knife?"

"This is no something I'm going to discuss with my mother." He picked the knife and skillet up from the floor and banged them on the table.

Niall appeared in the doorway behind his mother. "What's he done to Sìleas? If he's hurt her, I'll kill him."

Ian sighed and picked up the skillet again, in case he needed to defend himself.

"This is none of your business," his mother said in a sharp voice. "Go back to bed. I'll deal with Ian."

Niall stood clenching his fists and glaring at Ian for a long moment before he obeyed his mother. When the door finally closed behind Niall, Ian set the skillet down. It was all so ridiculous, that a smile tugged at his lips. "Ye will deal with me, will ye, mam? Aren't I a wee bit big for that?"

"I have some advice to give ye," she said, "and you'd best listen if ye don't want to lose your wife."

Heaving a sigh, Ian followed his mother into the hall and took a seat by the hearth. His head still pounded from the skillet. The lass had a good arm.

"You've hardly spoken to Sìleas since ye came home, and then ye go to her room demanding rights as a husband," his mother said, shaking her head.

"Mam, can you no respect my privacy? This is between Sìleas and me."

His mother waved her hand again. "What did ye do, jump on the poor lass?"

"No, mam. I didn't jump on her," Ian said, keeping his voice calm with effort. "But she is my wife."

"What kind of fool did I raise?" his mother said, tilting her head up as if beseeching Heaven.

"Ye made me marry her, and now ye are telling me I cannot act like a husband?"

"Ye know verra well that there are all kinds of marriages," his mother said, pointing her finger at him. "If ye want a happy one, you'll take my advice."

He thought of Alex's parents, who had been warring

for as long as he'd known them. "All right, mam. Tell me what ye think I ought to do."

"Ye broke her heart and hurt her pride," his mother said. "So now ye must seek her forgiveness and earn her trust."

"And how am I to do that?"

"Talk with her, spend time with her," his mother said. "Make her see that ye value her."

"I do value her," he said.

"I'm no sure she understood that when ye burst into her bedchamber in the middle of the night demanding your rights."

"I told ye, it wasn't like that."

"Sìleas knows ye were forced to wed her," his mother said, leaning forward. "So what ye must do is convince her that if ye could have any woman in the world, she is the one you'd choose."

He still wanted Sìl after she hit him in the head with a skillet—twice. Surely, that counted for something.

But would he choose Sìleas above any other woman? A week ago, he would not have believed it possible. Now, he wasn't so sure.

"Sìleas had a father who thought more of his dogs than he did of his daughter, and then she got a step-da who was worse," his mother said. "The lass needs a man who sees her worth and loves her. She deserves that. If you can't give her that, then perhaps ye should step aside."

Ian had always been fond of Sìleas. But he knew his mother was talking about something more than fondness. She was talking about what she and his father had.

His mother stood up and took his face in her hands. "I planned on the two of ye marrying long before that day your da and uncle caught ye sleeping in the woods with her."

Ian raised his eyebrows. "Perhaps ye should have told me."

"It would have done no good," she said, and kissed his forehead. "Ye and Sìleas were made for each other. Just don't ruin it by doing something else foolish."

CHAPTER 10

As soon as Ian sat down at the table to join his brother and Alex for breakfast, Niall jumped to his feet, sending his spoon clattering to the floor. After giving Ian a murderous look, he stormed across the room and out of the house, slamming the door behind him.

"Nothing quiet about this family," Alex said, his mouth twitching. He stretched his arms in a dramatic yawn. "A fearful noise woke me last night."

"I'm warning ye, Alex, not another word," Ian said.

"I take it that the wedding night did not go as well as ye hoped," Alex said. "Do ye need me to give ye pointers, cuz?"

Ian started to lunge across the table, but he checked himself when Alex shot him a warning glance.

"Good morning, Sìleas," Alex called out.

"Is it?" Sìleas said in a clipped tone. Ignoring the empty place beside Ian, she walked around to the far side of the table and sat next to Alex.

Alex raised an eyebrow at Ian and commenced to shovel porridge into his mouth.

Ian cleared his throat. "Morning, Sìl."

She pressed her lips into a tight line and set to stirring her porridge with a good deal of vigor. For the next several minutes, the only sound in the room was the scrape of spoons in bowls. For all the attention Sìleas gave her porridge, she didn't appear to be eating much.

Finally, she set down her spoon. Looking past Ian as if he weren't there, she said, "Where is Niall?"

Ian cleared his throat again. "I believe he went out for some fresh air." He tried desperately to think of something else to say to her.

"Some fresh air would do ye good as well," Alex said to her. "You're looking peaked. How about I take ye out fishing today and let the sea breeze put the color back in your cheeks?"

When Ian kicked him, Alex lifted the finger resting against his cheek to signal that Ian should be patient.

Sìleas narrowed her eyes, considering. Then she said, "I'd like that verra much. I haven't been fishing in years."

"Meet me on the beach in an hour, and I'll show ye how it's done," Alex said.

What the hell was Alex up to?

The door to the kitchen swung open, and Dina came in, wiping her hands on her apron. "Are ye finished?" With a sly smile for Alex, she added, "Or will ye be wanting more?"

"Can ye see to Payton's breakfast, Dina?" Sìleas said, as she got to her feet. "I have some things to attend to. And then I'm going fishing."

Without waiting for Dina to respond—or sparing a glance for Ian—Sìleas left them and disappeared up the stairs.

•   •   •

The icy wind froze Sìleas's cheeks and made her eyes water. Despite Alex's smooth, sure strokes with the oars, their little boat bobbed in the choppy water.

Sìleas's emotions were as wild as the sea today. She was furious with Ian for sneaking into her bed without even asking her. After keeping her waiting for five long years, he had expected her to be grateful—grateful!— that he had decided to "accept the situation."

She was not a "situation."

Ian's kisses had sent an unfamiliar storm of emotions raging inside her. She was so hungry for Ian's affection, and the desire he stirred in her was so overwhelming, that she had almost lost herself to it. But she knew that for him it was only a physical need. Ian wanted her, but for the wrong reason—or at least not for the reasons she needed.

"You're not afraid of a wee bit of weather, are ye?" Alex called out, grinning.

Sìleas shook her head. Like him, she was an islander and as comfortable on the sea as on land. "All the same, I'd say it's a poor day for fishing."

"Well, ye don't believe I brought ye out here for the fishing, do ye?" Alex said.

She shook her head again and watched as he skillfully maneuvered the boat around some rocks to a sheltered cove, where the sea was quieter.

"'Tis time we had ourselves a talk." He rested his oars and leaned forward. "You and I have some scheming to do."

She pushed back the hair whipping across her face. "Scheming?"

"Aye, scheming," Alex said, and waggled his eyebrows.

"Now, you and I both know that ye love Ian and always have."

"Ye don't know my feelings."

"I am on your side, lass," Alex said. "So let's not waste time lying to each other."

She folded her arms and looked out to sea. "I'll no spend my life hoping Ian will care for me."

"I'm no saying ye should accept less than your due," Alex said. "But I suspect Ian cares for ye more than he knows."

"Seems to me," she said between her teeth, "that not knowing that he cares is the same as not caring."

"Sometimes a man needs to be pushed a wee bit," Alex said. "Hitting him over the head with the skillet a couple of times was a good start."

Sìleas felt her cheeks grow warm. "Ian deserved it."

"I haven't a doubt that he did," Alex said. "But ye can't blame him for trying to get ye under the blankets."

"Hmmph."

A seal popped his head up and looked at her with its black eyes for a long moment before disappearing again below the waves.

"Do ye remember how the four of us lads used to sail to Knock Castle to take ye out fishing with us?" Alex said. "It was always Ian who talked us into it. Not that the rest of us didn't like ye, mind, but we were lads off having adventures. We wouldn't have brought ye along if Ian hadn't insisted."

"He just felt sorry for me," she said.

"Aye, Ian always did have a soft heart," Alex said. "But he liked having ye around. He was always talking about the funny things ye said or how quick ye were to learn something."

"I was a wee girl," she said. "He doesn't know me now."

"So give him time to get to know ye again," Alex said. "That's all I'm saying. Don't decide against him so quick."

"Why are ye trying to convince me?"

"Because I know ye will make Ian happy," Alex said, his expression serious for once. "He's a good man, Sìleas. That's why ye waited for him so long."

"Hmmph." She was more confused than ever.

Alex narrowed his eyes at the clouds on the horizon. "We'd best head back. A storm is coming."

The waves grew wild on the way back, bouncing them like an egg in a kettle at full boil. Sìleas held tight to the sides of the boat, enjoying the rush of the water and the sting of the sea on her skin.

"'Tis grand, isn't it?" Alex shouted, and they grinned at each other.

The rain was pelting the sea not far behind them as Alex rowed hard for the beach.

"Is that Ian?" Sìleas shouted over the wind, though she knew that was him pacing up and down the beach.

"Ahh, perfect," Alex said. "Even from here, I can see he's in a state."

Ian had seen them now and was standing with his hands on his hips, glaring out to sea in their direction.

"Shall we stay out a bit longer?" Alex said. "The man deserves to suffer, wouldn't ye say?"

"What are ye about, Alex?"

"'Tis all part of my plan to make Ian appreciate ye."

"Appreciate me? Ian looks as if he'd like to murder us both."

"What fills the eye fills the heart," Alex said. "Trust me, 'tis a good sign."

She crawled closer to Alex so she could hear him better over the wind. "Ye said ye had a scheme, but ye never told me what it was."

"Well, one part is to make him jealous," Alex said.

"Jealous? Of you?"

Alex laughed. "Believe it or not, most women find me irresistible."

Though Alex wasn't for her, it was easy to see the appeal of the sea-green eyes and Viking warrior looks combined with all that charm.

She turned to see Ian striding through the surf to meet them. He had that dangerous look about him that made her heart beat fast.

"Are ye sure this is a wise idea, Alex?" she asked.

"I'll make a wager with ye," Alex said. "If I'm right and ye have Ian groveling at your feet within a fortnight, ye must give me a big kiss on the mouth in front of him."

"Ye are a devil," she said, unable to keep from laughing, despite the tension she felt with Ian bearing down on them. "And if ye are wrong?"

A slow smile spread across Alex's face. "Why, the same, lass. The very same."

Ian must have been bewitched by faeries to let his cousin take Sìleas out in the boat alone.

You're no doing so well on your own, Alex had said to him. *Let me see if I can help her to see things your way. Ye know how persuasive I can be.*

Ian knew precisely how persuasive his handsome cousin could be. Women fell over each other to make fools of themselves with Alex.

The sea was rough, and heavy, black rain clouds were

rolling in as Ian paced the beach. Where in the hell were they? What was Alex doing keeping her out with this storm coming? The weather was getting worse by the moment.

He reminded himself that Alex had a second sense on the water, as if a Viking ancestor was whispering guidance in his ear. All the same, Alex shouldn't be taking chances with Sìleas in the boat.

Ian glanced again at the old, leaky boat resting high on the shore. He was almost desperate enough to take it out to look for them, when he caught sight of their boat as it appeared and disappeared between the troughs. By the saints, he was going to kill Alex.

As they neared shore, Ian waded out into the rough surf to help haul the boat in. Neither the icy water nor the cold, wet wind on his face cooled his temper. It burned hotter still when Sìleas moved to Alex's end of the boat and her laugh traveled across the water.

He caught hold of the side and steadied it as Alex dropped into the water. Instead of taking his side of the boat, Alex lifted Sìleas out. Alex headed for the shore, carrying her in his arms above the reach of the waves— and leaving Ian to drag the boat alone as if he were a damned servant.

"Mind the boat!" Alex shouted over his shoulder. "We don't want to lose her."

When Alex reached the sandy beach, he turned with Sìleas still in his arms to watch Ian do his work for him. For God's sake, why did the man not set her on her own two feet now? And there she was, smiling up at Alex, as if she were enjoying herself.

As soon as he had secured the boat, Ian stomped across the beach to join them. "Is my wife injured?"

"I wouldn't let harm come to my favorite lass, now would I?" Alex said with a broad wink at Sìleas. "But I couldn't risk letting her get tossed about in the surf. 'Tis a stormy day, if ye hadn't noticed."

"I suggest ye set her down before I break your arms," Ian said. "Better yet, I'll take her."

"I can stand," Sìleas said. "Put me down."

"Whatever ye say, lass," Alex said, and set her down.

Ian itched to give his cousin a clout across his smiling face, but he wanted some answers first. "What in the hell were ye doing, having her out on the water with that storm coming? And don't tell me ye didn't see it."

"'Course I saw it coming," Alex said, easy as could be. "I may have cut it a wee bit close, because we were having such a grand time, ye see. But we made it in all right."

Ian glared down at Sìleas and did not feel at all badly when she trembled. With her color high from the wind and her hair wild about her, she looked like a sea nymph come to shore hoping to be ravished.

"What were the two of ye doing out there so long?" he said to her. "I didn't see any fish in the damned boat."

"It was a poor day for fishing," she said.

Now that he thought of it, there wasn't even a net in the boat.

"Then just what were ye doing all this time?" he yelled, with the image of her arms around Alex's neck as he carried her to shore vivid in his mind. "Is it not enough that ye have Gòrdan Graumach eating out of your hand?"

"Ye may find it strange, but I enjoy being with a man who doesn't shout at me," she said, shouting herself.

"Enjoying Alex, were ye?"

With her green eyes flashing and her hair whipping

about her face, she looked like the magnificent Celtic warrior queen, Scáthach, herself.

"Ye have no call to accuse me of what ye are," she said, poking her finger into his chest.

Her statement calmed him a bit. Sìleas wouldn't lie to him.

"Ye should mind how it looks when ye go about with other men," he said. "I won't be made a fool of."

Sìleas sputtered what might have been curses but was lost in the wind. When he reached for her hand, she kicked him in the shin. He stood dumbfounded as she turned and ran up the beach to the path above.

Ian looked to his cousin, expecting commiseration— and the apology he was owed.

"What in the name of heaven is wrong with ye?" Alex said, raising his hands in the air. "Did ye have to yell at her?"

"Me? You're blaming me for this?"

"Accuse me of anything ye like," Alex said, with a hard edge to his voice. "But there's no excuse for insulting Sìleas."

"I hope you're telling me that nothing happened between ye out there," Ian said, clenching his fists.

"I was out there doing my best to persuade her that ye are not the idget that ye are. You've somehow managed, in spite of yourself, to get the perfect wife, and now ye seem to be doing all ye can to lose her."

Alex, who was usually hard to rile, was pacing back and forth and gesturing with his hands as he ranted.

"Sìleas is not just lovely, but she's sensible and kind as well," Alex said. "Adding to this miracle, your family adores the lass."

"I've told her I want her," Ian said. "What more does she want from me?"

"Why have ye done nothing to make amends to her?" Alex said, spreading his arms wide. "Would it be so hard to show her that ye admire her, that ye care for her? I tell ye, I'm disgusted with ye."

With that, Alex turned and left Ian alone on the beach staring after him. He was still standing there when the heavens opened up and drenched him.

CHAPTER 11

Sileas sat at the small table in her bedchamber with her letter to the now-dead King James and a clean sheet of parchment before her. How did one address a letter to a widowed queen who was also Regent? She brushed the feather of her quill against her cheek as she considered the question.

To Her Highness,

That should suffice. She bit her lip as she copied the rest of her original letter. It annoyed her that she had Ian to thank for the skill. Did she have no pleasant memories from her childhood that did not involve him?

Her mother had never been well long enough to teach her to write, and it wouldn't have crossed her father's mind to hire a tutor for her. When it was apparent that no one else would teach her, Ian did. For a boy who never liked to sit, he had been diligent, spending hours with her. The result was that while she did not have an elegant, feminine hand, she was a slow but competent writer.

She smudged the ink and had to start over on a clean sheet of parchment. When she finished, she blew on the letter and read it over again. It would do.

The problem now was how to get it delivered to the queen at Stirling Castle.

She started at the sound of a rap on her door and shoved the letters under the sheaf of accounts stacked on the table. "Who is it?" she called out.

Ian stuck his head through the door.

He gave her a smile that raised her heartbeat. Why did he have this effect on her? She had avoided him since yesterday—no small task when they were living under the same roof—because she feared seeing him would weaken her resolve.

"May I come in?"

When she failed to summon an answer, he stepped inside and closed the door behind him. Her cheeks flamed hot as she remembered her letter. She felt a pang of guilt for not telling him she was seeking royal assistance to annul their marriage—and stifled it.

"I promise, I won't shout at ye. And I won't touch ye..." Ian's voice trailed off as his gaze slid over her, as if he were remembering every part of her he'd had his hands on two nights before. "...unless ye want me to."

She could not get enough air. With his dark hair falling over one eye and the shadow of beard over his strong jaw, Ian looked rough and dangerously handsome.

He drew his brows together. "I wouldn't hurt ye. Surely ye know that?"

He would. He already had.

Ian's gaze drifted around the room. "You've made it nice in here." He sniffed and the corners of his mouth tipped up. "Smells much better than when I slept here as a lad. It used to smell of dogs and horses—and me, I suppose."

She remembered waking to the smell of him when he crawled into bed with her. The scent had lingered faintly in her bed, giving her a restless night.

She swallowed as Ian's gaze fell on the bed and remained there for a long moment.

"I came to ask ye about the accounts ye showed me," he said, bringing his gaze back to her.

How did a man get such blue eyes?

"I'm sure my da didn't record such things, though perhaps one of the men working for him did," Ian said. "So, you'll have to teach me."

She raised her eyebrows, since he had paid no attention the first time she tried to show him.

He lifted the stool that was against the wall with one hand, set it next to her, and sat down in one easy motion. The man moved as she imagined a lion would, all grace and rippling muscle.

She jumped when he scooted his stool closer.

As he reached across her for the pile of parchments, his arm and shoulder pressed against hers, sending heat radiating through her body. "Now let's have a look at these."

She awoke from her daze and grabbed the stack away from him.

"These are in order!" she said, her voice coming out high and squeaky.

He gave her an amused look, blue eyes sparkling, and raised an eyebrow.

To cover her embarrassment, she began explaining her

method of keeping track of the farm's livestock. "Ye see, I mark all the new calves here—"

He touched her hand, and the words dried in her mouth.

"Ye were always better at figures than me, Sìl."

"Only because ye lack patience." She attempted a severe look, though, despite herself, her heart swelled with the compliment.

"Impatience is a failing of mine." Ian gave her a slow smile as he dragged his finger up her forearm. "A failing I'm trying verra hard to cure."

She swallowed. "I know what ye are trying to do."

"Do ye now?" He brushed a stray curl from her cheek, sending a shiver all the way to her fingertips and toes.

"You're trying to seduce me."

"We should each do what we're good at," he said, his eyes glimmering. Without shifting his gaze from her face, he waved his hand toward the parchments. "You're good with figures, so ye should keep doing that."

She opened her mouth to tell him she would not be here to do it, but stopped herself. Ian was set on doing his duty to his family and clan, and he had decided that duty included making her his true wife. It was best, then, that he not know she was making other plans.

"And what are you good at?" she asked instead.

"Just as ye say," he said, leaning closer, his even white teeth gleaming. "Seducing my wife."

She felt herself blush to her roots. "I'm no your wife."

"But ye are," he said.

"Ye did not claim me for five years."

He slid a hand beneath her hair and cupped the back of her neck as he leaned toward her. "Well, I'm claiming ye now."

The saints protect her, Ian was going to kiss her. The memory of waking to his kisses sent an unfamiliar rush of desire through her. His lids were half lowered over eyes that held a molten heat like the blue in a hot fire. She felt herself leaning toward him, like a moth flying into the flame.

His kiss was soft and sensuous, caressing her lips with a tantalizing suggestion of all that a kiss could be. When he drew away, she followed him. He smiled against her lips, then ran his tongue lightly over her bottom lip. How could that small movement fill her with such a powerful yearning? She gripped the front of his linen shirt in her fists to steady herself.

He made a sound deep in his throat that she felt more than heard. When he pressed his mouth to hers this time, it wasn't a teasing brush of lips but a kiss that sent the blood pounding through her veins. She felt his heart beating beneath her hands as he pulled her against him.

Her own heart pounded in her ears as he deepened the kiss. She didn't remember opening her mouth to him, but their tongues were moving together in a rhythm that resonated deep inside her. She felt a growing urgency in him that was both frightening and exhilarating.

His fingers were buried in her hair, and his body was taut with the same tension that ran through hers. As he ran hot, wet kisses beneath her ear and down the side of her throat, she cupped his jaw with her hand. The rough day's growth of beard tickled the sensitive skin of her palm and sent shivers of pleasure up her arm.

She loved his face. Touching it now made her realize that she had been longing to hold it in her hands since the first night he returned.

She sucked in a shaky breath as he worked his way along the top of her bodice with his mouth. Now. She should stop him now.

But she was hungry for a man's touch. For this man's touch. For Ian.

She stopped breathing as he slowly slid his tongue over the curve of her breast. It was as if Ian read her body, for no sooner was she aware of a low ache between her legs than he made it worse by resting a warm, heavy hand on her thigh. When she made a sound at the back of her throat, he lifted his head to capture her mouth again.

She was light-headed, drowning in his kisses. How long they kissed she could never have said. When he pulled away, she became aware of his hand moving up her thigh and his breath hot in her ear.

"We need to move to the bed," he said, his voice rough with longing, and she wanted to go wherever he was taking her. "I don't want to make love to ye the first time in a chair."

Putting to words where this was headed finally brought her to her senses.

"No," she said, pushing him away.

He dropped his forehead on her shoulder. "Sìl, don't say no," he said, sounding as if he were in pain. "Please."

The room had become sweltering, and the only sound was their harsh breathing.

"I want ye something fierce." Though he didn't touch her except where his forehead rested on her shoulder, the air vibrated with the tension between them.

"I said no." She didn't try to push him away again, for fear that if she touched him she could not make herself let go again.

He drew in a deep breath and let it out slowly. "Whatever ye say," he whispered, then he leaned back on his stool. "But will ye tell me why?"

The heat in his gaze burned her skin. She bit her lip but wouldn't answer.

"Ye can't tell me ye don't like it when I kiss ye," he said, his voice rich like honey on her tongue. "Or that ye don't like the way I touch ye, because I can tell ye do."

His words sent another wave of heat through her.

"I believe ye would enjoy...the rest."

Oh, aye. She used to wonder if she would enjoy marital relations, but now she was quite certain she would—at least, she would if it were with Ian. Her heart was still pounding as if she'd run a race.

He ran a finger lightly up her arm, sending another bolt of heat low in her belly. "Is there something that worries ye? Something you're afraid of?"

There was, but she wasn't telling him.

"Ye might fear it will hurt the first time I bed ye," he said, "but I'm thinking it's something else that is holding ye back."

She swallowed, wondering how he had guessed.

"I can't fix it if I don't know what's wrong."

Ian sounded sincere, as best she could tell through the pounding in her ears. But she wasn't going to tell him. She had decided that she needed more from him than desire. Yet that wasn't what stopped her tonight. In truth, when he was kissing her like that, his lack of love and devotion couldn't have been further from her mind.

No, it was a different fear that had brought her back to her senses and given her the strength to bring a halt to what they both wanted.

.

"Ye used to trust me," he said, taking her hand and rubbing his thumb across the heel of her palm.

There was a time she would have told him anything. But not now.

Nothing could make her admit that what she feared was seeing the fire in his eyes cool when he saw her naked. In her ignorance, she used to think it would be possible to keep her clothes on when her husband took her to bed. But from the determined way Ian set about trying to get them off her, that seemed unlikely.

Most unlikely.

If he loved her, she might not be afraid to let him see her. If she didn't love him so much, it might not matter to her.

"Ye were fearless as a child," he said, his eyes softening with his smile. "Truth be told, ye used to scare me sometimes. It almost seemed as if ye got yourself into trouble just so I would have to save ye."

"It's true, I did." She choked on the words; it was a hard thing to admit. "I trusted ye utterly. But I don't trust ye now."

She saw the flash of hurt in his eyes before he pressed his lips together and nodded. Her mouth grew dry as the tense silence between them lengthened.

"I failed my family and my clan by not being home when I was needed. I want to make amends, to make things right, if I can," Ian said. "I want to be your husband—not just to have ye in my bed, though I'd be lying if I said that wasn't part of it. But I promise I'll try to be the kind of husband ye deserve."

Sìleas felt herself weakening, but one pretty speech should not be enough to make her forgive the years of neglect nor the hurt he'd caused her since coming home.

"What about what I want?" she asked with a quaver in her voice.

"I thought this was what ye wanted. You've been happy living here with my family." He leaned forward and gave her a soft smile. "And ye used to like me quite a lot."

What he didn't say, but they both knew, was that Ian had been the person she loved best in the world. And damn it, judging by how much her heart hurt, it was still true.

"I don't want ye to be my husband because ye were forced to do it." She swallowed and fixed her gaze on her hands in her lap. "Or because the clan needs my lands. Or because your mother is verra fond of me."

"I'm fond of ye as well." He reached out to tuck a loose strand of her hair behind her ear, but she pulled away.

"I don't want ye to be my husband because ye think I need protecting or because ye feel sorry for me," she continued. "Or because ye don't like to do figures yourself."

"I can promise ye, I'd want ye even if ye couldn't do figures," he said, brushing his knuckles against her cheek. When she looked up, he gave her a sizzling look that made her stomach tighten. "I do want ye, Sìl."

She took her hand from his and got to her feet.

All the reasons he wanted her might be enough if he were any other man. But they were not enough from Ian. She would not spend her life with a man, pining for her love to be returned.

She made herself walk out the door and close it behind her.

CHAPTER 12

Ian heard his father's raised voice as he opened the front door to the house.

"Look at what ye done to me!" Payton was shouting at Niall, who was trying to help him across the room. "Ye should have let me die like a man."

Sìleas stood on his father's other side, coaxing him forward. "It will be lovely to have ye take your meals with the family again."

"Will ye no come sit at the table, da?" Niall said.

The instant his father began to raise his cane to strike Niall, Ian started across the room, but Sìleas was closer. His heart stopped when she stepped between the two men.

"Don't ye dare touch him!" Sìleas shouted.

When his father checked the blow in time, Ian breathed again. His father still had the arms and shoulders of a powerful man. God in Heaven, he could have killed her.

Niall walked past Ian and out the front door without even seeing him. Sìleas locked gazes with his father, going nose to nose with him—or she would have, if she were taller. Neither appeared to take any notice of Ian's presence or the slamming door.

"If ye speak that way to Niall again, I swear I'll not forgive ye," Sìleas said. Her chest rose and fell in deep breaths as she and his father glared at each other.

"He should have let me die on the battlefield," his father said. "He took away my manhood, bringing me home like this."

She spoke in a slow, deliberate voice, and there was steel in her eyes. "Ye ought to be grateful to have such a son, after what he did for ye."

"Grateful? Look at me!" his father shouted, pointing at his missing leg.

"Shame on ye, Payton MacDonald, for wishing you could desert your family," she said. "'Tis long past time ye stopped feeling sorry for yourself."

She turned on her heel, her hair swinging out like a shooting flame, and stormed out of the house.

His father hobbled to the nearest chair, dropped onto it with a thump, and rubbed his hands over his face. Ian got the whiskey down from the cupboard and filled a cup.

"Here ye go, da," he said, as he set the cup on the table next to his father. He started to put the bottle back, then set it on the table as well.

His father clenched the cup as if holding a lifeline and stared at the wall.

"I'd best see to Niall," Ian said.

His father nodded without turning to look at him. "Do that, son."

It was raining buckets, so Ian hoped Niall hadn't gone far. He tried the old cottage first—and found Alex and Dina in the midst of enjoying the ways of the flesh. They didn't notice him. From there, he splashed through puddles to the byre.

The smell of cows and damp straw filled his nostrils as he peered into the dim, musty interior. He paused and listened. Behind the sound of the pounding rain, he heard the murmur of voices and followed it to the back of the byre, where he found Niall and Sìleas sitting side by side on a pile of straw between two cows. They didn't hear him approach.

"It's your father's pain speaking," Sìleas said. "He doesn't mean it like it sounds."

"He means precisely what he says." Niall slammed the side of his fist against the byre wall beside him. "He couldn't be plainer."

"Well, I am proud of ye, if that matters at all to ye." Sìleas put her hand to Niall's cheek. "I am so proud of what ye did that my chest fairly bursts with it every time I think of it."

"Ye mean it, Sìl?" Neill said, blushing bright red.

"Ach, of course I do!" she said with a wave of her hand. "I've watched you grow into a man we can all rely on. To tell the truth, I'm sick with jealousy over the woman who is going to have ye, because you're going to make the finest husband in all of Scotland."

Ian felt the bite of criticism in her words. *A man we can all rely on. The finest husband in all of Scotland.* He felt his shortcomings on both counts.

"But don't forget that it was your father who taught ye to be the man ye are," she added in a softer voice. "I'm spitting mad at Payton just now, but I'm also praying he'll get back to himself again. When he does, I know he'll regret every word he said to ye."

"So here ye are," Ian said, pretending he had just come into the byre.

They both turned as he stepped into view.

"I'm sorry da was so harsh with ye," Ian said.

"Do ye think I did the right thing, bringing da back?" Niall was looking up at him with earnest eyes, seeking his approval as he used to years ago.

Ian suspected he would feel the same way his father did. A man who couldn't fight was not really a man anymore. Still, in Niall's place, he would have done the same.

"I don't know if it was the right thing," Ian said. "But ye had no choice."

When Sìleas started to follow Niall out of the byre, Ian held her arm. He felt guilty when she turned to face him and he saw wariness replace the kindness that had been in her eyes when she spoke with his brother.

"Thank ye for speaking to Niall as ye did," he said. "Ye restored his pride."

Her expression softened at the praise, and he felt another wave of guilt. If paying her a well-deserved compliment was all it took to please her, he should have managed it before.

"The weather should clear soon," he said. "Will ye take a stroll with me later?"

"I've too much work to—"

"Ye have time to go with Gòrdan and Alex, but not with me?" he said, failing to keep the sharpness from his tone.

"I have a pleasant time with them," she said, her eyes snapping. "I see no cause to get behind with my chores to have an argument with you."

She tried to pull away, but he held her arm fast. "Ach, I don't mean to argue with ye," he said. "Will ye go with me to Teàrlag's cottage? Ye could take her a basket."

He knew from his mother that Sìleas and Duncan's sister took turns bringing the old seer food. Without it, Teàrlag wouldn't make it through the winter.

"I do need to visit her." Sìleas pressed her lips together, considering.

"So come along and keep me company," Ian said.

"I will," she said. "But what is taking ye to Teàrlag's cottage?"

"I'm meeting Connor and Duncan there," Ian said. "Can ye be ready in an hour or two? I have something to do first."

Sìleas bit back her irritation as she showed Dina where things were kept in the kitchen. In truth, *irritation* was far too mild a word for what she felt.

It wasn't that Dina was doing anything in particular to aggravate her—at the moment. Every time she looked at Dina, however, she saw her with her legs wrapped around Ian's bare backside as the pair rocked against the shepherd's hut.

Sìleas banged a pot onto the worktable—and then was doubly annoyed when she could not recall what she meant to do with it.

The fornicating pair had been too absorbed in what they were doing to notice the nine-year-old girl who was watching from a few yards away. At first, Sìleas had been too stunned to cover her eyes—which probably explained why her memory of it was crystal clear. Even when she finally covered them, she could hear Dina's odd gasps and her shouts of *Aye! Aye!*

"Aye?"

The sound of Dina's voice right next to her made Sìleas jump a foot.

Dina gave her a puzzled look. "Is this where Beitris hides the salt?"

Sìleas nodded without looking to see where Dina was pointing. She hated having this woman in the house. How dare Ian bring his former lover into their home? But then, this wasn't truly her home, was it?

And perhaps Dina wasn't Ian's *former* lover, either.

Sìleas started chopping turnips with a large knife. *Whack, whack, whack.*

She was angry with Ian for giving her that ugly memory of him and Dina. Ach, it was annoying that it upset her as much now as it had when she was a child. But everything changed between her and Ian after that. She paused in her chopping. No, the change had begun earlier.

As Ian left boyhood behind, he came to Knock Castle less and less often to take her for a ride on his horse or out in his boat. Then he was away at the university in the Lowlands for months at a time. And when he was home, he seemed to spend all his time practicing his battle skills with the men—or flirting with the lasses old enough to have breasts.

Or more than flirting.

"You're not getting much chopping done," Dina said, drawing her attention to the single chopped turnip on the table.

"Do ye think ye can get supper on alone?" Sìleas said, as she lifted her apron over her head. "I have an errand to run."

She fled the kitchen without waiting for Dina to answer

and went looking for Ian, intent on telling him she had changed her mind about going to Teàrlag's with him. She stopped in her tracks when she found him behind the byre with his father.

Her throat felt tight and tears stung the back of her eyes as she took in the scene. Damn Ian. Just when she was ready to accept that he had nothing left in him of the lad she had loved, he would go and do something like this.

Ian had carved a piece of wood and fitted it with leather straps to his father's half-missing leg. With one arm over Ian's shoulder, Payton was learning to walk with it.

The rest of them had treated Payton like the invalid they saw him to be. They fetched and carried for him and—until today—put up with his rage at finding himself less than the man he used to be. Ian was a warrior and understood his father better than they had.

She felt guilty as she realized this was the first Payton had been outside the house since Niall carried him home—and this was a man who was used to spending most of his waking hours outdoors.

She watched as Ian walked with his father at an excruciatingly slow pace, up and down the length of the byre, and then up and down again.

"Ye got it, da," Ian said.

Payton snorted. "Soon I will be dancing, aye?"

"Ye were always a terrible dancer, da."

At the sound of Payton's laugh, she felt her determination to resist Ian weaken another notch. This was so like the Ian she remembered. He had seen just the right thing to do to help his father and done it.

"Ye will be walking on your own in no time," Ian said. "As soon as ye do, we'll get a sword in your hand."

"Good. I'm a much better fighter than dancer," Payton said.

Ian was still laughing when he looked up and saw her. She managed to wipe her tears away before Payton noticed her as well.

"Ah, Sìleas," Payton said, with a smile that shone in his eyes. "'Tis a fine day to be out, is it not?"

It was bone-cold and damp.

"A very fine day, indeed, Payton," she said, her eyes blurring. "The best in a long, long while."

CHAPTER 13

•

Sileas's emotions felt raw, whipsawed between her anger with Ian and the warmth she felt toward him for what he'd done for Payton. She realized this walk to Teàrlag's was the first she had been alone with him since his return—except for the two times in her bedchamber, which hadn't been good for conversation.

"What will ye do to see that Connor is made chieftain?" she asked, for something to say.

"I'll do whatever it takes, for the sake of the clan," Ian said. "There's nothing I wouldn't do for Connor. He's like a brother to me."

If Ian had a plan, he wasn't sharing it with her.

"Teàrlag's is a good place to meet," she said. "I rarely see another soul on the path to her cottage."

"I suspect Connor and Duncan are staying in the cave on the beach below her cottage," Ian said. "That cove is a good place to hide Shaggy's boat as well."

"I remember that cave," she said, turning to him. "You lads used to hide there, pretending ye were wild pirates."

The other boys had been furious when she found them, until Ian suggested she could be the captive princess they held for ransom. At the time, being bound and gagged had seemed a small price to pay to be included in their game.

The path turned inland for the last mile, taking travelers through the valley to avoid the high sea cliffs on this stretch of the coast. Before taking the turn, Sìleas and Ian left the path to stand in a flat, grassy area at the top of the cliff.

"This is one of my favorite places," Sìleas said.

She breathed in the brisk sea breeze as she gazed at the mountains that rose up on the other side of the inlet. Excitement tingled at her fingertips as she listened to the crash of waves far below. Like many islanders, the wildness of the sea spoke to her soul.

"Shall we see if the log is still there?" Ian asked, pointing to their right, where a goat path continued along the cliff.

"Aye, let's."

Ian took her hand and smiled at her as he tucked it under his plaid to keep it warm. She knew he was remembering, as she was, how he used to take her hand along this path.

"I'm no likely to step off the edge now," she said, smiling back.

"All the same, I'll feel better if I have a hold on ye," he said. "The wind is strong, and it's a long way down."

The first part of the cliff path was wide enough for them to walk side by side between the cliff and the rock outcrop. After a short distance, the path veered around a huge boulder. It narrowed beyond that and then ended abruptly at the edge of a giant crevice that split the cliff.

"The log is still here," Ian said, sounding pleased.

In a long-ago storm, a tree that had once clung to the edge of the cliff fell across the thirty-foot fissure, forming a bridge of sorts. The only way to continue was to cross the log as the goats did.

Sìleas sucked in her breath as she peeked over the edge. "I can't believe you lads used to cross here, instead of going around by the main path."

"Ach, we were foolish. 'Tis a wonder we didn't kill ourselves," Ian said, pulling her back. "The only time I was truly frightened, though, was when ye followed us."

Sìleas remembered the feel of the slippery wood beneath her bare feet and the sound of the swell and crash of the waves against the rocks below. Ian had told her not to come, so she had hidden behind the boulder until all four boys had crossed over the crevice and disappeared down the path on the other side.

"It took a year off my young life when I turned around and saw ye on the log." Ian put his arm around her and pulled her tight against his side.

She had gotten halfway across the crevice before she looked down and froze.

"What made ye turn around that day?" she asked. His arm felt good around her. She couldn't help leaning into him.

"I felt a prickle at the back of my neck." He gave her a smile that made her stomach flutter and touched his knuckle under her chin.

Sìleas watched the water rise as another wave filled the narrow crevice, then crashed against the sheer walls. As it exploded into spray and foam, she tasted the dizzying fear that had gripped her when she stood on that log as a wee girl. That day, she had been unable to take her eyes off the rushing water thundering below her—until she heard Ian calling to her.

Don't look down, Sìl, Look at me. Look at me!

Biting her lip, she'd torn her gaze from the swirling water to meet Ian's eyes.

Don't be scared, because I'm coming to get ye.

Ian had walked across the log toward her, holding her with his gaze and talking to her all the while. Even now, her body recalled the surge of relief that went through her limbs when his hand finally clasped her wrist.

I've got ye now. I'll not let ye fall.

And he hadn't.

Sìleas realized she was holding her breath and blew it out. A swell of gratitude rose in her chest for the eleven-year-old boy who had crossed the log without a moment's hesitation to save her. Ian was always like that—fearless and decisive in a crisis. It was not the only time he had rescued her, just the most dramatic.

After that day, whenever she was in trouble, she no longer prayed to God to save her. Instead, she prayed for God to send Ian.

"Sìleas," Ian said, bringing her attention from the lad in her memory to the man beside her. He backed her up to the boulder and braced his arms on either side of her. "I think ye owe me a kiss for scaring me half to death that day."

Without waiting for her to agree, he lowered his head toward hers.

She couldn't resist him and didn't want to. Gripping the front of his plaid to steady herself, she tilted her head back to meet him. When his lips touched hers, she melted into him. The water crashing and churning below and the wind whipping the branches of the trees above echoed the tumult pulsing through her.

Her heart beat so fast she felt dizzy as he kissed her nose, her eyelids, her cheeks.

"Did ye bring me to this spot thinking the memory would make me soft on ye?" she asked.

"Aye," he said, nuzzling her ear. "Did it work?"

Beneath his vanity and that dangerous edge that seemed to make the air crackle around him, she caught glimpses of the good-hearted lad he used to be. Remembering that boy's blind disregard for his own safety to protect her, she could almost trust him.

Yet it wasn't the boy who had left her, but the man.

"Ye didn't used to smell so good," Ian said, kissing her hair. He ran his hands up her sides under her cloak, making her feel light-headed and breathless. "I like the feel of ye even better."

It was hard to think with his hands on her and his breath in her ear. Finally, she forced herself to brace her hands against his chest.

"I paid ye the kiss," she said. "Now it's time we were on our way."

"That kiss was for scaring me that day," he said, as he brushed light kisses along her jaw. "I'm afraid ye owe me several more for getting ye off the log."

Her heart raced as he brought his mouth back to hers. His lips were soft and warm and, once again, she turned liquid in his arms. When he ended the kiss, she peeled herself away from him, feeling flushed and confused.

"I'm verra glad I waited to collect the debt," he said, smiling at her with the devil in his eyes.

"I am not a trinket to be played with." Sìleas attempted to push him away, but he was as immovable as the rock at her back.

"I don't know what ye mean by that remark." he said, his smile gone and the edge of anger in his voice. "What makes ye think I take ye lightly?"

"Perhaps because ye ignored me and your vows for the last five years," she said. "And don't try to tell me ye had no women in France, for I'll no believe it."

"I didn't think of ye as my wife then." He took her chin in his hand and fixed intense blue eyes on her. "But I do now."

"Well, I don't." She darted under his arm and started around the boulder, but he caught her around the waist and hauled her back.

"Ye are my wife, like it or no," he said, towering over her. "So ye may as well like it."

"I don't like it," she said. "Not one bit."

"Ye lie, Sìl," he said, his eyes hot on hers. "Ye like it when I kiss ye. If ye have forgotten already, I'll have to show ye again."

Ian pulled her into his arms and proceeded to kiss her senseless. Every argument faded under the assault on her senses. It was as if she had been starving for his kisses without knowing it. Now that she had discovered what she craved, she had to taste it, touch it. She wanted to swallow him whole, take him inside her, and never lose him.

She clung to him, unable to get close enough.

"I want to feel you," Ian said, pushing back her cloak.

Wherever he touched, his hands burned her skin with a heat that drew her ever closer. He dropped his head and pressed his lips to where her pulse was beating madly at the base of her throat. She sucked in her breath as his hands covered her breasts.

"Ahhh," he breathed. "Your breasts were made for my hands."

He dipped his head lower, running his tongue in the valley between them. His lips were warm and wet on her skin. When he took her nipples between his fingers and thumbs, pure lust shot through her body and down her limbs, like whiskey on an empty belly.

Her head fell back against the boulder as she let the new sensations take her. When she felt the moist warmth of Ian's mouth on her breast, she started. He found the nipple through the cloth and flicked his tongue over it, and it felt so good she didn't want him to stop.

When he sucked her breast into his mouth, she felt it down to her toes. She had a fleeting sense of embarrassment when she realized she had groaned aloud, but it was soon lost in the swirl of sensations Ian was pulling from her. She was panting by the time he released her breast to move up her throat with hot, wet kisses.

"Ach, I love the sounds ye make," he said against her ear. "I want ye beneath me, Sìleas. I want to bury myself inside ye and bring ye such pleasure that ye cry out my name."

He kissed her until her lips felt swollen. When he pulled away, cold air chilled the heated skin beneath her clothes, leaving her with a physical longing for the body that had pressed against hers. She felt stunned, disoriented, and too aware of her body. Her breasts tingled, she felt wet and achy between her legs, and her fingertips itched for the silky feel of his hair and the rough cloth of his shirt.

"See, ye do like my kisses," Ian said, looking altogether too sure of himself. "And I promise ye, ye will like it still better when I take ye to bed."

She ran her tongue over her dry lips. "That doesn't mean I'll like being wed to ye."

"It's a verra good start," he said, with a gleam in his eye.

"Ye are a vain man, Ian MacDonald," she said, and turned her attention to straightening her gown.

She felt Ian go still and looked up to see his gaze fixed on something behind her. Holding a finger to his lips, he nodded in the direction of the road. She turned around and saw twenty men heading up the road toward them. Judging from the blades she could see, they were prepared for trouble—or to cause it.

At the front of the group, was none other than Hugh Dubh MacDonald.

She felt Ian's tension in the taut muscles of his body as he leaned against her, pressing her into the boulder.

"They're coming for Connor," he said next to her ear, as the group started around the bend in the road.

"God, no," she whispered. "What can we do?"

"'Tis quicker to Teàrlag's along the cliff path." He spun her around and gave her a quick, hard kiss. "I must warn Connor and Duncan. Wait here, and I'll come back for ye as soon as I can."

"I'm going with ye," she said. "Ye might need me."

"No, you're staying here. I don't have time to argue." He started to leave, but halted. "Damn it!"

She turned to see what had caught his attention. Four of Hugh's men were settling themselves down at the side of the road, instead of following the others.

"What are they doing?" she whispered.

"Hugh has remembered we used to take the goat path," he said in a hushed voice. "He's left these men to cut off Connor and Duncan's escape by this route."

When she looked up at him, Ian's jaw was set and his eyes cold-blue steel.

"Come," he said, taking her hand. "I can't leave ye here now."

CHAPTER 14

Ian stepped onto the log as if he were going up a door-step instead of walking off a cliff. When she told him earlier that she wanted to go with him, her only thought was that she didn't want to be separated from him. But fear gripped her belly now.

Ian stood sideways on the log and held his hand out to her. "Hold on, and we'll cross together."

Despite the chill in the air, her palms were sweaty. She wiped them on her cloak before reaching out to take his hand. The hand that enveloped hers was dry and warm and reassuring. Gingerly, she put one foot on the log.

"I don't know if I can do this."

"Just remember not to look down," Ian said. "We'll be on the other side before ye know it."

She took another step, and now both feet were on the log—and over the cliff. Although she kept her eyes fixed on Ian, she could hear the rushing water below.

"You're doing fine," Ian said. "I won't let ye fall."

She took another step.

" 'Tis easier to keep your balance if ye move quickly," he said, urging her along.

She took another step and another. It was getting easier. She dared to breathe again.

When she was halfway across, her foot hit a clump of moss and slipped. Though she recovered her balance almost at once, her gaze dropped to the churning water far below. Panic shot through her limbs and sweat prickled under her arms. Her feet would not move again.

"Look at me," Ian said in a tone that said everything would be all right. "I have ye, Sìl. I have ye."

With an effort, she wrenched her gaze from the crashing waves below to Ian's face. His expression was confident, reassuring.

"That's a good lass," Ian said. "We're nearly there."

Step by step, she followed him, squeezing his hand until her fingers ached. An eternity later, she reached the other side, and Ian was lifting her down. The feel of solid earth beneath her feet made her light-headed with relief.

"Ye are going to owe me a hundred kisses for that," he said, his voice hard and urgent. "We must hurry now."

Her trial was not over, for they still had to follow the cliff path the rest of the way to Teàrlag's cottage.

"Can ye let go?" she asked, as Ian pulled her along. "I've no feeling left in my fingers."

"No."

The path narrowed until it was a ledge barely as wide as her foot. They sidestepped over loose stones with the rock face at their backs. Beyond the toes of her shoes was nothing but air—and the gray swells and white foam far below.

Sìleas's heart pounded in her ears as she scanned the

sheer cliff below for shrubs growing out of the rock that she could grab hold of if she fell.

And then her heel slipped on the loose rock, and her foot shot out from under her. She screamed Ian's name as she fell to her death.

She continued screaming as her feet dangled in the air.

"I've got ye," Ian said, his voice strained.

She stopped screaming and looked up. Ian's knees were bent, and he had one arm spread across the rock wall for balance; his other hand still held her wrist. His jaw was clenched, and the muscles of his neck were taut with the effort of holding her.

With a grunt, he hoisted her back up onto the path. Her knees were shaking so violently she would have fallen again if Ian was not holding her up.

"We can't stop here," Ian said, looking hard into her eyes. "I told ye I would not let ye fall. Ye need to trust me."

She nodded. Ian had a firm hold on her arm; he would not let her go.

"Just a wee bit farther, love," Ian said, coaxing her along. "I can almost see Teàrlag's cottage now."

Sìleas's heart was in her mouth, but she moved with him.

"That's a good lass. Three or four more steps is all."

When the footpath finally opened onto the clearing behind Teàrlag's cottage, Sìleas wanted to sink to her knees and kiss the grass.

"For that, ye owe me a good deal more than kisses," Ian said, wiping his forehead with his sleeve. "Now we must find Connor and Duncan."

They ran into Teàrlag's cottage and found the two men sitting at her table eating stew from large wooden bowls.

"Time to run, lads," Ian said in a dead calm voice. "Hugh and twenty armed men are coming up the road."

Connor and Duncan were on their feet before Ian finished speaking.

"We'll be in the cave," Connor said, as he strapped on his claymore. "Make some noise to warn us if they start down to the beach."

"I will," Ian said. "Just go."

"Sorry, Teàrlag," Connor said over his shoulder, as he went out the door.

"Save my stew," Duncan said, as he grabbed an oatcake. He waved it at them as he followed Connor out.

Sìleas sank into the chair that was still warm from Connor sitting in it.

"Where's your whiskey, Teàrlag?" Ian asked.

"I'll get it," the old woman said.

Sìleas's limbs felt melded to the chair as she watched the other two go about their tasks with quick, controlled movements. In a blink, Ian dumped the stew from the bowls into the pot hanging over the hearth, wiped the bowls clean with a cloth, and set them on the shelf above the table.

While Ian did that, Teàrlag unearthed a jug from beneath her mending in the basket in the corner and poured a healthy measure of it into two cups on the table.

"Drink it down," Ian ordered Sìleas and tossed his own back.

Sìleas choked as the fiery liquid burned down her throat.

Ian wiped the cups clean, set them back on the shelf, and took the chair beside her. "Now, we are here having a nice, relaxing chat with Teàrlag."

A moment later the door burst open and several foul-smelling men crowded into the small room. The first was Hugh Dubh.

Sìleas had not seen him this close since she was a bairn. As Hugh surveyed the tiny cottage, she was struck by how much he looked like his brother, the former chieftain, and Ragnall. He had the same square face, impressive frame, and commanding presence, but there was something dark and sinister in Hugh's sea-mist eyes. The chieftain and Ragnall had been hard men, but they didn't have this evil in them.

"Where are they?" Hugh demanded.

The cow on the other side of the half wall mooed in complaint as one of Hugh's men pushed her aside and slashed at the straw with his claymore.

"If ye throw my cow off her milk, ye'll answer to me," Teàrlag said.

"The other three can't be far off, if you're here," Hugh said to Ian. "Why don't ye save us both a lot of trouble and tell me where my nephew is? Connor and I need to have a talk."

"I'm sure ye already know that Alex is staying with my family," Ian said, leaning back in his chair as if they were discussing how the fish were biting. "But I haven't seen Connor and Duncan."

"I have to ask myself why Ian MacDonald would be coming to see this old woman," Hugh said, tilting his head in Teàrlag's direction. "And the only answer that comes to me is that ye wouldn't. So I'm guessing that you're here because the others are hiding nearby."

Hugh waved to his men and headed for the door. "Come along lads, let's find them."

"I came with my wife," Ian said, resting his arm along the back of Sìleas's chair. When Hugh turned around, Ian added in a low voice, "Female problems, ye know."

Hugh raked his eyes over Sìleas, making her feel as if he could see beneath her clothes. "The lass looks fine to me."

"There's nothing's wrong with her," Teàrlag said, and all heads turned toward her.

"I knew Ian was lying," Hugh spit out and reached for his dirk.

" 'Tis true his wife brought him here." Teàrlag pursed her lips and shook her head. "Sometimes a lass has a problem with her husband, though I rarely see it in a man as young as Ian."

Ian coughed and banged the front legs of his chair to the floor.

"Teàrlag!" he said, glaring at the old seer.

"Are ye saying our lad Ian here is having trouble pleasing his pretty wife?" Hugh was grinning ear to ear.

"Nothing to fret about," Teàrlag said, sounding as if there was plenty to worry about.

Sìleas choked back a laugh and put her hand on Ian's leg to prevent him from rising from his chair.

"Sìleas is such a patient lass, waiting on her husband for five long years," Teàrlag said, looking mournful. "I'm sure she's willing to wait a wee bit longer for him to overcome his... battle injury."

"I wasn't injured there," Ian shouted. "There is nothing wrong with me parts."

Hugh and the other men roared with laughter.

"Sometimes the injury lies here," Teàrlag said, tapping her temple with her knobby finger. "But don't fret, I have a potion I'll mix for ye. It works... sometimes."

At the look of outrage on Ian's face, Sìleas had to bite her cheeks to keep from laughing.

Hugh and the other men were guffawing. The angrier Ian became, the more they believed Teàrlag's story.

"If ye lose patience with Ian, I can find ye a new husband," Hugh said, giving Sìleas a broad wink. "One who will be *up* to the task."

The men burst into a new round of laughter.

"Don't trouble yourself," Sìleas said, dropping her gaze to her lap. "I'm sure Ian will be right as rain soon."

"It's a hard rain she's hoping for," one of the men said, and he was rewarded with snorts and snickers.

"There's nothing wrong with me." Ian jumped to his feet and clenched his hands in front of him. "I'm ready to fight any man who says there is."

"You'd best save your strength," Hugh said, choking with laughter. He turned to Sìleas and added, "Don't forget my offer."

When Ian took a step toward Hugh, Sìleas stood up in front of him.

Ian's breathing was harsh, and the muscles of his arms were taut beneath her fingers. It would be foolish for Ian to attack Hugh with five of his men in the room and another fifteen waiting outside.

Hugh threw his head back, letting his laughter fill the tiny room. Sìleas was certain now that he was trying to bait Ian—and he was close to succeeding.

"'Tis not wise to laugh at the misfortunes of others," Teàrlag said, "especially when ye will be facing worse ones yourself."

Hugh's smile disappeared. "What are ye saying, old woman?"

"I see your death, Hugh Dubh MacDonald."

Hugh's face drained of color, and he took a step back.

Teàrlag reached into a small bowl on the shelf above the hearth and threw what looked like dried herbs on the fire, making it spit and smoke. Then her good eye rolled back into her head, and she began making an eerie high-pitched sound as she shifted from foot to foot.

"I see it clear as day," Teàrlag said in a distant voice, as if she were speaking to them from the other side. "Ye are laid out on a long table, and the women are preparing your body for the grave."

"Don't say it, witch!" Hugh held his hands up as he backed up to the cottage door.

"I see your death, Hugh Dubh MacDonald," Teàrlag called out, waving her arms. "I see your death, and no one is weeping!"

"Damn ye, woman! Ye know nothing. Ye see nothing," Hugh shouted, then turned and left the cottage. The other men stumbled over each other in their hurry to follow him out the door.

As soon as the men had gone, Ian turned blazing eyes on the old seer. "Why did ye find it necessary to tell them lies about my manhood, Teàrlag? All the men on the island will be having a good laugh at me by this evening."

"The women, too." Teàrlag's three good top teeth showed in a wide grin.

"Her story did divert them from looking for Connor and Duncan," Sìleas said in a soft voice, as she tried to hide her own smile.

"Ah well," Teàrlag said, waving her hand. "Ye deserve it after what ye done to Sìleas."

"What?" Ian said, banging his fist on the table. "I've done nothing to deserve being humiliated."

"Do ye not suppose the entire clan discussed how ye

left Sìleas the morning after ye wed?" Teàrlag said, shaking a nobby finger at him.

Ian sat down. After a long moment, he turned to Sìleas and took her hand. "Did the women tease ye, then?"

"Oh, aye," Sìleas said with a dry laugh. Pitching her voice high, she imitated their voices. "'Can ye no keep your man at home, Sìl?' 'What do ye suppose is keeping Ian?' 'If ye had given him a child, perhaps your husband would want to come home.'"

Ian brought her hand to his lips and kissed it. "I'm sorry. When I was in France, I still thought of ye as a young girl who would have no use for a husband."

If ye thought of me at all.

"Ian, go get the other lads now," Teàrlag said, taking the bowls down from the shelf. "They haven't finished their dinner."

It amused Sìleas to hear Teàrlag order Ian about as if he were a boy of ten and not a man three times her size. Her amusement faded as soon as Ian had gone and Teàrlag focused her single eye on her.

"So why have ye no taken that fine-looking husband to your bed yet?" Teàrlag said. "I know it isn't for the reason I gave that devil Hugh Dubh."

Sìleas felt her cheeks go hot, and she dropped her gaze to the floor.

"Give him time," Teàrlag said, covering Sìleas's hand with her gnarled one. "Ian has it in him to be the man ye want him to be. Do ye have that pouch I made for ye?"

Sìleas nodded.

"Ye sleep with it next to your heart?" Teàrlag asked.

She nodded again.

"Then ye know what to do, lass."

CHAPTER 15

Ian feared for his health.

Sìleas was driving him near witless with lust. It could not be good for a man to want a woman this much without satisfaction. Collecting the kisses he said she owed him only made the torture worse.

He lay awake at night imagining her creamy skin in the moonlight. Every time he heard her voice in the next room or caught a glimpse of her across the yard, he hoped she had come to seek him out, to tell him she was ready.

He imagined her walking toward him, slowly, with her hips swaying and a sparkle in her eyes. Then she would rest the flat of her hands on his chest and say, "I've made up my mind. I want ye in my bed, Ian MacDonald."

Ian shook his head and set down his hammer before he did damage to himself. Every time he backed her into a corner to steal a kiss, someone would come in and distract her. A few times he got his hand on her breast—ach, he was hard just thinking of that—but no further.

He could not take much more of this.

And he didn't have time to waste. With Samhain just over a fortnight away, they needed to do something dramatic. He had discussed it with Connor and Duncan when he went to get them from the cave that day at Teàrlag's. All of them agreed that the best way to sway their clansman into backing Connor was to take Knock Castle.

To justify attacking the MacKinnons, Ian needed to remove any question as to his right to Knock Castle as Sìleas's husband. Of course, they could take the castle without a rightful claim—it was done all the time—but that would draw the Crown into the dispute. Connor and the MacDonalds didn't need that kind of trouble on top of what they already had.

Which meant Ian needed to consummate his marriage. Bed his bride. 'Twas fortunate, indeed, that the needs of the clan matched his own precisely.

Everything was arranged. Ian had convinced his mother and Niall that taking his father out on a sail around Seal Island would do them all good. Of course, Alex had no trouble persuading Dina to disappear with him for the afternoon.

Finally, Ian would have Sìleas alone.

He found her in the kitchen. She was leaning over the worktable, pressing an oat mixture into the bottom of a flat pan. He sucked in his breath as he imagined lying on that table and having her work over him. She looked fetching with her hair pinned up, save for a few loose tendrils curling down her neck and the sides of her face.

"Smells good," he said. The kitchen was warm and smelled of oats and honey.

She started at the sound of his voice and looked up, wide-eyed. "I didn't hear ye come in."

"What's that you're making?"

"A treat for your da," she said with a smile. "He has a sweet tooth, ye know. And I'll have some left over to take to Annie up the road. She's just had a new babe."

Ian rolled up his sleeves and came around the table to stand beside her. "I used to help my mother in the kitchen."

She gave him a sideways glance. "I'm sure you were a verra big help to her."

"Ach, I'm hurt ye don't believe me," he said. "Come, I'll show ye how good I am."

She raised her eyebrows, showing him she suspected he wasn't just talking about his cooking skills.

He wasn't.

She dipped a wooden spoon into the honey jar and dribbled honey over the oat mixture.

"Dina was supposed to be helping me." She gave the wooden spoon a hard whack against the side of the pan. "There it's done."

"Ye won't be seeing Dina this afternoon," Ian said, taking the spoon from her to lick the honey off. "She and Alex are . . . keeping each other company."

Her hands stilled, and her cheeks turned a couple of shades of red. "So that's the way of it."

Ian was pleased for the opportunity to warn her off Alex. "I hope Dina doesn't expect to be the only one."

"I hope Alex doesn't, either."

He laughed, then added for good measure, "Alex is not the sort of man to stay in one woman's bed."

"I don't think ye are in a position to criticize Alex, when ye can hardly claim to have been living the life of a saint yourself." Sìleas picked up the pan and slapped it down so hard the table rattled. "That helps settle the mixture. I'll wait to cook it 'til they're home."

Ian leaned into her. "I'm living a monk's life now, if that's any comfort to ye."

"Ach, such a sacrifice," she said, as she moved ingredients around on the table for no purpose he could discern. "What has it been, all of a week?"

He moved behind her and took a firm hold of her hips. Ah, she felt good against him.

"A week seems a verra long time," he said as he nuzzled her neck, "when every moment of it I'm wishing I had ye naked."

He kissed the side of her neck and felt her pulse racing beneath his lips. She drew in a sharp breath when he pressed his throbbing erection against her buttocks.

"I'd love to lay ye back on the table here," he said, as he ran his hands up her arms.

"Shhh! Someone might come in and hear ye." She sounded scandalized, but she shivered at his touch.

"No one else is at home," he said, nipping at her earlobe. "'Tis just you and me."

Her breathing changed when he slipped his hands around her ribs and stroked the underside of her breasts with his thumbs.

"I'm thinking that the first time I make love to ye ought to be in our marriage bed," he said. "But if ye say here on the table, I'm a willing man."

Sìleas wiped her hands on her apron and made a show of pushing at his forearms. "Let me go now."

This was no serious resistance. When Sìleas told him no and meant it, she hit him with a skillet and stood over him with a blade in her hand.

He blew on the back of her neck and was rewarded when a "mmmm" escaped her lips. Her skin was soft and creamy as fresh butter and smelled of cinnamon and honey. Needing to taste her, he ran his tongue along her skin above the edge of her gown.

He cupped the soft fullness of her breasts and had to squeeze his eyes shut against the surge of lust that filled him. Oh, God, how he wanted her.

When he found her nipples, she made a low sound in the back of her throat that drove him mad—and he was determined to hear it again. As he rolled her nipples between his thumbs and fingers, she dropped her head back against his shoulder, and her breath came fast and shallow.

He tried to catch his own breath. She was like soft wax in his hands now, hot and molding to his touch. This time she was going to let him get under her skirts, he knew it. Heaven help him, he was going to explode right here if she kept moving against him like that.

It was time to take his wife upstairs. At last. Just as he was about to lift her off her feet to carry her up, he noticed a mark on her neck.

It was a white line, barely visible. A scar.

He ran a finger over it. "What's this from?"

She went rigid. When she tried to jerk away from him, he held her in place.

"How did ye get this?"

"'Tis nothing," she said. "Let me go, I mean it now."

He pushed the edge of her gown down an inch or two for a better look. The scar continued down her back, out of sight.

She turned around in his arms and rested her palms on

his chest. Looking up at him from under her lashes, she said, "I want ye to kiss me."

His gaze locked on her full, parted lips, and he was sorely tempted. But why was she so desperate to divert him? When she slid her hands up around his neck and leaned against him, it was damned hard to resist her.

He brushed her soft cheek with his thumb. "What is it that ye don't want me to know?"

She pressed her lips into a thin line and narrowed her eyes. Her brief game of seductress was over. A shame, that. But something here didn't sit right with him.

Each time he had kissed her, things had gone well—*very well*—until the moment he began unfastening buttons or hooks. As he thought about that, it came to him that this was the first time he'd seen her with her hair up.

"Ye can cooperate or no," he said, "but I'm going to have a look."

Her bottom lip trembled. Saints above, what was this about? Sìleas never cried. Even when she was a child of six and her father forgot her places, leaving her to find her own way home, she hadn't shed a tear.

He kissed the side of her face and gently turned her around.

"Don't," she said in a small voice, but he could tell she had given up expecting him to concede.

His fingers felt big and clumsy as he unfastened the tiny hooks. When he had them undone to her waist, he pushed the gown off her shoulders. The chemise she wore beneath it dipped low enough in the back for him to see what she was hiding.

Rage took him like a storm, pounding in his ears and making his hands shake. He reached around her to slam his fist on the table. "I'll kill him. I swear, I will kill whoever did this to you."

She was weeping silently, but he was so filled with violence that he was afraid to put his hands on her.

"Who did this to ye?" he asked. "Ye must tell me."

She wiped her face with her hand. "Who do ye think? My step-da."

"Ach, Sìl, why didn't ye tell me?" He wanted to throw his head back and howl in his outrage. She had still been a child when Murdoc did this. "If I'd known he was hurting ye, I would have done something."

But he *should* have known. He had always been her protector, and this had happened under his nose.

"When did he do this?" He strained to soften his voice, knowing anger was not what she needed from him now, but it was hard when his body still pulsed with it.

She took a shaky breath. "Mostly Murdoc didn't trouble himself with me. As ye know, he expected my mother to give him a son who would inherit Knock Castle."

Sìleas's mother had lost several babes before they reached a year. And Ian had no idea how many miscarriages the poor woman had.

"After she died losing that last baby, Murdoc got it into his head that he could keep my lands by wedding me to his son Angus. He gave me no peace after that. When I told him I would never marry a MacKinnon, let alone that disgusting son of his, he tried to beat me into agreeing to it."

Ian clenched his jaw until it ached to keep from shouting curses. Years ago, Angus MacKinnon had nearly caused a clan war by raping a woman from Ian's mother's clan, Clan Ranald. The matter had been settled with a hefty payment, but hard feelings remained—as did rumors of Angus's penchant for violence.

"But ye know how stubborn I am," Sìleas said, glancing over her shoulder to give him a bittersweet smile. "In the end, Murdoc locked me in my bedchamber and sent for Angus."

"And that was the day I found ye?" Ian asked, though he already knew the bitter truth.

She nodded. "Murdoc didn't know about the tunnel."

Christ, forgive me. All this time, he had blamed Sìleas for their forced wedding. He thought she'd caused it through some girlish foolishness that had gone farther than she expected. He'd had no notion she was in serious trouble that day.

But then, he hadn't made much effort to find out, either.

She covered her face and said in a choked whisper, "I knew ye would find me disgusting again once ye saw it."

"God help me, Sìl, how can ye say that?" He turned her around and pulled her against his chest. "Please tell me ye don't think so little of me."

He held her tight and kissed her hair until she ceased to weep. Then he lifted her in his arms and carried her to the stairs.

Sometimes words were not enough.

CHAPTER 16

Sileas rested her head against Ian's chest as he carried her up the stairs. She didn't know what she wanted anymore, but she felt safe nestled in his arms, and she needed to feel safe now.

Ian carried her into her bedchamber and kicked the door shut behind him. As soon as he set her on her feet next to the bed, he whisked her gown over her head, leaving her standing in her chemise. She was too drained to be embarrassed. He kept one hand on her shoulder to steady her as he folded back the blankets, then he lifted her onto the bed.

With a gentleness surprising in such a big man, he brushed the hair back from her face with his fingers. The gesture reminded her of his father's kindness that day he found them in the wood and knelt beside her, talking softly and holding her hand between his huge ones.

Beneath the dangerous, war-hardened man Ian had become, the kindness of the boy he once was lingered. He framed her face with his hands and leaned down to kiss her. She sighed as he brushed his lips over hers.

"I don't want ye to fret," he said in a soft voice, "but I'm coming into bed with ye."

Her mouth went dry as he unfastened his claymore and laid it on the floor next to the bed, where it would be close at hand. She knew he did it from habit, and yet that, too, made her feel safe. No one would get past the door while Ian was here.

She watched as he took off his boots and socks and then unwound his plaid and dropped it. He was standing in just his shirt, which fell to his thighs. She stared at his powerful legs, so different from how they were when he was a boy, then brought her gaze slowly back to his face. Ian had been a lovely boy, but he was so handsome now it made her ache to look at him.

When he met her gaze and his eyes went dark, she felt a stirring deep within her. Even if what he felt for her was mostly pity, she couldn't help reacting to his desire for her. Desire, pity, duty. If that was all that brought him to her bed and secured their marriage, he would never be content with her. At least not for long.

She drew in a shaky breath as Ian unfastened his shirt. He paused midway and dropped his hands.

He did not want her after all. The scars were too ugly.

"I'm no going to take your virginity this time, because ye are upset," he said. "I want ye to decide to have me as your husband with a clear head and heart."

The bed rocked as he climbed in beside her. Before she could catch her breath, he pulled her into his arms. The heat and power of him radiated through her from head to toe.

"What I am going to do," he said with his face so close she could feel the warmth of his breath on her lips, "is leave ye with no doubt that I want ye."

She swallowed. She strongly suspected his plan would involve removing the rest of her clothes.

"It's too light" was all she could manage to get through her tight throat.

"The first time I have ye naked, I want to see ye."

The first time. Would there be a second after he saw her back? He'd only seen a little of her scars in the kitchen. And even if the scars didn't trouble him, would she disappoint him in other ways?

"You're as lovely as your name, Sìleas." He said her name, drawing out the *shhh* sound. "I should have known you'd grow into it, just as ye have your teeth."

She didn't think it was possible to draw a smile from her, but this did. "And what is wrong with my teeth?"

"Nothing at all." He dragged his thumb over her bottom lip, making her breath hitch. "I'd like to feel them on my skin."

"Are ye joking?" She hadn't meant to say the words aloud.

He kept his eyes fixed on hers as he shook his head, and her heart skipped a beat. Taking her hand, he scraped his teeth over the pad of her thumb, sending a thrill of sensation through her.

When he covered her mouth with his, she found it hard to hang onto her worries.

He'd kissed her many times now, so she thought she was prepared. But kissing lying down was turning out to be a different experience altogether. She felt overwhelmed by his closeness, by the weight of him leaning over her, pressing her into the bed.

His lips were warm and soft. When she put her palm to his face to feel the rough bristles against her palm, he made a low sound in his throat. The thrust of his tongue in her mouth sent spirals of pleasure down to her belly. Her heart was beating too fast. And that was before she felt the warmth of his hand cover her breast.

She gasped for breath when he tore his mouth away from hers.

"Ahh, ye feel good, Sìl," he said in her ear.

He nipped at her earlobe, sending unexpected tingles through her, then kissed the side of her face. As he moved down her throat, he drew involuntary sighs from her lips. The moist warmth of his breath, his lips, his tongue on her skin, captured all her attention. But when she felt his mouth on the bare skin at the top of her breast, her eyes flew open.

When she started to sit up, Ian locked his hands around her wrists, pressed them to the bed on either side of her head, and proceeded to dissolve her resistance with endless kisses. She wasn't aware of when he released her hands, but she had them around his neck now, urging him closer.

She groaned in disappointment when he pulled away. He gave her a warm smile that shone in his eyes.

"We'd best get this next part over with, Sìl."

Before she knew it, he flipped her onto her stomach.

Guessing his intention, she gripped the sides of her chemise with both hands. "No, Ian. No."

Instead of jerking her chemise up as she expected, he drew her hair to the side and started kissing her neck. His lips were so soft, she sighed without meaning to. Then he kissed her bare shoulder. Straddling her on all fours, he slowly worked his way down, rubbing firm hands over her and kissing her through the cloth of her chemise.

She had been touched so little in her life. The intimacy

of the contact caused little flutters in her stomach. She started at the unexpected sensation when he nipped at her bottom through the chemise, with what felt very much like his teeth. When she rose up on her elbows to look over her shoulder, he gave her a devilish grin.

She let her head sink back to the bed. Closing her eyes, she concentrated on his hands as they slid over her hips and up and down her thighs. When he picked up her foot and kissed the bottom, it tickled and felt good at the same time. Her foot! Surely, he must care a little to do that.

He started back up her legs, but this time he was touching bare skin. She clenched her fists in her chemise again, but her fingers loosened as he kneaded the muscles of her legs.

"Your legs are tight," he said. "Ye work too hard."

"Mmmph."

His strong hands felt wonderful on her sore muscles— though she tensed every time his hand strayed to the inside of her thigh.

When he nipped at her bottom again, there was no cloth between it and his teeth. But it felt so good to be touched all over, she didn't object.

She was drifting in a liquid pool of warmth, when Ian leaned over her and said in her ear, "I have to do this."

She felt a gush of cold air on her back. Then she heard Ian suck in his breath and felt him go still above her.

"No!" She tried to get up, but Ian held her down by her shoulders.

He was quiet for a long time. Then he said in a strained voice, "Truly, I can hardly see the scars, they are so faint."

"You're lying to me. Ye can't bear to look at me."

"No, no, it's not that at all," he said.

She drew in a shaky breath and rested her head on the bed again.

"It's just that I can tell what they once looked like, what he did to ye," he said. "And it makes me so angry, I want to kill the bastard with my bare hands."

When she felt his lips touch her back with feather-light kisses, tears filled her eyes at his tenderness.

"I've been afraid Murdoc would come take me ever since your da came home injured." She glanced at Ian over her shoulder and saw him wince as if her words cut him.

"He will no get ye now," he said. "I won't let him."

"I know," she said against the pillow.

"Thank ye for that, Sìl," he said in a soft voice.

She hadn't felt comfortable in her own skin since the beating. After hiding her scars for so many years, she began to feel at ease in her nakedness as Ian moved over her back with his soft, warm kisses. While he kissed her, his hands moved in circles—up and down her sides, brushing the sides of her breasts and following the lines of her waist and hips.

"Ah, Sìleas," he said. "Ye are so beautiful. I want to touch every inch of ye."

Gòrdan and other men had told her she was beautiful, but she had never felt it. Ian's hands made her almost believe it. His touch was reverential and soothed her.

More, his acceptance began to heal the scar on her heart.

Five years ago, Ian's harsh words on the day of their wedding had been like the sting of alcohol on her fresh wounds. They had deepened the scar inside her. Perhaps that was the reason only he could heal her.

Ian moved off her to lie beside her, turning her with

him so that she felt the comforting heat of his body down her back and all around her. She closed her eyes, following the movement of his hand up her thigh and over the swell of her hip to her waist.

Then she felt something hard and urgent pressing against her backside—and her sense of peacefulness vanished. Her heart was beating twice as fast as before. Despite Ian's statement that he did not intend to take her virginity—*this time*—she suddenly felt her vulnerability, lying naked in bed next to an aroused man.

She licked her lips. "While this has all been verra pleasant, I should get up now."

She managed to sit up, but Ian sat up with her.

"Not yet," Ian said with a firm hand on her hip. "Trust me."

"I can guess what comes next," she said and tried to wriggle away from him.

"I don't think ye can," he said, pulling her closer. "But I'm looking forward to showing ye."

She turned to face him. "I know ye feel guilty for things that aren't your fault—like your father's lost leg and the scars on my back—and for a few things that may be your fault. But ye can't fix them by tying yourself to me now."

"I told ye, I won't take it that far," he said, cupping her face with his hand. "I know you're not ready. Ye can trust me."

Trust him or no, she let him coax her back down on the bed. She lay on her side again, with him behind her.

"I can smell summer heather on your skin," he said, as he nuzzled her neck.

She held her breath as his hand moved up her belly,

then let it out in a small gasp when his hand encompassed her breast. All her senses were ajar, with the heat of him surrounding her, pressed against her everywhere. His breathing grew harsh as he planted hot, wet kisses on the side of her throat. Then he held her tight against him so that her body moved with his in a slow rocking motion.

"I do want ye," he said in her ear. "Tell me ye know that."

"Aye." For certain he did, but he'd likely want any woman who was pressed up against him naked in bed.

He distracted her by rubbing his thumb over her nipple. The sensations shot to somewhere deep in her belly. Then he turned her on her back and took her breast in his mouth.

Did all men know to do this? She was breathing too fast. She was arching her back, her body begging him not to stop, as the sensations ripped through her and settled in a dull ache between her legs.

She wanted to feel his skin against hers. "Can ye not take off your shirt?"

"Do ye want to kill me, lass?" he asked, but he sat up and whipped his shirt off.

When he pulled her into his arms, she clenched her teeth, savoring the delicious sensation of his hard muscles and rough chest hair against her breasts. He kissed her until she felt as if she were floating.

His tongue moved against hers as he ran his fingers in slow circles from her hip to the top of her thigh. Each time his fingers brushed the place that ached between her legs it caused a burst of sensation. She felt so sensitive there it almost hurt—and yet she nearly groaned in disappointment each time his hand moved away.

When he finally slid his fingers between her legs,

the word "Aye!" came out of her mouth. Ian made a low sound in his throat and clamped his mouth over hers.

This wasn't the slow, sensual kiss of before but greedy, demanding. While he ravished her mouth, his fingers did a magic dance between her legs. She held on to him, wanting him closer, closer still, as the silvery sensations cascaded through her.

He broke the kiss and looked down at her with eyes that were dark with blue fire. "I want to see ye find your release," he said in a ragged voice. "Do ye know what that is?"

It was hard to concentrate with what he was doing to her with his hand, but she managed to shake her head.

"I want to give ye such pleasure that ye cry out."

"Do ye?" she asked doubtfully. "Are ye sure?"

"Oh, aye," he said, giving her a wicked smile that made her toes curl. "Trust me. Let me do this."

He gave her another deep kiss. Then he was running his tongue between her breasts, circling her nipple, all the while working his magic fingers between her legs. When he took her breast into his mouth and sucked, she heard herself making high-pitched pleading sounds. Whatever he was doing, she wanted more. Sensations coursed through her until every fiber in her being was strained with tension, waiting for something, something more.

Her body felt as if she might snap in two, but Ian was relentless.

And then she burst into a thousand pieces. She heard herself cry out as her body clenched in a spasm of intense pleasure that left her shaking. Before she could catch her breath, Ian was kissing her with a need and an urgency that sent a new surge of desire pulsing through her. His hands were everywhere, squeezing, stroking, as he devoured her with his kisses.

When he rolled on top of her and urged her legs apart with his knee, she didn't remind him of his promise. She wanted what he wanted. She wanted him inside her, to be joined with him, to be one with him.

A tear slid down the side of her face because this was Ian, the man who was always meant to be her husband. The man she wanted to be her first lover and her last. It could only be Ian. Always Ian, and no other.

When his shaft touched her center, desire surged through her like a wave crashing onto the shore. She pulled on his shoulders, urging him forward.

But he lifted his body away from hers and dropped his head to rest his forehead lightly on her breast bone. Her body was so tense that his breath prickled her damp skin.

"I'm trying hard to remember my promise," he said.

"I want ye to forget it. Please, Ian."

But he moved off her and dropped onto his back beside her. The air was charged with the tension between their bodies, and they were both gasping for breath.

"I just needed to stop a moment," he said.

She turned and tentatively rested her hand on the flat of his stomach. He started at her touch, then took her hand and brought it to his mouth to kiss her fingers.

He rolled to face her and laid his hand against her cheek. "Did ye like that?"

"Aye." She flushed, feeling embarrassed.

"Ye were wonderful to watch," he said, running his hand over her hair. "I love the sounds ye made, and the feel of ye under my hands."

At his words, she felt the tension growing in her again.

She swallowed. The intensity of his eyes on hers made it worse. When he put his hand between her legs again, her breath hitched.

Keeping his eyes fixed on hers, he said, "I like that ye are hot and wet for me, Sìl. You're a beautiful woman. You're everything I want."

"I don't know what to do. Shouldn't I..." She tried to hold on to the thought, but Ian was moving his fingers in that way that made it impossible to think of anything else.

"No love. This time is just for you," he said, as he rolled her on her back.

Then Ian's mouth was on hers, and she let herself be swept away by the magic.

CHAPTER 17

Ian greeted each man at the door of the church to be sure no one entered they didn't trust.

"Father Brian, it was brave of ye to agree to let us meet here," Ian said when the priest arrived. "But ye didn't need to risk coming here yourself tonight."

"I prayed over it, and God approves," the priest said, and went inside. Ian had heard the priest had a woman, and he supposed God had approved that as well.

It was time to begin.

Ian stepped out into the night and listened. When he heard nothing but the howl of the wind, he went back inside and signaled to Connor that all was ready.

Duncan and Alex joined him at the back, where they would be the first to meet any uninvited guests, while Connor took his place at the front. Because of the church's close proximity to Dunscaith Castle, only two candles were lit, one on either side of Connor. The men who were milling about found seats, and the room grew quiet.

Although the rest of the church was in deep shadow, Ian sensed that all eyes were on Connor.

"You have come here tonight," Connor said in a voice that filled the church, "because the MacKinnons have stolen Knock Castle from us, and ye know we must take it back."

Several of the men shouted and raised their fists or banged their claymores on the floor.

"Ye served my father when he was chieftain," Connor said when they grew quiet again.

"And he damned well wouldn't have let the MacKinnons take what belongs to us!" This outburst from one of the older men was followed by a loud murmur of agreement.

"We need Knock Castle to protect our lands to the east from invaders," Connor said. "It is a danger to all our homes not to have it in MacDonald hands."

Ian smiled in appreciation of how simply Connor put the matter before the men. He spoke a truth they all knew, in contrast to Hugh, who lied through his teeth whether he needed to or not.

"For the clan's protection, we must take it back," Connor said, and again there were murmurs of approval. "The question is how to go about it without a chieftain to lead us."

"It's time we had a chieftain willing to fight for us," one man shouted.

It was, but Connor was wise enough not to make that move yet.

Connor let the rumble grow before he put his hands up for silence. "Hugh has declared himself chieftain," he said, reinforcing in their minds that Hugh had not yet been chosen by the clan. "I don't want to put anyone in the position of going against the man who may well become our chieftain."

There were grumblings. So far, this was going just as they hoped.

"While Hugh has refused to fight for Knock Castle, he never said that others should not."

Connor paused to give the men time to consider this and come to the conclusion he wanted. He was good at this.

"There is one man here who has a clear right to that castle," Connor said. "And I say that a man with a right need not wait for his chieftain to act on his behalf, if he believes he can accomplish the deed himself."

Several men turned to peer at Ian in the shadows at the back of the church.

"And if some of his clansmen wish to lend him a hand, all the better!"

There were shouts of "Aye! Aye!"

One man stepped into the center aisle of the church and waited to speak until Connor acknowledged him with a nod.

"If ye are speaking of Ian MacDonald, he has no right to Knock Castle."

As soon as the man opened his mouth, Ian knew it was that damned Gòrdan.

"It is Sìleas who is the heir—Sìleas, and then her child. So far as I know," Gòrdan said, turning to look down the aisle at Ian, "the lass is no carrying Ian's child."

A child would make Ian's right certain. For now, he was claiming it on behalf of Sìleas and their future children.

"Ian's only been back a week," Alex shouted. "Give the man some time."

Alex's remark caused a round of laughter and an easing of the tension that Gòrdan's interruption had caused.

But Gòrdan wasn't finished.

"Ian deserted her," Gòrdan said. "If Sìleas has decided to take a different husband, no one can blame her."

"She has done no such thing, nor will she!" Ian struggled to shake off Duncan's arm so he could go up there and smash Gòrdan's face in.

"All I know," Gòrdan said, turning around again to be sure Ian didn't miss his words, "is that a man cannot get a woman with child if she's no sharing his bed."

This time, Ian broke free from Duncan's grip. He landed on Gòrdan, and the two crashed to the floor—but he only got in a few punches before Connor and Alex pulled him off. When Gòrdan sprang to his feet and tried to swing at him, Duncan caught Gòrdan from behind and held him.

"If ye haven't bedded her yet," Connor hissed an inch from Ian's face, "see that ye do before we gather the men to take the castle."

"I'll take care of it," Ian said between his teeth, as he glared at his cousin.

"As for you, Gòrdan MacDonald," Connor said, turning and grabbing Gòrdan by the front of his shirt. "If ye think Sìleas might choose you instead, I suggest ye keep your mouth shut and your sword sharp for the fight for her castle."

"Sìleas is my wife," Ian said, locking eyes with Gòrdan. "If Gòrdan wants to take her, he'll have to kill me first."

Ian shrugged Connor off and pushed past the others to stand at the front of the room.

"A MacDonald fights for what belongs to him," he shouted to the gathered men. "I ask you to join me in the fight for Knock Castle for the sake of our clan. But whether ye do or not, I will take it. For I am a MacDonald, and I keep what is mine."

Ian let his gaze travel slowly around the room, then drew his claymore and held it high. "I am Ian MacDonald, husband of Sìleas, and *I Will Take Knock Castle!*"

The floorboards of the church vibrated with the thumping of feet and the pounding of claymores as the men shouted with him, shaking the building with their battle cry.

"Knock Castle! Knock Castle! Knock Castle!"

CHAPTER 18

When Sìleas saw Ian and Alex coming up the path, she grabbed her cloak and ran out to meet them.

"Where have ye been?" she asked, taking Ian's arm and smiling up at him.

Alex waggled his eyebrows at her and grinned, as if he were responsible for the change between her and Ian.

"We stayed with Connor and Duncan last night," Ian said. "I confess we drank too much to make our way home."

Sìleas clicked her tongue. "Well, at least you're not lying to me about it."

Ian halted in the middle of the path, his eyes as warm as summer on her face. "I missed ye last night."

Alex took the hint and went on ahead toward the house.

"We need to talk," Ian said. "Not here."

Her heart did a little flip in her chest, knowing Ian wanted to settle things between them. She was ready. After staying awake half the night thinking about it, she had made her decision.

She felt a nervous excitement as Ian led her down the

path to the small beach below the house. Hopeful. That was what she felt. When he'd taken her upstairs, he had shown her the man she knew he could be, the man she believed in.

She couldn't fool herself into believing Ian loved her; he had other reasons for wanting to be her husband. But there was so much caring in his touch that she had reason to hope that one day he would. Even if he never did love her as she loved him, Ian had convinced her that he valued her and that he was determined to be a good husband to her from now forward.

It was too late, in any case. If she was going to leave him, she should have done it before he took her upstairs yesterday. He may have left her a virgin, but she'd lost her innocence. She longed to feel his weight on top of her again, to run her fingers over the muscles of his back, to see the stars spark against her eyelids as waves of pleasure pulsed through her.

What woman in her right mind could say no to the whole cake once she'd had a taste of that? The thought of sharing a bed with Ian every night sent tingles all the way to her toes.

Sìleas smiled to herself and fingered the special stone in her pocket for luck. When they reached the beach, Ian led her to the old lean-to that was hidden in the trees above the tide line. After ducking inside, they settled themselves on the low bench in the midst of a familiar assortment of fishing nets, ropes, and scraps for mending sails.

"I meant it when I said I missed ye," Ian said, fixing his intense blue eyes on her.

"I missed ye, too."

"I'll always want ye by my side," he said. "And I don't want to go another night without ye in my bed."

She held her breath, waiting for him to finish.

"What I'm saying—what I'm asking, I mean—is if ye are willing to be my true wife, starting tonight." He fumbled inside his plaid. "Here, I have something to give ye."

He took her hand and dropped a small silver ring into it.

"I didn't have a ring for ye the day we wed," he said. "I want to make that right now."

Sìleas turned it over in her palm, the traditional gift of a man to his bride. She ran her fingertip around the circle, the symbol of never-ending love. The ring was formed to resemble two ropes twisted together, intertwined as a couple's life would be.

"I know our wedding was no what it should have been," Ian said.

Sìleas had to laugh at that. "'Twas the worst day of my life."

Ian made a face. "It couldn't have been as bad as that."

"It was," she said. "Don't ye remember that gown your mother put me in?"

Ian's mouth twitched. "Three of ye could have fit inside it."

"And the color!" she said, rolling her eyes. "Nothing could have been worse."

Though they were laughing, it was a bitter memory for both of them. Still, it made Sìleas feel better to talk about it.

"But ye did get the man ye wanted, aye?" Ian said, squeezing her shoulders and giving her a wink.

"Having the groom say his vows with the point of a dirk in his back is not what a lass dreams of when she imagines her wedding day."

Ian's expression turned serious. "I'll make it all up to ye. The ring is just the start."

Looking into Ian's eyes was like being pulled into the sea—and she wanted to go wherever the current took her.

"I'm ready to be a good husband to ye," he said, taking her hand. "Tell me ye want to be my wife."

"I do."

Ian took the ring from her hand and slipped it onto her finger.

"It looks good on ye," he said, and raised her hand to his mouth. His lips were warm and soft on her fingers, reminding Sìleas of how they had felt on her belly.

She swallowed. "I have a gift for ye as well."

When his eyebrows shot up, she was pleased that she had surprised him. She pulled the crystal out of her pocket and held it out for him to see. It was no bigger than her thumb and a lovely misty color that was like seeing a green sea through a thick fog.

"Do ye know what it is?" she asked.

"A wee stone?" Ian said with a grin.

"It's a charm stone," she said in a hushed voice. "The MacDonald Crystal."

"I thought it was lost." He took it gingerly between his fingers and held it up, trying to see through it. "Isn't this the one they say was brought back from the Holy Land by Crusaders?"

"Aye. My grandmother had it." Sìleas dropped her gaze to her hands resting in her lap. "Ye see, she didn't like my father, and she knew my mother was weak. To keep it out of his hands, she gave it to the old seer to save for me. Teàrlag gave it to me after I came to live with your family. She says it protects the wearer."

"Then ye must keep it." Ian put the crystal in her hand, then closed his hand over hers.

Sìleas met his gaze and shook her head. "Ye tell me ye will protect me, and I believe ye. But who will protect you? This is my wedding gift to ye, and so ye must take it."

It was the most precious thing she owned. By giving it to him, she was showing him that she trusted him with her life—and with her heart.

"I will guard it and you," he said, meeting her eyes.

"Teàrlag made this pouch to keep it in." She pulled the leather thong from her pocket. "She said words over it to enhance the strength of the crystal."

Sìleas did not add that Teàrlag told her that if she slept with it next to her own heart first, his heart would remember hers. She hoped it was true.

When she opened the pouch for him, Ian dropped the crystal inside it. Tears stung at the back of her eyes as she reached up to put it around his neck.

She placed her hand over the pouch, where it rested over his heart.

"I can feel your heartbeat through it," she said, looking up at him. "Keep it close and be safe for me."

Ian gathered her in his arms. His breath was warm in her ear as he whispered, "Thank ye, Sìleas."

They held each other for a long while.

Then Ian kissed her softly and said, "I'll come to you tonight, then."

"Aye. Tonight."

Tonight. The start of their new life together.

CHAPTER 19

"Such a lovely babe Annie has," Sìleas said, as she walked arm in arm with Beitris on their way home from their visit to the neighbors. "Niall, it was sweet of ye to come with us."

Ian had planned to accompany them until Payton asked him to practice in the yard. It would be Payton's first attempt to use his claymore since his injury.

"You're looking happy today," her mother-in-law said, and winked at her. "Maybe you'll have a babe of your own to show off by this time next year."

Sìleas's heart lifted at the thought. Beitris had guessed that everything had changed between her and Ian—and was almost as happy about it as Sìleas.

When Niall gave her a searching glance, she blushed. She wasn't about to tell Niall that she and Ian were going to start sharing a marriage bed, though he and the rest of the household would know it by morning.

"Ach, look who's coming," Niall said with a sour look on his face.

It was Gòrdan, and he was marching straight for them,

looking like a man with something on his mind that would not keep. Sìleas took in a deep breath. She had feared they would see him, coming or going, since they had to walk past his house to get to Annie's.

" 'Tis best to set him straight," Beitris said in her ear just before Gòrdan reached them.

"Beitris. Niall." Gòrdan gave them each a brief nod. "Sìleas, may I have a word with ye? It's important."

"We'll walk slow," Beitris said to her. "Ye can catch up to us when you're done with your chat."

Gòrdan gave Sìleas a warm, hopeful smile that made her feel wretched. Beitris was right—'twas time to tell Gòrdan that things were settled between her and Ian. Gòrdan was a good man, and she owed him that.

"I can't go out walking with ye anymore," she said. "I've made my decision to stay with Ian."

"Say ye don't mean it." His eyes were wild as he gripped her arms. "Tell me it's not too late, that ye haven't given yourself to him yet."

She flushed, remembering all the things Ian had done to her. Though she was still a virgin, she had, indeed, given herself to him.

"Ian doesn't deserve ye," Gòrdan said. "He doesn't love ye as I do."

Ach, he was not making this easy. "Ian says he's ready to be a good husband to me, and I believe him."

"With his pretty face, Ian can have any of the lasses," Gòrdan said, waving his arm out to the side as if there were a line of women standing there. "But you should have a man who sees ye for the special woman that ye are."

She didn't want to hurt him, but softening the message would not help Gòrdan accept it.

"Ian cares for me," she said.

"Is that what he tells ye?" Gòrdan said, raising his voice. "It hurts me to see ye believe his lies."

"Stop it, Gòrdan. I know ye are upset, but you've no cause to call Ian a liar."

"You've always had a weakness for Ian, and it's made ye blind," he said, shaking his head. "What Ian values ye for is your lands."

"No. That's not true."

"He's come back to Skye to help Connor take the chieftainship." Gòrdan's voice was rough with emotion. "That's all this is about."

Icy fingers of doubt crept over her heart. "No, Ian wants to be my husband."

"Is that why he stayed away five years?" he asked. "Ye know Ian would do anything for Connor, and Connor wants your castle back in MacDonald hands."

"What are ye saying, Gòrdan?"

"The four of them—Connor, Ian, Alex, and Duncan—held a secret meeting last night in the church."

A shiver of fear went up her spine. "What about? Are they going to fight Hugh?"

"Connor is a clever one. He knows it's too soon to challenge his uncle directly," Gòrdan said. "Instead, he has Ian—as your husband—be the one to call on the men to take Knock Castle."

Why had no one told her of the plan to oust her stepfather from her castle? Why had *Ian* not told her? Instead, he'd led her to believe he'd spent the night drinking with Connor and the others.

"The four of them have it all planned out," Gòrdan said, raising his arms. "They know how much losing Knock

Castle hurt the clan's pride. Men came last night because they are angry that Hugh has not called for an attack. They all went home believing that unlike Hugh, Connor would never turn his back while our enemies took what belongs to us."

"Connor wouldn't," she said in a low voice.

"I'm telling ye," Gòrdan said, "the whole purpose of taking Knock Castle is to rally the men into supporting Connor for the chieftainship."

Sìleas felt like her throat was closing. Her voice came out high and tight as she asked, "Are ye saying this meeting was last night?"

"Aye."

And Ian had come back this morning with a ring, saying he didn't want to wait another night to be her true husband. She felt as if she were standing on the edge of a sandbar with the sand sliding out from beneath her feet.

"Connor needs a man with a husband's claim to justify the attack," Gòrdan said. "That is the reason Ian is claiming ye now."

In the back of her head, she heard Ian's voice. *There is nothing I would not do for Connor.*

Still, she said, "That doesn't mean Ian doesn't care for me."

"What Ian cares about," Gòrdan said, "is being the hero who saved the clan by putting Connor in the chieftainship."

His words rang true in her heart, for she knew Ian had a burning need to redeem himself.

"Just because Ian wants to help the clan doesn't mean that's the only reason he wants to be my husband."

"I'm telling ye," Gòrdan said, "Ian wants ye so he has the right to claim your lands and castle."

"That wasn't enough to make him want to wed me

five years ago, and I was heir to Knock Castle then." She could hear the desperation in her voice.

"That was before Flodden. Before Connor's father and brother died. Before Hugh Dubh took the chieftainship." Gòrdan hit each point relentlessly. "And it was before Connor had a chance at becoming chieftain."

She shook her head because she didn't want to believe it.

"Connor ordered Ian to take ye to bed, so he would have a husband's right to take Knock Castle," Gòrdan said. "I heard Connor say it."

I'll do whatever it takes, for the sake of the clan. There is nothing I would not do for Connor.

"Ian told Connor not to worry, he would 'take care of it.'"

She felt her checks flush with mortification.

"Ye know I've never lied to ye," he said.

"I won't hear this," she said, backing away from him.

"You've been a fool for Ian for five years," Gòrdan said. "I'm begging ye, don't be a fool for him for the rest of your life."

The long years of waiting still hurt. And for certain, Ian had not been faithful to her while he was in France. Did a ring and a few soft words make up for that?

"For God's sake, Sìleas, open your eyes and see the man for what he is." Gòrdan drew in a deep breath and blew it out. "If ye change your mind, I'll be waiting."

Her lip trembled as she watched Gòrdan turn away and walk up the path toward his home. No, she would not believe it. She knew Ian's heart. He wouldn't deceive her.

But as she ran toward the house, all she could remember was that Ian had not once told her he loved her.

CHAPTER 20

Ian hummed to himself as he poured the second pot of boiling water into the tub. In a wink, he stripped and tossed his dirty clothes into the corner, then settled into the steaming water with a long, satisfied sigh.

Tonight. Tonight would be the night he consummated his marriage and tied Sìleas to him for life. He wanted it all to be perfect for her. Of course, he couldn't be sweet-smelling like Sìleas, but at least he would be clean for her. He'd bring a flask of wine up to their bedchamber and set the room ablaze with candles.

He rested his head against the back of the tub and smiled to himself, thinking of the night ahead.

Damn. Was that the front door opening? With his da asleep and everyone else gone to see the neighbors' new babe, he expected to have the house to himself a while longer. Ach, he'd best get down to business before the women came into the kitchen to fix supper.

He sat up and scrubbed his face. After he dunked his head in the water to rinse the soap off, he felt fingers in his hair.

"Sìleas," he said, smiling like a fool with his eyes closed and water streaming down his face.

She laid her hands on his shoulders, and he sighed as she slid them down his chest. But something was not quite right...He sat bolt upright and spun around—and discovered it wasn't Sìleas who had her hands on him.

"Dina. What are ye doing here?"

"What's this?" Dina snapped the cord that held the crystal over his head before he could think to grab her arm to stop her.

"Ye need to leave—ye can see I'm bathing." He held his hand out. "Give that back to me before ye go."

She swung it in front of him, just out of his reach, then laughed and put it around her neck. "This would be a lovely gift for ye to give me in return for what I'm going to give ye."

"We're not giving each other anything, Dina," he said, losing his patience with her. "Now give that back to me."

"You didn't ask what I was going to give ye." She ran her finger down the cord to where the pouch that held the crystal lay in the cleavage between her breasts.

"By the saints, Dina, what do ye think ye are doing?"

"I couldn't help noticing ye been sleeping in the old cottage," she said. "Seems a shame to sleep alone, when ye don't have to."

"I'm not interested in what ye are offering," he said. "Now give me that and go."

He leaned forward and grabbed a handful of the skirt of her gown and pulled. "Give it to me."

She must have unfastened her gown already, because she stepped out of it as the damn thing came away in his hands. He looked up from the gown clenched in his fingers to see her standing in her chemise. Then, before he could say a word, the chemise was off.

Now, he was a man. He didn't mean to look. She wasn't the woman he wanted. But Dina did have attractive... attributes. And she was standing right in front of him stark naked. It didn't help matters that Sìleas left him in a constant state of frustration.

Against his will, his cock sprang to life. That did not mean he intended to use it.

"I want ye to give me that back, get your clothes on, and leave the kitchen, so I can finish my bath and get dressed."

"Come and take it." As she intended, his eyes went to the pouch, which was lying between her naked breasts.

He looked around for the towel. Damn, he'd left it on the stool on the other side of the table. Dina must have followed his gaze, for she ran around the table, breasts bobbing, and snatched up it up.

Ach! He wanted to strangle the woman.

"If ye will not get dressed and leave, then I will." He clenched the sides of the tub, hoisted himself up, and stepped out of the tub, streaming water. He was reaching for his clean shirt on the table when he heard a commotion behind him and turned.

Sìleas's scream filled the small room as he saw her in the doorway. Her eyes were impossibly wide, and she was screaming as if someone had stabbed her.

"Sìleas," Ian started for her, but then her gaze dropped to his groin and she screamed again. He'd forgotten he was naked. He grabbed his shirt from the table and covered himself. Although she was a virgin, he hadn't expected her to get this upset by her first good look at him naked.

"It's all right, Sìl," he said, walking toward her.

She backed away, not with fright in her eyes, as he expected, but with such hurt that his heart felt pinched in his chest.

When her gaze moved from him to fix on something behind him, he remembered Dina. In his concern for Sìleas, he had forgotten all about that damned woman. And then he realized what this must look like to Sìleas—and why she screamed.

"Ye gave her my stone," Sìleas said in a choked whisper.

Ian felt as if the walls of the room were crashing in on him, smothering him under their weight.

"No. No, I didn't," he said, as Sìleas turned and ran. "This is no what ye think!"

When he started after her, Niall took her place in the kitchen doorway, roaring, "Ye bastard!"

"Get out of my way," Ian said, and shoved his brother aside.

Unfortunately, both his feet and the floor were wet. When Niall tackled him, he slipped and fell backward to the floor. Then his brother proceeded to pound his head and torso, all the while shouting, "How could ye do it! How could ye!"

Ian was sorely tempted to beat the living shite out of his baby brother when Alex finally pulled Niall off him.

"What took ye so long?" Ian said, as he pulled his shirt over his head.

"Maybe I thought ye deserved it," Alex said.

"I didn't touch Dina." Ian turned around and shouted at her. "Tell them I didn't touch ye. Tell them!"

While his head was turned, Niall broke free from Alex's hold and landed a blow to the side of Ian's head that made his ears ring. He couldn't see to block the next punch.

He woke up on the floor by the hearth, with his mother hovering over him and his head pounding like the devil.

"Where's Sìl?" he said, starting to get up.

His mother put her hand on his chest. "Don't move, or I'll hit ye in the head myself."

"Mam, I need to see Sìl. She thinks I did something I didn't do."

"Give her time to calm down," his mother said. "Even then, you'll have a hard time convincing her. I'll tell ye, son, it didn't look good."

He supposed it didn't—not with he and Dina both naked, and his cock at full mast.

"Maybe ye should let me talk to her," his mother said.

"So ye believe me, mam?" He needed someone to believe him.

"You're like your da," she said, brushing his hair off his forehead. "Once ye find the woman ye want, ye quit looking." She turned as Alex came through the front door with a gush of cold air. "My sisters were no so lucky. I hope Connor and Alex don't follow their fathers' shameful examples."

"What's that you're saying?" Alex said, as he crossed the room. Then he leaned over Ian, grinning. "So, are ye finally awake? Next time we go 'a fighting, I want your brother with us."

"How long have I been lying here?" Ian bit back the nausea and sat up, despite his mother's protests.

Alex shrugged. "An hour?"

"I want Dina gone from this house," Ian said, as he stumbled to his feet.

God's blood, his head hurt, but he had to talk to Sìleas. He held onto the walls as he went up the stairs. When he reached her bedchamber door, he tapped softly.

"Sìl." He tapped again. "Sìleas. Let me explain. Please."

Nothing.

He went back three times.

When she still refused to answer the fourth time, he said, "I'm coming in."

He tried the door, but she'd pushed something against it. He rammed his shoulder against it, opening it a crack, but jarring his aching head something fierce. Hoping she didn't have a skillet, he poked his head through the opening.

The stillness of the room sent a prickle of unease up the back of his neck. He could see now that it was the chest she'd pushed against the door. After giving the door another shove, he stepped inside.

As he stood in the middle of the empty room, his gaze moved slowly from the clothes strewn across the bed to the yellow gown that she had been wearing, which lay in a heap on the floor. The pounding of his heart was loud in his ears against the silence of the room.

He turned to look for her cloak on the peg by the door, though he already knew it would be gone.

It was.

A blinding fury took hold of him as he guessed where she had gone—to the man waiting first in line to take her from him. After taking the stairs three at a time, he left the house without a word to the others.

By God, he was going to beat Gòrdan MacDonald to within an inch of his life. And then he was going to drag his wife back home—by her hair and screaming all the way, if he must.

CHAPTER 21

Sileas stumbled several times on the rocky path in the dark, but she kept running, as if putting distance between her and what she saw in the kitchen could dull the sharpness of the pain in her chest. But no matter how fast she ran, the vision of Ian and Dina was always before her.

The two of them. Together. Naked.

Seeing her crystal hanging between Dina's breasts was an even harder betrayal. She had denied Ian her bed. In time, she might have been able to forgive him for giving his body to yet another woman before they were sharing a marriage bed.

But the crystal was her wedding gift to him. It symbolized the gift of her heart, and Ian knew it.

The leather pouch tied to her waist slapped against her thigh as she ran along the dark path. She hoped she had stuffed enough coins in it to pay a fisherman to take her across the strait and buy a horse on the other side. Praise God she'd kept Niall's old clothes for cleaning out the byre. If anyone asked, the fisherman would say he'd taken a lad across.

What was that?

Over her breathing, she heard something behind her. A wolf? A bear? She remembered Ian telling her never to run from a wild animal because it made you look like prey. Damn him! Would she never be free of Ian's voice in her head?

She ignored it and ran faster.

The sound came closer the faster she ran. She screamed as the beast slammed into her, sending her sprawling to the ground. Its great weight landed on top of her, knocking the breath out of her and pinning her to the ground.

"Sìleas, stop kicking me! I'm trying to get off ye."

"Niall?"

The great weight rolled off her, and she sat up, gasping great lungfuls of air. Her limbs felt weak and boneless in the aftermath of fright.

"Ye scared the life out of me!"

"Did I hurt ye?" Niall asked.

"No, but why did ye come after me? Ye saw what I saw in the kitchen, so ye know I won't go back."

"I couldn't let ye go off alone, with no one to protect ye," Niall said. "I'm coming with ye, wherever you're going."

She wanted to weep at his kindness but refused to let herself. Once she gave in to tears, she feared there would be no end to them.

"I can't let ye come with me," she said. "Your family would not be happy with ye for helping me get away."

"Da is the one who sent me," Niall said. "He heard ye climb out the window and told me to follow ye and keep ye safe. He gave me money, too."

Dear Payton. This time, she did wipe a tear from her eye.

"Besides," Niall said with a smile in his voice, "I didn't want ye going to Gòrdan for help."

"There's nothing wrong with Gòrdan," she said, and wondered why she hadn't even thought of going to him.

"There's not enough right with him, either—not for you, Sìl." Niall stood and helped her to her feet. "So, just where are we going?"

"To Stirling."

Niall gave a long whistle. "That's a fair distance. What do ye want to go there for?"

Sìleas started walking. "I'm going to ask the queen to help me obtain an annulment from the church. And while I'm there, I'll also ask her help in removing my step-da from Knock Castle."

She didn't want to live in Knock Castle, but it was hers and she needed someplace to live.

"Asking the queen is a wee bit drastic, wouldn't ye say?" Niall asked. "You've got cause to leave Ian under Highland law. That should be enough."

"And before I know it, my chieftain will be telling me who I am to wed next," she said. "I won't let Hugh decide my fate, that is for certain. No, the only way to free myself is to put myself in the hands of someone more powerful. I praise God that happens to be a woman at the moment."

"But ye won't have to worry about Hugh for long," Niall said. "Connor is going to be chieftain."

"Connor wants Knock Castle in the hands of someone verra close to him," she said. "He'll decide I've no cause to leave Ian."

"Connor is a fair man," Niall said. "He'd let ye leave Ian so long as ye take another man in the clan—especially if the man is another close relative of his."

She snorted. "Are ye suggesting Alex? I'm verra fond

of him, but wedding Alex would be going from the frying pan into the fire."

"Take me," Niall said in a soft voice. "I'm as close a blood relation to Connor as either Ian or Alex."

Sìleas felt as if her chest were caving in on itself. She stopped and turned to look into his face, though she could barely make out his features in the dark.

"Aw, Niall," she said, reaching up to touch her fingers to his cheek, "ye can't mean it."

"What, do ye think I'm too young?" he said, sounding hurt. "Or is it that I'm not as good as my brother—even after what he's done to ye?"

"No, it's not that," she said, though he was far too young. She rested her hand on his arm. "I grew up wishing every day I had brothers and sisters. Having you become a brother to me has been one of the great blessings of my life. Don't ask me to give that up."

"You've been a sister to me as well," Niall said, and she could hear him fidgeting in the dark. "But . . . well, ye are so pretty that I believe I could overcome it."

"I do appreciate the offer," Sìleas said, taking his arm to hurry him down the path. "But I don't believe I'll want another husband for a verra, verra long time."

"Where is she?" Ian shouted, as he pounded on Gòrdan's door.

No candlelight shone in the window or under the door. If Gòrdan had taken Sìleas to his bed this very night, Ian would murder the devil's spawn on the spot.

He pounded the door again until the windows rattled. "Come out and face me like a man!"

When the door swung open, Ian clenched his fists,

ready to pound Gòrdan's pretty face to a pulp. He choked back his fury when Gòrdan's mother peered up at him from under her nightcap.

"I've come for my wife."

"Sìleas?" Gòrdan's mother clutched her nightshift about her throat. "Don't tell me the lass has left ye. I always knew she was trouble."

It occurred to him that Sìleas and Gòrdan would know this was the first place he'd look for them. If they weren't here, then he would track them down—to hell, if need be.

"I must ask ye to step aside, so I can have a look about," Ian said.

Gòrdan suddenly appeared behind his mother.

"What in God's name do ye think ye are doing," Gòrdan said, as he pushed his mother aside, "showing up at my door in the dark of night and threatening my mother?"

Ian slammed his fist into Gòrdan's face, dropping him backward into the house. As he stepped inside, he picked Gòrdan up by the front of his shirt.

"I'll ask ye but once," Ian said an inch from Gòrdan's nose. "Where have ye got my wife?"

"Sìleas? Is that what this is about?" Gòrdan said, wiping blood from his mouth with the back of his hand. "Has she finally left ye, then? Good for her."

"Don't try telling me ye didn't know it," Ian said, as he scanned the room. She was not in sight, so he released Gòrdan and crossed the room. "Where is she?" He stuck his head into the empty kitchen.

"No one's here but the two of us," Gòrdan's mother said.

Ian heard her fumbling with the lamp. When the flame took hold, Ian caught the look of worry on Gòrdan's face.

"She left in the night alone?" Gòrdan said. "What have ye done to her, man?"

A blade of fear cut into Ian's belly. "Are ye telling me the truth, that ye don't know where she is?"

"I swear it on my father's grave," Gòrdan said.

Ian swallowed. "I must find her before any harm comes to her." At the door, he turned and said, "Will ye tell me if she comes here?"

"I will," Gòrdan said. "But if Sìleas has chosen to leave ye, I won't send her back."

"Where could she have gone?" Ian ran his hands through his hair as he paced up and down the hall. He was always clearheaded in a crisis, but he couldn't think at all.

"Let's go up to her bedchamber and see if she left something that will tell us," Alex said.

Ian ran up the stairs with Alex on his heels.

When he reached the bedchamber, he picked up her gown from the floor. Before he could stop himself, he held it to his face and breathed in her scent. He closed his eyes. Missing her was a physical pain, like a razor's edge slicing into his heart.

How could she leave him?

"Take a look at this," Alex said behind him.

Ian joined Alex at the small table where Sìleas kept the accounts. Alex had ruined her neat stacks, tossing the parchments haphazardly across the tabletop.

"Read this one," Alex said, tapping his finger on a sheet that rested on top of the scattered parchments.

Ian's heart sank as he read it. God in Heaven, what was Sìleas thinking? It was a letter to the queen, begging for her support in obtaining an annulment from one Ian

MacDonald. She also asked for the crown's assistance in removing her stepfather from her castle and lands.

"It looks as though this was her first attempt," Alex said, pointing to where the ink was smudged. "I didn't find her final version."

"She must have taken it with her." The realization of where she had gone struck Ian with the force of a blow to the chest. "God help me, she's headed for Stirling."

Ian heard light steps on the stairs and turned to see his mother in the doorway. She remained there, worrying her hands. When she finally spoke, her voice was barely above a whisper.

"Niall is gone as well."

It took Ian a long moment to take in the meaning of his mother's words. "Niall? Niall is with Sìleas?"

"Your da says it's good that she's not alone," his mother said.

"God's blood!" Ian stormed up and down the bedchamber, feeling like a trapped animal. "What can the two of them be thinking? Stirling is not a jaunt down the road—it's a journey of several days. Christ above, they could be murdered along the way!"

Visions filled his head of Sìleas raped, the pair of them mercilessly beaten, and their mutilated bodies left beside the road for wild animals to feed upon.

"Niall is good with a sword," Alex said, guessing the direction of Ian's thoughts. "I'm sure your father taught him, same as he did you, to watch for trouble and travel unseen."

His mother's gaze rested on the yellow gown that was somehow still clenched in Ian's hand, then shifted to the bed. "Niall's old clothes that she wears to muck out the barn are gone. I washed them and left them folded on the bed for her."

"With Sìleas dressed like a lad, the risk is no so great," Alex said.

"Even if they do manage to reach Stirling in one piece," Ian said, raising his hands, "the town itself is a hive of hornets."

The untimely death of James IV at Flodden had left Scotland with a babe as king and his mother, the sister of the hated English king, as regent. Ian didn't need the Sight to know that powerful and ruthless men would be at court vying for control of the babe and his mother.

"I'm going after them," Ian said, starting toward the stairs. "And when I find them, I'm going to murder them myself."

Alex caught up with him in the hall. "It won't take us long to collect Connor and Duncan," he said.

Ian shook his head. "No. I don't know how long this will take, and the gathering for Samhain is only a fortnight away. The three of ye must stay here and make certain Connor is chosen chieftain."

"We're coming with ye." Alex put on his cap and lifted his mantle from one of the pegs by the door. "There's time to make it to Stirling and back, if we're quick."

Ian met his cousin's sea-green eyes, which were solemn for once.

"Connor and Duncan will say the same." Alex said.

Ian nodded his thanks and went out the door.

CHAPTER 22

Sìleas held onto Niall's arm as they walked their horses through the crowded, cobbled streets of Stirling. Despite being exhausted and filthy after days of travel, she stared about her. She'd never been in a town of this size before.

"Can ye let go of my arm?" Niall said in a low voice. "I don't like the way people are looking at us, with ye dressed like a lad and all."

Sìleas snatched her hand away. In her amazement, she had forgotten her disguise.

"It looks like a palace built for the gods," she said, looking up at Stirling Castle.

They had seen it for miles before they reached the town, perched on top of the towering rock cliffs that protected it on three sides. The side of the castle that faced the town was the only way it could be approached, and this was protected by a curtain wall and massive gatehouse.

"What if the queen isn't here?" Niall asked. "The royal family has more than one castle, ye know."

"Your da says that if the queen has any sense at all, this is where she's brought the baby king," Sìleas said. "He says not even the English can take Stirling Castle."

They retraced their steps to a tavern at the edge of town that had guest rooms upstairs and a stable behind for their horses. After paying for the night, they took their supper in the tavern.

Sìleas had never been among so many strangers in her life. Most of the men spoke in Scots, the English spoken by Lowlanders. Although she knew some Scots, they spoke it far too quickly for her to understand much. Most wore the English style of clothes.

"Will ye stop staring at their codpieces," Niall hissed and pushed her cap lower over her eyes. "You're going to get us hurt—or an unpleasant invitation."

Sìleas stifled a laugh behind her hand. She had heard that English noblemen wore a padded cloth over their private parts, but she had not truly believed it.

"I'll need a bath before visiting the queen." She looked down at her own clothes and sniffed. "I smell of horse, and that's the best part."

"I'll ask the tavern keeper to send up water," Niall said, getting to his feet. "It'll cost extra."

Sometime later, she saw a woman carrying two sloshing buckets up the stairs—the closest to a washing those stairs had gotten in a long, long while.

She and Niall followed the woman up to a small, serviceable room with a single cot. After warning Sìleas to bar the door, Niall returned to the tavern to wait while she had her bath.

Sìleas shook out the blue gown she'd stuffed in her cloth bag, pleased that in the chaos of her flight she had thought to bring her best gown for court. After spreading it out on the cot to air, she scrubbed herself clean as best she could in the small wooden tub and put on the chemise she would wear under the gown tomorrow.

When Niall returned, he insisted she take the cot. She lay with her back to him while he took his turn washing in the same water. When he was finished, he wrapped himself in his plaid on the floor in front of the door.

She blew out the candle and tried to make herself comfortable in the strange bed.

"Thanks for coming with me, Niall," she said into the darkness. "I don't believe I could have gotten here without ye."

"To tell ye the truth, I'm not sure we should have come at all," Niall said. "The town is filled with Lowlanders and worse—there are English here, starting with the queen herself. We've no notion what we're getting into. Perhaps we'd best go home and solve your problems there."

"After coming all this way, I'm going to see the queen," Sìleas said, but she closed her eyes and prayed hard for guidance. Was Niall right? Was coming here a mistake? She had never been this far from Skye. And she felt guilty for bringing Niall with her.

Niall was silent so long that she thought he had fallen asleep, when he said, "I've been thinking a lot about what we saw in the kitchen."

"And what about that did ye find worth considering?" she asked, her voice coming out sharp.

"Well, what if Ian was just taking a bath, and Dina came in, unexpected?" Niall said, hesitation in his voice. "Ye saw the tub, and Ian dripping water."

"Ye failed to mention that Dina was naked as well,"

Sìleas said between her teeth. "And don't try to tell me ye didn't notice."

"I could hardly help that, now could I? And at first I believed the same as you about what they were up to in the kitchen." From the discomfort in Niall's voice, she could tell he'd rather be rubbed with stinging nettles than discussing this with her. "But ye see, Dina is the sort of woman to drop her clothes without a man even asking."

Sìleas sat up in the bed and glared down at the dark shape on the floor. "And how would ye know this, Niall MacDonald?"

"Well...Dina did it for me," he said.

Sìleas's mouth fell open. How dare Dina work her wiles on Niall? He was a boy still—despite being over six feet tall.

And Dina's tendency to shed her clothes did not explain how the MacDonald Crystal ended up around her neck.

"Are ye expecting me to believe nothing happened in that kitchen?" she snapped. "Is that what happened when Dina took her clothes off for you, Niall? Nothing?"

Niall's silence confirmed his guilt.

"Your mother would be ashamed of ye." Sìleas lay back down and punched her pillow a few times to fluff it.

"I am not a married man," Niall said. "And what I do with a willing woman is no concern of my mother's."

"Hmmph. I'm disgusted with the lot of ye," she said, turning her back on him and pulling the blanket up to her ears.

The noise from the tavern below was all that interrupted the long silence between them, until, finally, Niall spoke again.

"If I had a wife like you, Sìl, I wouldn't have taken what

Dina offered." Niall paused. "That's why I keep thinking that maybe Ian didn't do anything he shouldn't have. Maybe ye ought to give him a chance to tell ye what happened."

Sìleas tossed and turned on the narrow cot half the night, slapping at the bugs in the straw mattress and thinking of what Niall had said. She had such an abiding weakness for Ian MacDonald that she could almost believe anything that would absolve him.

When she felt her resolve begin to fade, she made herself remember seeing Ian in all his naked glory, his cock standing at the ready, and Dina right behind him without a stitch on—except for the pouch with Sìleas's crystal hanging between her breasts.

Every time she managed to set aside her thoughts about Ian and Dina, she tossed and turned, worrying about meeting the queen. Was she on a fool's errand, bringing her problem to the queen? Ach, but she was tired of men deciding what to do with her. A woman was bound to be more concerned with her than with her castle.

Even if the queen chose not to help her, what harm could there be in asking?

When Sìleas got tired of slapping at the bugs and chasing her thoughts in endless circles, she got up and lay on the hard floor a little ways from Niall. She was grateful to him for staying with her and respecting her decision, even if what she did seemed foolish to him.

By annulling her marriage to Ian, she would also sever her formal tie with Niall. That was one more loss, and a hard one. She lay listening to him breathing, knowing Niall would always be the brother of her heart. She hoped he felt the same and that she would not lose him as well.

CHAPTER 23

Sìleas paced the tiny room above the tavern, regretting with every turn that she had let Niall talk her into waiting here while he delivered her letter to the castle. At the sound of a knock, she picked up her dirk from the bed and put her ear to the door.

"Sìleas, let me in."

It was Niall, so she slid the bolt back. "I was worried half to death. What took ye so long?"

"Don't ye look fine, now," Niall said, taking in her gown.

"Tell me what happened," she said. "Will the queen see me?"

"The guards laughed at me when I told them I would wait for the queen's answer," Niall said, as he dropped onto the cot. "But an hour later, they gave me the message that the queen will see us this morning."

Sìleas's stomach suddenly felt as if she had eaten a pound of lead instead of watery porridge for breakfast. She was actually going to see the queen.

"I've no mirror," she said. "Can ye help me with my hair?"

Niall's eyes went wide, but he dutifully took the pins from her hand. After she twisted her wild waves into a coil at the back of her head, he stood behind her and attempted to pin it in place. Niall could shoot a straight arrow, but he turned out to be all thumbs when it came to hair.

"I'll just tie it back with my ribbon," she said when it kept falling loose after three attempts. After she finished, she turned in a circle. "Do ye think this will do for court?"

"You're sure to be the loveliest lass there," Niall said, giving her a wide smile.

As they walked up the steep hill through the town to the castle, unease crept up Sìleas's spine and slowed her steps. No wonder Payton said the baby king would be safe in Stirling Castle. The gatehouse, which projected out from the curtain wall to form the castle's fortified entrance, was enormous. Sìleas's gaze traveled from the gatehouse's four round towers to the equally massive square towers at the corners of the wall that faced the town.

"We can go home," Niall said. "It's not too late to change your mind."

"We've come this far," she said. "It would be discourteous to refuse the queen's invitation—especially after I asked for it."

They crossed the drawbridge and showed their summons to the men standing guard at the entrance between the first two round towers. After checking the seal on the letter, the guards waved them through.

Sìleas felt as if she couldn't breathe inside the gatehouse with tons of stone above and on either side of her. As they passed through it, she saw that there was yet another set of massive round towers facing the interior of the castle. The pressure on her chest eased as they emerged into the light on the other side.

"This is where I waited yesterday," Niall said. "It's called the Outer Close."

In front of them was a building made of shining pink stone that was so beautiful it took Sìleas's breath away. The building was immense, yet graceful, with high windows and slender towers that appeared to be decorative rather than defensive. Carved figures of lions with crowns and a horned mythical creature she didn't know were perched at intervals along the center line of its peaked roof.

A guard who had followed them pointed to an arched gate next to the building. "Go through there."

Sìleas and Niall passed under the arch and entered the castle's inner courtyard. The building with the decorative towers was to their right. A second large building made of the same shining stone stood opposite. Bordering the far side of the courtyard was a smaller building with stained-glass windows that must be a chapel. Servants, soldiers, and well-dressed courtiers hurried across the courtyard looking as though they knew where they were going.

"Which building do ye suppose the queen is in?" she whispered to Niall.

He shrugged and nodded toward the building with the decorative towers. "This one's the biggest."

When they approached the guards, the men looked Sìleas up and down as if she might be hiding a dirk beneath her skirts—which of course she was. Still, she was relieved to see that they were Highlanders.

"We're looking for the queen," Niall said.

"This is the Great Hall, which is only used for grand

occasions." The guard who spoke was a man of about forty, with muscular legs the size of tree trunks and laughter in his eyes. "But since the lass has such a lovely smile, I'll let the two of ye have a wee peek."

After glancing left and right, he opened the door and motioned them inside.

Sìleas found herself in a room that was perhaps three stories high, with five fireplaces, and a roof with heavy wooden beams that crossed to form angled arches.

"The babe James V was crowned in here not long ago," the guard said. "'Tis the largest hall in all of Scotland— even larger than the one in Edinburgh Castle."

The guard spoke with as much pride as if he'd built the hall himself.

"'Tis a grand sight, and I thank ye kindly for letting us see it," Sìleas said. "But the queen is expecting us. Can ye tell us where we may find her?"

The guard opened the door and pointed across the courtyard. "She's keeping court across the way, in what is called the King's House."

When Sìleas started to follow Niall out, the guard stopped her with a touch on her arm.

"Let me give ye a wee bit of advice, lass," he said, leaning close enough for her to smell the onions on his breath. "Don't go in there with just the lad. Wait and come back with your father and a few other men of your clan."

"He's my brother, and he'll look out for me," she said, managing a smile.

The King's House was an impressive building, though it lacked the soaring elegance of the Great Hall. Well-dressed men and women moved along its covered wooden galleries, which served as outside corridors to the upper floors.

"We must keep our wits about us," Niall said in her ear, as they crossed the courtyard. "If the queen is at all like her godforsaken brother, she'll be crafty and willful."

"That describes most of the men I know," Sìleas said, "so I should be well prepared."

"Watch out for the Earl of Angus, Archibald Douglas, as well."

"The Douglas chieftain?" she asked. "Of what concern is he to us?"

"Last night while ye were washing up, I heard that the queen relies on him for advice." Niall leaned closer. "In fact, they say she has taken the Douglas to her bed."

Sìleas turned to stare at him. "But the king is hardly cold in his grave."

"Aye, and she carries the dead king's child," Niall said in a low voice. "All the same, they say the queen is quite taken with the Douglas—and that the Douglas is quite taken with the notion of ruling Scotland."

They had reached the entrance to the King's House, where they were met by another set of guards, who directed them to wait inside the hall until they were called.

Sìleas was immediately glad she wore an English-style gown, which was high-waisted and closer fitting than her everyday gowns, since all the women wore them. Hers, however, was simpler and far more modest than the ones the other women were wearing. Although there was a sprinkling of Highlanders dressed in saffron linen shirts and plaids, most of the men in the hall also wore English clothes.

Sìleas crossed the room, drawn by the spectacular view through the windows on the opposite side of the hall. When she reached the windows and looked down, it appeared that the King's House had been built on the very edge of the sheer cliffs.

"Ye can see for miles from here. Ach, that looks like Ben Lomond," Niall said, pointing.

"I believe it is." They both turned at the sound of a light, feminine voice behind them.

If the woman hadn't spoken to them in English, Sìleas would have thought she was looking at a faerie queen. She had hair the color of moonbeams and sparkles in her headdress, which framed a face with lovely, delicate features. A rose-colored gown with a silvery sheen floated about her—except for the tight-fitting bodice, which had a square neck that revealed the tops of small, perfect breasts.

Faerie or no, Niall was staring with his jaw hanging open, as if enchanted.

"You are new to Court, or I would know you," the woman said with a bright smile at Niall.

Either Niall was too enthralled to speak or his English was failing him. Sìleas's English was poorer than his, but she managed to say, "We have just arrived."

"Ah, you are Highlanders." The woman let her eyes drift over Niall again. "In truth, I knew by your size—and that wild handsomeness—that you were a Highlander."

Niall swelled like a toad at the blatant flattery.

"Welcome to Stirling," the woman said. "My name is Lady Philippa Boynton."

Philippa. The name was like a knife in Sìleas's heart. Philippa was the name of the young woman Ian had told her about that fateful night they slept in the woods.

"Have ye been in Stirling long yourself?" Sìleas asked, wondering if she could truly be having the bad luck to be meeting the woman Ian had wished to marry.

"Not long this time," the woman said, turning her sparkling eyes on Sìleas. "These days, I spend more time in London, but I have been to Stirling many times."

"Were ye here at the castle five years ago?" Sìleas asked in a tight voice.

The woman gave a laugh that made Sìleas think of tiny bells. "Why yes, I believe I was. I stayed here for several months about that time. How did you guess?"

Ach, it was her—the woman Ian had wished to marry.

The memory of that night came back sharply—the rough ground beneath her, the chill in the air, the night sky above her. But most of all, she remembered the wistfulness in Ian's voice as he spoke about a lady with a tinkling laugh and the grace of a faerie—and a beauty so enchanting that a young man who was not ready to marry would decide he was.

Ian had failed to mention that Philippa was English. If he had been willing to tell his father and chieftain he wished to wed an English lady, then Ian must have wanted her very badly indeed.

The faerie woman was looking at Sìleas as if she were waiting for a response. Sìleas had no recollection of the question, so she shook her head and let Lady Philippa believe she had not understood her English.

Sìleas was relieved when a young man in English livery interrupted them.

"Her Highness the Queen will see you now," he said, giving Sìleas a slight bow. "I'll escort you to her private parlor."

Sìleas nodded to Lady Philippa and took Niall's arm. As they followed the servant across the room, Niall stared at Lady Philippa over his shoulder.

The servant took them through an arched doorway, then stopped at the base of a circular stairs. "Only the lady is invited."

"She goes nowhere without me," Niall said.

"The audience will be in the queen's private apartments," the man said. "The queen and her ladies' privacy must be respected."

Sìleas tugged Niall to the side. "It will be all women in the queen's apartments, so there's nothing for ye to fret about."

Niall didn't look as though he liked it, but he didn't argue when she gave him a bright smile and picked up her skirts to follow the servant up the stairs.

A short time later, Sìleas found herself in the queen's bedchamber. Several ladies lounged on couches or on silk and brocade pillows on the floor, while the queen herself sat in a high-backed chair with her surprisingly tiny feet propped up on a stool and a ratlike dog in her lap. She was a buxom woman with beady eyes that matched her dog's and heavy, glittering rings on every plump finger.

Standing next to her, with a hand resting on the back of her chair, was a darkly handsome man of about Ian's age, with a well-groomed beard and hard eyes. Judging from his fine clothes and the way he held himself, Sìleas guessed this was the Earl of Angus, Archibald Douglas. She'd heard that his father had died at Flodden, making him the head of his clan—the Douglas, himself.

Sìleas's mouth was dry as she stepped forward and made her curtsy, hoping she was doing it correctly.

"You are Sìleas MacDonald from the Isle of Skye?" the queen asked.

Sìleas had not foreseen that the queen would have no Gaelic. Her husband, though a Lowlander, had won favor with Highlanders by learning to speak Gaelic. He had been a great lover of Highland music as well.

"She may have no English," the man Sìleas assumed was Archibald Douglas said.

"I do speak a little English," Sìleas said.

The queen gave an impatient sigh and rolled her eyes heavenward.

Sìleas took a deep breath to calm herself, then said. "Your Highness, I've come a long way to ask for your help in obtaining an annulment from the church."

While the queen scrunched her face up as if Sìleas were something her dog left behind, the Douglas looked her up and down as if she was standing in her chemise. What a rude pair these two were. As they say, *Put silk on a goat and it is still a goat.*

"So, you've found another man you wish to wed?" The queen turned to her ladies and added, "'Tis the usual reason."

Sìleas felt herself color. "No, Your Highness, I have not."

"So there's no urgency?" the queen asked, raising her plucked eyebrows. "You're not carrying another man's child?"

Sìleas's face felt burning hot. She shook her head violently this time.

The Douglas asked her in Gaelic, "So, you are a virgin?"

"That is an overly familiar question, sir," she answered in Gaelic, meeting his gaze.

The Douglas turned to the queen and graced her with a dazzling smile. "I know it's tedious for you to speak with someone who has such difficulty with English."

The man made Sìleas angry enough to spit. Her English was not as bad as that.

"It doesn't help that the lass is flustered speaking to

royalty for the first time." The Douglas spoke to the queen in a voice as smooth and slippery as melting lard. "Shall I take care of this problem for you?"

The queen flashed a sharp look at Sìleas, but she shifted her gaze away when the Douglas whispered something in her ear that made her neck flush. A moment later, he walked to the door that led outside to the gallery and flicked his hand at Sìleas, signaling for her to follow him.

Apprehension prickled at her skin as she followed him, but she didn't want to remain with the queen, either. Once they were on the gallery—and out of the queen's view—he held her arm against his body in a firm grip that increased her unease. She reminded herself that she was in a palace surrounded by soldiers and guards. Surely she had nothing to fear.

After passing three doors, he opened the fourth, which led into a small parlor. She was relieved to see two servants, who leapt to their feet and bowed as they entered. Sìleas glanced through the open door to her right—and her heart beat faster when she glimpsed an imposing bed with a dark wood frame and heavy crimson curtains.

"Go now," the Douglas said.

The servants disappeared though a second door. As it closed behind them, Sìleas felt for the dirk strapped to her thigh—and cursed herself for not finding a hiding place closer to hand. She'd tried, but there was no good place to stick a dirk in this gown—and certainly not in her dainty slippers.

The Douglas poured a cup of wine from an ornate silver pitcher on the side table and took a drink. She chided herself for letting her imagination get away with her. Nothing could be more normal than a man taking a drink.

"I have some business to discuss with ye, lass," he said, and handed her the cup. "Your letter to the queen said ye are heir to Knock Castle."

She decided to hold her tongue until she knew where this was leading.

"I knew about ye being the heir, of course, but I'd heard ye wed a MacDonald and thought the matter settled." Her surprise must have shown on her face, for he added, " 'Tis my business to know such things."

She didn't like this man knowing so much about her. Since he'd drunk the wine, it couldn't be poisoned, so she took a gulp. It did nothing to cure her dry throat.

"The queen will soon name me Protector of the Western Isles—which includes Skye, of course." He leaned closer and said in a soft voice. "That means, lass, that I am a good man to know. And the better ye know me, the better off you'll be."

Her heart was racing. Despite her inexperience, she had a fair notion of what he was suggesting.

He pried the cup from her hand and set it on the table. "I'm sure you've had a hard time of it, with both the Mac-Donalds and the MacKinnons trying to get their hands on you and your castle," he said. "Likely, the Macleods will have a try as well."

When he took a step closer, she took a step back.

"I am a powerful man," he said, resting a hand on her arm. "I can protect ye from the MacDonalds, the Mac-Kinnons, and all the others."

She backed up until her heels hit the wall. He was so close to her now that she could taste the wine on his breath and smell the musky odor of his skin beneath the scent he wore.

"You're a verra lovely lass." He ran a finger along her cheek. "And brave to come all this way, telling no one but that young lad who's waiting for ye in the hall."

If his intent was to make her realize just how alone she was—and how far from the protection of her clansmen— he had succeeded.

She swallowed back her fear and tried to keep her head. "I don't suppose the queen would be pleased to see ye touching me."

"No, I don't suppose she would," he said, his teeth gleaming white. "That's why I'll make sure she doesn't know about us. Nothing could be easier."

She ran her tongue over her dry lips. "'Tis time I was leaving."

"Come, lass, I deserve a reward for having to bed that Tudor cow." He cupped her face and dragged his thumb across her bottom lip. "And don't fret. If ye have a child, I promise I'll claim it."

Her mouth dropped open at this blunt statement of his intentions.

"Ye are a conniving bastard," she hissed in his face. "Ye just want Knock Castle for yourself, same as the rest of them."

"I can assure ye, lass," he said, taking hold of her shoulders and pressing her against the wall, "Knock Castle is not all I want from ye."

If she could have reached her dirk, she would have gutted him. As it was, she struggled against him, but he held her fast.

"Ye are a beauty," he said in a husky voice, as his mouth inched closer to hers. "And I find I'm partial to pretty virgins."

CHAPTER 24

Ian's every nerve and muscle was taut with tension as they rode into Stirling. He had expected to find Sìleas and Niall on the road, but the pair had moved fast, damn them. After days of hard travel and worry, he felt like a hide that had been stretched and beaten on a frame.

"We'll check all the taverns and inns," Connor said. "They'll be staying in one of them."

If they had made it to Stirling. Ian's headed pounded every time he thought of the dangers. "I'm going to the castle to look for them," he said.

"If they haven't gone there yet, we can still keep this quiet," Connor said.

Fear pulsed through him. "I don't care if I'm a laughingstock all across Scotland. I must find her quickly, before she comes to harm."

If harm had not already found her.

"They can't have arrived in Stirling more than half a day ahead of us," Alex said. "Sìleas cannot walk into the palace and receive an audience with the queen. More than likely, they'll make her wait a day or two—if they let her see the queen at all."

Ian agreed, reluctantly, to look first in the town. After stabling their horses at the first tavern they found, they went inside—and finally had their first bit of luck.

"Take the room upstairs on the end," the tavern keeper said, as he tucked the coins Ian gave him into the leather bag at his belt.

"Have ye seen a couple of lads, one almost as tall as me, and the other a wee thing with red hair?" Ian asked.

"Mayhap." The tavern keeper narrowed his eyes at Ian. "Why would ye be looking for them?"

Ian's heart beat faster. He wanted to grab the man and shake what he knew from him, but he was grateful for the tavern keeper's unexpected protectiveness toward the wayward pair.

"My brothers had an argument with our da and ran off," Ian said. "I've come to bring them home."

"'Tis good you've come," the man said, as he poured a cup of ale for another customer. "The big one looks like he could handle himself in a fight, but there are plenty of other dangers in Stirling, if ye know what I mean."

Ian did. Praise God he had found them.

"Which room are they in?" Ian said, starting toward the stairs.

"The younger lad might be up there, but the tall one left some time ago." He chuckled and shook his head. "Funny thing, he'd found himself a pretty lass and said they was going to visit the queen."

People on the street moved out of Ian's way as he strode toward the castle. Connor was beside him, matching him stride for stride, and the other two behind them.

"Mind your temper," Connor said, as they drew near the gatehouse. "If ye draw your blade, twenty guards will be on ye before ye can say her name."

They told the guards at the gatehouse they were looking for a clanswoman.

"She was with a big lad of fifteen, and she's so high," Ian said, holding his hand to his chin, "and has flaming red hair."

"Couldn't forget that lass, now could I?" one on the guards said. "Ach, she's a fair one."

Ian took a deep breath to keep from punching him.

"If that were my wife, ye can be sure I'd keep her home," another said.

Ian gritted his teeth while Connor and Alex talked the guards into letting them pass, then they hurried to the King's House. As soon as they got past another set of guards at the door, he saw Niall.

His brother's eyes widened as Ian and the others crossed the hall to him, but he stood his ground.

"Where is she?" Ian grabbed Niall by the front of his shirt. "Tell me now."

"A servant took her to the queen's private parlor," Niall said, and Ian saw the worry in his eyes. "He said men were not permitted to go there."

Ian knew from personal experience that was a lie. The queen's ladies sneaked men in all the time.

"I didn't like it, but it's only women in there, so Sìleas should be safe enough," Niall said, but there was a question in his voice. "But she's been gone a long while."

Ian turned to the others. "Can ye hold the guards for a wee bit?"

"Wait, I see an easier way in." Alex shifted his gaze

across the room. "I believe that is the English lass who used to have an eye for ye."

Ian followed Alex's gaze to a woman with a graceful figure and a delicate, perfectly proportioned face framed by very fair tendrils.

"Are ye speaking of Lady Philippa?" Niall asked in a wistful voice.

She was, indeed, Philippa, the woman Ian had once planned to marry. It seemed a lifetime ago.

"I'd wager Philippa can get ye into the queen's parlor in a wink, if she's a mind to it," Alex said, pushing Ian forward. "So make an effort to be charming."

Philippa turned her head and blinked several times when she saw Ian walking toward her. After whispering something to the man standing next to her, she swept across the room to meet him with a smile lighting her face.

"You are as handsome as ever, Ian MacDonald," she said, holding her gloved hand out to him. "How many other ladies' hearts have you broken since last we met?"

"I must speak with ye alone," Ian said, and took her by the elbow.

She glanced sideways at him and smiled as he led her into a darkened alcove. "Oh my, the ladies will be all atwitter—and green with envy."

Ian bit back his impatience.

"I never apologized for not coming back for ye." He owed her that—and it seemed politic to apologize before asking a favor. "I did mean to return and marry ye, but... it wasn't possible."

"Heavens, Ian, I couldn't have married you," she said, and laughed that tinkling laugh that used to enchant him. "I was one of King James's mistresses at the time."

Ian was stunned. He had thought her an innocent—and in love with him.

Philippa gave him a bittersweet smile. "I was doing as my family bid me. They sent me to court for that very purpose."

"I'm sorry your family used ye so poorly. It was wrong of them."

"Ah, Ian," she said with a sigh. "You are gallant. I always liked that in you."

"Since ye are here at court again, I assume the queen never discovered what ye were to the king," Ian said, hoping she was on good terms with the queen so she could help him. "I hear she is a vindictive woman, so ye are taking a chance being here."

"This time, it is my husband who sent me." She leaned forward to whisper next to his ear. "He says Archibald Douglas, the Earl of Angus, will soon have the power of the crown. That's why he wants me to lure the Douglas into my bed."

Ian stiffened. "Your husband asked ye to do that?"

"As if bedding the man would do us any good. Archibald Douglas is not a man to make decisions with his cock, or, alas"—she patted Ian's chest—"with his heart."

"Ach, 'tis a shame ye ended up with such a miserable husband."

She shrugged one delicate shoulder. "We are of a like mind on most things."

Ian didn't know what to say to that.

"Besides, I can take care of myself with the Douglas," she said. "Unlike the poor virgin he has in his clutches at the moment. The girl is such an innocent, she hasn't a chance against the likes of him."

A prickle ran up Ian's spine. "Tell me about this lass."

"Apparently, she is heir to a castle the Douglas wants. This morning, I heard him convincing the queen to help the girl end her marriage—and wed her to one of his Douglas cousins." She heaved a sigh. "I think I met her, and I fear that once the Douglas sees what a beauty she is, the cousin will not have her before he does."

Ian gripped her arm. "Philippa, I must get to her."

Philippa's eyes went wide, and her hand went to her chest. "Do not tell me...No, Ian, you cannot be the husband she is trying to get rid of, are you?"

"I am," he ground out. "I've come to take her home. Can ye get me inside the queen's apartments?"

She lowered her head. "I don't frighten easily, but the truth is that I am a bit afraid of Archibald Douglas."

"I promise ye," Ian said, leaning closer, "I would never tell who let me in."

"I suppose you would not, even under torture," she said, a faint smile returning to her lips. She held out her hand to him, "Come, we'd best hurry."

Philippa took him up the servants' staircase, which was hidden behind a screen. When she reached the top step, she turned to face him.

"I hope you won't blame her if..." She paused and bit her lip. "...if you find her too late."

Sweat broke out on his forehead. "Just tell me where to go from here."

"The queen has given the Douglas a set of rooms for his private use, just there." Philippa pointed to a door down the narrow back hallway.

"Be careful, Ian," she said and kissed him on the cheek. "There will be guards inside the door—and I hear that the Douglas is very good with a sword."

CHAPTER 25

Sìleas wished to God she had never left Skye.

"If it is all the same to you, Laird Douglas…" She attempted to lean farther away from him, but she had nowhere to go. "I'll withdraw my request for the queen's assistance and be on my way."

"Nonsense." The Douglas took a loose curl at the side of her face between his fingers, pulled it straight, and smiled as he let it loose and watched it spring back. "Tell me, lass, are ye as wild as your hair?"

She didn't like the way his eyes darkened when he said it.

"I'm a very proper lady." If ever there was a time to stretch the truth, it was now.

"Judging from your rash decision to travel across half of Scotland with only a boy as your escort, I'm guessing ye are a wild one."

Sìleas sucked in her breath to keep her chest from touching his as he leaned another inch closer. Sweat prickled down her back as she considered how unlikely she was to reach the dirk strapped to her thigh before he stopped her. In any case, lifting her gown seemed a foolish choice at present.

"You'll find there are a great many benefits to being my mistress," the Douglas said, easing his knee between her legs.

"I'm sure there are lasses who would appreciate the 'benefits,' but ye have nothing I want."

She didn't want to touch him, but when it appeared that he would not move away on his own, she pushed against his chest. He didn't seem to notice.

"You'll change your mind soon enough," he said, so close his breath was hot on her face. "I know how to please a woman."

Her heart pounded frantically in her chest as Douglas leaned toward her. She squeezed her eyes shut and prayed the same prayer she prayed when she was little.

Please God, send Ian.

"'Tis been a long time since I've had a virgin," he said in low, rough voice. "I'm looking forward to teaching ye all I know."

She flinched as the prickle of the Douglas's mustache grazed her upper lip.

"That is my wife you've got your hands on, Douglas."

By some miracle, Ian's voice filled the room. Hope took hold of her. Very slowly, she opened her eyes, afraid she had imagined it.

Her breath caught when she looked over Douglas's shoulder and saw the answer to her prayer filling the doorway. With his claymore drawn and murder in his eyes, Ian looked magnificent—and more dangerous than she had ever seen him.

"If ye will step away from her now," Ian said, "I'll assume ye did not know she is my wife—and let ye live."

Archibald Douglas arched his eyebrows at her. For a moment, Sìleas wondered if Ian knew he was threatening the Earl of Angus, one of the most powerful men in Scotland—and the queen's "special" friend besides. But of course he knew.

The Douglas spun around, taking her with him. He held her against him with one arm and the hilt of his sword in the other.

"Is this the husband ye want to be rid of?" Douglas said, an amused smile twitching at his lips. "The one ye say has left ye a virgin?"

"Make no mistake, that lass is my wife." Ian's voice was seething with such menace that the hairs on the back of Sìleas's neck stood up. "And she will remain so as long as there is breath in my body."

As long as there was breath in his body. Despite her precarious position, Ian's words sent a thrill through her.

"So you are Ian MacDonald of the Sleat MacDonalds," the Douglas said, narrowing his eyes. "Tell me, are ye as good a fighter as they say?"

"Better," Ian said. "Now, I asked ye verra nicely to step away from my wife. I'll no be so polite the next time."

It startled her when Archibald Douglas threw his head back and laughed.

"I appreciate a man who is fearless to the point of foolishness," the Douglas said. "I'll need men like you fighting with me when I come to the Isles to put down this latest rebellion."

"Ye won't live to fight another day if ye don't release my wife," Ian said. "My patience is gone."

"I'll call on ye when the time comes." The Douglas shoved her forward. "Take your bride, Ian MacDonald of Skye."

Ian took her wrist in a firm grasp and pulled her behind him.

"But for God's sake," the Douglas said, "don't leave her a virgin another night."

CHAPTER 26

Ian dragged Sìleas across the hall in front of the sniggering courtiers. He was practically wrenching her arm out of its socket, but she didn't care. She wanted to weep with relief that he was here, that he'd come for her, even if it was pride that made him do it.

Without breaking his pace, Ian signaled to someone. Sìleas barely had time to glance over her shoulder, but it was easy to spot the four tall men in Highland dress surrounded by a bevy of court ladies.

A surge of guilt went through her as she realized that Connor, Duncan, and Alex had come all the way to Stirling because of her, when they were needed at home. Although the three of them clearly saw her and Ian, they made no move to follow. Niall alone ran after them.

"Praise God, ye are all right—" Niall stopped in his tracks when Ian spun around.

Ian was in a fury as she'd never seen him.

"It was a close thing." Ian spoke between clenched

teeth, and the vein in his neck was pulsing. "The Douglas had his hands on her."

Niall turned wide eyes on her. "I should have gone with ye."

"What ye should have done," Ian bit out, "is never brought her to Stirling."

Even Niall had the sense not to follow them after that. Once they were outside, Ian headed toward an arched gate next to the chapel. On the other side of the arch, he continued down a set of steep steps built into the hillside. She nearly tumbled as she followed him down to an enormous grassy expanse that was enclosed by the castle's outer curtain wall.

Without glancing back at her, Ian proceeded to stomp across the field. She held her skirts up with her free hand and half-ran to keep up until they reached the wall. She thought surely he must stop now, but he pulled her behind him up the steps built into the side of the wall.

When he finally came to a halt at the top and turned to face her, she was gasping for breath.

"What in God's name did ye think ye were doing?" he shouted. "Do ye know who the Douglas is?"

She saw no guards patrolling this part of the wall, which was built directly over the sheer cliff. Apparently, Ian had brought her all the way here so he could yell at her without being heard or interrupted.

"The man could have used ye and left ye murdered on the street," Ian shouted, as he paced back and forth along the six-foot width of the wall walk, "and no one would have said a word about it."

He halted and looked out at the horizon. "God in Heaven, Sìl, what if I wasn't able to guess where you'd gone?" He paused, clenching his jaw. "What if I hadn't come in time?"

Keeping his gaze fixed in front of him, he climbed up onto the ledge of the wall and sat with his legs hanging over the side.

She went to stand next to him and watched his profile.

"So why did ye come for me?" she asked.

He turned blue eyes on her that were so intense the air seemed to vibrate between them. "Because ye are my wife, whether ye like it or no."

Her mouth went dry. Despite herself, her voice shook when she spoke. "I see. So ye have come because of your pride."

"Is that what ye think?" he said, sounding outraged.

"Aye." She licked her lips. "And because ye need me to justify taking Knock Castle."

"I won't say my pride didn't take a beating, because it did. And I won't say that we don't need to take Knock Castle, because we do," he said in a hard voice. "But that is not why I came for ye."

She lifted her gaze from her muddy slippers to meet his angry eyes. "Then why did ye come?"

"I came because it is my responsibility to protect ye," he said. "I cannot—*I will not*—fail you, my family, or my clan again. Even if ye weren't my wife—*which ye are*—it's my duty to keep ye from harm. I took on the task of being your protector long ago, and I'll not stop now."

Sìleas understood Ian's need to make amends. Still, she hoped she was more than a duty, more than a wrong he needed to make right. She drew in a deep breath and let it out slowly.

It was hard to ask what a woman wanted a man to tell her freely.

"Do ye care for me a little?"

"Of course I care for ye, damn it," he said, waving his arm out to the side. "I always cared for ye, since ye were a wee thing, and ye know it."

Like a favorite dog. A sigh of disappointment escaped her lips.

"And I want ye." His eyes went dark, and he gave her a look that burned right through her. "I want ye so much that sometimes I can't breathe when I look at ye."

He turned away again and stared off at the distant mountains. After a while, he said, "When ye left me, Sìl... well, nothing mattered but getting ye back."

Surely this was a good sign? A cause for hope? Even if Ian never came to love her as she wanted him to, he seemed to genuinely want her to be his wife now; there was no dirk at his back. He felt affection for her, desired her.

"Saints above, ye scared me half to death running off like that," he said, his anger flashing again. "I didn't know where ye were, or if ye were safe."

"Niall took good care of me," she said, feeling calmer now.

"Niall will be a man to be reckoned with one day, but he's young," he said, shaking his head. "He doesn't understand the danger of men like Archibald Douglas."

He stared into the distance for a long time before he spoke again.

"I know ye have your complaints against me, but I need to speak plainly to you," he said. "It was wrong of ye to bring our problems here. 'Tis dangerous to draw the attention of the crown—and the Douglas. Ye can never know where it will end."

She leaned against the ledge beside him and hugged

herself against the stiff wind. "Why did ye not tell me of your plans to take Knock Castle?"

"I didn't want ye fretting over it. Besides, we just made the plan." His tone was sour, but at least he didn't try to tell her that taking her family castle was none of her concern. "Now we won't have time to take it before the chieftain is chosen at the Samhain gathering."

"I wish Connor and the others hadn't come," she said.

"Bad as it was finding ye alone with the Douglas behind a locked door, it could have been worse," Ian said. "They knew I might need them, and we've always been loyal to each other."

Sìleas watched the clouds gathering around the mountains and thought about loyalty—specifically, Ian's.

"I'm ready to hear about Dina now," she said.

"Dina? I have nothing to say about Dina," he said. "She has naught to do with us."

She let the silence stretch and waited for his anger to pass.

"I wanted to be clean for ye on our wedding night," he said, and she heard the wistfulness in his voice. "I was taking my bath, when Dina came into the kitchen with her own plans."

"What about the crystal?" she asked. "I saw it on her."

"Dina came up behind me and snatched it from my neck when I wasn't expecting it."

This admission seemed to embarrass him more than being caught naked with Dina.

He dropped down from the wall ledge to stand before her.

"I got your stone back," he said, as he reached inside his shirt and tugged at a leather cord tied around his neck.

He opened the pouch and let the crystal drop into his palm for her to see.

"I swear I did not touch her," he said and held her gaze.

She closed his hand over the stone and wrapped her hands around his fist. "I believe ye."

"If ye stay with me, I promise I'll be faithful," Ian said. "I'll do my best to make ye happy."

It wasn't a pledge of undying love, but it was enough. Ian did care for her. As her husband, he would put her needs first, as a matter of honor. He would protect her with his life, if it came to it.

"If ye still want to leave me, I'll not fight ye," Ian said. "But these are troubled times, and ye must have a man to protect ye. If you wish to choose another husband, ye must do it quickly."

It wouldn't be fair to marry another man when she would always love Ian. What had made her think she could leave him?

"I made my choice a long time ago," she said. "For me, it has always been you, Ian MacDonald."

"Good." Ian slid the crystal back in the pouch, tucked it inside his shirt, and grabbed her hand.

Once again, Sìleas had to run to keep up with his long strides. He kept a firm grasp on her hand and forged ahead through the castle and then into the town, as if wolves were nipping at his heels.

"Where are we going?" she asked.

"I don't like the Douglas," Ian said without breaking his pace, "but I mean to take his advice as soon as possible."

Sìleas swallowed, remembering the Douglas's parting words.

For God's sake, don't leave her a virgin another night.

CHAPTER 27

Sileas saw Niall sitting at one of the tables as they entered the dark, noisy tavern. He stood as soon they entered.

"Stay out of trouble," Ian said, giving Niall a pointed look as he passed him. "I'll come find ye in the morning."

It was barely noon.

Niall grabbed her free arm. "Is this what ye want, Sìl?"

Brave lad. Her heart was thundering in her chest, but she managed a nod to reassure him.

Ian strode through the tavern with barely a glance right or left and led her up the stairs. At the last door, he scooped her up in his arms and carried her over the threshold.

Apparently, Ian was taking no chances with the bad luck that lurked in doorways.

He kicked the door shut and set her on her feet. While he shoved a chest from the far wall in front of the door, she glanced at the bed that seemed to fill the room. When he turned and focused his heated gaze on her, she swallowed. His body seemed to pulse with a barely contained energy.

She was aware of his chest rising and falling, the muscles in his jaw working, the tension running through every fiber of him. When he took a step toward her, she had to fight not to take a step back. His desire was palpable and dark, fanned hotter by his anger—anger that stemmed from the sting to his pride as well as fear for her safety.

Without a word, he crushed her against his chest and his passion exploded. His mouth ravished hers, demanding all and holding back nothing.

There was nothing in him of the gentle lover who pressed feather-light kisses over her scarred back. This time, Ian was letting her see the untamed violence of his hunger for her.

She felt overwhelmed by the force of his need, the assault on her senses. It frightened her, and yet something deep inside her craved his raw emotion, unchecked and unbound. She wanted to drown in the stormy passion of deep kisses, to feel the writhing need of the insistent hands gripping her hips.

Ian tore his mouth away to give her hot, wet kisses along the side of her throat. Clutching her bottom, he lifted her against him so that she felt his erection, full and hard.

"I want ye so badly," he said against her ear. "I may die right here if I can't have ye."

For the first time, she felt her power over him—and she liked it. She splayed her hands under his shirt and bit his lip, drawing a low groan from him.

"Well, ye can have me," she said, and pulled him into another deep kiss.

He backed her up to the bed, and they fell across it. Holding her face in his hands, he kissed her as if he might never have the chance again. Then his hands were running over her body, rough with wanting. Her chest felt tight, as if she could not get enough air. Her pulse pounded in her ears.

His hand was on her breast, his thumb seeking the nipple. When he found it, he lowered his head to suck on her breast through the bodice of her gown. She gasped as intense sensations spiraled through her. The world was suspended as every part of her being focused on his mouth on her breast. It was a torture, but a sweet torture that left her breathless and light-headed.

He jerked at the skirt of her gown until his hand touched her bare thigh. But it was not enough.

"I need ye naked," he said, his voice a low rasp deep in his throat. "Now."

He rolled her to the side and began unhooking the back of her gown, while his mouth assaulted hers with scorching kisses that left her dazed and wanting. The next thing she knew, she was lifting her arms and he was pulling the gown over her head. Cool air hit her hot skin—her chemise had come off with her gown.

Before she had time to feel embarrassed, he wrapped himself around her, engulfing her in the heat of his body and his passion. The rough cloth of his shirt made her sensitive skin tingle.

Her heart beat hard with anticipation as he paused to jerk his boots off and pull his shirt over his head. When he crushed her against him again, this time it was skin to skin.

Every inch of her was alive to his touch—and his hands were everywhere, running over her body, as he kissed her hair, her face, her throat. Their nakedness increased the urgency of his already burning need. She felt it in the tension of his muscles under her hands, in the hunger of his kisses.

"Ye are mine," he said, pausing to look at her with burning eyes. "And I'm claiming every inch of ye."

His hair slid over her skin as he moved down her body, planting hot, wet kisses down her breastbone, to the undersides of her breasts, and on her stomach. All the while, his hands played with her nipples, sending sensations straight to the aching place between her legs.

As his mouth and tongue traveled over her belly and down her hip, a sliver of unease crept into the swirl of sensations that swamped her. Her unease grew by a giant leap when he lifted her knee and she felt the bristle of his whiskers and the wet warmth of his open mouth on the inside of her thigh.

Tension mounted inside her as his mouth drew closer and closer to her center. Surely, he wasn't going to kiss her there. Her breathing grew shallow as he moved up, inch by inch. She was at his mercy, and she didn't care. Wherever he was taking her, she wanted to go.

Oh God! When he kissed her there, between her legs, her body jerked—whether from shock or because she was so sensitive, she didn't know. He groaned and tightened his hold on her thighs.

He ran his tongue over her, sending surges of pleasure through her that had her gripping the bedclothes in her fists. She tried to form the words to protest, but the sounds that came from her throat only seemed to encourage him to do more.

And the more he did, the more she never wanted him to stop.

She gripped the bedclothes tighter and held on for dear life as the tension built and built inside her. When she could stand no more, she strained against his hold.

But he was relentless. She came in pounding waves that blinded her.

Before she could catch her breath, he was on top of her. His hands were fisted in her hair, his ragged breath was on her face, and his eyes were dazed, unfocused. His chest pressed down on her sensitive breasts. But what had her attention was his manhood pressing against the sensitive place his mouth had been a moment before.

Of their own volition, her hips rose to meet him. He made a guttural sound deep in his throat and surged forward—but just as she felt him start to push inside her, he halted.

His face was strained as he looked down at her, blinking as if he had stepped into the light from a dark, dark place.

He lifted himself off of her slowly, as if he were pulling himself against a rushing current, and lay beside her.

When she turned to face him, he brushed the hair back from her face. Something had changed in him. The urgency of a few moments before was banked, though she sensed it still burned hot just beneath the surface.

"I've never bedded a virgin before, so I don't know how much this will hurt ye," he said. "Are ye frightened?"

She shook her head; it was mostly true.

Her gaze dropped to his groin, and she felt her eyes go wide as she got a good look at his shaft.

"Ach, it's bigger than I expected," she said, unable to take her eyes from it. "Will it fit?"

He chuckled deep in his throat and lifted her chin with his fingers. "Like a glove. We were made for each other."

She tilted her head to the side to take another look. "I'm no so sure..."

"Where's my brave lass?" he asked, with a smile in his eyes. "Do ye want to touch me?"

When she didn't answer, he said, "Come, give me your hand."

He sucked in his breath as he ran her fingers slowly up his shaft. It was strange how it felt rock hard at the same time that the skin was silky smooth. It was wet at the top.

"See? Nothing to be afraid of," he said, his voice strained.

When she looked up at Ian's face, he looked in pain.

"Does that hurt?" she asked as she stroked up and down, more firmly this time.

"It doesn't...pain me...exactly. But I can't stand it long, not until after I've had ye the first time."

She nodded, taking this in.

"Sit up, lass," he said, pulling her up. Then he dropped to his knees on the floor and pulled her to the edge of the bed so that her knees were on either side of his hips.

When he enfolded her in his arms, she was acutely aware of his shaft pressing against her. He kissed her face and leaned down to kiss the side of her throat. Then he gave her a slow, lingering kiss, his tongue moving in and out, exploring her mouth. The ache between her legs grew as he moved his hips back and forth, causing his shaft to move with exquisite slowness against her.

He covered her breasts with his hands, rolling her nipples between his thumbs and fingers as he continued moving against her. She felt spineless, hardly able to sit up. His shaft slid easily because she was so wet, but Ian didn't seem to mind.

He leaned back, and she felt the heat of his gaze on every intimate part of her. It made it hard to breathe.

"You're so beautiful," he said, his voice low and rough.

But Ian was the beautiful one. With his eyes darkened by desire to midnight blue, his black hair, and the hardened body of a young warrior, he could enchant the faerie queen herself.

"I want ye so badly," he said.

When he pushed her back on the bed, she was grateful because she didn't have the strength to sit up any more. He pulled her up further on the bed and hovered over her on all fours. Her breath came in shallow gasps when he cupped the sensitive spot between her legs and started moving his fingers over her in a circular motion.

When he leaned down to take her mouth, she slid her arms around his neck. Soon she was lost in deep kisses. She pulled him against her, wanting to feel his weight on her.

The breath went out of her in a huff when the tip of his shaft pressed against her opening. On their own, her legs went round him, urging him forward.

He broke the kiss. With his eyes on hers, watching her closely, he eased forward a fraction until something inside her stopped him. Sweat broke out on his brow.

"It will hurt a bit," he said.

"I don't care." She felt edgy, impatient.

"I think ye are ready," he said, breathing hard. "Do ye think ye are? Do ye want me to wait longer?" There was a strained, pleading quality to his voice.

"I want to feel ye inside me."

He made a strangled sound and surged forward. She felt a sharp pain, and something inside her ripped.

She must have cried out, because Ian covered her face with kisses. "Are ye all right, love?"

He called her "love."

"I am," she said. The sharp pain was gone, but she could feel every inch of him inside her, stretching her.

"You're so tight," he said.

"Too tight?" she asked, panic rising in her throat. "Will it be all right?"

"Ah, ye are perfect," he said, squeezing his eyes shut. "Ye can have no notion how good it feels."

Then he was kissing her, and she forgot everything except him. She groaned when he began moving slowly inside her, causing exquisite new sensations. His kisses were hungry, urgent, as he moved faster and harder against her. She lifted her hips and pulled at his shoulders, wanting him closer, deeper.

So many emotions were coursing through her veins that she felt as if she might burst into tears or shatter. Joy. Love. A closeness to another human being she had never felt before. She never imagined it would feel like this, encompassed in his arms, their bodies joined and moving as one. She could not tell where she ended and he began.

"Ye feel so good, Sìl." His words came in soft bursts. "I...I can't wait, love."

She held onto him as he thrust into her faster and faster. She felt the pressure building inside both him and her.

"You're mine," he gasped. "Mine. Mine. Forever mine."

Forever. She had loved him forever.

"Sìleas," he cried, as he surged against her, and she shattered in his arms. Stars sparkled against her eyelids as her body squeezed around his. She called his name as waves of pleasure coursed through her.

He collapsed over her. Though he was heavy, she welcomed the weight of him, the certainty that he was here, that he was hers.

Ian had claimed her as his at last.

In truth, she had always been his. Always.

Oh God, he was a bad man and a poor husband. For certain, he'd been too rough with her—and she a virgin. But he'd never needed a woman like that. Never. At least he had stopped himself from plunging into her and taking her hard and fast as he'd wanted to.

He should have talked to her and been gentle from the start. Ach, he probably frightened her half to death attacking her the way he did the moment the door was closed. And then he shocked her by tasting her. He smiled to himself. Nay, he couldn't regret that part—and he was quite sure she didn't, either.

When she found her release…there was nothing like it in this world, and probably not in the next one, either. He was still shaking from what making love to her had done to him. He was a blessed man to have a woman who could make him feel like that.

He pulled her close so that her head was resting on his chest, breathed in the scent of her hair, and started to drift off to sleep.

"I met the English lady ye wanted to wed."

Her words jarred him from his stupor. "What?"

"Philippa," she said in a soft voice. "She's all that ye said she was."

"I can't remember what I said about her." Why was she talking about Philippa?

In a small voice, she said, "Do ye still regret that ye were prevented from marrying her?"

"Sìl, I don't want any woman as my wife but you." After what had just passed between them, how could she be asking this? Women could be very hard to understand at times.

"I've told ye there will never be another woman," he said, "but I cannot change the past."

And that was the problem. Their past was precisely the reason she needed reassurance.

He rolled her onto her back and leaned over her. "Ye have no cause to be jealous of Philippa," he said, looking into her eyes. "And it's not just that ye are more beautiful than she is."

"Ach, now I know ye are lying to me," she said, making a face.

"Ye don't know how lovely ye are." She was beautiful with her hair all wild on the pillow and her cheeks rosy from their lovemaking.

She sucked in her breath when he leaned down and flicked his tongue over her nipple. It stood up for him, begging for more. He pressed his cock against her side so she would feel how hard she made him.

"Wedding Philippa would have been a terrible mistake," he said.

She licked her lip and asked in a breathy voice. "Why is that?"

"Because ye are the woman who was made for me." He rolled on top of her, pushing her legs apart. "If ye have any doubt, let me show ye again."

CHAPTER 28

Ian winked at Sìleas and squeezed her leg under the table as he scooped up the last of his porridge. He knew he looked like a lovesick fool to the other guests, who were having breakfast or a cup of ale before going about their business for the day, but he couldn't wipe the grin off his face.

"Ye look pretty this morning," he said, brushing a stray strand of hair from her face. He couldn't keep his hands off her, either, though he knew it embarrassed her.

"Will we collect the others and leave Stirling this morning?" Sìleas asked.

He was about to suggest they could go back to bed for another hour or two first, when a man entered the tavern and scanned the crowded room. Damn, with that bushy black beard, he looked like a Douglas. Then the man's gaze settled on Ian, and he strode through the tavern toward them. Damn again.

"The Douglas has a wedding gift for ye," the man said, sounding more like he was delivering a threat than a felicitation.

Ian took the parchment the man handed him and broke the seal. It was a charter for Knock Castle and the surrounding lands signed by the queen, as regent.

"Give my thanks to the Douglas," Ian said, rolling the parchment back up and sticking it inside his shirt for safekeeping. "I don't suppose ye know if it's the only one?"

The crown had a bad habit of giving charters for the same property to more than one clan, which tended to fuel the conflicts already burning between clans.

The man ignored his question and sat down next to him on the bench. "Donald Gallda MacDonald of Lochalsh is raising trouble again."

Donald Gallda was leading this latest rebellion against the crown. Like his father and cousin before him, Donald sought to resurrect the MacDonalds to their former glory, when their chieftain was Lord of the Isles. After his father's failed rebellion, Donald was taken by the king to be raised in the Lowlands, which was why Highlanders called him Donald *Gallda*, the Stranger.

"The days of the Lord of the Isles are long past," the Douglas man said. "Siding with the rebellion will do you and the MacDonalds of Sleat nothing but harm."

Ian agreed, though he wasn't about to share his thoughts on the matter with a stranger. It had been twenty years since the Lord of the Isles had been forced to submit to the king of Scotland. Since then, the MacDonald clan had broken into several branches, each with their own chieftain, and there was no going back from that. The MacDonald's former vassals—the Macleods, the Camerons, and the Macleans, among them—were used to their independence as well.

"I hear Donald Gallda ousted the royal garrison and took Urquhart Castle," Ian said.

"Ach, they're devils," the man said. "Starting this fight on the heels of our bloody losses to the English."

"I've a new bride, so the rebellion doesn't concern me much one way or the other today," Ian said, putting his arm around Sìleas. Would the man never leave?

"We share enemies," the Douglas man said.

That was true, though a man would need a chart like Sìleas kept for the sheep and cows to keep track of the shifting alliances among the clans. The Macleods of Harris and Dunvegan, however, were long-standing rivals of the MacDonalds of Sleat, and they were supporting the rebellion. Lachlan Cattanach Maclean of Duart, otherwise known as Shaggy Maclean, had taken the rebel side as well—and Ian had a personal grudge against Shaggy, having spent time in his dungeon.

"If the Douglas could be certain your cousin would support the Crown," the man said, "he could be convinced to lend a hand when Connor is ready to take the chieftainship from his uncle."

"I'll be sure to give Connor my best advice," Ian said.

When the man finally got up and left, Ian blew out his breath. "I can see that taking the chieftainship from Hugh Dubh will just be the start of Connor's troubles."

"Aye," Sìleas said. "But the sooner he is chieftain the better."

"My wife is a wise woman," Ian said, lifting her chin with his finger. "What do ye say to going back to our room?"

Ahh, her eyes were so green. And, better yet, they were telling him just what he wanted.

He was halfway off the bench when a heavy hand rested on his shoulder. Who now? Brushing the hand off, he turned to find a wild-haired man who smelled as if he'd been living rough far too long.

"I saw ye talking to one of the Douglases," the man said, in a voice so deep the bench vibrated when he spoke.

"He was giving me a wedding gift," Ian said, losing patience. "And if ye don't mind, I'm taking my bride back to bed now."

"A moment, friend," the man said, not sounding friendly at all. "Go home and tell your chieftain that we're counting on the MacDonalds of Sleat to fight with us against the Crown."

God's beard, how many men must he argue with before he could take his bride back upstairs?

"Ye don't think the English killed enough Scots at Flodden that we must kill each other now?" Ian took a long drink of his ale and slammed his empty cup down. "All in all, your timing seems verra poor to me."

"We must strike now, while there is no king to fight us," the man said. "Even Lowlanders won't follow an English woman into battle."

"I suspect it will not be the queen, but Archibald Douglas, who will be leading them," Ian said. "I don't like the man, but I wouldn't make the mistake of underestimating him. The Douglas has iron in his eyes."

When the second man finally left them, Ian took Sìleas's hand. "We'd best hurry."

"Ach, they've come for us," she said.

Ian turned to see Connor and the others entering the tavern. He heaved a sigh, knowing his friends had already given him more time than they ought. They could not afford to delay their departure longer. It was, however, a small comfort to see the disappointment on Sìleas's face.

· · ·

Sìleas fought to keep her eyes open as they sat around the campfire. Niall had lost the fight and was snoring with his head against a log while the others talked. The only thing that kept Sìleas awake was her rumbling stomach— and her sore behind. After one day, it felt as if she had been on that damned horse a week.

Although the men attempted to restrain their pace out of consideration for her, Sìleas felt their urgency. Samhain—and the gathering to select the new chieftain— was less than a week away. They could ill afford the days lost fetching her from Stirling. And yet, none of them uttered one word of complaint against her.

Nor would they.

Because Ian had claimed her as his wife, the others simply accepted her. She could almost feel the tight bond that connected the four men wrap around her and encompass her within their protection. It was unspoken and subtle, but she knew with utter certainty that any one of them would die to protect her.

Although she had known Connor, Alex, and Duncan when they were lads, she was coming to know them as men now. She let her gaze rest on each of them as they talked, starting with Alex, who looked like one of his marauding Viking ancestors—until he laughed, which was often. Then there was Duncan, a huge man, who could play the sweetest music you'd ever want to hear, but had a shadow of sadness in his eyes. When she asked, Ian told her Duncan had been in love with Connor's sister, who was wed to the son of an Irish chieftain.

Finally, she turned her gaze to Connor, who looked so much like Ian they could be mistaken for each other by someone who didn't know them well. If the men made him chieftain, it would be because he was a strong warrior and very clever. But Sìleas believed Connor would be a great chieftain because he also had the humility to listen to the wise counsel of others and felt compassion for even the lowliest members of his clan.

"I had as many men taking my measure in Stirling as I do at home on Skye," Connor said as he turned the spit with the rabbits over the fire.

"They want to place their wager on the right horse," Duncan said. "What worries me is that they'll be expecting a portion of the winnings."

"With the Crown in the hands of a babe, it's every man for himself," Connor said, shaking his head, "and the scavengers feeding on the weak."

"The Douglases and the Campbells are the worst," Alex said. "They're like two dogs with one bone."

"Aye, and I feel their teeth in me," Connor said, and they all laughed.

"Ye should have put Alex to work on the queen," Duncan said. "Then we could all have fancy titles like the Douglases."

"Ye offend my honor," Alex said. "I only do my duty for the clan with the pretty ones."

After the laughter died down again, Connor said. "We'd best keep our heads down, lads. We have enemies to spare without adding more."

The smell of the rabbits roasting finally woke Niall, who sat up and stretched. "Are they cooked yet? I'm famished."

"I'd best serve Sìleas first," Connor said, as he lifted the spit from the fire. "Her stomach is so loud it's disturbing the horses."

Her mouth watered as Connor held the spit out and Ian cut off a big slice for her with his knife. Though she enjoyed the men's easy banter, as soon as her hunger was sated, she grew too tired to follow it.

"Your wife is going to choke to death if she keeps falling asleep with her mouth full," Connor said.

She opened her eyes with a start to find the men all smiling at her.

"That would be a shame, after we went to the trouble of fetching her," Duncan said.

"Goodness, Duncan, is that two jokes I heard ye make tonight?" she said, and they all laughed.

Ian handed her a flask of ale and rubbed her back as she took a drink to wash down the rabbit.

"Let's get ye off to bed." He set the flask aside and scooped her up in his arms.

"Night, Sìleas," and "Sleep well," the others called to her as Ian carried her off into the darkness beyond the firelight.

When Ian had found a secluded spot some distance from the others, he set her down and spread their blankets. She thought she would fall asleep as soon as her head hit the ground. Instead, she lay in Ian's arms listening to the wind in the trees and the faint sound of Duncan playing a tune on his whistle.

When Ian lifted her chin and gave her a soft kiss, she opened her mouth to him and pressed against him. How she loved him.

He pulled back. "Are ye sure you're not too tired?"

"Aye. I want ye, Ian MacDonald." She ran her hand up his erect shaft to show him how certain she was.

It was the same each night of their return to Skye. After riding so many hours that she could barely stand, they would eat and talk with the others. Then Ian would lead her off to make their bed away from the others.

As soon as she lay down with him, her tiredness evaporated like the morning mist and they would make love half the night. What Ian did to her was a constant wonder to her, a magic she feared the faeries would envy.

By the time they reached the coast, she was in an exhausted fog of happiness. They found a distant cousin of Alex, one of the MacDonnells, who was willing to take them across the Sound of Sleat in his boat. Despite the cold, wet wind on the sea, Sìleas fell sound asleep to the rocking of the boat with Ian's arms about her.

She awoke to an awareness of tension in Ian's body. When she opened her eyes, she saw Knock Castle shrouded in low clouds up the coastline to the north.

"I hope ye believe I would want ye as my wife whether or not ye were heir to Knock Castle," he said.

She ignored the grain of doubt that remained in her heart and nodded.

"But we must take it back," he said.

She tightened her grip on Ian's arm. Even if she had Ian with her, would she be able to live in a place that held such sorrow for her? Could it ever be cleansed of her mother's suffering or her stepfather's malevolence?

Could she and Ian be happy in a castle that made a ghost weep?

She understood the importance of the castle and her claim on it to the clan, but just the sight of it made her stomach tighten into knots. Knowing Murdoc and Angus were there now made her feel worse.

"They can't see us from the castle, can they?" she asked, though it made her feel foolish.

"They'll see the boat, but there are many boats in these waters," Ian said. "This isn't one they'll know."

Ian kept his gaze fixed on Knock Castle until it disappeared from view. "I'll not let the man who hurt you keep your home."

But Knock Castle had never been a true home to her.

CHAPTER 29

Shouts of greeting filled the house as soon as Ian opened the front door.

"Praise God, all of ye are safe and that ye brought her home to us," his mother said. She hugged him and each of the other men in turn, while his father embraced Sìleas.

"Is my thick-headed son treating ye better now?" his father asked, with his arm about her shoulders. "Sometimes a man needs a good scare to clear his head."

"Then my head must be verra clear, for she had me scared witless, da," Ian said, laughing.

Ah, it was good to be home.

They caught up on news over dinner. Though no one was told of their departure, as happens on Skye, everyone knew of it within a day or two.

"Hugh's supporters spread the rumor that Connor's left for good," his father said. "We hear from Duncan's sister that Hugh is making promises he's not likely to keep in order to gain support. Unfortunately, it seems to be working."

That didn't bode well at all. From the start, it was always going to be a challenge for Connor to take the chieftainship from his uncle, but they had counted on taking Knock Castle to swing support in Connor's favor. Men love a victory. But it was too late now to gather men and mount an attack.

"With Samhain but two days away," Alex said, slapping Connor on the back, "we'll have to move quickly to let the men know you're home and ready to take your place as chieftain."

Time was too short. Still, there had to be a way to convince their clansmen that Connor was the right man to choose—or that Hugh was the wrong choice.

They discussed their strategies for the gathering over supper. But when they were done eating, they set aside the uncertainties ahead to celebrate coming home and the start of Ian and Sìleas's life together.

Duncan pulled out his whistle, and the rest of them took turns singing verses to the old songs they all knew. As Sìleas sang and clapped with the others, there was a glow about her that warmed Ian's heart.

He leaned back in his chair, watching the others. He caught his father winking at his mother and knew how pleased his parents were that matters were settled between him and Sìleas. Even Niall had come around. Although Niall had been cautious around him the day they left Stirling, his brother had warmed once he saw how happy Sìleas was.

Ian felt at peace here at home with Sìleas, his friends, and his family. He couldn't remember a time when he felt so content.

"We'd best say our good-byes now," Connor said,

getting to his feet. "Duncan, Alex, and I will leave early in the morning—long before our pair of lovebirds are up. We'll talk to as many men as we can before the Samhain gathering."

"I'll meet up with ye before the gathering," Ian said.

"Sìleas, lass," Duncan said in his gruff voice, "will ye be wearing that new gown ye was telling us about to the gathering?"

Ian almost fell off his chair. Duncan was a good man, making such an effort to bring Sìleas into the circle of their friendship.

"I must have been light-headed with weariness to be speaking about gowns with ye," Sìleas said, a pretty blush coloring her cheeks. "I didn't think ye were listening to my blathering about it."

"I don't talk all the time like some," Duncan said, turning to raise an eyebrow at Alex, "so I heard ye well enough. It's green to match your eyes, am I right?"

Ian exchanged glances with Alex and Connor, who appeared to be as startled as he was by Duncan's conversation.

"It is green," Sìleas said, giving Duncan a huge smile. "Tell me, will ye play your whistle at the gathering?"

"Ach, this little whistle is for when I travel light," Duncan said, patting where he kept it on a cord inside his shirt. "When Connor is made chieftain, I'll play my pipes—and perhaps my harp as well. My sister has been keeping them for me."

The men stood up, preparing to go to the old cottage for the night.

Sìleas rose up on her toes and kissed Duncan's cheek. "I'll see ye at the gathering."

"Careful, lass," Duncan said. "I don't want Ian's dirk in my back."

"I'll risk it," Alex said, opening his arms to her. "Remember, ye promised me a kiss when we were on the boat."

"What promise—" Before Ian could get the question out, Alex had lifted Sìleas off the ground and kissed her right on the mouth.

No sooner had Ian pried her loose from Alex, than Connor said, "Since we're leaving early, I'd best get my kiss now as well."

Connor, wise man, settled for a friendly peck on the cheek.

"I've had enough of ye handling my wife," Ian said, putting his arm around Sìleas and pulling her close.

"But I didn't get my turn," Niall said, stepping forward.

"Ye were alone with my wife overnight and lived to tell the tale," Ian said, lifting his hand to ward off his brother. "Ye'd best be content with that."

After the men left for the cottage and his parents had settled into quiet conversation near the hearth, Sìleas took Ian aside.

"I want to tell Gòrdan about us," she said. "It's not right that he should hear of it from someone else."

Ian nodded. "All right. I'll take ye up there in the morning."

"I'd rather go now and get it over with," she said. "Do ye mind?"

Ian recalled what his brother said about a long line of men waiting for Sìleas to lose patience with him. If she was in a hurry to tell the first man in that line to stop waiting, well, that was fine with him.

"I'll walk up with ye and wait outside," he said. "I don't want ye out alone."

A short time later, Ian was leaning against a tree under a moonless sky and watching his wife rap on Gòrdan's door.

When Gòrdan opened it, a shaft of light fell over Sìleas and across the dark yard. Ian heard their murmured voices as they talked in the doorway.

Then he heard Gòrdan's mother shouting, "The wicked lass has left her husband for ye, hasn't she?"

Gòrdan was patient, as always, with his mother.

"Quiet, mam. I can't explain now," he called to her, before he stepped outside and shut the door.

The two spoke in quiet voices a while longer, then Sìleas left Gòrdan to walk toward the tree where Ian waited. Ian felt Gòrdan's eyes on him in the darkness.

"Be good to her," Gòrdan called out.

"I will."

Ian held Sìleas's hand as they walked home along the dark path. He didn't ask about her conversation with Gòrdan; if she wanted to speak of it, she would.

Before they reached the house, he stopped in the path and turned to her. He brushed back the hair whipping about her face, but it was too dark to see her expression.

"I never meant to shame ye by not coming home," he said.

"I know ye didn't," she said.

But the truth was that he had given her feelings little thought at all, and they both knew it.

"If I had it to do over again, I wouldn't be such an arse."

"Are ye sure?" she said with a smile in her voice.

It was like her to try to ease his conscience by making light of it. He pulled her into his arms and rested his chin on her head. "I'm sorry I hurt ye. I wish we hadn't been forced to wed back then before we were ready, so we could do it now, and do it right."

"'Tis true I wasn't ready," Sìleas said. "But I always wanted you to be my husband in the end."

"That's because ye are wiser than me," Ian said, rubbing his chin against her hair. "I hate knowing that my wife will always remember the start of our marriage as the worst day of her life. I'd do anything to change that."

Sìleas leaned away from him, and he felt the soft touch of her fingertips graze his cheek. "Then let's count our marriage as starting now, and not five years ago."

Ian realized she was right for wanting to tell Gòrdan tonight, to have all that done and behind them. They were embarking on their new life together, now that they were home.

Ian held her tight against him. "I'll try to make it up to ye every day from now on."

CHAPTER 30

Sìleas understood why Ian was saying these things to her. It wasn't that she didn't believe him when he said he wanted to make her happy—he did. But Ian had a hole inside him. Until he redeemed himself for being gone when they needed him, he could not forgive himself. That only made her love him more.

Watching him tonight, laughing and talking with his friends and family, Sìleas knew she could sit across the breakfast table from him for fifty years and never tire of it. But love was not always equal. If Ian cared for her and did his best to be a good husband, that was better than what most women got from the men they devoted their lives to—and far better than Sileas's poor mother ever had.

The feelings between them when they made love were so powerful that she believed Ian could come to love her in the way she loved him. When he was inside her, he called her "love" and the beautiful endearment, *a chuisle mo chroí*, pulse of my heart.

She'd heard many a young woman tell of a man who

spoke of love in the throes of passion and was gone before the babe came. Someday, Ian might say these words to her at other times—perhaps across the table or while he held a child of theirs on his knee—and she would know he meant them.

In the meantime, she would take the warm affection he gave her—and, aye, the passion in the night as well—and be glad for it.

But she would wait for that day when he gave his heart to her wholly.

Ian was glad to find the house quiet when they returned. When he opened their bedchamber door for Sìleas, the room was filled with the warm glow of a dozen lit candles. He smiled at his mother's thoughtfulness.

He took Sìleas's face in his hands as they stood beside the bed. When he made love to her for the first time in Stirling, his pent-up lust for her had made their coupling frantic, intense. If he were honest with himself, there was an edge of anger to his need to possess her that first time—until the wonder of it took hold of him and shook him to his soul.

On their way home to Skye, they had made love every night in the dark, under his plaid on the cold, damp ground. Each time, there was still the frantic need, the sense that there could never be time enough.

But tonight they were home, in their own bed for the first time as man and wife. Looking into her eyes, he felt an overwhelming tenderness for her.

"I want to make love to you slowly tonight." He rubbed his thumb across her cheek.

When he leaned down to kiss her, she tilted her head

back to meet him. Her lips were soft and warm. Desire stirred in him, but he could take his time to savor her. She would be here always. She was his.

He ran his hands down the slope of her back to the dip of her waist and the flare of her hips. When she put her arms around his neck, he deepened the kiss. For long minutes, they stood by the bed, lost in deep, lingering kisses.

She pulled away to rest her head against his chest and gave a long, contented sigh that made him smile.

"Ye have such lovely hair." He ran his hand through the long strands, watching the colors slide over his fingers in the candlelight. It had every color of red in it, from gold to ginger to copper and wine.

"Will ye unhook my gown for me?" she asked.

As he reached around her and unfastened the hooks running down her back, it pleased him to think he would be doing this every night. He pushed the gown off her shoulder and kissed her warm, milky skin. When she leaned back to look at him, he could see tiny flecks of gold in the green of her eyes.

The desire he saw in them sent a jolt of lust through him.

"Let's go to bed, Ian."

He swallowed as she let her gown fall to the floor and stepped out of it. Before he could get his breath, her chemise followed it.

Apparently, his wife had decided to set a tone for the nights of their marriage. It seemed like a fine one to him. And he was pleased that she'd ceased to fret over her scars as well.

He let his gaze travel over her, from her shining mass of wavy hair, which fell over her bare shoulders and breasts like a wood nymph, to the tight curls that covered her secret place, and then down her long legs, all the way to her slender ankles and feet.

"Ach, ye are beautiful, Sìleas."

"Your clothes now." When he sat down on the bed and reached for his boot, she pushed him back. "I'll do it."

He never knew how provocative it could be to have a naked woman at his feet pulling his boots off. The glimpse of heaven she gave him had his cock standing straight. When she knelt between his legs and ran her hands up his thighs, he unfastened his belt and tossed it aside without looking to see where it fell.

He was breathing hard as her hands moved up his legs, under his long shirt. Of course, he wore nothing under it. His cock pushed up the cloth calling attention to itself.

Please, Sìl. He bit his lip to keep from begging her to touch him.

She locked eyes with him as she ran her hands up the sides of his hips. "Your shirt?"

"Aye!" He rose up enough to pull it out from under him and whipped it off.

This time, she tortured him by running her hands over the tops of his legs, along the sides of his hips, and then over his chest. Finally, she wrapped her hand around his cock.

As she moved her hand up and down his shaft, he gripped her shoulders and kissed her with all the passion he felt. It was long moments before he remembered he had meant to make love to her slowly. When she broke the kiss, it came back to him... but it was hard to hold on to the thought. Her hair brushed his thighs and belly as she kissed his chest.

When her kisses drifted lower, his mind stopped working altogether.

"Ahh!" The air went out of him when he felt the soft touch of her lips on the tip of his shaft.

"Is that how it's done?" she asked.

He couldn't answer, but she must have taken his groan as encouragement for she continued her efforts. They were quite good, but finally, he was able to get the words out to offer a suggestion. "Ye can use your whole mouth, love."

Sìleas had good instincts and needed no more instruction. Ian lay back on the bed, panting. Vaguely, the thought came to him that he should stop her and make love to her properly, but he couldn't make himself. What she was doing felt too damned good.

He came in an explosion that nearly killed him—and left him grateful. He pulled her up on the bed and wrapped his arms around her. "Ah, love, that was...that was...verra, verra nice..."

He fought the weight of his eyelids, but he hadn't slept much for close to a fortnight.

He awoke to the smell of the summer heather in her hair. When he opened his eyes, she was sitting up, leaning on one arm and watching him with a smile on her face. She looked pleased with herself.

"Tell me I didn't sleep long."

"No. Just a wee doze."

Judging from the height of the candles, she was telling him the truth. Still, he must have dreamed of her, because he woke up wanting her. He rested a hand on her thigh.

"How did ye know to do that?" Thinking of her mouth on him made him harder.

"I heard the married women talking about how men liked it."

He'd never appreciated women's gossip before.

"They were laughing, so I wasn't sure if they were joking." She gave him a crooked smile. "I guess they weren't."

The candlelight played across her skin. Her nipples were rosy and peaked, and her eyes went dark when he cupped her breast and rubbed his thumb over the hardened nipple.

"I did like it," he said.

He pulled her down into a deep kiss and slid his hand between her thighs. She was hot and wet for him. From the way she was kissing him, she didn't want to wait.

Next time, for certain. Next time, he would take her slowly.

He did. And the time after that as well. They dozed between bouts of lovemaking.

When he awoke for the last time, the candles were gone, and the first light of dawn was coming through the window. He propped himself up on one elbow to watch her sleep. Though her tangled hair looked like a wild storm across the pillow, her face was peaceful.

Ian felt so much tenderness for her that it was like an ache inside him.

Though he'd told her in Stirling he would let her choose another man if she didn't want him, he knew that now for the lie that it was. He could never have let her go.

He loved her. He didn't know when it happened, but he suspected it was long before he realized it. With the back of his hand, he brushed a strand of hair from her face.

Sìleas didn't know her own value. He loved her strength, her good heart, her curiosity, and her courage. Though she didn't like to hear it, he also loved her for her devotion to his family, for there was such goodness in it.

He liked that she said her mind and stood up for herself. And that she gave herself to him without holding back. When she was a wee thing, she trusted him to rescue her from mishaps. And now that she was a woman, she trusted him with her heart.

He would do his best to deserve it, now and always.

When he smelled porridge and heard the murmur of male voices coming from downstairs, he knew he had to get up. Still, he let himself watch Sìleas's face and the steady rise and fall of her chest for a few moments more. It was hard to make himself leave her, even though he knew he would sleep with her again tonight—and most nights for the rest of his life.

But Ian needed to talk with his father before Connor and the others left. A suspicion too horrible to believe at first had taken root in Ian's mind about what really happened at Flodden. He hoped his father's memory had improved with his health.

CHAPTER 31

Sileas hummed to herself as she washed up at the basin and dressed. How late had she slept? It was quiet downstairs, giving her hope she would find Ian alone. Her face grew warm at the thought of facing Beitris and Payton after last night. What if they had heard her through the walls?

Her limbs were so loose that her legs wobbled as she went down the stairs.

Her foot had barely touched the bottom step when Alex banged through the front door, holding his side. She blinked, unable to take in what was happening for a moment.

Good God, that was blood dripping through his fingers! As Ian and Niall helped Alex to a chair, she bolted for the kitchen to get a cloth and basin of water. By the time she returned, Ian had removed Alex's plaid and cut his shirt open, revealing a deep red gash down Alex's side and another on his thigh.

"Ian, ye must go for Connor and Duncan," Alex said,

speaking in short bursts between gasps for air. "They're hurt far worse than me."

Alex winced as Sìleas began to clean the wound on his side with the wet cloth.

"Where will I find them?" Ian said.

"We were ambushed on the path, less than a mile north of here," Alex said. "But they're in no shape to walk."

"Let's go," Ian said to Niall. "We'll take the horses."

"Ian." Alex's voice stopped him at the door. "They left us for dead, so I don't think they'll be back. But keep a sharp eye, all the same."

"How many men?" Ian asked.

"Twenty when they attacked us," Alex said. "A few less now."

Beitris had come into the room in the midst of this exchange and immediately set to helping Sìleas staunch the blood from Alex's wounds.

After the door slammed behind Ian and Niall, Sìleas said, "We'll need ye to lie down, Alex, so we can sew up that cut on your face. It looks deep."

"There's no need," Alex said, but he let them help him to the floor by the fire.

"Careful now," she said, "I think ye may have broken a rib or two."

Sìleas built up the fire while Beitris went to get needle and thread.

"We'll need to work fast," Beitris said when she returned, "so we're ready when they bring in Connor and Duncan."

Fear hammered at Sìleas's heart as she washed blood and dirt from the wound on Alex's cheek. If Alex was the least hurt, what must the other two look like?

"Can ye tell me what happened?" she asked to divert him from what she was doing.

"They were looking for us." Alex sucked in his breath as she took the first stitch to close the gash. "I'm guessing someone saw us crossing the water yesterday."

"Was it Hugh?" she asked.

"No." Alex winced as she drew the needle through again. "It was the MacKinnons and a few of their good friends, the MacLeods."

Sìleas's fingers froze. "Are ye sure? What would they be doing here, so far into MacDonald territory?"

"That's a verra good question," Alex said. "Your step-da Murdoc was with them. And that ugly ox Angus as well."

Sìleas swallowed back the panic rising in her throat and forced herself to keep her hand steady as she finished up the stitches. Then she took the salve Beitris handed her and rubbed it gently over the wound.

"There ye go," she said, wiping her hands. "Ye might have a scar, but that will just make ye more interesting to the lasses."

They worked quickly to clean and bind his other wounds.

"Lie still," Beitris told Alex, as she got up from her knees. "Now we'd best get clean water and blankets for the others."

No sooner had they gathered the blankets than Ian burst through the door carrying Duncan. The huge, red-haired man's head lolled against Ian's arm, as if he were a sleeping child. Sìleas spread a blanket on the floor by the hearth where Alex had lain a few moments before. Ian dropped to his knees and gently laid Duncan down between them.

"I need to help Niall with Connor." Ian met her eyes. "He's verra bad."

The blood from Duncan's wounds was already soaking the flagstones of the hearth.

"God help us," she whispered, as Beitris took Ian's place on the other side of the moaning man.

"He's trying to wake," Beitris said. " 'Tis a good sign."

Sìleas suspected Beitris was saying that to give them hope. Taking the knife her mother-in-law had brought in from the kitchen, she began cutting away Duncan's blood-soaked shirt. She swallowed back bile when she saw the wound beneath.

"Oh God, no," she said, covering her mouth.

"Let me do that." Alex hobbled over and pushed her aside. "I've tended wounds like this before."

Before she could argue with Alex, Ian backed through the door with Connor. He was supporting Connor's head and shoulders, while Niall followed carrying his legs.

Mary, Mother of God! No wonder the MacKinnons had left him for dead. If it weren't for the straight black hair that was so like Ian's, Sìleas would not have known this broken man was Connor.

Ian laid him on the blanket she spread for him. Using his dirk, he cut Connor's clothes off, tossing the pieces of blood-soaked cloth into the fire as he worked. Connor was covered with so much blood, Sìleas could not tell where his wounds were. But the shallowness of his breathing frightened her more than all the blood.

Like Alex, Ian worked with a brisk efficiency that bespoke experience. She knew they had fought in France—and in the Borders before that—but the dangers they faced had never seemed real to her before.

"Can ye get the whiskey?" Alex called out to her from where he and Beitris worked over Duncan.

"There's a good lass," Alex said when she got it down from the shelf. "Now pour it onto a couple of cloths for us."

She did as he said and then stoked the fire to a roaring blaze to keep the injured men warm.

"His whistle saved him," Alex said, holding it up. The whistle, which hung about Duncan's neck from a leather cord, was bent in the middle where it had been struck by a sword.

Duncan's body bucked as Alex and Beitris cleaned his wounds with whiskey-soaked cloths. Though his pain made her cringe, the fight in Duncan reassured her.

Connor only shivered as Ian cleaned his wounds. Sileas prayed hard while she handed Ian clean cloths.

"Do ye think he'll live?" she asked Ian in a choked whisper.

"I will no let him die," Ian said.

She helped him bind the bandages around Connor's head and chest, and then his arms. Ach, Connor's skin had a gray cast to it. He'd lost far too much blood.

Lord Jesus, have mercy. Connor is a good man, and the hope of our clan. Do not take him from us.

Ian tried to make a plan as he worked to stem the flow of Connor's blood. He had to get the injured men to safety. Connor was most likely the target, but whoever had done this had meant to kill them all.

"We'll need to hide the three of ye while ye recover," he said over his shoulder to Alex. "It is best that the men who did this believe they succeeded in their treachery."

"It was the MacKinnons, with a few of the MacLeods,"

Alex said. "But I suspect Hugh made a devil's agreement with them to do it, or they wouldn't risk attacking us so far into MacDonald territory."

"I have the same suspicion," Ian said, as he pulled tight the last knot of the bandage around Connor's arm. "Proving it will be another matter."

"It would be even harder to prove if we were dead," Alex said.

Alex caught his eye and tilted his head to the side, signaling he wanted a word outside of the others' hearing. When Ian crouched beside him, Alex said, "Did ye notice the MacKinnons and MacLeods didn't take time to gather their dead? Something scared them off."

"Aye. All the more reason to get the three of ye away from here." Ian wiped his forehead with his sleeve. "I'll take ye by boat to Teàrlag's cottage. She is the best healer, and ye can hide there, same as before.

"Niall, get the wagon so we can get them down to the water," he called out to his brother, as he returned to where Connor lay.

He looked down at Connor's battered face, and rage swept through him. Earlier, he had been so focused on staunching the blood to save Connor's life that he had not truly seen how badly beaten he was.

"I should have killed Hugh Dubh outside the church that day," Ian said, clenching his fists. "I swear to God, I will have his blood for this."

His mother came to kneel beside Sìleas on the other side of Connor. Her mouth tightened as she laid her fingers against Connor's cheek.

"Ye must get the priest before ye take him away," she said.

"There's no time for that," Ian said.

"This is my dead sister's only son," his mother said, looking up at him, "and I'll not have him meet his Maker with his sins upon him."

"Connor is not dying."

"I fear he might, son," she said in a soft voice. "What's more, ye will hurt what chance he has by moving him."

Ian looked at Connor as he weighed the risks. "No, I'm taking him. I'll not have him dragged from this house and slaughtered in the yard like an animal."

Alex nodded his agreement. In the chaos, Ian hadn't noticed that his father had come into the room until now.

"Ian's right," Payton said, laying a hand on his wife's shoulder. "If those men hear Connor survived and is here, they'll come for him."

A rush of cold air sent the flames of the hearth dancing as Niall came through the door. "I've got the cart just outside."

Ian rubbed his forehead. His parents and Niall should be safe enough at home, so long as they weren't hiding Connor here. But he didn't like leaving Sìleas here with Murdoc in the area.

But what was he to do with her? With Hugh and the MacKinnons set on murdering Connor, taking her with them could put her in greater danger than leaving her. Besides, there was barely room for the injured men in the tiny fishing boat.

There was only one choice. "Niall, I need ye to take Sìleas up to Gòrdan's."

Ian looked down at Sìleas, where she knelt on the floor holding Connor's hand like some angel. God in Heaven, he loved this woman. He went down on one knee and touched her cheek.

"It's not safe for ye here at the house, with MacKinnons about," he said. "They'll not think to look for ye at Gòrdan's, and I know he'd protect ye with his life."

She bit her lip and nodded.

"After ye take her," he said to Niall, "find the priest and ask him to come to Teàrlag's cottage after nightfall—tell him he must not be seen."

That would comfort his mother, and it couldn't hurt to have the priest praying over the men either way.

"I'll help ye get them down to the boat before Sìl and I go," Niall said.

"I can help with the others," Alex said.

Ian saw the sheen of sweat on Alex's forehead as he struggled to his feet. Alex was hurt worse than he wanted them to know.

As they rolled the cart down to the beach, the cold wind snapped the ends of the blankets that were wrapped around the injured men. Sìleas followed the cart down to the water. While he and Niall carried first Duncan and then Connor from the cart to the boat, she found a stick for Alex to lean on and helped him into the boat.

Ian looked at the three injured men, Alex slumped over and the two others lying across the small boat at the edge of the shore. God only knew how he would get them up the steep steps from the beach to Teàrlag's cottage, but he would.

He squeezed his brother's shoulder and turned to say good-bye to Sìleas.

"Ye are the best of men, Ian MacDonald," she said, her voice firm and her eyes dry and clear. "If anyone can save them, ye will do it."

•

She had always had such faith in him—and he needed it now.

"I'll return as soon as I can." He took her face in his hands and kissed her hard on the mouth. "Be safe, *mo chroí*."

CHAPTER 32

"Take this dirk," Niall said, handing it to her as they left the beach. "Put it up your sleeve, just in case."

They took the fork in the path toward Gòrdan's house and walked at a brisk pace without speaking again, their thoughts on the loved ones they had just left. Relying on Gòrdan to protect her must have been bitter medicine for Ian to swallow, but he hadn't hesitated to put her safety before his pride.

Sìleas looked over her shoulder and caught a glimpse through the trees of Ian on the beach pushing the boat out into the water. A shiver went through her.

Please, God, watch over Ian and keep him safe for me. Do not let these young men perish.

It was only a half mile to Gòrdan's, but the path rose and turned so that one could not see from one house to the other. As they rounded a bend, a dozen men on horses appeared in the distance, coming in their direction.

Sìleas sucked in her breath. Was that her stepfather and Angus at the front of the riders? Even from this distance, they would know her by her hair. She could feel their eyes on her. What she had feared for years was coming true.

They were coming for her.

"Run," she said to Niall. "They are going to take me, and there is nothing ye can do to prevent it."

"We can make it back to the house," Niall said, tugging at her arm.

"No! If they come to the house, they'll see the others leaving in the boat," she shouted. "They'll kill them all."

The MacKinnons had tried to murder Connor once. When they saw that they had failed, they would kill every man in the boat. Ian was the best of fighters, but there were too many of them. He would die trying to save the others. Likely, Payton and Beitris would run out to help and be killed as well. She couldn't let that happen.

"Please, Niall," she said. "I'm begging ye to go. It's me they want."

"Not without ye." She heard the familiar whisper of a steel blade as Niall drew his claymore from his back.

"Ye must go so ye can tell Ian they've taken me," she said, holding his arm.

The hooves of the approaching horses vibrated through her feet and echoed in her head.

"It's too late. Get behind me," Niall said, shoving her back.

In another moment, a dozen MacKinnon men surrounded them.

"He's a brave one," one of the men said with a laugh, as they dismounted. He jumped back, though, when Niall swung his claymore within an inch of his chest.

"Come, laddie, there's no need for ye to die today," another man said, "but the lass belongs to us."

The men moved aside as Murdoc pushed through them on his horse.

"Ye have a lot to answer for, Sìleas," he said in a hard voice, as he looked down at her. Glancing at Niall, he said, "Who's the foolish lad ready to die for ye?"

Before she could think of a lie, Niall said in a defiant voice, "I am Niall MacDonald, son of Payton and brother to Ian."

"Take him," Murdoc said.

Sìleas screamed as the men closed in on Niall from all sides. Niall sliced one man's arm and nicked another, but there were too many of them. It wasn't long before they held him.

"He's yours," Murdoc said, turning to Angus.

Panic pounded through Sìleas's veins as Angus dismounted from his horse. It was no use pleading with him, for Angus enjoyed hurting people and wasn't one to think about the consequences. Murdoc was the calculating one. Killing Niall was not important to him; she needed to give him a reason not to do it.

"Ye will regret it if ye hurt him," she shouted.

Murdoc raised his hand, signaling Angus to halt. "And why would I regret one less MacDonald in this world?"

"Ian MacDonald is a stubborn man," she said. "Ye must have heard he stayed away for five years just because he was forced to wed me."

"I've heard he's even refused to bed ye." Murdoc laughed and the others joined in. "Luckily, Angus here is no so particular."

Sìleas could not let herself look at Angus for fear she would lose her nerve.

"'Tis true Ian doesn't want me." She stretched out her

arm, pointing at Niall. "But this lad is Ian's only brother. If ye harm a hair on his head, I can promise ye Ian will come after ye. No matter how long it takes, one day he will catch ye unawares. He's that stubborn."

"Enough talk," Angus said, pulling his sword.

Fear seized her heart as Angus started toward Niall. "Murdoc, ye gain nothing by harming him."

"If Ian has treated ye so poorly," Murdoc asked, narrowing his eyes at her, "why do ye care what happens to his brother?"

"Because he's like a brother to me as well," she said, letting the truth of it show in her eyes.

"If your mother had not been so useless," Murdoc said, his anger flashing, "ye would have a true brother."

Sìleas felt for the dirk up her sleeve. If Murdoc didn't stop Angus she would have to stab the brute as he walked by her. She'd have only one chance, but she didn't know where best to stick him. Her heart raced as she tried to think. Angus had too much belly—if she stuck him there, it might not stop him. No, it had to be in his thick neck.

"Angus, we've got what we came for," Murdoc said, then turned to the other men. "Tie the lad to a tree. If he rots before he's found, so be it."

Sìleas's limbs felt weak from the relief surging through her. *Praise God!* She watched as the men bound and gagged Niall, despite his kicking.

"Come, Sìleas. We've no more time to waste," Murdoc said. "Ye will ride with Angus."

It wasn't easy to keep her courage up when Angus smiled, showing his brown and broken teeth, and crooked his finger at her.

"Let me say good-bye," she blurted out. Before anyone

moved to stop her, she ran to the tree where Niall was tied and threw her arms around his neck.

"Tell Ian I'll be waiting for him," she said in Niall's ear, as she dropped the dirk behind his back.

An instant later, Angus's rough hands jerked her to her feet.

CHAPTER 33

Connor lay so still that Ian watched for the shallow rise and fall of his chest as he guided the boat in to shore. Connor was still alive, but not much more.

He and Alex exchanged a worried look, but there was nothing to say. As soon as he hauled the boat onto the beach, he lifted his cousin's limp body in his arms. His stomach tightened; it was hard to see Connor like this.

Leaving Alex to watch over Duncan, he started up the treacherous steps of the sea cliff. He thought of all the times they had raced up and down these steps when they were lads. As men, the two years between him and Connor made no difference. But as a lad, Ian had looked up to his older cousin. Though as brave as anyone, Connor had always been the most sensible of the four of them. They lived to manhood only because Connor managed to discourage their most foolhardy adventures—or at least some of them.

When Ian neared the top of the bluff, he looked up to see Teàrlag and Duncan's sister Ilysa clutching their arms against the wind and peering over the side.

"I saw ye coming," Teàrlag called out, and he knew she was referring to the Sight for which she was well-known.

The women rushed him inside and directed him to lay Connor on blankets they had already laid out before the fire. Ilysa went almost as pale as Connor when she saw the condition he was in.

"Go fetch the others," Teàrlag said, waving him off.

When he returned to the boat, he was relieved to find Duncan was awake and able to hold onto Ian's back. He was a huge man, though, and Ian nearly lost his balance more than once on the slick rock steps. The wind was blowing a thin, icy rain now. By the time they reached the top, Duncan was shivering violently. His body, already taxed to the limit, could not take the cold and wet.

Ian banged through the cottage door and staggered across the room to deposit his burden onto Teàrlag's bed. It was a box bed built into the partial wall that separated the main room of her cottage from the byre, where her cow was mooing in complaint.

Ilysa threw a blanket over her brother while Teàrlag shoveled a hot stone from the fire to place at his feet.

Without pausing to rest, Ian returned to the beach for Alex.

"I can walk up, if ye give me a hand," Alex said.

"No, I'll take ye on my back," Ian said. "It'll be quicker, and I'm in no mood to argue."

Alex didn't like it, but that was how it was going to be.

Ian grunted as he hefted Alex onto his back. "God help me, the three of ye must eat like horses."

Ian's legs were cramping by the time he reached the cottage the third time. Alex insisted on sitting in a chair. He made no complaint, however, when the women whisked a blanket around his shoulders, a warming stone under his feet, and a cup of hot broth into his hands.

Ian sat down heavily on a stool by the table. He had succeeded in getting all three men here alive, though Connor was hanging on by a thread and Duncan was not much better. Ian was grateful that both women were skilled at healing, though he suspected there was little that could be done now except keep the men warm and feed them broth.

And pray.

"Ye mustn't tarry," Teàrlag said, fixing her good eye on him. "Your wife is in danger."

Sìleas. He jumped to his feet, feeling as if he'd been kicked in the stomach.

"What can ye tell me?" he asked.

"Only that she's very frightened," Teàrlag said.

"Take this," Ilysa said, shoving a wrapped cloth of oat-cakes into his hand as he went out the cottage door.

The heavens opened on his return trip, soaking him to the skin. He shouted in frustration when it forced him to bring down the sail and row. As he strained against the oars, his heart seemed to race in time to the rain pelting his face.

If Sìleas had not left the dirk with Niall, she would stab Angus with it now. The foul smell of the man surrounded her, suffocating her as they rode. She looked down at the massive thigh rubbing against hers and imagined plunging her blade into it over and over again. Every time he moved the arm around her waist up to press against the undersides of her breasts, she rammed her elbow into his ribs.

Angus made no sign he noticed.

"How many little girls have ye raped since the last time I saw ye?" she said, and jabbed him again.

"I don't count them," he said, sounding amused. "Shame ye have grown up, Sìleas. You'll do, but I liked ye better before."

"Ach, ye are a disgusting beast! Ye will burn in hell for sure."

"I confess to the priests," he said. "When I hold a blade to their throats, the penance is no so bad—except for that damned Father Brian. He's a self-righteous bastard."

"My husband is going to kill ye before ye have a chance to confess again," she said. "Ye will die with your soul black with sin."

"Your marriage is a sham, and everyone on Skye knows it." He leaned down until his filthy whiskers touched the side of her face and his breath choked her. "But you'll soon have a real husband—the kind who knows what he's supposed to do with a wife."

The taunts she had used to hold back her fear left her. Ian would come for her, but when? He thought she was safe, in Gòrdan's care. How long would she be inside Knock Castle with Angus and Murdoc before Ian learned she was there?

As if to dampen her hopes, a cold rain began to fall.

As Knock Castle rose out of the misty rain on the headland, fear weighed down on her chest, making it hard to breathe. She had not been inside the castle since the day she escaped through the tunnel after Murdoc beat her. As they crossed the drawbridge, she looked up at the massive iron and wooden gates and shivered. Dear Lord, how would Ian ever get her out?

Sileas wondered if the ghost of the castle would appear to her as she used to. The legend was that the Green Lady, as she was called for the pale green gown she wore, would smile or weep, depending on whether good news or bad was coming to the family who occupied the castle.

The ghost had always wept for Sìleas.

CHAPTER 34

By the time Ian finally neared the shore below his parents' home, the muscles of his arms and shoulders felt ready to tear from the bone. He narrowed his eyes to peer through the freezing rain still pelting his face. Someone was on the beach waving his arms.

It was Niall. Ian's heart dropped to his boots. Teàrlag was right. Something had gone wrong. He jumped out of the boat and splashed toward shore, hauling the boat with him, as Niall waded into the rough surf to help.

"They've got Sìleas," Niall shouted over the wind and rain whipping around them, as he grabbed the other side of the boat.

"Who has her?" Ian shouted back.

"The MacKinnons and her step-da," Niall said, and Ian could see that his brother was near tears. "Angus was with them."

Ian slammed his fist against the boat. *God, no!*

As soon as they had lugged the boat above the tide line, Niall told him in a rush of words what had happened.

The MacKinnon devils had taken Ian's wife—and almost killed his brother.

"I tried to save her," Niall said in a choked voice.

Ian clenched his jaws against the rage surging inside him and squeezed his brother's shoulders. "I know ye did."

"Ian! Niall!"

At the shouts, Ian looked up to see Gòrdan running toward them along the path above the shore.

"Tell me the MacKinnons did not take her," Gòrdan called out, as he scrambled down the bank to them.

How did Gòrdan know it was the MacKinnons? Murder pulsed through Ian's veins. He pulled his dirk and started toward Gòrdan. "What do ye know of this?"

Niall held Ian's arm. "Gòrdan wouldn't harm Sìleas. Let him talk."

Gòrdan had the wild eyes of a distraught man, and he had come to find them. Ian lowered his dirk, but he did not put it away.

"When Sìleas came to talk to me last night, my mother thought she was making plans to leave ye—to marry me," Gòrdan said, looking pained. "She sent the boy who works for me out in the night to Knock Castle. She gave him a message for Murdoc, telling him that the four of ye had brought Sìleas back from Stirling and were here at your folks' house. The boy just told me about it now."

After Niall told Gòrdan what happened, Gòrdan sank to the wet sand and held his head. Ian left him on the beach without a backward glance. Damn Gòrdan and his mother.

"Murdoc will have Sìleas inside Knock Castle by now," he said to Niall, as they headed up to the house. "I've got to get her out."

Ian clenched his fists, remembering the scars Murdoc put on her back. He was going to kill him, regardless. But if Murdoc had laid a hand on her, he would tear him limb from limb.

"Ian," his brother said, turning worried eyes on him. "She let Murdoc believe that ye don't care for her and that ye never...well, that your marriage was not completed."

Ian waited for the rest.

"He intends to wed her to Angus."

The thought of Angus's meaty hands on Sìleas's delicate skin made his own hands shake with fury. He had to rescue her—and quickly. If he did not save her before Angus raped her, he would never forgive himself. Never.

He could not allow his rage to cloud his thinking. He forced himself to focus his thoughts on the problems before him. The first thing he had to do was make a plan to get Sìleas out of Knock Castle. Then, once he had her safe, he needed to save his clan from Hugh. With the others injured, there was no one else to do it.

He took what comfort he could from her whispered message to Niall. *Tell Ian I'll be waiting for him.* She believed he could not fail her.

He'd always had Connor, Duncan, and Alex at his side. As bairns, they played together. As lads, they learned to sail and to swing their first claymores together. As men, they fought side by side. Through the years, they had taken countless foolish risks together and saved each others' lives. They watched each others' backs.

Now, when Ian needed them more than ever before, he was on his own.

"Ye have me and da," his brother said, as if reading his thoughts.

Ian almost laughed. If he added Father Brian, he'd have a new foursome. But a one-legged man, a fifteen-year-old lad, and a priest were poor substitutes for experienced Highland warriors in their prime.

"Should I gather what men I can?" Niall asked.

"Men were willing to fight with us because they believed Connor could be our new chieftain," Ian said, shaking his head. "Hugh will be spreading the word that Connor is dead or gone. Until Connor is on his feet again, it would put him in danger for us to let it be known he survived the attack."

"Then what will we do?" Niall asked.

"We'll do what Highlanders always do when our enemy is stronger," Ian said, meeting his brother's eyes.

"What's that?" Niall asked.

"We'll use deceit and trickery, of course."

CHAPTER 35

Mice skittered out of the rushes as Murdoc dragged Sìleas down the length of the room. The castle's hall was even filthier than she remembered.

"Get some food on this table!" Murdoc shouted at a woman cowering in the corner. He kicked at two dogs fighting over a bone and turned to Sìleas. "We'll have the wedding after we eat."

"Ye can't do this," Sìleas said. "I am already wed. And it was no trial marriage—a priest wed Ian and me."

Murdoc's lips curled into a sneer. "So ye believed that drunk your chieftain found was a priest?"

Sìleas was stunned. "Of course he was."

Even as she said it, she remembered how the priest fumbled through the words and the threat in the chieftain's eyes when he looked at the man. Other things fell into place that had been buried beneath worse memories of that day: the priest tripping over robes that were far too long for him; his attempt to follow, rather than lead them up the stairs to sprinkle the bed with holy water—before Ian threatened to toss him down the stairs.

"Ye are as easily fooled as your mother was," Murdoc said.

She was indeed a fool.

"Ian and I said vows to each other, and that makes us husband and wife under Highland custom." She swallowed. "And no matter what ye heard, I could be carrying his child."

She instinctively put a hand over her abdomen as the truth of her words struck her.

"Ye think I care whose child it is?" Murdoc shrugged. "But if Angus doesn't want to claim your brat as his own, well, babes die all the time."

She gaped at him openmouthed. She hadn't believed even Murdoc capable of such evil.

"If ye aren't pregnant now, ye soon will be," Murdoc said. "One way or another, ye are going to give me the MacKinnon child your mother should have. We need that child to have a clear right to the castle."

"I promise ye, Murdoc, ye will never have your hands on a child of mine."

"Don't think ye can escape this time, because I've blocked the tunnel." He gave her a hard shove. "Go help get food on the table. The men are hungry."

Ian pulled his plaid over his head as he passed within sight of Dunscaith Castle on his way to the church.

Luck was with him, for he found the priest alone on his knees before the church's simple altar. "Sorry, Father, but this cannot wait."

The priest crossed himself and got to his feet.

"Are ye that desperate to confess your sins, Ian Mac-Donald?" Father Brian asked, as he brushed off his knees.

"No, Father. I haven't time for it."

"I thought as much," the priest said. "'Tis a shame, for I suspect it would be a good deal more interesting than what I usually hear."

"One day I'll give ye hours of confession over cups of whiskey, if ye like," Ian said. "But right now I need a different kind of help."

"What kind is that?" the priest asked.

"Are ye on good terms with the MacKinnons?"

"Whether I am or no, I serve all the clans in these parts," Father Brian said with a shrug. "As a matter of fact, I was planning to visit the MacKinnons next, as I do every year."

"Will the MacKinnons let ye into Knock Castle?" Ian asked.

"If they have sins to confess or weddings to be blessed, they'll open their gates to me," Father Brian said. "Why do ye ask?"

Ian's stomach knotted at the priest's mention of weddings to be blessed. He hated to think that Murdoc's plan to wed Sìleas to Angus might serve as the key to the gate.

"Murdoc MacKinnon is holding my wife at Knock Castle," Ian said between clenched teeth. "I need to get her out. Will ye help me, Father?"

When the priest did not answer at once, Ian said. "He plans to give her to Angus MacKinnon."

"Ach, not Angus. I've seen what that man has done to young lasses," the priest said, his eyes snapping with anger. "What would ye have me do?"

"We'll talk on the way." Ian hoped a plan would come to him soon. God had sent him Father Brian, and that was a start.

Ian crossed himself before he left the church. *Please, God, keep her safe until I can get to her.*

CHAPTER 36

Sìleas's eyes widened when she saw the woman leaning against the wall by the stairs that led down to the kitchens.

"Dina," she whispered. "What are ye doing here?"

"One of the MacKinnon men took a liking to me," Dina said. "I had nowhere else to go."

"I'm sorry for it." Though Sìleas had reason to wish the worst for Dina, she was unhappy to see any woman living in this hellhole.

"I am sorry to see ye here as well," Dina said.

"Will ye help me then?"

"I can't get ye out," Dina said. "They're keeping guards at the gate."

"Then I need to find a way to divert them until Ian comes for me," she said.

"You're that sure he'll come for ye?" Dina asked.

"I am."

"I wouldn't have done what I did if I knew ye wanted Ian," Dina said. "Since ye weren't giving him what he wanted, I saw no harm in it."

They were interrupted by Murdoc's bellow from across the hall. "Where's our dinner?"

When his metal cup hit the wall by Sìleas's head, she and Dina started down. It was dark on the stairs, but there was light and the sound of voices and pans coming from the kitchen below.

"I have some poison," Dina said close to Sìleas's ear.

"Poison?" Sìleas halted and turned to stare at Dina. "How did ye get poison?"

"Teàrlag gave it to me," Dina said. "I went to see her to ask for a charm before I came here. I didn't tell her where I was going, but she said, 'A lass as foolish as you is likely to need something stronger than a good luck charm.'"

Dina leaned down and reached into the side of her boot. "That's when she gave me this wee vial. We can pour it in the ale, aye?"

"I don't want to murder them all," Sìleas said.

"Teàrlag said a drop or two will make a man ill." Dina handed her the vial. "The pitchers of ale will be on a tray by the door. I'll distract the men in the kitchen while ye do it."

"How will ye do that?"

Dina laughed. "You'll see. Nothing could be easier."

Sìleas followed Dina under the low vaulted ceiling of the undercroft into the noisy kitchen. She stayed by the door while Dina crossed the kitchen, hips swaying, toward a beefy man who had a cleaver in his hand and was shouting orders to the other kitchen servants.

He stopped shouting midsentence when he saw Dina coming.

"I'm starving, Donald," she said with a purr in her voice. She laid her hand on the cook's shoulder. "Do ye have something...special...for a hungry lass?"

Everyone else in the kitchen paused in the midst of their tasks to watch Dina as she leaned closer to the cook and spoke to him in a low, suggestive voice. Sìleas saw a half-dozen pitchers of ale on the table next to her, ready to be taken into the hall. Turning her back to the room, she pulled the tiny stopper from the vial.

How many drops should she put in each? It was hard to guess how much each man would drink from the shared pitchers. Her hands shook as she poured a few drops into each.

"What are ye doing there?" The harsh voice behind her startled Sìleas, and she spilled the rest of the poison into the last pitcher.

"Murdoc told her to bring more ale to the table," Dina said, "so you'd best let her go."

Sìleas lifted the tray and hurried out of the kitchen, sloshing ale. At the bottom of the stairs, she paused to draw in a deep breath to steady herself. It would do no good to poison the ale if she spilled it all on the floor.

Before she could get to the table, men started snatching pitchers from her tray.

"Stop it, ye animals!" she shouted and lifted her tray higher, fearful they would take it all.

She had only one pitcher left when she reached the table—but it was the one with the extra poison. She tried to hide her smile as she set it between Murdoc and Angus.

Another man shoved her aside and grabbed the last pitcher. Fury burned in her chest as she watched ale drip off his chin while he gulped the ale straight from the pitcher.

"Take my ale, will ye?" Angus punched the man in the belly and jerked the pitcher from his hands.

Hope rose in her heart as Angus lifted the pitcher to his mouth—and sank again when nothing came out of the pitcher. Angus threw it against the hearth and commenced to beat the man who took it about the head.

"Get more," Murdoc said and slapped her behind hard enough to sting through the layers of her gown. "And tell that worthless cook I'll take my dirk to him if he doesn't get food up here now."

She had made a grave error. What she should have done was saved all the poison for Murdoc and killed him. Without him, the other men would run around confused, like a chicken with its ugly head cut off.

Murdoc turned and caught her glaring at him. "What are ye doing looking at me?" he said and slammed his fist on the table. "Go!"

Sìleas stood against the wall with Dina, watching the men eat and waiting for them to show some sign of illness. Her time was running out.

She chewed her lip. "Why isn't the poison working, Dina?"

"I don't know. Maybe it's too soon."

Sìleas jumped when Murdoc stood and banged his cup on the table. When he had the men's attention, he shouted, "'Tis time for a wedding!"

He scanned the room until he found Sìleas and then motioned her to come forward. When she did not move, he nodded to two burly men.

"I've heard Angus can't perform unless a woman is screaming and crying," Dina said, squeezing her hand. "So lie still."

Sìleas looked frantically for a means of escape as the

two men came toward her. Despite Dina's warning, she screamed as they dragged her across the hall to stand before Murdoc and Angus.

"You'll say your vows now," Murdoc said.

"I won't," Sìleas said, meeting his eyes. "If ye couldn't make me do it at thirteen, ye must know ye cannot now."

"Perhaps ye will be more willing after the bedding." Murdoc shrugged. "But if not, all we truly need is a MacKinnon child by ye."

"My husband Ian will kill ye if ye let a man touch me," she said. "And the MacDonalds won't rest while ye hold Knock Castle."

"Ye are so naïve it pains me," Murdoc said, shaking his head. "Hugh MacDonald and I made an agreement. I get you and Knock Castle in exchange for killing his nephew Connor."

A well of anger rose up from deep inside her. With it came words she did not know were there.

"In the name of my mother, I curse ye, Murdoc MacKinnon," she shouted, stretching out her arm and pointing at Murdoc. Then she turned slowly and swung her arm in a wide circle. "I curse every one of ye! Ye shall suffer for snatching me from my husband and for taking what belongs to me and my clan. Every one of ye shall suffer!"

The hall went quiet. Every man's eyes were upon her, and a few crossed themselves.

"Angus!" Murdoc's deep voice broke the silence, filling the hall and reverberating in her chest. "Take her upstairs."

Panic flooded through her when Angus picked her up with one arm and tossed her over his shoulder. With her head hanging down, blood pounded in her ears as she screamed and beat her fists on his back. The men's laughter faded as he climbed the enclosed spiral staircase that led to the family's private rooms above.

When Angus carried her into the bedchamber that had been her mother's, true hysteria took her. It blinded her to everything but the image in her mind of her mother lying on the bed with blood soaking her shift and the sheets beneath her. Sìleas saw the tiny droplets that fell from the bed to the floor as her mother died.

Sìleas clawed and screeched like a wild animal. When she sank her teeth into Angus's hand, he let go long enough for her to scramble off the bed and sprint for the door.

She ran headlong into Murdoc in the doorway. He held her fast.

"No, not here," she pleaded, flailing her arms and legs. "Please, not here, not where she died."

Murdoc did not heed her pleading any more than he had her mother's.

How many times had she stood on the other side of the door and heard her mother weeping? Her mother had suffered the attentions of two husbands who wanted an heir to this castle and did not care if they killed her in the process.

For years, Sìleas had pushed the memories of her mother's suffering to the far recesses of her mind. Her mother had seemed so unlike her—beautiful, frail, compliant. In truth, Sìleas had blamed her mother for the choices that had led to their misery. Now she realized her mother must have felt as trapped as she did now.

As Murdoc dragged her back to the bed, she saw her mother's strawberry blond hair fanned out on the pillow, its beauty a stark contrast to the dark blood on the sheets. The smell of blood and the sweat of illness filled her nose. She saw the deathly pale skin and limp arms of a woman too weak to weep anymore.

When Murdoc dropped her on her back on the bed, Sìleas felt her body sink into the mattress, heavy with the weight of her grief. She saw her mother as she had the very last time, with her eyes open but unseeing, and one thin arm stretched out across the bed, as if she were still hoping someone would take her hand and rescue her from the nightmare that was her life.

In the end, it was God who had mercy and took her to join her dead babes.

Sìleas lay unblinking, her gaze fixed on the beams of the ceiling. She felt immune to the men now, drenched in grief for her mother, grief that she had denied until now.

CHAPTER 37

The darkening sky increased Ian's sense of urgency as he scanned the top of the walls of Knock Castle.

"Only two men on the wall," his father said beside him.

Ian nodded. "Are ye ready, Father Brian?"

"Aye."

Ian climbed into the handcart and crouched down next to the barrel of wine. God's bones, what was he doing?

"We should have used the horse cart, so da and I could go in with ye," Niall complained, not for the first time.

"The guards would be more suspicious of a large cart," Ian said. "I'll open the gate for ye to join us as soon as I can."

The truth was that Ian did not know if there were two men or forty waiting on the other side of the gate, and there was no point in all of them being killed.

"God be with ye," Father Brian said, and flung the tarp over Ian as if he were spreading a cloth over an altar. Then he tucked it around Ian and made sure it didn't cover the wine barrel.

Their trick was as old as the ancient Greeks. It seemed unlikely, however, that Murdoc or Angus had studied the classics.

Father Brian grunted as he picked up the handles and pushed the cart forward. 'Twas a good thing the priest was a strong man, for it was a hundred yards from the trees to the castle out on the headland.

With the wine barrel sloshing next to his head, Ian wondered if the Trojans had been as cramped in their wooden horse. He held on to the edges of the tarp to keep it in place as the cart bumped over the boards of the drawbridge. When Father Brian brought the cart to a jerking halt and dropped the handles to the ground, Ian had to brace his feet against the sides to keep from sliding out the back.

Through a hole he poked in the tarp with the point of his dirk, he watched the priest bang on the wooden gate. A voice responded from the other side, but Ian couldn't distinguish the words.

"I am making my rounds of Skye, as I do every year," Father Brian said in his deep, rumbling voice. He gestured toward the cart. "I've a barrel of wine from the monastery on Iona I was bringing to my bishop, but it's too far to carry. I'm willing to sell it to ye."

The gate creaked open. Ian gripped the hilt of his dirk as Father Brian picked up the cart handles and pushed it forward.

"Since we're celebrating a wedding, I'm sure ye will be wanting to make a gift of that wine," a guard said.

The blood in Ian's veins turned to ice at the mention of a wedding, and he prayed he was not too late to save Sìleas from rape.

"There will be no taking the wine until I have payment

in my hand for the good monks' work," Father Brian said, as he brought the cart to a halt inside the bailey yard.

As Ian had predicted, the guards were not inclined to wait. When the first one lifted the tarp, Ian stuck his dirk under the man's raised arm and killed him before he could utter a sound. There were only five other guards around the cart. As he sprang to his feet, he drew his claymore and swung into one of them.

The others who had crowded around the cart, intent on relieving the priest of his wine, stepped back quickly. The ever-helpful Father Brian stuck his foot out, causing one of them to fall backward with a shout. When one of his companions turned to look, Ian's sword whooshed through the air, nearly severing the man's head from his body.

By now, the other guards had their swords out and ready. There were only two of them standing, though. Ian moved toward the pair swinging, anxious to finish the job.

From the corner of his eye, he saw the man Father Brian had tripped get up and charge the priest with his blade drawn. A moment later, the guard lay at Father Brian's feet, and the priest was wiping blood from his attacker's blade on his robe.

Ian swung in a full circle, and one of his opponents shrieked as Ian's blade struck the man's side. Damn, they were making too much noise. The last guard charged, believing Ian would not be quick enough to recover from his last swing.

It was the last mistake the man would ever make.

Ian scanned the walls. When he didn't see anyone, he assumed the two who had been on the wall earlier had come down for the wine and were among the dead. He ran to the gate and waved to signal his father and brother.

"Ye weren't always a priest, were ye, Father?" Ian said, as the two of them dragged the bodies of the dead men into an empty storeroom built against the wall.

"I thought I'd put my fighting days behind me," the priest said. After they had moved the last man, he crossed himself and wiped his hands on his robe. "There should have been more guards here. Where do ye suppose all the other men are?"

"Inside the keep."

Celebrating a wedding.

Angus's massive frame appeared at the edge of Sìleas's vision. As if from a great distance, she saw him drop his plaid and lift his shirt. She shivered, her body sensing the danger, as she struggled to push aside the images of her mother and the weight of the grief that pinned her to the bed.

But when Angus's beefy hands gripped her thighs, she came back to herself with a jerk. She could not bear to have this vile man touch her. Before she could gather herself to fight him, Angus looked over his shoulder.

"What?" Angus said. "Are ye going to stay and watch me?"

"I want to be sure it's done. Capturing her does us no good unless she bears a child."

She could not see beyond the mammoth man standing between her legs at the edge of the bed, but it was Murdoc's voice she heard.

"I can't do it when she's staring at me like the dead," Angus complained.

"We both know what ye need to take a woman," Murdoc said. "So do it."

At Murdoc's words, Dina's advice came back to her: *Lie still.* As Angus turned back to her with his arm cocked to strike her, she steeled herself to take the blow.

But then, Angus froze in place, his eyes fixed on something above her. As an eerie keening filled the bedchamber, Sìleas looked up to see the translucent form of the Green Lady floating above her. She was weeping, making a pitiful sound.

Angus staggered back from the bed. "The wretch has called up a ghost with her curse!"

Angus held his arms in front of his face as the Green Lady's wailing grew louder. The sadness in the ghost's voice was enough to make the angels weep.

"She's coming for me!" Angus stumbled over his own feet as he turned and fled from the room.

Sìleas sat up and met her stepfather's eyes. The Green Lady's intervention had given her time to get her courage—and her anger—back.

"It is you who makes her weep," she said. "You have always made her weep."

Murdoc crossed the room in three long strides and shoved her down on the bed.

"Her weeping never stopped me before," he said. "And it will not now."

Sìleas stared up at him, terror gripping her heart. "I am your wife's daughter. Not even you would commit such a grave sin."

Murdoc held her shoulders fast and leaned over her until she felt the heat from his body.

"I will tell ye the same as I told your mother," he hissed in her face. "I need a child of my blood."

The Green Lady's weeping had grown soft, as if she knew it would do no good against Murdoc.

"After being such an ugly child, ye have become a pretty thing," Murdoc said, leaning back to fix his hard black eyes on her breasts. "If Angus can't do the job, I'm sure I'll have no trouble."

CHAPTER 38

"We'll see if the wine works a second time," Ian told the others. "Father Brian, are ye willing to take the barrel into the hall to distract them?"

The priest nodded.

"Once all the men inside gather around Father Brian, we'll go in as quietly as we can," he said to his father and Niall. "If Sìleas is in the hall, we'll take her and be gone before most of them notice we're there."

Or so he hoped.

"If she's not in the hall..." Ian swallowed at the thought of what that would mean. "Then Niall and da will guard the stairs while I go up and fetch her."

It was a poor plan, but he could think of none better.

Father Brian said a quick prayer for them, and they all made the sign of the cross. As Ian and the priest carried the cart up the steps of the keep, he turned to watch his father crossing the bailey yard. Seeing how slowly his father moved, he feared he was leading all the men of his family to their deaths.

"God is on our side." The priest patted Ian's arm as he spoke, then opened the door and wheeled his cart inside, calling, "Good evening to ye, MacKinnons!"

Ian waited a few moments, every muscle taut, before he eased the door open and slipped inside. No guard was posted at the door—or if there was one, he had left his post to join the throng of men gathered around Father Brian and his barrel. When Niall poked his head inside, Ian waved him forward and moved along the wall into the shadows.

He scanned the dimly lit hall, searching for Sìleas. There were fifty MacKinnon men in the hall, to his four, but there were almost no women—and Sìleas was not among them. His stomach tightened when he realized that Angus and Murdoc were also missing from the hall.

His eyes went back to one of the women. What was Dina doing here? Her gaze was fixed on him. His muscles tensed as he waited for her to give them away.

After glancing about her, Dina removed the torch from the wall bracket beside her and dropped the torch onto the rushes on the floor. Then she met Ian's eyes again and nodded toward the stairs.

She was telling him they had Sìleas upstairs.

As he ran through the arched doorway to the stairs, the rushes were already beginning to flame. The spiral of the stone staircase was built clockwise to give the advantage to the defender, who could swing his sword arm freely, while a right-handed attacker going up had his sword arm cramped against the middle of the spiral. The advantage was lost, however, when the attacker had taught himself to swing equally either way. As Ian sprinted up the stairs, he shifted his sword to his left hand.

Other footsteps echoed above him. An instant later, a huge man barreled into him, sending them both tumbling down the stairs. When Ian saw that the man on top of him was Angus MacKinnon, rage nearly blinded him.

"What have ye done to her?" he shouted, as he plunged his dirk into Angus's gut.

Angus was strong, but he fought with wild, panicked punches, as if he were mad. In no time, Ian was sitting on Angus's chest with his dirk at the man's throat.

"I asked what ye have done with my wife." Ian pressed his blade against Angus's throat until he drew blood.

"I saw her ghost!" Angus cried out. "It was hovering over me."

Ian's heart stopped in his chest. He had feared they would rape Sìleas, but he'd never thought they would murder her.

He heard an eerie, unnatural sound, and a coldness passed over him. God, no. Don't let her be dead! Ian slashed his blade across Angus's throat and ran up the stairs.

When he reached the next floor, the open door from the stairs led into a large bedchamber. Through it, he saw a man leaning over the bed, a woman's bare knee, and a bit of bright blue fabric hanging over the side of the bed. The blue was the same shade as the gown Sìleas was wearing when last he saw her.

White hot rage pounded through him. With a roar, he burst into the bedchamber swinging his claymore.

CHAPTER 39

Murdoc clamped his hand over Sìleas's mouth as she fought to get out from under him. She could not hear the Green Lady's weeping over his harsh breathing.

Even the castle's ghost had deserted her.

"Your mother was a weak vessel," Murdoc said. "Poking her was dull work. But a lively lass like you will surely give me a strong son."

Murdoc suddenly released her as a murderous war cry rolled through the room like a thunderclap. Relief washed over her.

Ian had come for her.

Murdoc spun and drew his sword with lightning quickness. Although he blocked Ian's thrust from reaching his heart, blood seeped down his arm, soaking the sleeve of his shirt. The clank of swords filled the room as the two men moved back and forth.

Sìleas hugged her knees to her chest as she watched and prayed.

Ian looked glorious, with his dark hair flying, and his

blue eyes as piercing as a hawk dropping from the sky for a kill. The muscles of his body clenched and released as he swung the heavy two-handed sword in deadly, rhythmic arcs.

Behind the controlled violence, she felt Ian's pulsing rage. Time and again, he attacked, his blade slicing through the air with lethal force. Another slash and blood ran from the top of Murdoc's thigh, near his groin. Another, and his shoulder bled. Yet Murdoc fought his way back each time. He was a strong man and an experienced warrior, and he was fighting for his life. The men grunted with the effort of their swings.

Blood sprayed the bed as the fight moved closer. When Murdoc fell backward against the bed, she scrambled to get out of his way. But Murdoc's arm shot out, and she shrieked as he caught her ankle in an iron grip.

"Arrgh!" Murdoc screamed as Ian's sword went through his belly, pinning him to the bed. In quick successive moves, Ian grabbed Murdoc by the hair, drew his dirk across Murdoc's throat, and pulled his sword from Murdoc's gut with a great sucking sound.

Ian stepped over Murdoc's body and lifted Sìleas off the bed into his arms. She held onto him with all her strength.

"Hush, hush. I'm here now." He soothed her with soft murmurs as he rubbed her back and kissed her hair. "I'll keep ye safe."

"Ian! We must go."

At the sound of a man's deep voice, she turned and saw Father Brian in the doorway. Smoke was billowing out of the stairwell behind him.

"Hurry," the priest shouted. "The castle is burning."

Ian lifted her in his arms. As he carried her out, she looked over his shoulder at the bedchamber that had been the place of so much of her mother's suffering. Smoke was filling the room so rapidly she could barely make out Murdoc's body on the floor. The last thing she saw gliding through swells of gray was the flash of a pale green gown.

The smoke was so thick in the stairwell that she could not see Father Brian ahead of them, but she heard him coughing. Her eyes watered and her throat burned. When they reached the bottom, Niall and Payton were waiting for them just inside the hall.

The two were surrounded by the bodies of dead men.

As soon as Ian set her on her feet, the four of them ran along the wall toward the front door of the keep. The smoke was not as thick in the hall, because the fire was hot here. Everything that could burn—rushes, tables, overturned benches—was ablaze. As she watched, flames shot up from the high table and ignited the wooden ceiling.

She prayed that Dina had escaped, for there was no one else in the hall but the dead.

"I'll go first. They may have men just outside, ready to cut us down as we come out," Ian warned before he opened the door.

That was what he would have done, but when he stepped outside, it appeared that the MacKinnons had abandoned the castle altogether. The bailey yard was empty save for Dina, a goat, and a few squawking chickens.

"Ye should have seen Niall," his father said, as he came down the steps of the keep one at a time. He was covered in blood and leaning on Niall for support, but he was grinning as if he'd never been happier. "We stood together, with him covering my weak side, and cut down every MacKinnon who dared come near the stairs."

Ian tightened his arm around Sìleas. He couldn't join in their good humor over their success. The vision of his wife held down on a bed with a man standing between her legs was still with him—and would likely haunt his dreams for a long, long time to come.

"Father Brian was a sight to behold," Niall said, laughing. "He didn't want to use a sword or dirk, so he went 'round hitting MacKinnons on the head with a silver candlestick holder."

"There was little fight left in them by then," Father Brian said. "Between retching and the fire, they fled like rabbits."

"Dina and I poisoned their ale," Sìleas said in a quiet voice.

"Clever lasses," his father said, beaming at her.

While the others continued sharing stories, Ian pulled Sìleas against his chest and closed his eyes. *Praise be to God he had found her.*

His eyes flew open at the sound of boots on the wooden planks of the drawbridge. He pushed Sìleas behind him and drew his claymore just before a dozen men poured through the gate.

"It's Gòrdan," Sìleas said.

Ian relaxed his stance when he saw that it was, indeed, Gòrdan, and he was leading a group of MacDonald men.

"We've taken Knock Castle!" his father greeted them, raising his sword to the sky.

The men took in the smoldering keep and the bailey yard empty of MacKinnons and lowered their weapons. To a man, they looked disappointed.

"I could only gather a dozen men quickly," Gòrdan said, as he approached them.

"I'm grateful to ye for coming," Ian said and saw the pain in Gòrdan's eyes when they flicked to Sìleas.

Gòrdan turned away and fixed his gaze on the smoke billowing out of the open doors of the keep. "I thought ye would need help, but I can see ye didn't."

"I do need your help," Ian said.

Gòrdan turned back. "Good. What would ye have me do?"

"It's near dark, so we'll have to stay here overnight," Ian said. "But in the morning, I must see my family home and get Connor to the gathering. Can ye hold the castle for me for a time?"

"Aye. The guardhouse hasn't been touched by the fire, so we can sleep there," Gòrdan said. "I'll send one man to the gathering tomorrow night to speak for all the men here." His gaze roved over the smoldering keep again. "With so much stone, the keep won't burn long. We'll save what we can, but I suspect there won't be much."

Ian thought of all the bad memories Sìleas had of this castle, which was to be their home. He didn't want to keep a single stick of furniture, sheet, or floorboard.

"Let the men have anything they can salvage," he said. "Sìleas and I will start anew."

From the way Sìleas squeezed his hand, he knew he had made the right decision.

"Are ye all right, lass?" his father asked her.

While Sìleas talked with his father and Niall, Ian drew Gòrdan away for a private word.

"There's another favor I'd ask of ye," he said in a low voice.

Gòrdan looked at the ground and kicked at the dirt with the toe of his boot. "Ye know I owe ye after what my mother did."

"Can ye take care of Dina after we leave in the morning?" When Gòrdan's head snapped up, Ian added, "Just until I can find someone else to take her in."

"Is she your mistress?" Gòrdan hissed, his nostrils flaring. "I said I owe ye, but I'll no help ye deceive Sìleas."

"Ye misunderstand me," Ian said, putting a hand up. "There will never be another woman for me but Sìleas."

Gòrdan's lips were pressed into a hard line, but he was listening.

"I doubt we would have all gotten out alive without Dina's help," Ian said. "I don't like leaving her unprotected. Will ye watch over her and see that's she's safe?"

Gòrdan looked over at Dina, who was standing alone, hugging herself against the fine mist that had begun to fall.

"She's made mistakes," Ian said. "But we all deserve a chance to redeem ourselves."

"Aye, we do," Gòrdan said with a tight nod. "I'll see her safe."

CHAPTER 40

It was damp and cold in the gatehouse, but they didn't go hungry that night. Gòrdan had brought dried fish, oatcakes, and cheese, and Father Brian—bless him—had the presence of mind to wheel the wine barrel out of the keep when he was escaping the fire.

After their cold supper, Father Brian led them in prayer. They bowed their heads to pray for the lives of Connor, Alex, and Duncan, and for the survival of their clan.

While the others dropped off to sleep or spoke in low voices, Ian huddled against the wall with Sìleas, where he could watch the door. He couldn't be certain the MacKinnons would not return. Although he'd barred the gate and left a few men out on the wall in the rain to keep watch, he wouldn't rest easy tonight. He didn't have enough men to hold the castle against a full attack.

He wrapped his plaid tighter around Sìleas and kissed her hair as she rested against his chest. Every time he thought of how close he had come to losing her, he felt as if a great fist squeezed his heart.

"There is something I need to tell ye," Sìleas said in a low voice.

Blood pounded in Ian's ears as he braced himself to hear what he knew would be past bearing. But he must bear it and be strong for her.

"Was it Angus or Murdoc?" he asked in a choked voice. For as long as he lived, he would never forgive himself for being too late to save her from being taken in violence.

Sìleas touched her fingers to his face. "No. That didn't happen."

Would she lie to spare him? He didn't want to press her now. When he had her safe, with hours before them to talk, he would find out all that had happened in the castle.

"I speak the truth," she said. "I wasn't certain ye would find me before one of them raped me, but ye did."

Relief flooded through him. Men had their hands on her and frightened her, but at least she had not suffered the worst violation.

"I never doubted ye would rescue me in the end," she said. "Ye always have."

Her faith in him overwhelmed him. Ian lifted her hand and kissed her fingers.

"And tomorrow, ye will make certain Hugh Dubh does not become our chieftain," she said in a determined voice. "Ye will do it for the clan, for Connor, and for all the others. And ye will do it for me."

"I'll do my best."

"What I wanted to tell ye is that Murdoc admitted he had an agreement with Hugh," Sìleas said. "Hugh let him have Knock Castle—and me—in exchange for murdering Connor."

"I knew it," Ian said, pounding his fist on the dirt floor. "I promise ye, I will not let Hugh become chieftain."

He'd murder Hugh before he let that happen.

She let her head drop against his chest again. "I want to stay awake just to feel your arms around me," she said in a soft voice. "But I'm so tired, I can't keep my eyes open."

"Shhh. Sleep, *mo chroí*," he murmured, as she fell asleep in his arms.

Ian roused the men at first light. He was anxious to get his wife to a safer place and to see how Connor and the others fared. And there was no time to spare. The dark days of November were almost upon them; the celebration of Samhain would begin at sunset.

"Ian," Niall called from the gate. "Come see this."

Ian heard the urgency in his brother's voice and ran to join him on the drawbridge.

"There," Niall said, pointing out to sea, where three war galleys were sailing toward shore.

Damn, damn, damn. Ian squinted through the rain, trying to see who they were. God's blood, the man standing in the prow of the front ship was none other than his former jailor, Shaggy Lachlan Cattanach Maclean.

Why would Shaggy be coming here? With three galleys loaded with clansmen, it did not appear to be a friendly visit.

"Christ above," Ian said, "I don't have time to deal with a pack of murdering Macleans this morning."

Ian turned as Father Brian joined them on the drawbridge.

"I'm sure ye meant to call on the Lord's help, rather than take His name in vain," the priest said. "Because we'll be needing divine intervention, that's for certain."

Indeed they would, for the Macleans were landing.

"Quick, I need every man up on the wall!" Ian shouted, as he ran inside. "Each of ye take a dead man's shield with ye. The Macleans are coming, and we must make them believe there are more of us than there are."

He didn't object when Sìleas and Dina followed Gòrdan up a ladder carrying shields. If Shaggy's men did break through, they would be safer up on the wall.

"I'm going down there," Ian called out to the others.

The rain and extra shields would only fool Shaggy from a distance, which meant he needed to keep Shaggy on the beach.

Shaggy was the sort who could smell weakness, so Ian made a point of walking as if he had all the time in the world as he made his way down to where Shaggy and his men had landed their boats.

"A bit far from home, aren't ye, Shaggy?" he said when he reached them.

He was glad to see that the younger man beside Shaggy was Hector, Shaggy's eldest son. Hector had a reputation for being both more sensible and more trustworthy than his father.

"What kind of fool faces three war galleys full of men alone?" Shaggy said, glaring at him from under his black eyebrows. "But then, I heard that the Douglas says ye are fearless to the point of foolishness."

Sometimes news traveled faster than men in the Highlands.

Ian shrugged. "I'm just curious about why ye are sailing these waters."

"I'm searching for that sweet little galley ye stole from me," Shaggy said. "I didn't see it when I sailed by your house, so I'm still looking."

Ian had the answer to one question. It must have been the sight of Shaggy's three war galleys off shore that had sent the MacKinnons running after they attacked Connor and the others. He didn't believe, however, that Shaggy had come just for his missing boat.

"I can't offer ye the kind of hospitality I'd like to," Ian said. "We had to burn the keep in the process of taking the castle, so the dungeon is in verra poor shape."

Shaggy started toward him, but his son grabbed his arm.

"I've a proposition for ye," Ian said. "And if ye aren't as mad as they say, you'll take it."

Hector held his father back a second time. "Let's hear it first, da."

"You've backed the wrong man in helping Hugh take the chieftainship from Connor. We escaped your dungeon, and now we've taken Knock Castle." Ian paused to let Shaggy consider this, before he said, "I suggest ye change sides while ye still can."

Shaggy growled, which Ian took as sufficient encouragement to continue.

"Hugh sat by while the MacKinnons took Knock Castle, which is why you were thinking you could come and take it yourself," Ian said. "If we have a chieftain who will not protect our lands, then the MacKinnons and the MacLeods will overrun us—and that will be the end of the MacDonalds on Skye."

Ian paused for a long moment. "Have ye thought about what the MacKinnons and their more powerful brothers, the MacLeods, would do if they had all of Skye?"

"What do I care what the damned MacLeods do?" Shaggy said.

Ian spread his hands. "If they don't have to worry about the MacDonalds on their doorstep, they'll be looking south to your lands on the Isle of Mull."

From the sideways glance Hector gave his father, Ian suspected Hector had given Shaggy precisely the same warning. Any man with sense knew maintaining a balance was important, with friends as well as enemies. In the Highlands, one often became the other.

"But that won't happen, because Connor will be chieftain." Ian folded his arms as if he hadn't a care in the world. "Connor is not a man ye want as your enemy. So if ye have any notion of attempting to take Knock Castle, you'd best reconsider."

Shaggy exchanged glances with his son.

"Hugh says he'll join the rebellion against the Crown," Shaggy said. "Would Connor?"

"Ye can't believe a word Hugh tells ye." Ian shrugged. "I can't speak for Connor, but he'll do whatever is best for our clan."

Shaggy fixed his eyes on Ian as he scratched his face through his beard. Despite the rain and cold wind blowing off the sea, sweat trickled down Ian's back. Time was growing short. He was anxious to have the Macleans gone so he could be on his way to get Connor.

All the same, he tilted his head back as if he were considering the weather until, at last, Shaggy spoke.

"Connor hasn't taken a wife yet, has he?"

Ian was so surprised by the question that he nearly laughed. Still, it wasn't hard to guess why Shaggy asked it. With the number of wives Shaggy had wed and then put aside over the years, he probably had an abundance of daughters to marry off.

"Connor isn't married...yet," Ian said, rocking back on his heels, and wishing the man would take his damned boats and leave.

"If Connor were to wed one of my daughters—assuming he does become your chieftain," Shaggy said, "I could be persuaded to let him keep that galley as a wedding present."

"That galley is a fine, fast boat," Ian said. "I'll speak to Connor about your daughters."

"Tell him he can use the galley when he comes to fetch one of them." Shaggy's crooked teeth showed in the midst of his bushy beard, in what Ian took for a smile.

"When Connor comes for the wedding," Shaggy called back as he headed to his boat, "we'll discuss his position on the rebellion."

Poor Connor. He would have his hands full when he became chieftain.

If he still lived.

As soon as Ian was back inside the gate, he got his horse.

"I may not make it to Dunscaith Castle before the gathering begins," he said to his father, as he mounted. "Can ye delay the ceremony to choose the chieftain until I can get there with Connor?"

"The *seannachie* will tell stories of the clan from ancient times to the present," his father said. "When he comes to Connor's da, I'll add my own tales to honor my old friend, and I'll encourage the other older men to do so as well. It will be awkward for Hugh to cut us off. All the same, ye'd best have the wind at your back."

"I'm going with ye," Sìleas said, reaching her hand up to him.

"Good. I want ye with me." He helped her up onto his horse.

Last time, he had left her, thinking that would keep her safe. He wouldn't risk being parted from her again. Whatever happened today, they would face it together.

As soon as Shaggy's boats rounded the bay and were out of sight, Ian and Sìleas galloped over the drawbridge. The sun was a lighter circle of gray in the heavy clouds ahead. It was raining between here and Dunscaith Castle, which meant there was a reasonable chance Hugh would not see the smoke from Knock Castle and learn that his plans had gone afoul.

Ian was counting on it. To have any hope of success, he needed surprise on his side.

CHAPTER 41

"Ye look as poor an excuse for a man as I've ever seen," Ian said, leaning over the bed to squeeze Connor's good shoulder. "But ye never looked better to me."

Connor was weak and battered, but he was alert.

"He's no fit to go anywhere yet," Ilysa said, her brows pinched together. "And poor Duncan is as weak as a kitten."

Despite the direness of their situation, he and the other men exchanged amused glances. Even badly injured, no one but Duncan's sister would compare him to a kitten.

"And Alex's leg wound frets me something fierce," Ilysa said, pointing an accusing finger at the offending patient.

"Ach, we'll all be fine," Duncan said, though he was so pale that the freckles stood out on his face.

"Do ye think ye can travel?" Ian asked Connor. "The gathering is starting."

Wee thing that she was, Ilysa stood between him and Connor and put her hands on her hips. "Ye can't mean to get him out of this bed, Ian MacDonald."

"I can make it to the gathering," Connor said between his teeth, as he tried to sit up.

Duncan caught his sister's arm as Ian went to help Connor. "Connor has to go," Duncan said. "We all do."

The effort to sit up had cost Connor; he was breathing hard and sweat beaded on his brow.

"We must go, but the question is how," Alex said from his stool across the tiny room. "I hate to admit it, lads, but we won't strike fear in the hearts of our enemies in our present condition."

Ian looked them over. Duncan and Alex had two good legs between them and one good sword arm, and it was doubtful Connor could stand at all.

"Alex is right. If Hugh sees ye coming looking like this, he'll finish ye off before we make it into the castle," Ian said. "We need to get the three of ye inside without anyone seeing ye.

"We have two things in our favor," he continued. "First, Hugh isn't expecting ye because he thinks you're dead."

"And the second," Sìleas said, "is that it's the eve of Samhain, so we can dress ye in disguises."

Half the clan would be wearing costumes—whether to imitate the dead or ward them off, Ian was never sure.

"We can paint our faces black," Duncan suggested. "A lot of the young men do that."

"If I arrive with three men of your size and hair color—especially yours, Duncan—I fear blackened faces won't be enough to prevent someone from guessing who ye are."

Teàrlag, who had been bent over something boiling in the iron pot over her fire, turned and spoke for the first time. "Ilysa, I haven't yet given away the clothes of the last person we helped lay out. They should do, aye?"

"My braw brother won't like it," Ilysa said, a slow smile spreading over her face. "But I believe we'll get ye into the castle without anyone recognizing ye."

Ian steered Shaggy's fine little galley around the point. Luckily, there was a stiff breeze so he didn't have to row.

"Ye look fetching," Alex said, choking back a laugh as Duncan held his bonnet against the wind. "I fear it will be hard keeping the men at a distance."

Duncan was wearing the clothes of a well-known gossip who had died a few weeks earlier and who, fortunately, had been enormous. Duncan and Alex had drawn straws for the privilege.

"Any man that touches me will find himself on his arse," Duncan said with a sour look.

"I don't want to hurt your feelings, but I think ye will be safe from untoward advances," Ian said. "But just in case, I hope ye have a dirk hidden beneath your skirts."

"Hmmph." Duncan snorted and glared at the castle.

Alex put on one of the masks Teàrlag had fashioned from scrap cloth to cover Connor's and Alex's bruised faces. "I hate to hide my pretty face, when all the lasses of the clan will be at the gathering."

Connor was lying in the bottom of the boat, fast asleep. Even though Ian had carried him most of the way, the trip down to the boat from the cottage had sapped what little strength he had.

"Best get him up now," Ian said.

Duncan and Alex helped Connor sit up, and Sìleas put on his mask for him.

Ian didn't need to hide his own identity, since people would expect him to be at the gathering. All the same, he kept his cap low over his eyes as he guided the boat up to the castle's sea entrance. Earlier, there would have been a line of boats waiting, but the afternoon light was gone, and evening had settled in. The torches inside the sea gate shone on the boat ahead of them, the only other latecomer.

Ilysa had returned to the castle earlier by the road, since it might raise alarms if she was missing when it was time to set out the food for the gathering.

The water sloshed between the boat and the sea steps as one of the guards grabbed the coiled rope from the front of their boat and tied it to an iron peg. This was the most dangerous moment. Ian was prepared to reach for his claymore and cut the guards down if he had to.

The other guard was a small wiry fellow, who gamely offered his hand to Duncan. "Big lass, aren't ye now?"

Duncan looked as if he was going to squeeze the life out of the guard rather than take his hand. Ach, this was going to be trouble. Ian tensed as the guard turned his head, letting his gaze rove over each of them in turn. When his eyes met Ian's, his face broke into a wide grin that showed several missing teeth.

"It's me, Tait," the man said in a low voice. "Ilysa sent me down to help at the sea gate."

In the light from the torches behind the guard, Ian could just make out the features of Tait, the man who hated Hugh for violating his sister.

"I can handle this last boat and lock the sea gate," Tait called to the other guard. "Ye don't want to miss the bonfire, now do ye?"

This time when Tait offered his hand, Duncan took

it. The boat dipped as Duncan stepped on the side of the boat then rose again when he stepped off.

"Glad to see ye here, lads," Tait said as soon as the other guard disappeared up the stairs. "That damned Hugh Dubh has been parading around the castle all day like a damned rooster."

Tait climbed into the boat to help him with Connor. As they half-carried Connor between them, Ian looked over his shoulder to see Sìleas helping Alex.

"By now, everyone will be outside in the yard for the bonfire," Tait said.

Ian looked up the long flight of steps, lit by torches that lined the walls on either side. Unfortunately, they would have to go up through the keep to get to the bailey yard. All that was on the dank sea level of the castle was the dungeon—a place Ian hoped they wouldn't see the inside of tonight.

Alex went first, managing well enough on his own. Duncan was next, dragging his leg, with Sìleas hovering beside him.

"I think I can go up myself," Connor said in a tight voice, but a groan escaped him as Ian and Tait helped him up the first step.

"Save your strength," Ian said. "You'll be needing it soon."

"Word is that Hugh has his men watching for ye, Ian," Tait said, as they inched their way up the steps behind the others.

It was taking an eternity to get the men up the damned stairs.

"He's heard that some of the men intend to put your name forward to be chieftain, now that they think Connor is dead—even though ye aren't of the chieftain's blood," Tait said.

"Why do ye suppose I went to such trouble to get Connor here tonight?" Ian joked.

Connor stopped where he was and turned. "Maybe ye should take it, Ian. I'm in no shape to lead the clan."

"No, ye will not be giving me the miserable task of leading this stubborn rabble," Ian said, pulling Connor up the next step. "You're the right man for it. The only one."

The Samhain bonfire raged in the middle of the castle's bailey yard, just as it had every year of Sìleas's life. It seemed odd, when so much else had changed.

No one gave them a second look as they merged into the shadows at the back of the circle gathered around the fire. Many in the crowd wore garish costumes or carried lanterns made of hollowed-out turnips with carved faces to ward off evil spirits.

A few women were throwing bones or roasting nuts to divine whom they would marry, for Samhain was a time for divination. Many a lass told her young man aye or nay following Samhain, depending on what the signs revealed this night.

The children were enjoying themselves as they usually did, but Sìleas sensed the tension behind the adults' revelry. Hugh had made it known he would call on every man to make a pledge of loyalty to him before the night was over.

"When we go inside for the ceremony, I want ye to find Ilysa and stand with her," Ian said to her in a low voice. "She'll know how to get ye out if things should turn violent."

"I will." She understood it would help him not to have to worry about her when the time came.

At the sound of pipes and drums, the crowd turned their attention to Hugh, who stood facing the crowd with the great fire behind him.

"Samhain is a time when we come together to celebrate the final harvest of the year and remember our dead," Hugh said, holding his arms out.

"I am grateful for the long stories that so many of you have shared in remembrance of my dear, departed brother," he said, emphasizing the *long* and the *many*, with a glance toward a group of older men that included Ian's father. "But Samhain is also when we mark the beginning of our New Year. And on this Samhain, we also celebrate the beginning of a new era for the MacDonalds of Sleat."

Sìleas tapped her foot. Hugh was in fine form tonight.

"I've laid a place at the head table for my dead brother and my nephew Ragnall, as is our tradition, so their spirits can join us for this special Samhain night."

Sìleas thought calling on the memory of their former chieftain was bold on Hugh's part, for most members of the clan knew Hugh had resented his brother from the day he was born. Still, blood ties were respected in the Highlands.

Hugh put his hand over his heart. "I know my brother would be pleased to see me take his place as chieftain."

Alex and Duncan both made choking noises. Hugh glared in their direction, but they were safe from discovery here in the shadows.

"It is time now for all of us to set aside our sorrow, hard as it may be," Hugh said, "and to swear fealty to your new chieftain."

"Does he think he can avoid taking a vote altogether?" she whispered to Ian.

"Aye, but the men don't like it."

From the low grumbling around them, it was clear Ian was right.

"We'll have our feast as soon as the oaths are taken," Hugh said. "To the hall!"

"Move about among the men and be ready," Ian said to Tait. Then he turned to Connor and the others. "Don't let anyone see ye until I signal."

"Grá mo chroí," Ian said to Sìleas, and squeezed her hand before disappearing into the crowd. Love of my heart.

Sìleas waited with the three men until most of the crowd was inside. The rumble of voices was loud in the hall as they moved inside and found a place to stand against the back wall.

She leaned forward to look at the three of them. They appeared to be an odd but unremarkable, drunken threesome—two men in Samhain masks and an enormous woman in a large bonnet—leaning against the wall and holding on to each other for support.

Connor lifted his mask and leaned over to speak in her ear. "Ye shouldn't be near us now, when things are coming to a head."

His voice sounded stronger than before, and he was staying upright. That much was good. She squeezed his arm and went to join Ilysa and Beitris, who were standing with the other women.

She had a good view of Hugh, who sat in the chieftain's chair on a raised platform at one end of the hall. She didn't know the rough-looking men who stood on either side of him, but assumed they were companions from his pirating days. They glared at the crowd, looking as if they were eager to force the oath from any man who didn't give it freely.

"Who wants the honor of being first?" Hugh called out.

The hall grew quiet as everyone waited to see who would be the first to come forward. There was an audible intake of breath from the crowd as Ian stepped into the space that had been left in front of Hugh and the guards flanking him.

"Well, ye have more sense than I gave ye credit for, Ian Aluinn," Hugh said, using the nickname the women had given Ian years ago in an attempt to ridicule him. "I thought my men would have to 'persuade' ye to do what ye must."

Instead of bending his knee to take his oath, Ian turned to face the crowd. There was fire in his eyes, and he stood with his legs apart as if he was ready to fight half a dozen men at once—which he probably was. Ach, her husband was breathtaking.

"It is our tradition to allow men to speak before the selection of a new chieftain," Ian said in a voice that reached every corner of the hall. "I intend to speak."

A loud murmur of agreement rose from the crowd.

Hugh drummed his fingers on the arm of his chair, as if he were itching to give the order to cut Ian down. But Hugh was no fool. It was clear from the reaction to Ian's statement that the clan expected him to follow the traditions, even if they believed the outcome was certain.

"Speak if ye must," Hugh said with an impatient wave of his hand. "But as I am the only man here of chieftain's blood, I see little point in it."

Ian turned to look over his shoulder at Hugh. "Can ye be so sure my uncle did not leave another son or two that ye don't know about?"

There were barks of male laughter around the room,

for everyone knew their chieftain, like his father before him, had bedded countless women over the years.

"But no, I've not disrupted the evening to tell ye about a new claimant to the chieftainship." Ian raised his fist in the air. "I've here to tell ye I've taken Knock Castle back from the MacKinnons!"

The hall erupted as men waved their claymores, and the crowd roared their approval. Hugh stood and raised his hands for quiet, but it was some time before he could be heard.

After the cheering died down, Hugh said, "Just saying ye took the castle doesn't make it so."

Sìleas was startled to see Gòrdan emerge from the crowd to stand beside Ian at the front. His clothes were streaked with soot, and he looked as if he had ridden hard to get here.

"Most of ye know I've had my differences with Ian," Gòrdan said. "So ye can trust my word when I say he did take Knock Castle yesterday."

A few men shouted, but Gòrdan put his hand up to signal he wasn't finished. "Shaggy Maclean is plying the waters nearby, so I hope some of ye will join me at Knock Castle in the morning. We don't want to lose it to the Macleans after we've just taken it back from the MacKinnons."

The hall again was filled with whoops and swords raised high. His speech done, Gòrdan gave a stiff nod and moved back into the crowd.

"This is a proud day, indeed, for the MacDonalds of Sleat." Hugh spoke as if he were responsible for the victory, though everyone knew he had stood by while the MacKinnons held Knock Castle.

All eyes, however, were on Ian, who had won the crowd's

goodwill. He walked the few feet to the high table, where the two places had been set for the dead.

"Before we choose a new chieftain," Ian said, in a slow deliberate voice, "we must settle the matter of the death of our last chieftain—and of his son, Ragnall."

A chill went through the room at his mention of the dead, for the veil was thin between the dead and the living on Samhain. Sìleas could almost see the chieftain and Ragnall—big, muscular, fair-haired men with grim faces—standing on either side of Ian.

"Those of us who were at Flodden know what happened," Hugh said, his hard, gray eyes sweeping the crowd. "While Ian here was drinking fine wines and dallying with the ladies in France, we were being slaughtered by the English!"

Ian waited for the murmur that followed to grow quiet. Then, in a voice choked with rage, he said, "Our chieftain and his son were not slaughtered by the English."

The blood drained from Hugh's face, and he stared at Ian openmouthed, before he caught himself and snapped his mouth shut. The crowd was stunned into silence.

Ian stretched out his arm, pointing at Hugh, and shouted in a voice that reverberated through the hall. "I accuse you, Hugh Dubh MacDonald, of murdering our chieftain and his son at Flodden!"

The crowd was in an uproar.

Hugh tried to speak several times before he could be heard. "I fought at Flodden," he said, clenching his fists and fixing murderous eyes on Ian. "How dare ye accuse me of the vilest crime, when I sank in Scots' blood to my ankles, fighting, while you deserted the clan in our hour of need."

Hugh turned and shouted to his guard, "Seize him!"

Sìleas gasped and started forward, but Beitris and Ilysa held her.

Then Tait's voice came from the other side of the hall. "Let's hear what Ian has to say!"

Several others followed, shouting, "Aye! Let him speak! Let him speak!"

Hugh put his hand up as if to stop his guards, though they had been slow to follow his order.

"'Tis easy to make accusations," Hugh said to Ian, "with nothing to back them up."

"But I do have proof." Ian paused, giving everyone time to take in his words, before he said, "I ask my father, Payton MacDonald, to come forward."

Sìleas squeezed Beitris's and Ilysa's hands as Payton made his way to the front of the room. Despite his limp and his graying hair, he was still a formidable man with powerful shoulders and battle scars on his face and hands. Her heart burst with pride to see father and son, fine and honorable men, standing together before their clan.

"Da," Ian said, "can ye tell us which of our clansman fought near ye in the battle."

"I fought on our chieftain's left and Ragnall fought on his right, just as we always did," his father said. "We were in the front—again, same as always."

There was a rumble of agreement among the men, for they knew the three always fought like that.

"And who was behind ye?" Ian asked.

"This time, it was Hugh Dubh and a few of his men."

Payton's answer caused a murmuring in the crowd, though Hugh's being behind the men who were killed proved nothing in itself.

"Can ye tell us how the chieftain and Ragnall were killed?"

Payton shook his head. "I didn't see who struck the blows, but they came from behind us. I've puzzled on that ever since."

The hall was so quiet that Sìleas could hear her own breathing.

"The English came at us hard, and we were fighting for our lives," Payton said. "All the same, I don't know how English soldiers could have gotten behind us without us knowing it."

Ian shrugged his shoulders. "In the heat of battle, ye can't always see."

"But the three of us were used to fighting together. We watched each other's backs. I can understand one of us not seeing an English soldier slip behind us—but none of us?" Payton shook his head. "No, that doesn't seem possible."

Several men grunted in agreement, for the three men had been known as remarkable fighters who had survived many a battle when others had not.

"The three of us were struck at almost the same moment," Payton said. "I saw our chieftain fall forward at the same time that I heard Ragnall cry out. Before I could reach either of them, I took a blow to the back of my head."

"In the back, from behind," Ian repeated. "Do ye know who struck ye, da?"

Payton shook his head. "I woke up a fortnight later in bed with no leg."

"This is proof?" Hugh interrupted, lifting his arms. "'Tis a shame that my brother and Ragnall were lost at Flodden, but you're wasting our time dwelling on the past."

Ian pointed to three older men in the front. "Would ye

say ye have fought against the English and other High-landers often enough to know the difference in their weapons?"

"Don't be a damned fool," one of them said. "Of course we can."

"Then can ye tell us what weapon made the scar on the back of my da's head?"

Payton took off his cap and turned around. His head had been shaved around a five-inch wound.

"Lucky he caught ye with just the tip of his sword, or you'd be a dead man," one of them said. "Your moving to reach the chieftain and Ragnall as the blow fell is probably what saved ye."

"Can ye tell what kind of sword it was?" Ian asked.

"This was made by a claymore, not an English blade," the man said, and the other two nodded. "Ye see how thick the cut is? Aye, that was done by a claymore."

The noise in the hall was deafening until Ian raised his hands for silence.

"We have plenty of enemies among the clans, and most of them were there that day," Hugh said. "Our chief-tain was my brother, and Ragnall, my nephew. I'd never raise my hand against my own blood."

"Is Connor not your own blood?" Ian said, stepping toward Hugh with his hands clenched into fists. "Why don't ye tell our clansmen what ye did to Connor?"

"I haven't laid eyes on Connor in more than five years."

"I know what ye did," Ian said, his eyes narrow blue slits. "First, ye asked Shaggy Maclean to kill the four of us before we got to Skye. But we surprised ye, when we escaped Shaggy's dungeon."

Hugh started to speak, but Ian shouted over him. "So

ye made a deal with that devil Murdoc MacKinnon. Ye told him he could keep Knock Castle—*and take my wife*—in exchange for murdering Connor."

Every man in the room had wondered why Hugh did not fight for Knock Castle; Ian had just given them an explanation they could believe.

"You're a liar," Hugh said, but sweat was beading on his forehead.

"Murdoc MacKinnon admitted the treachery to my wife."

"A woman will tell ye what she thinks ye want to hear." Hugh's eyes darted around the room. "What I think happened is that Connor and the other two decided to return to France soon after the four of ye came home."

"Then why have ye been spreading the word that they were murdered by the MacKinnons?" Ian asked. "Shall I call on Connor, Alex, and Duncan to tell us the tale?"

The high, sweet sound of a whistle started at the back of the hall, causing everyone to turn and look. At the back of the room, stood Connor, Alex, and Duncan, without their disguises. Men gasped and women drew back their skirts to let them pass as the three started forward.

"It's Samhain, uncle," Connor called out. "Are ye prepared to meet the dead?"

Hugh's eyes went wide, and he made a strangled sound, while his men crossed themselves and backed away. Though the three men limped and their faces were bruised, there was no mistaking that these were warriors to be reckoned with.

"Ye should have murdered me yourself," Connor said, when he reached his uncle at the front. "Only a fool would rely on a Maclean or MacKinnon for such an important task."

When several clansmen surrounded Hugh, he looked to his guards to protect him. But Hugh's men, who as pirates were known for vanishing into the mists to avoid capture, had disappeared into the crowd. In no time, Hugh was disarmed and dragged to the side.

Every eye in the room was fixed on the four Highland warriors who had returned from France. Despite their injuries, they were hard-muscled men in their prime, a new generation of MacDonald men, ready to take their place as leaders and protectors of their clan.

Ian's father began pounding his cane rhythmically on the stone floor. Immediately, others began to stomp and clap to the same rhythm. *Clap. Clap. Clap. Clap.* Deep voices filled the hall, shouting in time to the stomping and clapping. "Chief-tain! Chief-tain! Chief-tain!"

Connor stepped forward and raised his arms as the crowd roared louder and louder, proclaiming him as their choice.

It was a miracle Connor managed to stand alone as long as he did. Sìleas didn't think the crowd noticed when he started to weave, but Alex and Duncan limped forward to stand on either side of him.

Ian stood a little apart, his eyes searching the hall until he found her.

They had succeeded. Connor would be the next chieftain of the MacDonalds of Sleat.

Ian felt as if a great weight had been lifted from his shoulders—a weight he had carried since the moment he first learned of the calamity at Flodden. He had redeemed himself by saving his clan from certain disaster.

The fight was not over. Hugh still had supporters—some in the hall and others who slipped out of the castle in the chaos. They would have to be dealt with eventually, but they would cause no more trouble tonight.

Ian wanted to share this moment with Sìleas. Smiling, he turned to look for her.

His heart swelled when he saw her, because she was smiling back at him, her eyes shining. People moved out of his way as he pushed through the crowd toward her. Suddenly, her gaze shifted to something behind him, and she screamed.

He spun around in time to see a flash of steel behind Connor, Alex, and Duncan, where the men were holding Hugh. In the midst of the tumultuous jubilation, no one else seemed to notice when one of the men holding Hugh sank to the ground with blood gushing from his throat. A moment later, the second man holding Hugh doubled over, with blood seeping between his lips.

Neither did anyone heed Ian's cry of warning as Hugh pulled the dead man's dirk from his belt. Ian was already pushing through the crowd, racing to get to Connor before Hugh did.

Though Ian was running as fast as he could, he saw everything with piercing clarity, as if time had slowed. He saw each person who fell out of his way, Duncan's hands clapping, Alex's head thrown back in laughter—and Hugh moving toward Connor with the point of his blade aimed at Connor's back.

"No!" Ian shouted, as he took the last three steps at a dead run and flew through the air.

He felt the sting of a blade glancing off his back as he crashed to the floor on top of Connor with a hard thump. When he looked up, with his dirk ready in his hand, Duncan and Alex were holding Hugh above him. Screams and shouts echoed off the walls, and every dirk and claymore in the hall was unsheathed.

"I appreciate ye saving my life," Connor grunted from beneath him. "But do ye think ye could get off of me now? I feel as if a horse fell on me."

"I hope I didn't break open any of your wounds," Ian said, as he got up. "Ach, from the blood it looks as though I did."

"The blood is yours this time," Connor said after Ian helped him up. "Turn 'round and let's see how bad he cut ye."

"I don't even feel it," Ian said, looking over his shoulder at his bloody shirt.

"Connor, what do ye want us to do with this murderer?" Alex asked, and gave Hugh a shake.

"My father was a great chieftain, and my brother Ragnall would have been an even greater one," Connor said, looking at his uncle. "You have deprived the clan of their leadership."

Ian thought Connor would be a better chieftain than either of them, but it wasn't the time to say it.

"You haven't the hardness it takes to be chieftain," Hugh spat out. "Your father at least had that."

"I won't mar tonight's celebration with an execution— but say your prayers, Hugh, for you'll die in the morning." Connor turned to several clansmen who were standing nearby. "Take him to the dungeon. He's a slippery one, so mind him closely."

The noise in the hall was deafening as men carried Connor around in the chieftain's chair. In the wake of the revelation of their former chieftain's murder, the clan's choice was clear. That did not mean no one had doubts about Connor's leadership, but none would express them tonight.

They chose Connor because he was his father's son and Ragnall's brother—and because he was not Hugh. Most members of the clan did not know Connor's mettle yet. In time, he would prove himself to them. Once they knew him as Ian did, they would follow Connor because of the good man he was and the great man he was destined to be.

For tonight, Connor and the clan were safe. The celebrations would go on through most of the night, but Ian did not need to stay for them. He had one more thing he must do to make up for the past, one last step to redeem himself with the person who mattered most.

He found Sìleas elbowing her way through the throng of men crowded around the front. When she felt his gaze, she gave him a broad smile, as before. After all the ways he had failed her, her smile was a small miracle, a gift he hoped to earn in time.

He lifted her in his arms and carried her out of the hall.

Most of the guests would be sleeping on the floor of the hall tonight, but Ian intended to take one of the few bedchambers. Connor owed him that.

CHAPTER 42

As soon as the chamber door was closed behind them, he pulled Sìleas into his arms. He buried his face in her hair and breathed in the familiar scent of her hair and skin. While she was in danger, all his focus was on rescuing her. Then he had to turn his mind to getting Connor to the gathering and making him chieftain.

"I almost lost you."

Only now that his tasks were completed and the dangers passed, did it fully hit him. His knees felt weak at the thought of how close it had been. He ran his hands over her to assure himself that she was whole.

"I should have prevented Murdoc from taking ye," he said.

"Ian, ye can't blame yourself for everything that happens." Sìleas leaned back and looked at him with her honest green eyes. "And ye did save me."

"I've failed ye so many times—starting with the day I found ye outside the tunnel and didn't believe ye were in danger," he said. "I never should have left ye to deal with everything alone while I went off to France. I don't know how to tell ye how sorry I am for it all."

"Ye returned home precisely when we needed ye most," she said, touching her fingers to his cheek. "If ye had been here all along, ye might have been killed at Flodden with the rest of them. And where would we be now without ye? Your da would still be lying in bed spewing venom at Niall, Hugh would be chieftain, and I'd likely be wed to that brute Angus."

The thought of Angus's hands on her sent a wave of cold fury through him. If he could kill him again, he would. "I don't know how ye can forgive me."

"Do ye know why I waited five long years for ye, Ian MacDonald?" she asked with a soft smile lighting her face.

It was a wonder to him that she had.

"It's because I always knew ye were special. I could see it in ye from the time I was a wee bairn. Even when ye made mistakes, I believed in that lad who had so much courage and kindness in his heart. I knew the man ye could be."

He cradled her face in his hand. He felt an overwhelming gratitude for her faith in him—for the wee bairn who trusted him to rescue her from every mishap, for the brave thirteen-year-old lass who threw her fate in with his without thinking twice. And most of all, for the young woman who waited for him to return, and who, when he failed her again, gave him yet another chance to prove himself.

He had come home seeking only atonement, and she had given him the wonder of love. "I'll do my best to be the man ye believe I can become."

"Ye already are," she said.

He felt a powerful need to make love to her, to show her how much he cared. But she would need time, after what she had been through. The image of Murdoc standing between her legs would be with him for a long, long time. How much worse the memory must be for her. Would it ever fade enough for her to want him again?

"Let me help ye to bed, *a chroí*. Ye need your rest," he said. "But if ye can bear to have me touch ye, I'd like to sleep holding ye in my arms."

He wanted much more than that, but he brushed his lips across her forehead.

He was already hard with wanting her before she slid her arms around his neck. When she rose up on her toes and leaned into him, he held himself in check and gave her a chaste kiss. But when she pulled him down into a deep kiss, thrusting her tongue into his mouth with an urgency that sent his blood pounding through his veins, he was a lost man.

Finally, he forced himself to break the kiss. "Ye don't have to do this to please me. Ye should r—"

"I want ye something fierce," she said, pulling him to her by the front of his shirt. "Don't ye dare tell me I must rest."

Ian trusted his wife to know what she wanted.

Sìleas needed him to make love to her to wipe away the fear that had dogged her since Alex burst into the house bleeding the morning before. She had kept up a brave front most of the time, but she had feared rape and degradation and death; she had feared for the lives of Ian's family and friends, who were now her family and friends. And most of all, she had feared she would die and never see Ian again.

She felt desperate to hold him, to feel him inside her and all around her. They fell to the bed, kissing and running their hands over each other as if they might never get the chance again—because it had almost been true. They tore at each other's clothes until at last they lay skin to skin. But it wasn't enough.

She needed to feel his weight on her. When she tugged on his shoulder, he rolled to cover her. She closed her eyes and drew in deep breaths. It was as if she needed to feel him pressing down on her, touching her from head to toe, to believe he was truly here with her.

She felt safe at last.

And she wanted him as she had never wanted him before. He slid his hands between her legs and groaned when he found how wet she was for him.

"I need ye inside of me," she said, her voice coming out hoarse. "I need us to be one."

When he brought the head of his shaft to touch her center, he shuddered with the effort not to plunge into her. But when she clamped her legs around him, he gave in to what they both wanted. She gasped as he thrust deep inside her.

For a long moment, they held still, and she reveled in the intensity of the sensation of him inside her, and the anticipation of his moving again.

"*Mo chroí.*" He held her head between his hands and kissed her eyelids, her cheeks, her hair. "Do ye know how much I love ye?"

"Aye." She did know it now. His love shone in his eyes, his voice, his touch. It was all around her, encompassing her in its warmth.

Ian's heart was worth waiting for. *He* was worth waiting for.

With his eyes locked on hers, he began moving slowly inside her. The pouch holding the crystal she gave him dragged across her chest as if connecting their hearts as he moved over her again and again. His breathing was ragged, and the muscles of his face were straining.

"Harder." She arched her back and pulled on his shoulders, urging him closer, deeper. She clung to him with all her strength and love.

"Mo shíorghrá…mo shíorghrá…"

He whispered endearments to her as he moved inside her, but she felt too much now to speak. Tears streamed down the sides of her face from emotions too strong to contain. Ian captured her mouth and swallowed her cries as they melded together in an explosion of white fire.

Ian rolled with her until she lay sprawled on top of him. His heart thumped wildly in her ear, and his hand shook as he brushed the hair back from her face.

"We are one," he said. "We always will be."

The gray light of dawn was coming through the narrow window when she awoke. Ian lay behind her, his arms wrapped about her and one hand cupping her breast. She snuggled closer and felt his shaft press against her. When she turned in his arms to face him, he traced her skin with his fingers and kissed her with a tenderness that squeezed her heart.

"This time, I'm determined to make love to ye slowly," he said with a gleam in his eye, "and you're going to let me have my way."

"I will," she said, smiling back at him.

Ian sat up and took her hand. "I have something I want to ask ye first."

The seriousness of his expression sent a frisson of anxiety through her. She sat up cross-legged to face him and pulled the blanket over her shoulders. "Aye, what is it?"

Ian licked his lips. She'd never seen Ian look nervous before in her life, and it put her on edge to see it now.

"What I want to ask ye is, would ye like to do it over again?" he said. "Get married, I mean. With friends and neighbors coming to wish us well, a big feast, music and dancing."

Sìleas was too stunned to speak.

"I'd like to do it right this time," he said.

Tears stung at the back of her eyes. Her voice came out as a whisper. "Ye mean it?"

"I do," he said, his eyes soft on hers. "When I give ye my vows before all our friends and neighbors, they will know I give them freely and that I mean to keep them."

She had tried not to let what others said hurt her, but in an island clan where everyone knew everyone else's business, it had been hard. Ian had found a way to restore her pride by honoring her before their clan.

"Murdoc said that wasn't a real priest who wed us that day," she said.

"Ach, I should have guessed my uncle would do that. Then we'll ask Father Brian to bless our marriage." Ian lifted her chin with his finger. "I want ye looking your loveliest in a fine gown, and every man eating his heart out because ye are mine."

Sìleas thought of the ill-fitting red gown that sagged at her bosom and made her skin look blotchy and her hair orange.

"I'll wear a gown of blue, the color of my true love's eyes," she said, letting a slow smile spread across her face.

"It will be so gorgeous that the women will talk of nothing else for weeks."

"Ye will do it then?" Ian asked. "Marry me again?"

Sìleas threw her arms around his neck. "I'd marry ye a thousand times over, Ian MacDonald."

Ian held her tight against him.

"When I was a lad, Teàrlag predicted I would wed twice," he said with a laugh in his voice. "Teàrlag could have saved me a good deal of trouble if she'd told me it would be to the same woman both times."

Sìleas looked up at him from under her lashes. "So which wife is it that ye intend to make love to slowly?"

"It will have to be you, *mo chroí*," Ian said, as he kissed her below her ear and eased her back on the bed, "and you again."

CHAPTER 43

Sìleas and Beitris greeted the last group of women as they entered the gatehouse of Knock Castle. The women cooed and clucked as they surveyed the presents that were laid out for that very purpose.

"Ach, the stitching on that pillow is lovely, Margaret," one woman said to another.

"But not as useful a gift for a bride as the fine iron pot ye gave her," her friend replied.

It was only three days since Connor was made chieftain, so the women had barely had time to prepare their gifts. But after Sìleas's long wait for a real wedding celebration, none of them was complaining. Despite the mild smell of charred wood that lingered in the air, Sìleas was glad now that Ian had insisted they not wait until the keep was livable to have their wedding.

Once the women had finished viewing the gifts and complimenting each other, Beitris called out, "Time for the washing of the bride's feet!"

Sìleas laughed as the women sat her down on a stool

before a wooden tub—a wedding present from Ilysa—pulled off her shoes and stockings, and stuck her feet into the cold water.

Sìleas had not grown up in the company of women. She had always felt awkward among them, particularly in the years when she didn't fit in with either the unmarried lasses or the women with husbands. More than a few had made thoughtless remarks to her about Ian's long absence. But today, she felt accepted for the first time—and she was enjoying herself.

Sìleas watched as her mother-in-law twisted off her wedding ring and tossed it into the tub.

"You have the happiest marriage I know, so your ring is sure to bring me the best of luck." Sìleas took Beitris's hand and smiled up at her. "I am blessed to have a mother-in-law who is like a mother to me."

Beitris sniffed and wiped her nose as the women cheered.

Then all the women in want of husbands gathered around the tub. Sìleas shrieked as they took turns scrubbing her ticklish feet and searching the bottom of the tub for the ring. Though Ilysa was younger than she and a widow, Sìleas was surprised to see her standing in line to take a turn. Ilysa had never shown any interest in remarrying before.

Ilysa, however, never got her turn.

"I have it!" Dina shouted. The other women exchanged glances, for they were all quite aware of how Dina lost her last husband.

"Good luck to ye, Dina," Sìleas said. "May ye be as happy as I am."

The women finally deigned to notice Ian and the other

men who, by tradition, were crowded around the doorway, joking with each other and trying to peek inside. Ian let the women drag him into the room and sit him down on a stool on the other side of the tub from Sìleas.

Ian's gaze was warm on hers as he put his hand over his heart and mouthed, *a chuisle mo chroí.* There was a good deal of sighing from the women, but that didn't stop them from covering his feet in ashes before putting them in the tub.

The feet washing and gift viewing were supposed to take place the eve before the wedding, but they had decided to do it all on the same day so Father Brian could be on his way.

Ian took her hands and helped her to her feet. As they stood together in the tub, he gave her a kiss that made her forget the others were watching—until she heard them shouting their approval.

"I think he could give my Donald a lesson or two," one of the older women said, causing another round of laughter.

"Out with ye, Ian Aluinn," another woman said, and Ian let a matron half his size push him out the door.

Before they could close it on him, he blew Sìleas a kiss. "I'll be waiting for ye in the yard, *a chroí.*"

"You're a lucky lass," Dina said, as the women helped her out of the tub and dried her feet. From the way the other women's eyes had followed Ian, Sìleas suspected Dina wasn't the only woman in the room who would have been more than glad to change places with her.

Sìleas wondered where Beitris had gone when she saw her return from the corner of the room with a shimmering silk gown the color of bluebells.

"Ahh, it's gorgeous," Sìleas breathed, as she fingered the fine material. "When did ye have time to make it?"

Beitris's smile was so broad she looked as if her face might split. "I started working on it the night Ian came home from France."

Sìleas didn't bother asking how her mother-in-law had known she would be needing it. She lifted her arms as two of the women pulled her gown over her head, leaving her in her chemise.

"Beitris, this one will give ye many grandchildren," an old woman with pure white hair said, as she pinched Sìleas's hip.

"She'll have beautiful babes," Beitris said, as she dropped the gown over Sìleas's head.

The gown floated over her in a swirl of cool silk. It fit perfectly, clinging to every curve as if it had been stitched by faeries. Sìleas met Beitris's eyes and knew they were both thinking of the awful red gown she had worn to her first wedding.

"Thank ye, Beitris," she said, as they grinned at each other.

"Ach, such luck you'll have!" the women exclaimed again and again, for a wedding gown that fit well was a sign of good luck.

The women slid thin stockings up her legs and combed her hair. As a last touch, Ilysa tied a sprig of white heather in her hair, another token of good fortune.

Then all the women cooed and sighed, telling her, as they did all brides, that she was the loveliest bride they'd ever seen. When she stepped out into the bailey yard and Ian looked at her, she felt as if it were true.

He was so handsome that the sight of him made her

feel as if something had slammed against her chest. The crystal she had given him had been fashioned into a pin that held his plaid at the shoulder, and he wore a sprig of white heather in his cap like the one she wore one in her hair.

Duncan, Connor, and Alex were next to him, dressed in their best and looking fine. Being young and healthy, they were recovering quickly from their injuries, though their bruises still told the tale.

When Duncan raised his eyebrows at her, she nodded and he began to play. His pipes filled the bailey yard with a song of hope and joy. All eyes were on her as she joined Ian to stand before Father Brian.

"I, Ian Payton MacDonald, take ye, Sìleas MacDonald, to be my wife. In the presence of God and before these witnesses, I promise to be a loving and faithful husband to ye until God shall separate us by death."

Sìleas said her vows in turn. When the priest had blessed them, Ian kissed her and the crowd erupted into cheers.

Connor was the first to congratulate them. "May ye be blessed with long life and peace."

Sìleas squeezed Ian's hand. Between the rebellion brewing and Hugh's escape, peace seemed unlikely, but she would hope for a long life together.

"May ye grow old with goodness and with riches," Duncan said, giving them another of the usual blessings.

When it was Alex's turn, he said to Ian, "Ye saved yourself a lot of trouble by marrying a MacDonald. As they say, 'Marry a lass and ye marry her whole clan.' "

"I'm glad ye mentioned that," Connor said, resting his hand on Alex's shoulder. "That is precisely the reason I need ye to marry a woman from another clan. I'll be calling on ye soon to do your duty."

"Not me," Alex said, putting his hands up and taking a step back. "I live by the saying, 'The smart fellow's share is on every dish.'"

They all pretended not to hear Alex's parents, who had gone off to the far end of the bailey yard to shout at each other.

They had the feast in the yard, too, since the guardhouse was too small for all the guests. Though it was chilly, it wasn't raining, and the food the women brought was tasty and plentiful. They warmed up afterward with music and dancing. All the men kissed Sìleas, giving her pennies, until Ian put a stop to that particular tradition.

"Let's get the priest," he whispered in her ear.

They found Father Brian and sneaked away without anyone noticing—or at least they pretended not to notice. When they reached the makeshift bedchamber Ian had set up for them on the upper floor of the gatehouse, he carried her over the threshold.

He set her down, and they waited while Father Brian sprinkled the bed with holy water.

"Do your part," he said to Ian with a wink, "and ye will have many fine children."

As soon as Ian closed the door behind the priest, Sìleas burst out laughing. "I already put the fertility charm Teàrlag gave me under the bed."

Ian pulled her into his arms. "We'll have to do our best not to waste so much luck."

EPILOGUE

NINE MONTHS LATER

Fear was an unnatural state for Ian.

His mother came downstairs periodically to report that his wife was well and all was proceeding as expected. Despite her reassurances, an unfamiliar sensation of panic flooded through his limbs every time he heard his mother's step on the stairs.

"Sit down, Ian, before ye wear out your new floor," Alex said.

Why had he got Sìleas with child? What was he thinking? It wasn't of children, that was for certain. But God help him, her mother had died in childbirth.

"She is a strong lass," his father said. The sympathy in his eyes showed that he understood in a way the others, who had no wives, could not.

Sìleas screamed again, and his heart stopped in his chest.

"'Tis only when they're too weak to scream that ye have cause to fret," his father said.

His father could be lying to him, but the strength of Sìleas's voice was reassuring.

"I think I hear her cursing," Duncan said, looking nearly as worried as Ian. "That's a good sign, aye?"

"How long does this take, da?" Ian ran his hands through his hair as he paced. "I shouldn't have brought her back here to Knock Castle. What if it's bad luck?"

"First ye had Father Brian bless every nook and corner," Alex said. "Then ye kept poor old Teàrlag here for three days making silly spells for protection."

"That was to comfort Sìleas," Ian said—and ignored the snorts from the others.

"If the two of ye have been unhappy here," Connor said, "you've done a good job of fooling everyone."

They'd been too happy. Ian feared they'd made the faeries jealous.

"Ian," his mother said from doorway. "Ye can come up now."

She stepped aside to let him run by her, and he took the stairs three at a time. When he entered their bedchamber, Sìleas was propped up on pillows, flanked by Ilysa and Dina.

His wife looked tired but radiant. *Praise God!* He never wanted to go through this again.

Ilysa moved aside so he could take her place next to the bed. "We'll leave ye alone," she said. "Just call if ye need me."

"I'll say good-bye, because Gòrdan will be coming to fetch me soon." Dina patted her own expanding belly and gave them a broad wink. "He's a very…*attentive*…husband."

When Ian asked Gòrdan to watch over Dina, he never suspected he was fostering a lasting union. It appeared to be a love match as well. Having a steady man like Gòrdan had settled Dina, and Dina added a spark to Gòrdan. The shouting matches between Dina and Gòrdan's mother, however, were the stuff of legends.

When the door closed behind the two women, Ian brushed his fingers against Sìleas's cheek. "Are ye all right, *a chuisle mo chroí*?"

"I am," she said.

"Ach, ye sounded as if ye were being tortured."

"I was," she said, but when she smiled up at him, Ian's heart did a turn in his chest. Sìleas had an inner glow that made her unbearably beautiful.

"Ye haven't looked yet," she said.

The blanket over the bundle in her arm shielded the babe's face from him.

"What is it?" he asked. "A boy or a girl?"

He hoped for a boy, only because the thought of having a girl frightened him half to death. What if she was a bairn like her mother, falling into trouble at every opportunity? He'd be an old man before his time.

"Take your daughter," Sìleas said.

When he lifted the bundle from her arm, the babe weighed nothing at all.

"She is a wee tiny thing, isn't she?" He pushed the blanket back to see her face—and his daughter held his heartstrings from that moment. "Ah, but she is a beauty! She's going to have lovely orange hair, just like you."

"My hair is not orange."

It was, but he didn't argue.

"Do ye want to see the other one now?" she asked.

"What? There's more?"

"Just one more. Another girl."

He hadn't noticed the bundle in his wife's other arm until now. She lifted it up and rested it in the crook of his arm.

"This one has orange hair, too," Ian said as he looked at his second lovely daughter. He grinned at his wife. "There're going to be trouble, aren't they?"

"More than likely," she said, sounding quite complacent about it. "You're going to be a wonderful da."

Sìleas always had such faith in him.

"What shall we name them?" he asked.

"I'd like to name one Beitris, after your mother," Sìleas said. "What about Alexandra for the other, after Alex?"

"Fine," he said, smiling down at his wee girls. "Duncan and Connor are not good names for a lass."

"We should have sons after this," she said. "We'll need at least four."

"Four sons? Why do we need any sons at all?" Overjoyed as he was with their two babes, he wasn't anxious to risk his wife's life again.

"So we can name them after Connor, Duncan, Payton, and Niall, of course." She touched his arm. "After being an only child, I want a houseful of children."

He nodded, hoping it would be easier next time, but expecting it wouldn't. "If we do two at a time, it won't take long."

He heard a tinkle of laugher and looked up to see what looked very much like a woman in a pale green gown floating above the bed.

"It's the Green Lady—she's come back," Sìleas said, sounding pleased at finding a ghost in their bedchamber. "I've never seen her smile before."

Ian decided he could live with a smiling ghost if it made his wife happy.

As he leaned down with his babes in his arms to give his beloved Sìleas a kiss, he could have sworn that the Green Lady winked at him.

HISTORICAL NOTE

Last summer, I was lucky enough to take a trip to Scotland. One memorable afternoon, I drove across the Sleat Peninsula of Skye, from the ruins of Knock Castle to the ruins of Dunscaith Castle, on a one-lane road that had more sheep than cars. Seeing the castles I was writing about was an amazing experience, and the island is breathtakingly beautiful. The landscape hasn't changed much over the centuries, so I found it easy to imagine my heroes traipsing over the hills or sailing the shores.

Researching clan histories of five hundred years ago proved far more challenging. Not much was recorded in a written record at the time. While there is a rich tradition of oral histories, clans often have different versions of the same long-ago events. And clan alliances, including marriages between chieftains' families, were made and broken with a frequency that is hard to follow.

The MacDonalds of Sleat are a prime example of the complex family relationships. Hugh (Uisdean), the first MacDonald of Sleat and the grandfather of my fictional character Connor, had six sons by six different women, all from prominent families. If I have this right, Hugh, one of his sons, and one of his grandsons all married daughters of Torquil MacLeod of Lewis—and another of Hugh's sons married Torquil's former wife.

As is often the case, Hugh's proliferate ways did not lead to family harmony. Hugh's first son hated his half brothers so much that upon his death he turned the clan's lands over to the Crown to keep the others from inheriting them. The lack of legal title to their lands caused later chieftains problems for years. Two of Hugh's other sons were murdered by their brothers, and another was murdered by Hugh's grandsons.

In this series, I've kept the family animosity, but changed the details and timing of these events. I've also changed the name of one of Hugh's sons from Archibald to Hugh. A number of other secondary characters in *The Guardian* are real historical figures, including Shaggy Maclean and Archibald Douglas. I embellished freely upon what I knew of their personalities.

For ease of reading, I used anglicized versions of Gaelic names for some of my fictional characters. For the same reason, I did not follow the practice of calling a person by different names when he was with his mother's clan, his father's clan, or somewhere else.

Finally, I confess that I shortened travel times to suit the needs of my story and that Knock Castle was still known as Castle Camus, or Caisteal Chamuis, in 1513. I did not, however, make up the legend of the Green Lady of Knock Castle.

Look for the second book of
this sizzling series featuring
the fearless Highlanders!

⁓

Please turn this page
for a preview of

THE SINNER

Available in November 2011.

CHAPTER 1

BARRA ISLAND,
Scottish Highlands
Spring 1515

"Can ye hurry with your stitching?" Glynis asked, as she peered out her window. "Their boat is nearly at the sea gate."

"Your father is going to murder ye for this." Old Molly's face was grim, but her needle flew along the seam. "Now stand straight."

"Better dead than wed again," Glynis muttered under her breath.

"This trick will work but once, if it works at all." Old Molly paused to tie a knot and rethread the needle. "'Tis a losing game you're playing, lass."

Glynis crossed her arms. "I won't let him marry me off again."

"Your da is just as stubborn as you, and he's the chieftain." Old Molly looked up from her sewing to fix her filmy eyes on Glynis. "Not all men are as blackhearted as your first husband."

"Perhaps not," Glynis said, though she was far from convinced. "But the MacDonalds of Sleat are known philanderers. I swear on my grandmother's grave, I'll no take one of them."

"Beware of what ye swear, lass," Old Molly said. "I knew your grandmother well, and I'd hate for ye to cause that good woman to turn in her grave."

"Ouch!" Glynis yelped when a loud banging caused Old Molly to stick her needle in Glynis's side.

"Get yourself down to the hall, Glynis," her father shouted from the other side of the door. "Our guests are arriving."

"I'm almost ready, da," she called out.

"Don't think ye can fool me with a sweet voice," he said. "What are ye doing in there?"

Glynis risked opening the door a crack and stuck her face in it. Her father, a big, barrel-chested man, was looking as foul-tempered as his reputation.

"Ye said I should dress so these damned MacDonalds won't soon forget me," she said. "That takes a woman time, da."

He narrowed his eyes at her, but he let that pass. After all these years of living with a wife and daughters, females were still largely a mystery to him. In this war with her father, Glynis was willing to use whatever small advantage she had.

"Their new chieftain didn't come himself," he said in what for him was a low voice. "But it was too much to hope a chieftain would take ye, after the shame ye brought upon yourself. One of these others will have to do."

Glynis swallowed against the lump in her throat. Having her father blame her for her failed marriage—and believe she had dishonored her family—hurt more than anything her husband had done to her.

"I did nothing shameful," she said through clenched teeth. "But I will, if ye force me to take another husband."

"Ye were born obstinate as an ox," her father shouted through the six-inch crack in the door. "But I am your father and your chieftain, and ye will do as I tell ye."

"What man will want a woman who's shamed herself?" she hissed at him.

"Ach, men are fools for beauty," her father said. "Despite what happened, ye are still that."

Glynis slammed the door shut in his face and threw the bar across it.

"Ye will do as I say, or I'll throw ye out to starve!"

That was all she could make out amidst his long string of curses before his footsteps echoed down the spiral stone staircase.

Glynis blinked hard to keep back the tears. She was done with weeping.

"I should have given ye poison as a wedding gift, so ye could come home a widow," Old Molly said behind her. "I told the chieftain he was wedding ye to a bad man, but he's no better at listening than his daughter is."

"Quickly now." Glynis picked up the small bowl from the side table and held it out to Molly. "It will ruin everything if he loses patience and comes back to drag me downstairs."

Old Molly heaved a great sigh and dipped her fingers into the red clay paste.

Alex stretched out and closed his eyes to enjoy the sun and sea breeze a little longer. It was a long sail from the Isle of Skye to the MacNeil stronghold on Barra, but they were nearly there.

"Remind me how Connor convinced us to pay a visit on the MacNeils," Alex said.

"We volunteered," Duncan said.

"Ach, that was foolish," Alex said, "when we know the MacNeil chieftain is looking for husbands for his daughters."

"Aye."

Alex opened one eye. "Were we that drunk?"

"Aye," Duncan said with one of his rare smiles.

Duncan was a good man, if a wee bit dour these days—which just went to show that love could bring the strongest of men to their knees. Alex had known the big, red-haired warrior since they were bairns. They and Alex's cousins, Connor and Ian, had been fast friends all their lives.

"I swear," Alex said, "since Connor became chieftain, he grows more devious by the day."

"Drunk or sober, we would have agreed," Duncan said. "We couldn't let Connor come himself."

A chieftain didn't travel the Western Isles without war galleys full of men—the risk of being taken hostage or murdered by another clan was too great. With Connor's uncle Hugh Dubh still threatening to take the chieftainship, Connor had to keep most of his warriors at home to defend Dunscaith Castle.

The four of them—Alex, Duncan, Ian, and Connor—had returned from France to find Connor's father dead, his blackhearted Uncle Hugh living in the chieftain's castle, and their clan in a dire state. While they had succeeded in driving Hugh Dubh from the castle and making Connor chieftain, Hugh Dubh had escaped. Worse still, Hugh had returned to pirating with his brothers. Now, at a time when their clan was badly in need of allies, Connor's uncles were harassing clans all over the Western Isles.

Alex and Duncan's task, as Connor's emissaries, was to assure the other chieftains that Connor's uncles weren't raping and pillaging their shores on their new chieftain's orders.

"Ye could make this easy by marrying one of the Mac-Neil's daughters," Duncan said, the corner of his mouth quirking up.

"I see ye do remember how to make a joke." Not many men teased Duncan, so Alex did his best to make up for it.

"Ye know that's what Connor wants," Duncan said. "He has no brothers to make marriage alliances for him—so a cousin will have to do. If ye don't like one of the MacNeil lasses, there are plenty of other chieftains' daughters."

"I'd take a blade for Connor," Alex said, losing his humor, "but I'll no take a wife for him."

"Connor has a way of getting what he wants," Duncan said. "I'll wager you'll be wed within half a year."

"Ye must still be drunk." Alex sat up and grinned at his friend. "What shall we wager?"

"This galley," Duncan said.

"Perfect." Alex loved this boat, which was smaller and sleeker than a war galley and sliced through the water like a fish. They had been arguing over who had the better right to it ever since they had stolen it from Shaggy Maclean.

The MacNeil castle, which sat on a rock island in a bay off the coast of Barra, was in sight now.

"You're going to miss this sweet galley," Alex said, as he guided the boat into the bay.

A short time later, a large group of armed MacNeil warriors were escorting them inside the castle's keep.

"I see we've got them scared," Alex said in a low voice to Duncan.

"We could take them," Duncan grunted.

"Did ye notice that there are twelve of them?" Alex asked.

"I'm no saying it would be easy."

Alex laughed, which had the MacNeils all reaching for their swords. He was enjoying himself. Still, he hoped he and Duncan wouldn't have to fight their way out. These were Highland warriors, not Englishmen or Lowlanders, and everyone knew MacNeils were mean and devious fighters.

Almost as mean and devious as MacDonalds.

But the MacNeils had more dangerous weapons in their arsenal. Alex heard Duncan groan beside him as they entered the hall and saw what was waiting for them.

"God save us," escaped Alex's lips. Three twittering lasses were sitting at the head table. The girls were pretty, but young and innocent enough to give Alex hives.

One of them wiggled her fingers at him, then her sister elbowed her in the ribs, and all three went into a fit of giggles behind their hands.

It was going to be a long evening.

"Quiet!" the chieftain thundered, and the color drained from the girls' faces.

After exchanging greetings with Alex and Duncan, the MacNeil introduced his wife, an attractive, plump woman half his age, and his young son, who sat on her lap. Then he waved his arm toward the girls, saying, "These are my three youngest daughters. My eldest will join us soon."

The missing daughter would be the one they'd heard about. She was rumored to be a rare beauty who had been turned out by her husband in disgrace.

She sounded like Alex's kind of woman.

Before the chieftain could direct them where to sit, Alex and Duncan took seats at the far end from the three lasses. After a cursory prayer, wine and ale was poured, and the first courses were brought out.

Alex wanted to get their business done as soon as possible—and leave. "Our chieftain hopes to strengthen the friendship between our two clans and has sent us here on a mission of goodwill," he began.

The MacNeil kept glancing at the doorway, his face darker each time. Though he didn't appear to be listening to a word, Alex forged ahead.

"Our chieftain pledges that he will join ye in fighting the pirates who are harassing all our shores."

That caught the MacNeil's attention. In a sour tone, he asked, "Isn't it his own uncle who leads them?"

"His half uncle," Duncan put in, as if that explained it all.

The MacNeil chief tilted his head back to take a long drink from his cup, then slammed it on the table, sputtering and choking.

Alex followed the direction of his gaze—and almost choked on his own ale when he saw the woman. Ach, the poor thing had suffered the worst case of pox Alex had ever seen. The afflicted woman crossed the room at a brisk pace, her gaze fixed on the floor. When she took the place at the end of the table next to Alex, he had to move over to make room for her. She was quite stout, though not in a pleasing sort of way.

Alex tried not to stare at the pockmarks when he turned to greet her. But he couldn't help it. God's bones, these weren't old scars—the pox were still oozing! Blood never troubled him at all, of course, but he was a wee bit squeamish about oozing sores.

"I am Alexander MacDonald." He put on a bright smile for her, which she missed altogether because she kept her gaze on the table before her.

He waited, but when she didn't introduce herself, he asked, "And you are?"

"Glynis."

Since she refused to look at him, Alex could stare freely. The longer he looked, the more certain he was that the pockmarks weren't oozing—they were melting. Amusement tugged at the corners of his mouth.

"I confess, ye have me curious, Glynis," he said, leaning close to her ear. "What would cause a lass to give herself pockmarks?"

Glynis jerked her head up and stared at him. Despite the distracting red boils that were easing their way down her face, Alex couldn't help noticing she had arrestingly beautiful gray eyes.

"It is unkind to poke fun at a lady's unfortunate looks," she said.

It was disconcerting to hear such a lovely voice come out of that alarming face. Alex let his gaze drift over her, taking in the graceful swan neck and the long, slender fingers clenching her wine cup.

"Your secret is safe with me, lass," Alex said in a low voice. "But I suspect your family already knows it's a disguise."

He was hoping for a laugh, but he got none.

"Come," he said, waggling his eyebrows at her. "Ye must tell me why ye did it."

She took a deep drink from her wine, then said, "So ye wouldn't want to marry me, of course."

Alex laughed. "I fear ye went to a good deal of trouble for no purpose, for I have no intention of leaving here with a wife. But does it happen to ye often that men see ye once and want to marry ye?"

"My father says men are fools for beauty, so I couldn't take the risk."

The woman said this with utter seriousness. Alex hadn't been this amused in some time—and he was a man easily amused.

"No matter how lovely ye are beneath the padding and paste," Alex said, "ye are quite safe from finding wedded bliss with me."

She searched his face intently, as if trying to decide if she could believe him. The combination of her sober expression and the globs sliding down her face made it hard not to laugh, but he managed.

"My father was certain your new chieftain would want a marriage between our clans," she said at last, "to show his goodwill—after the trouble caused by the MacDonald pirates."

"Your father isn't far wrong," Alex said. "But my chieftain, who is also my cousin and good friend, knows my feelings about matrimony."

Alex realized he'd been so caught up in his conversation with this unusual lass that he'd been ignoring her father and the rest of the table. When he turned to join their conversation, however, he found that no one else was talking. Every member of Glynis's family was staring at them.

Alex guessed this was the first time Glynis had tried this particular method of thwarting a potential suitor.

Glynis nudged him. When he turned back to her, she nodded toward Duncan, who, as usual, was putting away astonishing quantities of food.

"What about your friend?" she asked in a low voice. "Is he in want of a wife?"

Duncan only wanted one woman. Unfortunately, that particular woman was living in Ireland with her husband.

"No, you're safe from Duncan as well."

Glynis dropped her shoulders and closed her eyes, as if he'd just told her that a loved one she'd feared dead had been found alive.

"'Tis a pleasure to talk with a woman who is almost as set against marriage as I am." Alex lifted his cup to her. "To our escape from that blessèd union."

Glynis couldn't spare him a smile, but she did raise her cup to his.

"How could ye tell my gown was padded?" she asked.

"I pinched your behind."

Her jaw dropped. "Ye wouldn't dare."

"Ach, of course I would," he said, though he hadn't. "And ye didn't feel a thing."

"How did ye know I didn't feel it?" she asked.

"Well, it's like this," he said, leaning forward on his elbows. "A pinch earns a man either a slap or a wink, and ye gave me neither."

She gave a laugh that was all the more lovely for being unexpected.

"Ye are a devil," she said and poked his arm with her finger.

That long, slender finger made him wonder what the

rest of her looked like without the padding. He was a man of considerable imagination.

"Which do ye get more often, a wink or a slap?" she asked.

"'Tis always a wink, lass."

Glynis laughed again and missed the startled looks her father and sisters gave her.

"Ye are a vain man, to be sure." She took a drumstick from the platter as she spoke, and Alex realized he hadn't taken a bite himself since she sat down.

"It's just that I know women," Alex explained, as he took a slab of roasted mutton with his knife. "So I can tell the ones that would welcome a pinch."

She pointed her drumstick at him. "Ye pinched me, and I didn't want ye to."

"Pinching your padding doesn't count," Alex said. "You'd wink if I pinched ye, Mistress Glynis. Ye may not know it yet, but I can tell."

Instead of laughing and calling him vain again, as he'd hoped, her expression was tense. "I don't like the way my father looks."

"How does he look to ye?" Alex asked.

"Hopeful."

Alex and Duncan slept on the floor of the hall with a score of snoring MacNeils. At dawn, Alex awoke to the sound of soft footfalls crossing the hall. He rolled to the side and leaped to his feet, leaving his host kicking into air where Alex had been lying.

"You're quick," the MacNeil said, with an approving nod. "I only meant to wake ye."

"That could have gotten ye killed," Alex said, as he

slipped his dirk back into his belt. "And then I'd have no end of trouble leaving your fine home."

Duncan was feigning sleep, but his hand was on the hilt of his dagger. If Alex gave the signal, Duncan would slit their host's throat, and the two of them would be halfway to their boat before anyone else in the hall knew what had happened.

"Come for a stroll with me," the MacNeil said. "I've something to show ye."

"I could use some fresh air after all the whiskey ye gave me last night."

It was difficult to discover a man's intentions when he was sober, so Alex had matched the MacNeil drink for drink far into the night. No doubt the MacNeil chieftain had attempted to drink him under the table with the same goal in mind. Neither had succeeded.

"No one forced it down your throat," the MacNeil said, as they left the hall.

"Ah, but ye knew I am a MacDonald," Alex said. "We don't like to lose, whether it be drinking games or battles."

The MacNeil cocked an eyebrow. "Or women?"

Alex didn't take the bait. His problem had never been losing women, but finding a graceful way to end it when the time came—which it always did.

Alex followed the MacNeil out the gate and onto the narrow causeway that connected the castle to the main island.

The MacNeil halted and pointed down the beach. "My daughter Glynis is there."

Alex's gaze was riveted to the slender figure walking barefoot along the shore with her back to them. Her long hair was blowing in the wind, and every few feet she stopped and leaned over to pick up something from the beach. Ach, she made a lovely sight. Alex had a weakness for a woman who liked to get her feet wet.

"Ye strike me as a curious man," the MacNeil said. "Don't ye want to know what she truly looks like?"

Alex did want to know. He narrowed his eyes at the MacNeil. He was more accustomed to having fathers hide their daughters from him. "Are ye not fond of your daughter?"

"Glynis is my only child by my first wife. She's very much like her mother, as difficult a woman as was ever born." The MacNeil sighed. "God, how I loved her.

"The other girls are sweet, biddable lasses who will tell their husbands they are wise and clever and always in the right, whether they are or no. But not Glynis."

The younger sisters sounded too dull by half.

"I didn't raise Glynis any different, she just is," the chieftain said. "If we were attacked and I was killed, the other girls would weep and wail, helpless creatures that they are. But Glynis would pick up a sword and fight like a she-wolf to protect the others."

"So why are ye so anxious to see Glynis wed?" Alex asked. She seemed the only one worth keeping to him.

"She and her stepmother are like dry kindling and a lit torch. Glynis needs her own home. She doesn't like being under the thumb of another woman."

"Or a man's," Alex said. "Judging from what I heard she did to her former husband."

"Ach, he was a fool to tell the tale," the MacNeil said with a wave of his hand. "What man with any pride would admit his wife got her blade into his hip? Ye know what she was aiming for, of course."

Alex winced. He'd had women weep and occasionally toss things at him, but none had ever tried to cut off his manly parts.

But then, Alex had never married.

THE DISH

Where authors give you the inside scoop!

♥ ♥ ♥ ♥ ♥ ♥ ♥ ♥ ♥ ♥ ♥ ♥ ♥ ♥ ♥

From the desk of Margaret Mallory

Dear Reader,

I was a late bloomer.

There, I've said it. That single fact defined my adolescence.

When I entered high school at thirteen-going-on-fourteen, I looked like a sixth grader. Was it the braces? The glasses? The flat chest? The short stature? Red hair and freckles did not lend sophistication to this deadly combination. I have a vivid memory of one of my mother's friends looking at me that summer before high school and blurting out, "What a funny-looking kid."

To my *enormous* relief, I entered tenth grade with breasts, contact lenses, and no braces. Boys looked at me differently, girls quit ridiculing me, and adults ceased to speak to me as if I were eleven. And older guys—who had utterly failed to notice my "inner beauty" before—appeared out of nowhere

Although it took my self-esteem years to recover, suffering is never wasted on a writer. With THE GUARDIAN, I wanted to write a story with a heroine who goes through this awkward stage—along with several dangerous adventures—and eventually comes out the other side as a confident, mature woman who feels loved and valued for her beauty inside and out.

Of course, I had to give Sìleas, my ugly-duckling heroine, a hero to die for. Ian MacDonald is the handsome young Highlander she has adored since she could walk.

Sìleas is an awkward, funny-looking thirteen-year-old when Ian rescues her from her latest round of trouble. Ian is not exactly pleased when, as a result of his good deed, he is forced to wed her. Although Sìleas lives in the Scottish Highlands in the year 1513, I knew exactly how she felt when she overheard Ian shouting at his father, "Have ye taken a good look at her, da?"

When Ian returns years later, Sìleas is so beautiful she knocks his socks off. Not surprisingly, Ian finds that he is now willing to consummate the marriage. But as Sìleas's self-confidence grows, she knows she deserves a man who loves and respects her.

Our handsome hero has his hands full trying to win his bride while also saving his clan. Eventually, Ian realizes he wants Sìleas's heart as much as he wants her in his bed. I admit that I found it most gratifying to make this handsome Highland warrior suffer until he proves himself worthy of Sìleas. But I had faith in Ian. He always did have a hero's heart.

I hope you enjoyed Ian and Sìleas's love story. THE GUARDIAN is the first book in my *Return of the Highlanders* series about four warriors who return home from fighting in France to find their clan in danger. Each brave warrior must do his part to save the clan in the troubled times ahead—and to win the Highland lass who captures his heart.

Happy Reading!

Margaret Mallory

www.margaretmallory.com

From the desk of Roxanne St. Claire

Dear Reader,

Character notes? Character notes! Where did I put my character notes for Vivi Angelino? Oh, that's right. I never had any. She wrote herself.

I have never subscribed to the theory that "a character tells her own story," despite the number of times I've heard writers discuss that phenomenon. Sure, certain characters are vivid in the writer's head and have personality traits that, for whatever reason, make them standouts on the page. They're fun people to write, but letting them take over the book? Come on! Who is the boss here? Whose fingertips are on the keyboard? Whose imagination is at work? A good author should be able to control their character.

And then along came Vivina Angelino. From the first book in the Guardian Angelinos series, Vivi was not only vivid and three-dimensional to me, she seemed to liven up every scene. (Make that "take over" every scene.) When I could finally give her free rein as the heroine of FACE OF DANGER, I did what any writer would do. I buckled up and hung on for the ride. There were daily surprises with Vivi, including her back story, which she revealed to me as slowly and carefully as she does to the reader, and the hero.

The interesting thing about Vivi is that she is one of those people—or appears to be on the surface—who knows exactly who she is and doesn't give a flying saucer what other people think. I think we all kind of envy that bone-deep confidence. I know I do! She scoots around Boston on a skateboard (and, yes, this is possible, because this is precisely how my stepson transports himself from home to work in downtown Boston), wears her hair short and spiky, and has a tiny diamond in her nose...not because she's making a statement, but because she likes it. She's a woman, but she's not particularly feminine and she has little regard for fashion, makeup, and the "girlier" things in life. I wanted to know why.

About five years ago, long before I "met" Vivi, I read an article about a woman who looked so much like Demi Moore that she worked as a "celebrity look-alike" at trade shows and special events. Of course, the suspense writer in me instantly asked the "what-if" question that is at the heart of every book. What if that look-alike was truly mistaken for the actress by someone with nefarious intentions? What if the look-alike was brave enough to take the job to *intentionally* attract and trap that threatening person?

I held on to that thread of a story, waiting for the right character. I wanted a heroine who is so comfortable in her own skin that assuming someone else's identity would be a little excruciating. Kind of like kicking off sneakers and sliding into stilettos—fun until you try to walk, and near impossible when you have to run for your life. When Vivi Angelino showed up on the scene, I knew I had my girl.

No surprise, Vivi told this story her way. Of course, she chafed at the hair extensions and false eyelashes, but that was only on the surface. Wearing another woman's identity forced this character to understand herself better and to do that, she had to face her past. More importantly, to find the love she so richly deserves, she had to shed the skin she clung to so steadfastly, and discover why she was uncomfortable with the feminine things in life. When she did, well, like everything about Vivi, she surprised me.

She pulled it off, though, and now she's FBI Agent Colton Lang's problem. I hope he can control her better than I could.

Enjoy!

Roxanne St. Claire

www.roxannestclaire.com

♥ ♥ ♥ ♥ ♥ ♥ ♥ ♥ ♥ ♥ ♥ ♥ ♥ ♥ ♥ ♥ ♥ ♥

From the desk of Isobel Carr

Dear Reader,

Do you ever wonder what happens to all the mistresses who are given up by noble heroes so they can have their monogamous happily-ever-after with their virginal brides? Or how all those "spares" get on after they've been made redundant when their elder brother produces an heir? I most certainly do!

In fact, I've always been intrigued by people who take charge, go out on a limb, and make lemonade when the universe keeps handing them lemons. So it comes as little surprise that my series—The League of Second Sons—is about younger sons of the nobility, the untraditional women they fall in love with, and what it takes for two people who aren't going to inherit everything to make a life for themselves.

The League of Second Sons is a secret club for younger sons who've banded together to help one another seize whatever life offers them and make the most of it. These are the men who actually run England. They're elected to the House of Commons, they run their family estates, they're the traditional family sacrifice to the military (the Duke of Wellington and Lord Nelson were both younger sons). They work—in a gentlemanly manner—for what they've got and what they want. They're hungry, in a way that an eldest son, destined for fortune and title, never can be.

Leonidas Vaughn, the hero of the first book, RIPE FOR PLEASURE, is just such a younger son. His father may be a duke, but Leonidas not going to inherit much beyond the small estate his grandfather bequeathed him.

My heroine, Viola Whedon, took a chance on young love that worked out very badly indeed. Since then, she's been level-headed and practical. A rough life in the workhouse or a posh life as a mistress was an easy decision, and keeping her heart out of it was never a problem...until now. Brash seduction at the hands of a handsome man who promises to put her desires first sweeps her off her feet and off her guard.

I hope you'll enjoy letting Leo show you what it means to be RIPE FOR PLEASURE.

Isobel Carr

www.isobelcarr.com

From the desk of Katie Lane

Dear Reader,

When I was little I used to love watching *The Andy Griffith Show* reruns. I loved everything about Mayberry—from Floyd's barbershop, where all the town gossip took place, to the tree-lined lake where Andy took his son fishing. I would daydream for hours about living in Mayberry, eating Aunt Bea's home cooking, tagging after Barney to listen to his latest harebrained scheme, or just hanging out with Opie. And even though my life remained in a larger city, these daydreams stuck with me over the years. So much so that I ended up snagging a redheaded, freckle-faced Opie of my own... with one tiny difference.

My Opie came from Texas.

Welcome to Bramble! Mayberry on Texas peyote.

You won't find Andy, Barney, or Aunt Bea in town. But you will find a sheriff who enjoys grand theft auto, a matchmaking mayor, a hairdresser whose "exes" fill half of Texas, and a bunch of meddling townsfolk. And let's not forget the pretty imposter, the smoking-hot cowboy, the feisty actress, and the very naughty bad boy.

So I hope you'll stop by because the folks of Bramble, Texas, are just itchin' to show y'all a knee-slappin' good time. GOING COWBOY CRAZY, my first romance set in Bramble, is out now.

Much Love and Laughter,

Katie Lane

www.katielanebooks.com

Find out more about Forever Romance!

Visit us at
www.hachettebookgroup.com/publishing_forever.aspx

Find us on Facebook
http://www.facebook.com/ForeverRomance

Follow us on Twitter
http://twitter.com/ForeverRomance

NEW AND UPCOMING TITLES

Each month we feature our new titles
and reader favorites.

CONTESTS AND GIVEAWAYS

We give away galleys, autographed copies,
and all kinds of exclusive items.

AUTHOR INFO

You'll find bios, articles, and links to personal websites
for all your favorite authors—and so much more.

GET SOCIAL

Connect with your favorite authors, editors, and
other Forever fans, and share what's important to you.

THE BUZZ

Sign up for our monthly romance newsletter,
and be the first to read all about it.

VISIT US ONLINE

@ WWW.HACHETTEBOOKGROUP.COM.

AT THE HACHETTE BOOK GROUP WEBSITE YOU'LL FIND:

CHAPTER EXCERPTS FROM SELECTED
NEW RELEASES
•
ORIGINAL AUTHOR AND EDITOR ARTICLES
•
AUDIO EXCERPTS
•
BESTSELLER NEWS
•
ELECTRONIC NEWSLETTERS
•
AUTHOR TOUR INFORMATION
•
CONTESTS, QUIZZES, AND POLLS
•
FUN, QUIRKY RECOMMENDATION CENTER
•
PLUS MUCH MORE!

BOOKMARK HACHETTE BOOK GROUP
@ WWW.HACHETTEBOOKGROUP.COM.